FUNDAMENTALS OF English Grammar

Azar 英文文法系列（中階）第四版

U0108274

敦煌書局
CAVES BOOKS

PEARSON

Betty S. Azar
Stacy A. Hagen

To my sister, Jo

B.S.A.

For D. P. and H. B.
with appreciation

S.H.

目　錄

第四版前言

《Azar英文文法系列—中階》是一部標榜漸進式技巧培養的文法書,適合中低階至中階的語言學習者。本書以文法為基礎,融入溝通式教學法,以多樣方法促進語言技巧的全面發展。從瞭解形式和意義的基礎部分開始,學生可針對與自身相關的真實活動、真實事物和真實生活,在課堂上進行有意義的溝通交流。《Azar英文文法系列—中階》原則上可作為課堂教學用書,也是一本多面向且適合師生使用的參考書。

同本書之前三版,書中練習題的編寫風格兼容並蓄,並保持其豐富多樣性,但此第四版加入了創新的方法,特別是:

- **文法表格前的暖身活動**

  為第四版新增的練習。此創新的練習活動置於文法表格前,介紹接下來要教授的文法重點。每個暖身活動均精心設計過,有助於學生在進行該活動時,「領會」設定的文法目標。

- **聽力練習**

  大量的聽力練習能幫助學生在不同的情境中作口語互動,情境範圍從輕鬆、非正式的日常對話到更具學術性的內容。書後附上完整的聽力練習文字。

- **閱讀文章**

  學生可閱讀及回應著重目標文法結構的多元化文章。

- **寫作練習**

  每一章節都有針對目標文法結構設計的全新寫作活動,且每一個寫作習題之前都有寫作範例供學生參考、遵循。

- **大量的口說練習活動**

  在第四版中,學生可以有更多的機會分享他們的生活經驗、表達他們的看法,並將目標文法與個人生活作連結。本書經常在文中引用學生自身的生活經驗當作練習情境,也常介紹有趣的話題,以激勵學生在設定好架構的開放性小組討論中自由表達自己的看法。

・語料庫指引的內容

本書文法內容根據我們語料庫的研究結果，加以增減或修改，以反映口語和書面英語的言談模式。

使用本書中全新題型的訣竅：

・暖身活動

暖身活動練習是介紹每個表格前的簡要教學工具，每個練習都著重於其後表格中將介紹的重點。在開始介紹前，教師們會想熟悉表格中的內容。然後，在教師的引導之下，學生在完成暖身活動練習的同時，便得以發現許多，有時甚或是全部的新文法句型。在學生完成練習題之後，教師或許會發現不再需要更多的解釋，因為表格本身就是非常有用的參考資料。

・聽力練習

聽力練習是為了幫助學生了解真實的美式口語英文而設計的。因此，聽力練習包含了發音弱化以及部分自然、輕鬆的日常口語英文中的其他現象。因為聽力部分的英文口說速度比學生習慣的來得更快，在完成練習題的同時，他們或許需要每個句子都聽兩到三次。

聽力練習並不鼓勵立即的口語發音（除非這些練習與特定的發音習題做了連結）。語言接受性技巧必須比產出性技巧先建立；學生能夠先聽懂各式各樣的口語表達方式，然後再用到自己的口語中，這是很重要的。

鼓勵學生在第一次聽較長的文章時先不要看書，教師之後可以再解釋學生未接觸過的單字。在第二次聆聽的過程中，學生可以著手完成練習題，教師則應該適度地暫停播放 CD。依照班上學生的程度，亦可在每句之後或甚至一句之間作暫停。

CD 中說話者的口音有時候很難避免地會與教師的不同，無論是因為語體風格或區域上的差異。一般情況下，如果教師希望學生可以聽另外一種口音，或是學生自己提出疑問，也可呈現不同的語音範例。

本書後面附有完整的聽力練習文字。

・閱讀文章

閱讀文章賦予學生在延伸的文章情境中接觸文法結構的機會，其中一種方法是先讓學生獨自閱讀文章一次，然後他們可以分小組或全班一起討論未學過的單字，且或許會需要第二次閱讀文章的機會。接下來，多樣化的閱讀習題能讓學生檢視自己對文章的理解力，讓學生使用目標文法結構，並進一步延伸應用於口說或寫作上。

・寫作練習

當學生有信心使用目標文法結構時，教師可以鼓勵他們用完整的段落表達自己的看法。每個習題都有範例段落以及提示問題來幫助學生發展他們的想法。

同儕間互相訂正可以是批改的一種方法。以下為一個有用的方法：將學生兩兩分作一組、讓他們交換完成的作業，然後大聲唸出「搭檔」所寫的段落文字。如此一來，寫的學生便可以「聽見」唸出的內容是不是自己當初想要表達的。這個方法也防止寫作者在唸的同時，自行修改內容。（如果寫作者在唸的時候，不自覺地進行自我修改，便有可能產生問題。）

對於沒有太多寫作經驗的班級，教師可以將學生分成小組。各組組員一起完成一段文字，教師將該作業收回，並加註評語，再影印一份給組內每位組員。然後，學生再「各自」訂正該段文字。

在批改學生所寫的作業時，教師應該著重於該章節所教的文法結構。

・口說練習

每個口說練習活動都遵照下列形式進行：**兩人一組**、**小組**、**全班活動**、**訪談**或是**遊戲**。成功的語言學習需要社交互動，而這些練習都鼓勵學生與他人述說自己的想法、日常生活以及周遭事物。當學生可以將語言與自己的知識和經驗做連結時，他們將更能輕鬆、自在地以該語言表達。

・檢視學習成果

在一個章節的最後，學生可以進展到整句式訂正的程度，並藉由更正此程度中常見的錯誤，學習相關的校訂技巧。這些練習可以當作回家作業或分小組完成。

檢視學習成果的練習可以輕易地設計為遊戲。教師任意說出一個題號，學生分組訂正該句子，然後最先正確修改完句子的組別贏得一分。

《Azar 英文文法系列—中階》配有：
- *Workbook*：提供內容豐富的自學用練習本。
- *Azar Interactive*：這是一套與本書內容相對應的電腦程式，提供易於瞭解的內容、全新的練習、文章、聽力與口說活動以及綜合測驗。
- *AzarGrammar.com* 專屬網站：提供多樣化的課堂補充教材，同時也是教師們彼此交流知識和經驗，相互支援的園地。
- *Fun with Grammar* 課堂活動：這是由 Suzanne Woodward 所編寫的教師資源，提供適用於 Azar 英文文法系列之各種溝通式活動。請至 *AzarGrammar.com* 專屬網站下載。

Azar 英文文法系列包括：
- 《Azar 英文文法系列—進階》（藍色封面）：高級程度學生適用。
- 《Azar 英文文法系列—中階》（黑色封面）：中級程度學生適用。
- 《Azar 英文文法系列—初級》（紅色封面）：程度較低或初學者適用。

感謝的話

如果沒有許多才智出眾的專業人士的幫助，我們就無法順利完成第四版。我們依據下列評論家優秀的洞察力和建議，開始進行這次的改版：Michael Berman，蒙哥馬利學院；Jeff Bette，威徹斯特社區學院；Mary Goodman，艾弗瑞斯特大學；Linda Gossard，DPT 商學院（丹佛校區）；Roberta Hodges，所羅馬州立美國語言中心；Suzanne Kelso，波夕州立大學；Steven Lasswell，聖塔芭芭拉城市學院；Diane Mahin，邁阿密大學；Maria Mitchell，DPT 商學院（費城校區）；Monica Oliva，邁阿密日落成人教育中心；Amy Parker，密西根大學；Casey Peltier，北維吉尼亞社區學院。

我們非常榮幸能擁有優秀的專業編輯團隊，他們監控著本書的整個過程，從初期計畫階段到最後實際印刷出版。我們想向以下所有人致謝：Shelly Hartle，傑出的執行編輯，她嚴密且敏銳的編輯能力造就了本書的每一頁；Amy McCormick，編輯總監，她對這套系列叢書的洞察力、關注以及用心引導了我們撰寫的方向；Ruth Voetmann，研發編輯，她提供了銳利的見解、寶貴的建議，並有無限的耐心；Janice Baillie，傑出的文字編輯，她詳細審閱及反覆斟酌每頁的字句；Sue Van Etten，才華出眾的業務經理及網站管理負責人；Robert Ruvo，培生集團裡技術純熟且熱情的出版部經理。

我們同時也想向補充教材的作者們表達感激之意：Rachel Spack Koch，編寫了練習本；Kelly Roberts Weibel，編寫了題庫系統；以及 Martha Hall，撰寫了教師手冊。他們用自己創新的點子和創造力大大地豐富了此系列叢書。

最後，我們想要感謝培生集團裡，負責指導此次改版工作且貢獻良多的領導團隊：Pietro Alongi、Rhea Banker 以及 Paula Van Ells。

色彩豐富的插畫則要感謝 Don Martinetti 和 Chris Pavely 的巧思與才華。

最後，我們想要感謝我們的家人，他們在此次改版過程中的每個階段都支持及鼓勵著我們，也是創作靈感綿延不絕的來源。

Betty S. Azar
Stacy A. Hagen

第一章
現在式

☐ Exercise 1. 聽力與閱讀

第一部分 聆聽 CD 播放 Sam 和 Lisa 的對話。他們是在加州唸書的大學生,將接受爲期一週的宿舍管理員 (resident assistants⋆) 訓練。他們將訪問彼此,之後再將彼此介紹給小組其他成員。

CD 1
Track 2

SAM: Hi. My name is Sam.

LISA: Hi. I'm Lisa. It's nice to meet you.

SAM: Nice to meet you too. Where are you from?

LISA: I'm from Boston. How about you?

SAM: I'm from Quebec. So, how long have you been here?

LISA: Just one day. I still have a little jet lag.

SAM: Me too. I got in yesterday morning. So — we need to ask each other about a hobby. What do you like to do in your free time?

LISA: I spend a lot of time outdoors. I love to hike. When I'm indoors, I like to surf the Internet.

SAM: Me too. I'm studying Italian right now. There are a lot of good websites for learning languages on the Internet.

LISA: I know. I found a good one for Japanese. I'm trying to learn a little.
Now, when I introduce you to the group, I have to write your full name on the board. What's your last name, and how do you spell it?

SAM: It's Sanchez. S-A-N-C-H-E-Z.

LISA: My last name is Paterson — with one "t": P-A-T-E-R-S-O-N.

SAM: It looks like our time is up. Thanks. It's been nice talking to you.

LISA: I enjoyed it too.

⋆*resident assistant* 意指「住在學校宿舍,並且協助其他住宿學生日常生活相關事宜的在校學生;也可簡稱爲 R. A.」。

第二部分 閱讀第一部分的對話。用對話中的資訊，幫助 Sam 完成要對全班同學介紹 Lisa 的短文。

SAM: I would like to introduce Lisa Paterson. Lisa is from ___Boston___ . She has been here

_____ . In her free time, she _____

_____ .

第三部分 現在換 Lisa 要為全班介紹 Sam。她會說什麼呢？用 "I would like to introduce Sam." 開頭，寫一段介紹 Sam 的短文。

❏ **Exercise 2. 口說：訪談**

訪問一位同學，然後將你的搭檔介紹給全班認識。在認識其他同學的同時，將他們的名字寫在一張紙上。

找出搭檔的：

    name
    native country or hometown
    free-time activities or hobbies
    favorite food
    reason for being here
    length of time here

❏ **Exercise 3. 寫作**

寫出下列問題的答案，然後參考此練習最後所附的建議，和老師一同討論如何運用你剛才所寫的答案。

1. What is your name?
2. Where are you from?
3. Where are you living?
4. Why are you here (in this city)?
    a. Are you a student? If so, what are you studying?
    b. Do you work? If so, what is your job?
    c. Do you have another reason for being here?
5. What do you like to do in your free time?
6. What is your favorite season of the year? Why?
7. What are your three favorite TV programs or movies? Why do you like them?
8. Describe your first day in this class.

寫完上述練習後的建議：

a. 將寫完的作品給一位同學看過，該名同學可以摘要其中資訊，對小組進行口頭報告。
b. 兩人一組互相訂正彼此作品中的錯誤。
c. 將你的作品在小組中大聲唸出來，並回答任何相關的問題。
d. 將你的作品交給老師，老師會訂正其中錯誤，再發還給你。
e. 將你的作品交給老師；當你的英文在學期末有所進步時，老師會發還給你，讓你訂正自己的錯誤。

Exercise 4. 暖身活動（表 1-1 和 1-2）

閱讀下列敘述，並圈選 *yes* 或 *no*。選出符合自身情況的敘述，並和一位搭檔分享你的答案
（例：*I use a computer every day.* 或 *I don't use a computer every day.*）。你的搭檔將向全班報告與
你相關的資訊（例：*Eric doesn't use a computer every day.*）。

1. I use a computer every day.   yes   no

2. I am sitting in front of a computer right now.   yes   no

3. I check emails every day.   yes   no

4. I send text messages several times a day.   yes   no

5. I am sending a text message now.   yes   no

1-1 現在簡單式與現在進行式 Simple Present and Present Progressive

現在簡單式	(a) Ann **takes** a shower *every day*.	現在簡單式用來表達日常習慣或經常性活動，如：例 (a) 及例 (b)。
過去　現在　未來 XXXXXXXXXXX	(b) I *usually* **read** the newspaper in the morning.	現在簡單式亦用於陳述一般事實，如：例 (c)。
	(c) Babies **cry**. Birds **fly**.	一般而言，現在簡單式用以描述無論在現在、過去、及未來，都是永久性、經常性及習慣性的事件或情況。
	(d) 否定句： It **doesn't snow** in Bangkok.	
	(e) 問句： **Does** the teacher **speak** slowly?	
現在進行式	(f) Ann can't come to the phone *right now* because she **is taking** a shower.	現在進行式表示某活動此刻正在進行中（或發生中）。
開始　現在　結束？ 進行中	(g) I **am reading** my grammar book *right now*.	當說話者說此句話時，所述事件亦同時進行中。此事件始於過去、現在正在進行，且可能持續到未來。
	(h) Jimmy and Susie are babies. They **are crying**. I can hear them *right now*. Maybe they are hungry.	形式：**am, is, are + -ing**
	(i) 否定句： It **isn't snowing** *right now*.	
	(j) 問句： **Is** the teacher **speaking** *right now*?	

	現在簡單式	現在進行式
直述句	I **work**. You **work**. He, She, It **works**. We **work**. They **work**.	I **am** working. You **are** working. He, She, It **is** working. We **are** working. They **are** working.
否定句	I **do** not **work**. You **do** not **work**. He, She, It **does** not **work**. We **do** not **work**. They **do** not **work**.	I **am** not working. You **are** not working. He, She, It **is** not working. We **are** not working. They **are** not working.
疑問句	**Do** I **work**? **Do** you **work**? **Does** he, she, it **work**? **Do** we **work**? **Do** they **work**?	**Am** I working? **Are** you working? **Is** he, she, it working? **Are** we working? **Are** they working?

縮寫

代名詞 + be 動詞	I + am = **I'm** working. you, we, they + are = **You're**, **We're**, **They're** working. he, she, it + is = **He's**, **She's**, **It's** working.
do + not	does + not = **doesn't** She **doesn't** work. do + not = **don't** I **don't** work.
be 動詞 + not	is + not = **isn't** He **isn't** working. are + not = **aren't** They **aren't** working. (am + not = am not★ I am not working.)

★註：am 和 not 不可縮寫。

□ **Exercise 5. 聽力與文法**（表 1-1 和 1-2）

CD 1
Track 3

聆聽 CD 播放的下一頁文章，討論斜體字動詞描述的是常態性活動 (usual activity)，抑或是發生於此刻的活動 (happening right now)。

Lunch at the Fire Station

It's 12:30, and the firefighters *are waiting* for their next call. They *are taking* their lunch
                              1   2
break. Ben, Rita, and Jada *are sitting* at a table in the fire station. Their co-worker Bruno
                                  3
is making lunch for them. He is an excellent cook. He often *makes* lunch. He *is fixing* spicy
    4   5   6
chicken and rice. Their captain *isn't eating*. He *is doing* paperwork. He *skips* lunch on busy
                                     7   8   9
days. He *works* in his office and *finishes* his paperwork.
        10   11

❑ **Exercise 6.** 聽力 (表 1-1 和 1-2)

CD 1
Track 4

聆聽 CD 播放關於 Irene 及其工作的敘述，判斷該敘述中的動作屬於常態性活動，抑或是發生
於此刻的活動，並圈選正確答案。

例：你會聽到：Irene works for a video game company.
　　你要圈出：(usual activity)　　happening right now

1. usual activity　　　　happening right now

2. usual activity　　　　happening right now

3. usual activity　　　　happening right now

4. usual activity　　　　happening right now

5. usual activity　　　　happening right now

❑ **Exercise 7.** 文法 (表 1-1 和 1-2)

用括弧內動詞的現在簡單式或現在進行式，完成下列句子。

1. Shhh. The baby (*sleep*) ___is sleeping___. The baby (*sleep*) ___sleeps___ for ten
   hours every night.

2. Right now I'm in class. I (*sit*) ___am sitting___ at my desk. I usually (*sit*)
   ___sit___ at the same desk in class every day.

3. Ali (*speak*) ___speaks___ Arabic. Arabic is his native language, but right
   now he (*speak*) ___is speaking___ English.

4. A: (*it, rain*) ___Does it rain___ a lot in southern Spain?
   B: No. The weather (*be*) ___is___ usually warm and sunny.

5. A: Look out the window. (*it, rain*) ___Is it raining___?
   B: It (*start*) ___is starting___ to sprinkle.

現在式　　**5**

6. A: Look. It's Yumiko.

   B: Where?

   A: Over there. She (*walk*) ___is walking___ out of the café.

7. A: Oscar usually (*walk*) ___walks___ to work.

   (*you, walk*) ___Do you walk___ to work every day too?

   B: Yes.

   A: (*Oscar, walk*) ___Does Oscar walking___ with you?

   B: Sometimes.

❑ **Exercise 8. 口說** (表 1-1 和 1-2)

老師會要求一名學生做動作，並要另一名學生用現在進行式描述該動作。

例：stand next to your desk
對學生 A 說：Would you please stand next to your desk?（學生 A 起立）
對學生 B 說：Who is standing next to his/her desk? 或 What is (Student A) doing?
學生 B：(Student A) is standing next to his/her desk.

1. stand up
2. smile
3. whistle
4. open or close the door
5. read your grammar book
6. shake your head "no"
7. erase the board
8. hold your pen in your left hand
9. knock on the door
10. scratch your head
11. count aloud the number of people in the classroom
12. look at the ceiling

❑ **Exercise 9. 聽力** (表 1-1 和 1-2)

聆聽 CD 播放的問題，並寫下聽見的字詞。

CD 1
Track 5 **A problem with the printer**

例：你會聽到：Is the printer working?

你要寫下：___Is___ the printer working?

1. _____ need more paper?

2. _____ have enough ink?

3. _____ fixing it yourself?

4. _____ know how to fix it?

5. _____ have another printer in the office?

6. Hmmm. Is it my imagination or _____ making a strange noise?

❏ **Exercise 10. 遊戲：知識問答比賽** （表 1-1 和 1-2）

分小組進行。用括弧內動詞的正確形式，完成下列句子。對的敘述圈 T；錯的則圈 F。答對最多題的小組獲勝。★

1. In one soccer game, a player (*run*) _____ seven miles on average.   T   F

2. In one soccer game, players (*run*) _____ seven miles on average.   T   F

3. Right-handed people (*live*) _____ 10 years longer than left-handed people.   T   F

4. Mountains (*cover*) _____ 3% of Africa and 25% of Europe.   T   F

5. The Eiffel Tower (*have*) _____ 3,000 steps.   T   F

6. Honey (*spoil*) _____ after one year.   T   F

7. The letter "e" (*be*) _____ the most common letter in English.   T   F

8. It (*take*) _____ about seven seconds for food to get from our mouths to our stomachs.   T   F

9. A man's heart (*beat*) _____ faster than a woman's heart.   T   F

10. About 145,000 people in the world (*die*) _____ every 24 hours.   T   F

❏ **Exercise 11. 口說** （表 1-1 和 1-2）

成兩人一組。使用現在進行式，輪流描述自己的圖片，並找出兩張圖片不同之處。學生 A：遮住自己書本上學生 B 的圖片。學生 B：遮住自己書本上學生 A 的圖片。

例：

學生 A   **學生 B**

學生 A：In my picture, the airplane is taking off.
學生 B：In my picture, the airplane is landing.

★請見解答本中的 *Trivia Answers*。

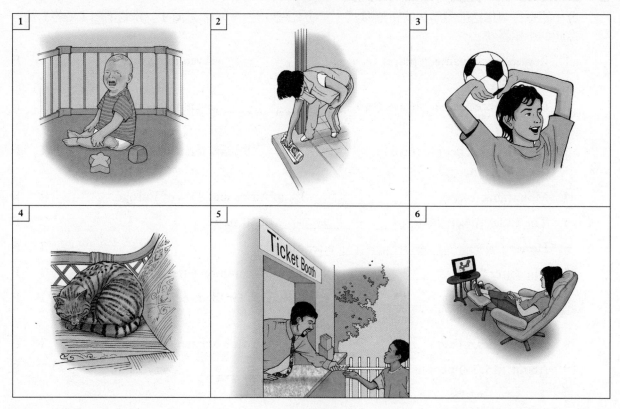

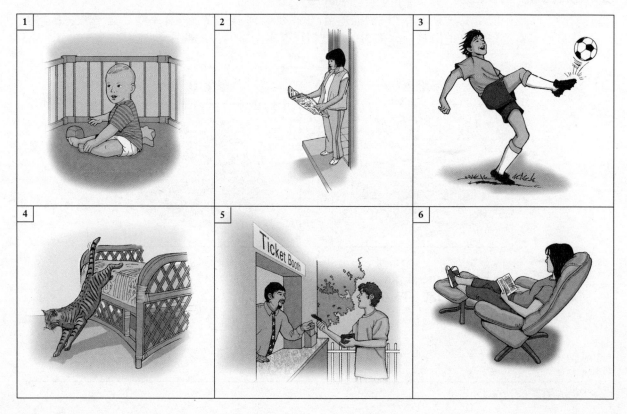

❏ **Exercise 12. 閱讀與寫作** (表 1-1 和 1-2)
第一部分　閱讀以下段落，並回答問題。

Hair Facts

　　Here are some interesting facts about our hair.　Human hair grows about one-half inch per month or 15 centimeters a year.　The hair on our scalp is dead.　That's why it doesn't hurt when we get a haircut.　The average person has about 100,000 strands of hair.*　Every day we lose 75 to 150 strands of hair.　One strand of hair grows for two to seven years.　After it stops growing, it rests for a while and then falls out.　Hair grows faster in warmer weather, and women's hair grows faster than men's hair.

問題：
1. How fast does hair grow?
2. Why don't haircuts hurt?
3. About how many strands of hair are on your head right now?
4. Where is a good place to live if you want your hair to grow faster?

第二部分　選擇身體的一部份，如：指甲、皮膚、眉毛、眼睛、心臟、肺臟等，列出該部分的趣味知識。運用這些趣味知識撰寫一個段落，並用以下的主題句作為該段落的開頭。註：如果你用網路尋找資料，搜尋這個主題："interesting _____ facts" (e.g., interesting hair facts)。

主題句：Here are some interesting facts about our _____.

❏ **Exercise 13. 暖身活動** (表 1-3)
你有多常做下列活動？寫出百分比 (0% → 100%)。老師將會詢問你經常做的 (always do)、偶爾做的 (sometimes do) 或是從不做 (never do) 的活動。

1. _____ I take the bus to school.

2. _____ I go to bed late.

3. _____ I skip breakfast.

4. _____ I eat vegetables at lunch time.

5. _____ I cook my own dinner.

6. _____ I am an early riser.**

---

*strands of hair 意指「一些頭髮」。

**early riser 意指「早起的人」。

100%　 　　　┌ always 　　　│ almost always 　　　│ **usually** 肯　　│ **often** 定　　│ **frequently** 　　　│ **generally** 50%　│ **sometimes** 　　　└ **occasionally**	頻率副詞通常置於句子中間，且有特定位置，如下列例 (a) 到例 (e) 所示。 左列**粗體**的頻率副詞也可以置於句首或句尾。 　*I sometimes get up at 6:30.* 　*Sometimes I get up at 6:30.* 　*I get up at 6:30 sometimes.*
┌ seldom 　　　│ rarely 否　　│ hardly ever 定　　│ almost never 0%　　└ not ever, never	左列沒有加粗的頻率副詞，幾乎不會出現在句首或句尾，通常出現在句中。
主詞　＋　頻率副詞　＋　動詞 (a) Karen　　**always**　　**tells**　the truth.	頻率副詞通常置於主詞與現在簡單式動詞之間。 （*be* 動詞除外） 錯誤：*Always Karen tells the truth.*
主詞 ＋ BE 動詞 ＋ 頻率副詞 (b) Karen　　**is**　　**always**　　on time.	動詞為 *be* 動詞的現在簡單式（*am, is, are*）和過去簡單式（*was, were*）時，頻率副詞置於 *be* 動詞之後。
(c) Do ***you always*** eat breakfast?	在疑問句中，頻率副詞緊接在主詞之後。
(d) Ann ***usually doesn't*** eat breakfast.	在否定句中，頻率副詞大部分置於否定動詞之前（*always* 和 *ever* 除外）。
(e) Sue ***doesn't always*** eat breakfast.	***always*** 接在否定助動詞，如：例 (e)，或否定 *be* 動詞之後。
(f) 正確：Anna ***never eats*** meat. 　　 錯誤：*Anna doesn't never eat meat.*	表否定意味的頻率副詞（*seldom, rarely, hardly ever, never*）「不與」否定動詞連用。
(g) — *Do* you ***ever take*** the bus to work? 　　 — Yes, I do. I often take the bus.	***ever*** 用在問及頻率的疑問句中，如：例 (g)，意指「在任何時刻」。
(h) I ***don't ever*** walk to work. 　　 錯誤：*I ever walk to work.*	***ever*** 也與 ***not*** 連用，如：例 (h)。 ***ever*** 「不用於」直述句中。

❑ **Exercise 14. 文法與口說**（表 1-3）

第一部分　依據自己在 Exercise 13. 的作答，運用表 1-3 所列的頻率副詞，寫出完整的句子。

例：1.　0% = *I **never** take the bus to school.* 或
　　　　50% = *I **sometimes** take the bus to school.*

第二部分 在教室裡走動，找出從事這些活動的頻率和自己相同的人。

例：
說話者 A：I **always** take the bus to school. Do you **always** take the bus to school?
說話者 B：No, I don't. I **sometimes** take the bus to school. Do you **usually** go to bed late?
說話者 A：Yes, I do. I **usually** go to bed late.

❏ **Exercise 15. 口說**（表 1-3）

回答下列問題，並討論頻率副詞的字義。

What is something that . . .
1. you seldom do?
2. a polite person often does?
3. a polite person never does?
4. our teacher frequently does in class?
5. you never do in class?
6. you rarely eat?
7. you occasionally do after class?
8. drivers generally do?
9. people in your country always or usually do to celebrate the New Year?

❏ **Exercise 16. 文法**（表 1-3）

用各題所列的頻率副詞改寫各題句子：將這些副詞置於句中正確的位置，並將句子做適當的變化。

例：Emily doesn't get to work on time.
    a. usually → Emily *usually* doesn't get to work on time.
    b. often → Emily *often* doesn't get to work on time.

1. Kazu doesn't shave in the morning.
    a. frequently   d. always   g. hardly ever
    b. occasionally   e. ever   h. rarely
    c. sometimes   f. never   i. seldom

2. I don't eat breakfast.
    a. usually   c. seldom
    b. always   d. ever

3. My roommate isn't home in the evening.
    a. generally   c. always
    b. sometimes   d. hardly ever

❑ **Exercise 17. 文法**（表 1-3）

依照表格中的資訊，運用頻率副詞來描述 Mia 一週的活動。

Mia's Week	S	M	Tu	W	Th	F	S
1. wake up early				x			
2. make breakfast		x	x		x		
3. go to the gym	x	x		x		x	x
4. be late for the bus		x	x	x	x		
5. cook dinner	x	x	x	x	x	x	x
6. read a book	x	x	x	x		x	x
7. do homework			x			x	
8. go to bed early							

1. Mia _seldom/rarely wakes_ up early.

2. She _____ breakfast.

3. She _____ to the gym.

4. She _____ late for the bus.

5. She _____ dinner.

6. She _____ a book.

7. She _____ her homework.

8. She _____ to bed early.

❑ **Exercise 18. 口說：兩人一組**（表 1-1 → 1-3）

成兩人一組。運用頻率副詞來介紹自己，並詢問你的搭檔問題。

例：walk to school
學生 A（書本打開）：I usually walk to school. How about you? Do you usually walk to school?
學生 B（書本闔上）：I usually walk to school too. 或
　　　　　　　　　　I seldom walk to school. I usually take the bus.

　　　　　　　　　　　　　　　　　　　　　　　　角色互換

1. wear a suit to class
2. go to sleep before 11:00 P.M.
3. get at least one email a day
4. read in bed before I go to sleep
5. speak to people who sit next to me on an airplane

6. wear a hat to class
7. believe the things I hear in the news
8. get up before nine o'clock in the morning
9. call my family or a friend if I feel homesick or lonely
10. have chocolate ice cream for dessert

❑ **Exercise 19. 暖身活動**（表 1-4）

將下列字詞合併為句子，並視情況加上字尾 **-s**。不要添加任何其他字詞。

1. A dolphin \ swim

2. Dolphin \ swim

1-4 單／複數 Singular/Plural

(a) 單數：*one bird*	單數＝數量為一	
(b) 複數：*two birds, three birds, many birds, all birds, etc.*	複數＝數量為二、三或更多	
(c) *Birds* sing.	**複數名詞**的字尾加 **-s**，如：例 (c)。	
(d) A bird *sings*.	**單數動詞**的字尾加 **-s**，如：例 (d)。	
(e) A **bird** *sings* outside my window. **It** *sings* loudly. **Ann** *sings* beautifully. **She** *sings* songs to her children. **Tom** *sings* very well. **He** *sings* professionally.	單數動詞接在單數主詞之後。 如果主詞符合下列條件，現在簡單式動詞字尾須加 **-s**。 (1) 單數名詞（例：*a bird*、*Ann*、*Tom*），或 (2) *he*、*she* 或 *it* ＊。	

＊he、she 和 it 為第三人稱單數代名詞。更多關於人稱代名詞的資訊，請見第 164 頁，表 6-10。

❑ **Exercise 20. 文法**（表 1-4）

仔細看下表中以 **-s** 結尾的字，並判斷該字是名詞還是動詞，是單數還是複數。

句子	名詞	動詞	單數	複數
1. Plants grow quickly in warm weather.	✗			✗
2. Ali lives in an apartment.		✗	✗	
3. Bettina listens to the radio every morning.				
4. The students at this school work hard.				
5. An ambulance takes sick people to the hospital.				
6. Ambulances take sick people to the hospital.				
7. Cell phones offer text-messaging.				
8. The earth revolves around the sun.				

Exercise 21. 聽力 (表 1-4)

聆聽 CD 播放的敘述句，視情況加上字尾 **-s**，如果不用則寫上 **Ø**。

CD 1
Track 6 **Natural disasters: a flood**

1. The weather __Ø__ cause __s__ some natural disaster __s__ .

2. Heavy rains sometimes create _____ flood _____ .

3. A big flood _____ cause _____ a lot of damage.

4. In town _____ , flood _____ can damage building _____ , home _____ , and road _____ .

5. After a flood _____ , a town _____ need _____ a lot of financial help for repair _____ .

❑ **Exercise 22. 暖身活動** (表 1-5)

在正確的類別標題下，寫出下列動詞的第三人稱形式。你知道何時該加字尾 **-s**、**-es** 和 **-ies** 嗎？

| mix | speak | stay | study | take | try | wish |

加字尾 **-s**   加字尾 **-es**   加字尾 **-ies**

_____   _____   _____

_____   _____   _____

_____

1-5 拼寫規則：字尾加 -s 或 -es Spelling of Final -s/-es

(a)	visit → **visits** speak → **speaks**		在大部分的情況下，動詞字尾加 **-s**，而非 **-es**。 錯誤：visites、speakes
(b)	ride → **rides** write → **writes**		動詞字尾是 **-e** 時，加上 **-s** 即可。
(c)	catch → **catches** wash → **washes** miss → **misses** fix → **fixes** buzz → **buzzes**		動詞字尾是 **-ch**、**-sh**、**-s**、**-x** 和 **-z** 時，字尾加 **-es**。 發音規則：字尾 **-es** 唸作 /əz/，多了一個音節。★
(d)	f**ly** → **flies**		若動詞字尾是子音字母加 **-y** 時，改 **-y** 為 **-i**，然後加 **-es**，如：例 (d)。 錯誤：*flys*
(e)	p**ay** → **pays**		若動詞字尾是母音字母加 **-y** 時，只須加 **-s**，** 如：例 (e)。 錯誤：*paies* 或 *payes*
(f)	go → **goes** do → **does** have → **has**		**go**、**do** 和 **have** 等動詞的單數形式為不規則變化。

★更多關於字尾 -s/-es 的發音資訊，請見 147 頁，表 6-1。

**母音字母為 a、e、i、o、u，子音字母則為其餘字母。

❑ **Exercise 23. 文法**（表 1-4 和 1-5）

以底線標示出下列句子中的動詞，並視情況加上字尾 **-s/-es**，不要改變其他字詞。

1. A frog jump^s .

2. Frogs jump. → (*no change*)

3. A boat float on water.

4. Rivers flow toward the sea.

5. My mother worry about me.

6. A student buy a lot of books at the beginning of each term.

7. Airplanes fly all around the world.

8. The teacher ask us a lot of questions in class every day.

9. Mr. Cook watch game shows on TV every evening.

10. Water freeze at 32°F (0°C) and boil at 212°F (100°C).

11. Mrs. Taylor never cross the street in the middle of a block. She always walk to the corner and use the crosswalk.

❑ **Exercise 24. 文法與聽力**（表 1-5）

CD 1
Track 7

在以下動詞加上 **-s/-es/-ies**，並和一位搭檔核對答案，然後再聆聽各動詞的發音。

1. talk _s_____   6. kiss _____   11. study _____
2. fish _es____   7. push _____   12. buy _____
3. hope _____   8. wait _____   13. enjoy _____
4. teach _____   9. mix _____   14. try _____
5. move _____   10. bow _____   15. carry _____

❑ **Exercise 25. 口說：兩人一組**（表 1-5）

成兩人一組。邊看下列圖片，邊與搭檔做對話練習。輪流當學生 A 和 學生 B。遵照下列範例，並視情況使用 *he*、*she* 或 *they*。

學生 A：What is he doing?
學生 B：He _____.
學生 A：Does he _____ often?
學生 B：No, he doesn't. He rarely _____.

Exercise 26. 遊戲 (表 1-4 和 1-5)

老師將會給每位學生一個項目編號。（如果少於 20 位學生，部分學生則會有兩個號碼。如果多於 20 位學生，部分學生會有相同號碼。）在下列清單中找到自己的號碼，並在一張紙條上寫下號碼旁的字詞，然後闔上書本。

在教室內走動，告訴其他同學你寫下的字詞，並尋找能與你寫的字詞組成完整句的另一組字詞。當你找到有另一組字詞的同學時，將你們紙條上的片斷內容合併為一句。在黑板上或一張紙上寫下該句，並視情況做動詞變化。

例：1. A star
2. shine in the sky at night
   → *A star shines in the sky at night.*

1. A car
2. causes air pollution.
3. stretch when you pull on it.
4. A hotel
5. support a huge variety of marine life.
6. A bee
7. Does exercise
8. cause great destruction when it reaches land.
9. A river
10. improves your health?
11. An elephant
12. A hurricane
13. produce one-fourth of the world's coffee.
14. Oceans
15. use its long trunk like a hand to pick things up.
16. Brazil
17. supply its guests with clean towels.
18. A rubber band
19. collects nectar* from flowers.
20. flows downhill.

❏ **Exercise 27. 暖身活動** (表 1-6)

圈選可完成句子的正確答案。

CHARLIE: Shhh! I _____ something on our roof.
    a. hear   b. am hearing

I _____ there is a person up there.
    a. think   b. am thinking

DAD: I _____.
    a. don't know   b. am not knowing

It _____ more like a small animal, maybe a cat or squirrel.
    a. sounds   b. is sounding

---

*nectar 意指「花蜜」。

1-6 非動作動詞 Non-Action Verbs

(a) I **know** Ms. Chen. 錯誤：*I am knowing Ms. Chen.* (b) I'm hungry. I **want** a sandwich. 錯誤：*I am wanting a sandwich.* (c) This book **belongs** to Mikhail. 錯誤：*This book is belonging to Mikhail.*	有些動詞不能使用進行式，這些動詞稱作「非動作動詞」*； 用來表示存在的狀況，而非進行中的動作。

非動作動詞

hear	believe	be	own	need	like	forget
see	think	exist	have	want	love	remember
sound	understand		possess	prefer	hate	
	know	seem	belong			agree
	mean	look like				disagree

比較下列句子： (d) I **think** that grammar is easy. (e) I **am thinking** about grammar right now. (f) Tom **has** a car. (g) I**'m having** a good time.	有時 **think** 與 **have** 可以用進行式。 在 (d) 句中，**think** 表示「認為」時，不可用進行式。 在 (e) 句中，**think** 表示某人當下正有該想法時，可用進行式。 在 (f) 句中，**have** 表示「擁有」時，不可用進行式。 在 (g) 句中，**have** 不用來表示「擁有」時，可用進行式。 類似的情形有：*have a good time*、*have a bad time*、*have trouble*、*have a problem*、*have lunch*、*have a snack*、*have company*、*have an operation* 等。

*非動作動詞也稱作「無進行時態」(non-progressive) 或「靜態」(stative) 動詞。

❑ **Exercise 28. 文法** (表 1-6)

圈選正確的答覆。

1. A: What do you like better: coffee or tea?
    B: I _____ tea.
        a. am preferring   (b.) prefer

2. A: Can you help me set the table for dinner?
    B: In a minute. I _____ my report.
        a. am finishing   b. finish

3. A: Are you busy?
    B: I _____ a few minutes.
        a. have   b. am having

4. A: _____ a good time?
        a. Are you having   b. Do you have
    B: Yes, I _____ myself.
        a. am enjoying   b. I enjoy

5. A: There's goes Salma on her new racing bike.
   B: Yeah, she really _____ bikes.
      a. is loving   b. loves
   A: That's for sure! She _____ several.
      a. is owning   b. owns

❑ **Exercise 29. 文法** (表 1-6)
用 ***think*** 和 ***have*** 的現在簡單式或現在進行式，完成下列句子。

1. A: How is your new job going?
   B: Pretty good. I (*think*) ___think___ I am doing okay.

2. A: You look upset. What's on your mind?
   B: I'm worried about my daughter. I (*think*) _____ she's in trouble.

3. A: You look far away.* What's on your mind?
   B: I (*think*) _____ about my vacation next week. I can't wait!

4. A: Hey, there! How's the party going?
   B: Great! We (*have*) _____ a lot of fun.

5. A: Could I borrow some money?
   B: Sorry, I only (*have*) _____ a little change** on me.

❑ **Exercise 30. 文法** (表 1-6)
用括弧內動詞的現在簡單式或現在進行式，完成下列句子。

1. Right now I (*look*) ___am looking___ out the window. I (*see*) ___see___ a window washer on a ladder.

2. A: (*you, need*) _____ some help, Mrs. Bernini?
      (*you, want*) _____ me to carry that box for you?
   B: Yes, thank you. That's very nice of you.

3. A: Who is that man? I (*think*) _____ that I (*know*) _____ him, but I (*forget*) _____ his name.
   B: That's Mr. Martinez.
   A: That's right! I (*remember*) _____ him now.

---

*look far away 意指「若有所思；做白日夢」。

**change 意指「零錢」。

4. A: (*you, believe*) _____ in ghosts?

   B: No. In my opinion, ghosts (*exist*) _____ only in people's imaginations.

5. Right now the children (*be*) _____ at the beach. They (*have*) _____ a good time. They (*have*) _____ shovels, and they (*build*) _____ a sandcastle. They (*like*) _____ to build big sandcastles. Their parents (*lie*) _____ on the beach and (*listen*) _____ to music. They (*listen, not*) _____ to their children's conversations, but they (*hear*) _____ them anyway.

❏ **Exercise 31.** 暖身活動 (表 1-7)
圈選下列問句的正確答覆。

1. Does Janet eat fish?
   a. Yes, she does.   b. Yes, she is.   c. Yes, she eats.

2. Do you eat fish?
   a. No, I don't.   b. No, I am not.   c. No, I don't eat.

3. Are you vegetarian?
   a. Yes, I do.   b. Yes, I am.   c. Yes, I like.

1-7 現在式動詞：Yes/No 問句的簡答

		問句	簡答	詳答
DO/DOES 為首的問句		*Does* Bob *like* tea?	Yes, he **does**. No, he **doesn't**.	Yes, he likes tea. No, he doesn't like tea.
		Do you *like* tea?	Yes, I **do**. No, I **don't**.	Yes, I like tea. No, I don't like tea.
BE 動詞為首的問句		*Are* you *studying*?	Yes, I **am**.★ No, I **'m not**.	Yes, I am (I'm) studying. No, I'm not studying.
		Is Yoko a student?	Yes, she **is**.★ No, she **'s not**. 或 No, she **isn't**.	Yes, she is (she's) a student. No, she's not a student. 或 No, she isn't a student.
		Are they *studying*?	Yes, they **are**.★ No, they **'re not**. 或 No, they **aren't**.	Yes, they are (they're) studying. No, they're not studying. 或 No, they aren't studying.

★在肯定簡答中，am、is 和 are「不可」與代名詞合併縮寫。
　錯誤簡答：*Yes, I'm.*、*Yes, she's.*、*Yes, they're.*

❑ **Exercise 32. 文法**（表 1-7）

用括弧內動詞的現在簡單式或現在進行式，完成下列對話，並視情況以簡答回答問題。

1.　A: (*Tanya, have*) ___Does Tanya___ have a bike?

　　B: Yes, ___she does___ . She (*have*) ___has___ a racing bike.

2.　A: (*it, rain*) _____ right now?

　　B: No, _____ . At least, I (*think, not*) _____ so.

3.　A: (*your friends, write*) _____ a lot of emails?

　　B: Yes, _____ . I (*get*) _____ lots of emails all the time.

4.　A: (*the weather, affect*★) _____ your mood?

　　B: Yes, _____ . I (*get*) _____ grumpy when it's rainy.

★*affect* 為動詞，如：The weather **affects** my mood.

　effect 為名詞，如：Warm, sunny weather has a good **effect** on my mood.

5. A: (*Jean, study*) _____ at the library this evening?

B: No, _____ . She (*be*) _____ at the gym. She

(*play*) _____ table tennis with her friend.

A: (*Jean, play*) _____ table tennis every evening?

B: No, _____ . She usually (*study*) _____ at the library.

A: (*she, be*) _____ a good player?

B: Yes, _____ . She (*play*) _____ table tennis a lot.

A: (*you, play*) _____ table tennis?

B: Yes, _____ . But I (*be, not*) _____ very good.

□ Exercise 33. 聽力 (表 1-7)

第一部分 聆聽 CD 播放的下列範例。注意斜體片語的弱化發音。

CD 1
Track 8 **At the doctor's office**

1. Do you	→	*Dyou*	*Do you have* an appointment?
2. Does he	→	*Dze*	*Does he have* an appointment?
3. Does she	→	*Duh-she*	*Does she have* an appointment?
4. Do we	→	*Duh-we*	*Do we have* an appointment?
5. Do they	→	*Duh-they*	*Do they have* an appointment?
6. Am I	→	*Mi*	*Am I* late for my appointment?
7. Is it	→	*Zit*	*Is it* time for my appointment?*
8. Does it	→	*Zit*	*Does it* hurt?

第二部分 用聽見字詞的非弱化形式，完成下列問題。

例：你會聽到：Do you want to tell me what the problem is?

你要寫下： _____*Do you*_____ want to tell me what the problem is?

1. _____ have pain anywhere?

2. _____ hurt anywhere else?

3. _____ have a cough or sore throat?

4. _____ have a fever?

5. _____ need lab tests?

6. _____ very sick?

7. _____ serious?

8. _____ need to make another appointment?

9. _____ want to wait in the waiting room?

10. _____ pay now or later?

---

*更多關於口語英文中含 *be* 動詞的問句，請見第 5 章。

❏ **Exercise 34. 口說：訪談** (表 1-7)

用下列字詞寫出問句；然後在教室內走動，詢問及回答問題。答案必須有簡答和詳答兩種形式。

例：be \ Texas \ in South America?
說話者 A：Is Texas in South America?
說話者 B：No, it isn't. Texas is in North America.

1. the earth \ revolve \ around the sun \ right now?
2. the moon \ revolve \ around the earth \ every 28 days?
3. be \ the sun and moon planets?
4. be \ Toronto in western Canada?
5. whales \ lay \ eggs?
6. your country \ have \ gorillas in the wild?
7. be \ gorillas \ intelligent?
8. mosquitoes \ carry \ malaria?
9. you \ like \ vegetarian food?
10. be \ our teacher \ from Australia?
11. it \ rain \ outside \ right now?
12. be \ you \ tired of this interview?

❏ **Exercise 35. 聽力** (表 1-7)

CD 1
Track 9

聆聽 CD 播放的內容，圈選正確的答覆。

例：你會聽到：You look hot and tired. Are you thirsty?
你要圈出： (a.) Yes, I am.
  b. Yes, I do.

1. a. Yes, I want.
   b. Yes, I do.

2. a. Yes, I am.
   b. Yes, I do.

3. a. Yes, it is.
   b. Yes, it does.

4. a. Yes, we do.
   b. Yes, we need.

5. a. Yes, he does.
   b. Yes, he is.

6. a. Yes, they are.
   b. Yes, they do.

❏ **Exercise 36. 文法** (第 1 章)

用括弧內動詞的現在簡單式或現在進行式，完成下列句子。

1. A: My sister (*have*) ___has___ a new car. She bought it last month.

   B: (*you, have*) ___Do you have___ a car?

   A: No, I ___don't___. Do you?

   B: No, but I have a motorcycle.

2. A: What are the children doing? (*they, watch*) _____ TV?

   B: No, they _____. They (*play*) _____ outside.

3. A: Jacob, (*you, listen*) _____ to me?

   B: Of course I am, Mom. You (*want*) _____ me to take out the garbage. Right?

   A: Yes, and I mean now!

4. A: Hey, Becky, where (*be*) _____ you?

   B: I (*be*) _____ in the bedroom.

   A: What (*you, do*) _____?

   B: I (*try*) _____ to sleep!

5. A: What (*you, think*) _____ about at night before you fall asleep?

   B: I (*think*) _____ about my day. But I (*think, not*) _____ about anything negative. What (*think*) _____ about?

   A: I (*think, not*) _____ about anything. I (*count*) _____ sheep.*

6. A: A penny for your thoughts.

   B: Huh?

   A: That means: What (*you, think*) _____ about right now?

   B: I (*think*) _____ about my homework. I (*think, not*) _____ _____ about anything else right now.

   A: I (*believe, not*) _____ you. You (*think*) _____ about your wedding plans!

7. A: (*you, know*) _____ any tongue-twisters?

   B: Yes, I _____. Here's one: She sells seashells down by the seashore.

   A: That (*be*) _____ hard to say! Can you say this: Sharon wears Sue's shoes to zoos to look at cheap sheep?

   B: That (*make, not*) _____ any sense.

   A: I (*know*) _____, but it's fun to say.

---

*count sheep 意指「藉由閉眼數想像中羊隻的數目，而自然入睡。」

❑ **Exercise 37. 閱讀、文法與聽力** (第 1 章)

第一部分 閱讀以下文章，圈選正確的字詞。

Aerobic Exercise

Jeremy and Nancy believe exercise is important. They go to an exercise class three times a week. They like aerobic exercise.

Aerobic exercise is a special type of exercise. It increases a person's heart rate. Fast walking, running, and dancing are examples of aerobic exercise. During aerobic exercise, a person's heart beats fast. This brings more oxygen to the muscles. Muscles work longer when they have more oxygen.

Right now Jeremy and Nancy are listening to some lively music. They are doing special dance steps. They are exercising different parts of their body.

How about you? Do you like to exercise? Do your muscles get exercise every week? Do you do some type of aerobic exercise?

1. Jeremy and Nancy *(think,)* *are thinking* exercise is good for them.

2. They *prefer, are preferring* aerobic exercise.

3. Aerobic exercise *makes, is making* a person's heart beat fast.

4. Muscles *need, are needing* oxygen.

5. With more oxygen, muscles *work, are working* longer.

6. Right now Jeremy and Nancy *do, are doing* a special kind of dance.

7. *Do you exercise, Are you exercising* every week?

8. *Do you exercise, Are you exercising* right now?

第二部分 聆聽 CD 播放的文章，並用聽到的字詞完成下列句子。用一張紙遮住第一部分。

CD 1
Track 10

Aerobic Exercise

Jeremy and Nancy _____ exercise is important. They _____ to
         1   2
an exercise class three times a week. They _____ aerobic exercise.
                                              3

Aerobic exercise _____ a special type of exercise. It _____ a
                    4   5
person's heart rate. Fast walking, running, and dancing _____ examples of aerobic
                                                            6
exercise. During aerobic exercise, a person's heart _____ fast. This
                                                        7
_____ more oxygen to the muscles. Muscles _____ longer when they
        8   9
_____ more oxygen.
   10

Right now Jeremy and Nancy _____ to some lively music. They
                                         11
_____ special dance steps. They _____ different
         12   13
parts of their body.

24 第一章

How about you? _____ you _____ to exercise? _____ your
                        14   15   16
muscles _____ exercise every week? _____ you _____ some type
                  17   18   19
of aerobic exercise?

❑ **Exercise 38. 檢視學習成果**（第 1 章）
校訂以下文章，訂正錯誤的動詞時態。

Omar's Visit

(1) My friend Omar ~~is owning~~ *owns* his own car now. It's brand new.★ Today he driving to a
small town north of the city to visit his aunt. He love to listen to music, so the CD player is
play one of his favorite CDs—loudly. Omar is very happy: he is drive his own car and listen to
loud music. He's look forward to his visit with his aunt.

(2) Omar is visiting his aunt once a week. She's elderly and live alone. She is thinking
Omar a wonderful nephew. She love his visits. He try to be helpful and considerate in every
way. His aunt don't hearing well, so Omar is speaks loudly and clearly when he's with her.

(3) When he's there, he fix things for her around her apartment and help her with her
shopping. He isn't staying with her overnight. He usually is staying for a few hours and then is
heading back to the city. He kiss his aunt good-bye and give her a hug before he is leaving.
Omar is a very good nephew.

★brand new 意指「全新的」。

第二章

過去式

❑ **Exercise 1. 暖身活動** (表 2-1)

勾選 (✓) 符合你自身情況的敘述,並與搭檔分享彼此的答案。

1. ＿＿＿ I stayed up late last night.

2. ＿＿＿ I slept well last night.

3. ＿＿＿ I was tired this morning.

2-1 表達過去的時間:過去簡單式 The Simple Past

(a) Mary **walked** downtown *yesterday*. (b) I **slept** for eight hours *last night*.	過去簡單式用以描述在過去時間開始並結束的活動或情況 (如:*yesterday*、*last night*、*two days ago*、*in 2010*)。
(c) Bob **stayed** home yesterday morning. (d) Our plane **landed** on time last night.	大多數過去簡單式的形式是在字尾加 **-ed**,如:例 (a)、(c) 和 (d)。
(e) I **ate** breakfast this morning. (f) Sue **took** a taxi to the airport yesterday.	有些動詞的過去式為不規則變化,如:例 (b)、(e) 和 (f)。請見表 2-4。
(g) I **was** busy yesterday. (h) They **were** at home last night.	**be** 動詞的過去簡單式形式是 **was** 與 **were**。

規則動詞的過去簡單式形式

直述句	I, You, She, He, It, We, They **worked** yesterday.
否定句	I, You, She, He, It, We, They **did not** (**didn't**) **work** yesterday.
疑問句	**Did** I, you, she, he, it, we, they **work** yesterday?
簡答	Yes, I, you, she, he, it, we, they **did**. 或 No, I, you, she, he, it, we, they **didn't**.

Be 動詞的過去簡單式形式

直述句	I, She, He, It **was** in class yesterday. We, You, They **were** in class yesterday.
否定句	I, She, He, It **was not** (**wasn't**) in class yesterday. We, You, They **were not** (**weren't**) in class yesterday.
疑問句	**Was** I, she, he, it in class yesterday? **Were** we, you, they in class yesterday?
簡答	Yes, I, she, he, it **was**.　　Yes, we, you, they **were**. No, I, she, he, it **wasn't**.　　No, we, you, they **weren't**.

❏ **Exercise 2. 文法** (表 2-1)

製作屬於自己的文法表格。寫出下列斜體字的否定句和疑問句形式，並省略句中其他字詞。

	否定句	疑問句
1. *He needed* water.	*He didn't need*	*Did he need*
2. *She drank* tea.		
3. *They played* baseball.		
4. *I left* early.		
5. *They wore* boots.		
6. *We had* time.		
7. *It was* fun.		
8. *You were* late.		

❏ **Exercise 3. 口說** (表 2-1)

下列所有句子皆含錯誤訊息。用以下兩種句型，寫出符合事實的句子：

(1) 否定句
(2) 含有正確訊息的肯定句

1. Thomas Edison invented the telephone.
   → *Thomas Edison didn't invent the telephone.*
   → *Alexander Graham Bell invented the telephone.*

2. I came to school by hot-air balloon today.

3. The students in this class swam into the classroom today.

4. (*Teacher's name*) is a movie director.

5. I slept in a tree last night.

6. The Internet became popular in the 1970s.

❏ **Exercise 4. 聽力** (第 1 章和表 2-1)

CD 1
Track 11

聆聽 CD 播放的句子，並圈選可完成句子的正確字詞；該字詞可能不只一個。

例：你會聽到：It snows . . .
　　你要圈出：(in the winter.)　　every day.　　now.

1.	French.	together.	last week.
2.	right now.	yesterday.	last summer.
3.	in the evening.	last night.	behind the mountains.
4.	at this moment.	our class.	yesterday.
5.	two weeks ago.	right now.	at this moment.

❑ **Exercise 5. 聽力**（表 2-1）

CD 1
Track 12

在英文口語中，很難聽出 **was/wasn't** 和 **were/weren't** 的差別。否定縮寫中 "t" 的聲音常常被省略，你可能只會聽到 /n/ 的聲音。

第一部分　聆聽 CD 播放的下列範例。

1. I was in a hurry.　I wasn't in a hurry.
2. They were on time.　They weren't on time.
3. He was at the doctor's.　He wasn't at the doctor's.
4. We were early.　We weren't early.

第二部分　圈選聽見的字。在開始前，你或許會想先確定自己是否認識這些字：*wedding*、*nervous*、*excited*、*ceremony*、*reception*。

At a wedding

1.	was	wasn't	6. was	wasn't
2.	was	wasn't	7. was	wasn't
3.	were	weren't	8. was	wasn't
4.	were	weren't	9. were	weren't
5.	was	wasn't	10. were	weren't

❑ **Exercise 6. 暖身活動**（表 2-2）

你知道下列動詞的拼字規則嗎？

第一部分　在正確的類別標題下，寫出各個動詞的 **-ing** 形式（現在分詞）。

die	give	hit	try

去 **-e**，加 **-ing**。	重複字尾子音字母，加 **-ing**。	把 **-ie** 改成 **-y**，加 **-ing**。	直接加 **-ing**。
＿＿＿＿＿	＿＿＿＿＿	＿＿＿＿＿	＿＿＿＿＿

第二部分　在正確的類別標題下，寫出各個動詞的 **-ed** 形式（過去式）。

enjoy	tie	stop	study

重複字尾子音字母，加 **-ed**。	把 **-y** 改成 **-i**，加 **-ed**。	直接加 **-ed**。	只加 **-d**。
＿＿＿＿＿	＿＿＿＿＿	＿＿＿＿＿	＿＿＿＿＿

2-2 拼寫規則：字尾加 *-ing* 或 *-ed* Spelling of *-ing* and *-ed* Forms

動詞字尾字母	重複字尾子音字母	原形	*-ing*	*-ed*	
-e	NO	(a) smil**e** hop**e**	smiling hoping	smil**ed** hop**ed**	*-ing* 形式：去 *-e*，加 *-ing*。 *-ed* 形式：只需加 *-d*。
兩個子音字母	NO	(b) he**lp** lea**rn**	helping learning	help**ed** learn**ed**	以兩個子音字母結尾的動詞， 只需加 *-ing* 或 *-ed*。
兩個母音字母＋一個子音字母	NO	(c) ra**in** he**at**	raining heating	rain**ed** heat**ed**	以兩個母音字母＋一個子音字母結尾的動詞，只需加 *-ing* 或 *-ed*。
一個母音字母＋一個子音字母	YES	單音節動詞			以一個母音字母＋一個子音字母結尾的單音節動詞，則重複字尾子音字母後，再加 *-ing* 或 *-ed*。★
		(d) sto**p** pla**n**	stop**p**ing plan**n**ing	stop**ped** plan**ned**	
	NO	雙音節動詞			若雙音節動詞的重音在第一音節，則不需重複子音字母。
		(e) ví**s**it óf**f**er	visiting offering	visited offered	
	YES	(f) prefér admít	prefer**r**ing admit**t**ing	prefer**red** admit**ted**	若雙音節動詞的重音在第二音節，則必須重複子音字母。
-y	NO	(g) pla**y** enjo**y**	playing enjoying	play**ed** enjoy**ed**	若動詞字尾是母音字母＋ *-y*，保留 *-y*。 不需將 *-y* 改成 *-i*。
	NO	(h) wor**ry** stu**dy**	worrying studying	worr**ied** stud**ied**	若動詞字尾是子音字母＋ *-y*， *-ing* 形式：保留 *-y*，再加 *-ing*。 *-ed* 形式：把 *-y* 改成 *-i*，再加 *-ed*。
-ie		(i) d**ie** t**ie**	dying tying	died tied	若動詞字尾是 *-ie*， *-ing* 形式：把 *-ie* 改成 *-y*，再加 *-ing*。 *-ed* 形式：只需加 *-d*。

★例外：字尾子音字母為 "w" 或 "x" 時，不需重複該子音字母，如：*snow*、*snowing*、*snowed*、*fix*、*fixing*、*fixed*。

❑ **Exercise 7. 拼寫**（表 2-2）

寫出下列動詞的 *-ing* 和 *-ed* 形式。

	-ing	*-ed*
1. wait	_____	_____
2. clean	_____	_____
3. plant	_____	_____
4. plan	_____	_____
5. hope	_____	_____
6. hop	_____	_____

7. play   _____   _____

8. study   _____   _____

9. try   _____   _____

10. die   _____   _____

11. sleep   _____   _slept (no -ed)_

12. run   _____   _ran (no -ed)_

❏ **Exercise 8. 聽力** (表 2-2)

用聽到的動詞完成下列句子；要特別注意拼寫。

CD 1
Track 13

1. Shhh. The movie is _____.

2. Oh, no. The elevator door is stuck. It isn't _____.

3. Here's a letter for you. I _____ it accidentally.

4. I'm _____ to the phone message that you already _____ to.

5. Are you _____ to me or telling me the truth?

6. We _____ the party.

7. I'm _____ the nice weather today.

8. You look upset. What _____?

❏ **Exercise 9. 暖身活動** (表 2-3 和 2-4)

每個動詞都有四種主要形式。你能完成下列表格嗎？

原形	過去式	過去分詞	現在分詞
1. help	_helped_	_helped_	_helping_
2. stay	_____	_____	_____
3. take	_took_	_taken_	_taking_
4. give	_____	_____	_____
5. be	_____	_____	_____

2-3 動詞的主要形式 The Principal Parts of a Verb

規則動詞

原形 (SIMPLE FORM)	過去式 (SIMPLE PAST)	過去分詞 (PAST PARTICIPLE)	現在分詞 (PRESENT PARTICIPLE)
finish	finished	finished	finishing
stop	stopped	stopped	stopping
hope	hoped	hoped	hoping
wait	waited	waited	waiting
play	played	played	playing
try	tried	tried	trying

不規則動詞

see	saw	seen	seeing
make	made	made	making
sing	sang	sung	singing
eat	ate	eaten	eating
put	put	put	putting
go	went	gone	going

動詞的主要形式

（1）原形	英文動詞有四種主要形式，查字典時找到的是**原形**，它是最基本的形式，沒有字尾變化（不加 **-s**、**-ed** 或 **-ing**）。
（2）過去式	規則動詞的過去式是「動詞 + **-ed**」結尾。大部分的動詞是規則動詞，但也有很多常用動詞是不規則變化，常見不規則動詞變化表請見下頁，表 2-4。
（3）過去分詞	規則動詞的過去分詞也是「動詞 + **-ed**」結尾；有些動詞的過去分詞則為不規則變化。過去分詞用在完成式（請見第 4 章）及被動語態（請見第 10 章）。
（4）現在分詞	規則動詞和不規則動詞的現在分詞都是直接加 **-ing**。現在分詞用在進行式中（如：現在進行式和過去進行式）。

2-4 常見不規則動詞變化表

原形	過去式	過去分詞	原形	過去式	過去分詞
be	was, were	been	lend	lent	lent
beat	beat	beaten	let	let	let
become	became	become	lie	lay	lain
begin	began	begun	light	lit/lighted	lit/lighted
bend	bent	bent	lose	lost	lost
bite	bit	bitten	make	made	made
blow	blew	blown	mean	meant	meant
break	broke	broken	meet	met	met
bring	brought	brought	pay	paid	paid
build	built	built	put	put	put
burn	burned/burnt	burned/burnt	quit	quit	quit
buy	bought	bought	read	read	read
catch	caught	caught	ride	rode	ridden
choose	chose	chosen	ring	rang	rung
come	came	come	rise	rose	risen
cost	cost	cost	run	ran	run
cut	cut	cut	say	said	said
dig	dug	dug	see	saw	seen
do	did	done	sell	sold	sold
draw	drew	drawn	send	sent	sent
dream	dreamed/dreamt	dreamed/dreamt	set	set	set
drink	drank	drunk	shake	shook	shaken
drive	drove	driven	shoot	shot	shot
eat	ate	eaten	shut	shut	shut
fall	fell	fallen	sing	sang	sung
feed	fed	fed	sink	sank	sunk
feel	felt	felt	sit	sat	sat
fight	fought	fought	sleep	slept	slept
find	found	found	slide	slid	slid
fit	fit	fit	speak	spoke	spoken
fly	flew	flown	spend	spent	spent
forget	forgot	forgotten	spread	spread	spread
forgive	forgave	forgiven	stand	stood	stood
freeze	froze	frozen	steal	stole	stolen
get	got	got/gotten	stick	stuck	stuck
give	gave	given	swim	swam	swum
go	went	gone	take	took	taken
grow	grew	grown	teach	taught	taught
hang	hung	hung	tear	tore	torn
have	had	had	tell	told	told
hear	heard	heard	think	thought	thought
hide	hid	hidden	throw	threw	thrown
hit	hit	hit	understand	understood	understood
hold	held	held	upset	upset	upset
hurt	hurt	hurt	wake	woke/waked	woken/waked
keep	kept	kept	wear	wore	worn
know	knew	known	win	won	won
leave	left	left	write	wrote	written

❑ **Exercise 10.** 文法 (表 2-4)

填入適當的過去式不規則動詞，以完成下列句子。答案可能不只一個。

1. Alima walked to the office today. Rebecca ___*drove*___ her car. Olga _____ her bike. Yoko _____ the bus.

2. It got so cold last night that the water in the pond _____ .

3. Katya had a choice between a blue raincoat and a brown one. She finally _____ the blue one.

4. My husband gave me a painting for my birthday. I _____ it on a wall in my office.

5. Last night around midnight, when I was sound asleep, the telephone _____ . It _____ me up.

6. The sun _____ at 6:04 this morning and _____ at 6:59 last night.

7. I _____ an email to my cousin after I finished studying last night.

8. Ms. Morita _____ chemistry at the local high school last year.

9. Oh, my gosh! Call the police! Someone _____ my car!

10. The police _____ the car thieves quickly and _____ them to jail.

11. The earthquake was strong, and the ground _____ for two minutes.

12. A bird _____ into the grocery store through an open door.

13. My dog _____ a hole in the yard and buried his bone.

14. I don't have any money in my wallet. I _____ it all yesterday. I'm flat broke.★

15. Ann does funny things. She _____ a tuxedo to her brother's wedding last week.

★*flat broke* 意指「身無分文」。

❏ **Exercise 11. 文法** (表 2-1 → 2-4)

創造屬於自己的表格。寫出下列斜體字的過去式、否定句及問句形式，並省略句中其他字詞。

	過去式	否定句	問句
1. *He skips* lunch.	He skipped	He didn't skip	Did he skip
2. *They leave* early.	_____	_____	_____
3. *She does* a lot.	_____	_____	_____
4. *He is* sick.	_____	_____	_____
5. *We drive* to work.	_____	_____	_____
6. *You are* right.	_____	_____	_____
7. *I plan* my day.	_____	_____	_____

❏ **Exercise 12. 口說：兩人一組** (表 2-1 → 2-4)

成兩人一組；運用 **Yes** 和完整句回答下列問題。

A broken arm

想像你昨天在冰上滑倒，今天手上裹著一大塊石膏上學。

1. Did you have a bad day yesterday? → *Yes, I had a bad day yesterday.*
2. Did you fall down?
3. Did you hurt yourself when you fell down?
4. Did you break your arm?
5. Did you go to the emergency room?

互換角色。
6. Did you see a doctor?
7. Did you sit in the waiting room for a long time?
8. Did the doctor put a cast on your arm?
9. Did you pay a lot of money?
10. Did you come home exhausted?

❏ **Exercise 13. 文法** (表 2-1 → 2-4)

用括弧中字詞的正確形式，完成下列對話。

1. A: (*you, sleep*) __Did you sleep__ well last night?

   B: Yes, __I did__. I (*sleep*) __slept__ very well.

2. A: (*Ella's plane, arrive*) _____ on time yesterday?

   B: Yes, _____. It (*get*) _____ in at exactly 6:05.

3. A: (*you, go*) _____ away last weekend?

 B: No, _____. I (*stay*) _____ home because I (*feel, not*)
 _____ good.

4. A: (*you, eat*) _____ breakfast this morning?

 B: No, _____. I (*have, not*) _____ enough time. I
 was late for class because my alarm clock (*ring, not*) _____.

5. A: (*Da Vinci, paint*) _____ the *Mona Lisa?*

 B: Yes, _____. He also (*paint*) _____ other famous
 pictures.

❑ **Exercise 14. 文法** (表 2-1 → 2-4)
閱讀下列每個人的日常活動，並以列舉動詞的正確形式，完成下列句子。

情境 1：旋風 Wendy (Whirlwind Wendy) 總是充滿活力，且做事迅速。以下是她典型的上午作息。

Activities:
 wake up at 4:00 A.M.
 clean her apartment
 ride her bike five miles
 get vegetables from her garden
 watch a cooking show on TV
 make soup for dinner
 bring her elderly mother a meal
 read the day's paper
 fix herself lunch

Yesterday, Wendy . . .

1. ___*woke*_____ up at 4:00 A.M.

2. ___*didn't clean*_____ her car.

3. _____ her bike ten miles.

4. _____ vegetables from her garden.

5. _____ a comedy show on TV.

6. _____ soup for dinner.

7. _____ her elderly mother a meal.

8. _____ a book.

9. _____ herself a snack.

情境 2：懶惰蟲 Sam (Sluggish Sam) 總是偷懶，動作又慢，一天做不了幾件事。以下是他典型的一天。

一日作息：

sleep for 12 hours   come home
wake up at noon   lie on the couch
take two hours to eat breakfast   think about his busy life
go fishing   begin dinner at 8:00
fall asleep on his boat   finish dinner at 11:00

Yesterday, Sam . . .

1. _____*slept*_____ for 12 hours.

2. _____*didn't wake*_____ up at 5:00 A.M.

3. _____ two hours to eat breakfast.

4. _____ hiking.

5. _____ asleep on his boat.

6. _____ home.

7. _____ on his bed.

8. _____ about his busy life.

9. _____ dinner at 5:00.

10. _____ dinner at 11:00.

❑ **Exercise 15. 口說：兩人一組** (表 2-1 → 2-4)

成兩人一組。學生 A 指示學生 B 表演一個動作，學生 B 做完動作後，學生 A 再用過去式問學生 B 一個問題。

例：Open your book.
學生 A：Open your book.
學生 B：(*opens his/her book*)
學生 A：What did you do?
學生 B：I opened my book.

互換角色。

1. Shut your book.
2. Stand up.
3. Hide your pen.
4. Turn to page 10 in your book.
5. Put your book in your lap.
6. Nod your head "yes."
7. Tear a piece of paper.
8. Spell the past tense of "speak."
9. Write your name on the board.
10. Draw a triangle under your name.
11. Shake your head "no."
12. Invite our teacher to have lunch with us.
13. Read a sentence from your grammar book.
14. Wave "good-bye."
15. Ask me for a pencil.
16. Repeat this question: "Which came first: the chicken or the egg?"

❏ **Exercise 16. 聽力**（表 2-1 → 2-4）

CD 1
Track 14

第一部分　did 置於問句開頭時，該字的發音常常會弱化；接在 did 後面的代名詞發音或許也會改變。聆聽與 did 結合後的弱化音。

1. Did you	→	*Did-ja*	Did you forget something?
		Did-ya	Did you forget something?
2. Did I	→	*Dih-di*	Did I forget something?
		Di	Did I forget something?
3. Did he	→	*Dih-de*	Did he forget something?
		De	Did he forget something?
4. Did she	→	*Dih-she*	Did she forget something?
5. Did we	→	*Dih-we*	Did we forget something?
6. Did they	→	*Dih-they*	Did they forget something?

第二部分　你將會聽到 CD 播放的問句；用聽到動詞的非弱化形式，完成下列答句。

1. Yes, he ___did___ . He ___cut___ it with a knife.

2. Yes, she _____ . She _____ it all yesterday.

3. Yes, I _____ . I _____ them yesterday.

4. Yes, they _____ . They _____ it.

5. Yes, you _____ . You _____ it.

6. Yes, she _____ . She _____ them.

7. Yes, he _____ . He _____ it to him.

8. Yes, I _____ . I _____ them yesterday.

9. Yes, he _____ . He _____ it.

10. Yes, you _____ . You _____ her.

❏ **Exercise 17. 聽力**（表 2-1 → 2-4）

CD 1
Track 15

聆聽 CD 播放的問句，用聽到動詞的正確形式，完成下列答句。

Luka wasn't home last night.

1. Yes, he ___went___ to a party last night.

2. Yes, he _____ a good time.

3. Yes, he _____ a lot of food.

4. Yes, he _____ a lot of soda.

5. Yes, he _____ some new people.

6. Yes, he _____ hands with them when he met them.

7. Yes, he _____ with friends.

8. Yes, he _____ with his friends and _____ .

Exercise 18. 文法 (表 2-1 → 2-4)

用過去式重寫以下段落，用 ***Yesterday morning*** 作爲新段落的開頭。

The Daily News

Every morning, Jake reads the newspaper online. He wants to know the latest news. He enjoys the business section most. His wife, Eva, doesn't read any newspapers on her computer. She downloads them on her ebook* reader. She looks at the front pages first. She doesn't have a lot of time. She finishes the articles later in the day. Both Jake and Eva are very knowledgeable about the day's events.

Exercise 19. 聽力 (表 2-1 → 2-4)

CD 1 Track 16

第一部分 回答下列問題，然後闔上書本，聆聽 CD 播放的文章。

Did you get the flu** last year?

Were you very sick?

What symptoms did you have?

第二部分 打開你的書本，並閱讀下列敘述。對的敘述圈選 T；錯的則圈 F。

1. The flu kills a lot of people worldwide every year.   T   F

2. The flu virus from 1918 to 1920 was a usual flu virus.   T   F

3. Most of the people who died were very young or very old.   T   F

第三部分 再次聆聽此篇文章，並用聽到的字詞完成下列句子。

A Deadly Flu

Every year, the flu _____ 200,000 to 300,000 people around the world. But in
1

1918, a very strong flu virus _____ millions of people. This flu _____ in
2 3

1918 and _____ until 1920. It _____ around the world, and between
4 5

20 million and 100 million people _____. Unlike other flu viruses that usually
6

_____ the very young and the very old, many of the victims _____ healthy
7 8

young adults. This _____ unusual and _____ people especially afraid.
9 10

---

*ebook 意指「電子書 (electronic book)」。

**the flu 爲「流行性感冒」；通常伴隨的症狀爲發燒、疼痛、倦怠、咳嗽及流鼻水。

❏ **Exercise 20. 暖身活動：聽力** (表 2-5)

第一部分 聆聽 CD 播放的各組動詞，並判斷各個動詞字尾的發音是否相同。

例：你會聽到：plays　played

你要圈出：same　(different)

1. same　different　　　3. same　different

2. same　different　　　4. same　different

第二部分 聆聽 CD 播放的句子，各句皆含過去式動詞。字尾 *-ed* 的發音應該是：/t/、/d/ 或是 /əd/？

例：你會聽到：Jack played a game of tennis.

你要圈出：/t/　(/d/)　　/əd/

1. /t/　　/d/　　/əd/　　　3. /t/　　/d/　　/əd/

2. /t/　　/d/　　/əd/　　　4. /t/　　/d/　　/əd/

2-5 規則動詞：字尾 *-ed* 的發音

(a) talked	=	talk/*t*/
stopped	=	stop/*t*/
hissed	=	hiss/*t*/
watched	=	watch/*t*/
washed	=	wash/*t*/

字尾 *-ed* 接在「無聲音」的字母之後，要發 /t/ 的音。
藉由推擠空氣穿過嘴巴，便能發出「無聲音」。
你的喉嚨不會發出任何聲音。

「無聲音」有：/k/、/p/、/s/、/ch/、/sh/。

(b) called	=	call/*d*/
rained	=	rain/*d*/
lived	=	live/*d*/
robbed	=	rob/*d*/
stayed	=	stay/*d*/

字尾 *-ed* 接在「有聲音」的字母之後，要發 /d/ 的音。
用喉嚨發出「有聲音」，且喉頭會震動。

「有聲音」有：/l/、/n/、/v/、/b/，以及所有的母音。

(c) waited	=	wait/*əd*/
needed	=	need/*əd*/

字尾 *-ed* 接在發 /t/ 和 /d/ 兩個音的字母之後，要發 /əd/ 的音。
添加 /əd/ 的音，會讓該字增加一個音節。

❏ **Exercise 21. 聽力** (第 1 章和表 2-5)

聆聽 CD 播放的句子，並圈選聽到的動詞形式。

例：你會聽到：I needed more help.

你要圈出：need　needs　(needed)

1. agree　　agrees　　agreed　　　5. end　　ends　　ended

2. agree　　agrees　　agreed　　　6. stop　　stops　　stopped

3. arrive　　arrives　　arrived　　　7. touch　　touches　　touched

4. explain　　explains　　explained

□ **Exercise 22. 聽力**（第 1 章和表 2-5）

CD 1
Track 19

聆聽 CD 播放的句子，並圈選可以完成句子的正確字詞。

例：你會聽到：We worked in small groups . . .

你要圈出：right now.　　(yesterday.)

1. every day.　　　　　yesterday.

2. right now.　　　　　last week.

3. six days a week.　　yesterday.

4. now.　　　　　　　last weekend.

5. every day.　　　　　yesterday.

6. every day.　　　　　yesterday.

□ **Exercise 23. 聽力與發音**（表 2-5）

CD 1
Track 20

聆聽 CD 中播放的過去式動詞發音。寫下聽到字尾 **-ed** 的發音：/t/、/d/ 或是 /əd/。最後再做這些動詞的發音練習。

1. cooked /t /　　　5. started /　　/　　　9. added /　　/

2. served /　　/　　6. dropped /　　/　　10. passed /　　/

3. wanted /　　/　　7. pulled /　　/　　11. returned /　　/

4. asked /　　/　　8. pushed /　　/　　12. pointed /　　/

□ **Exercise 24. 聽力與口說**（表 2-1 → 2-5）

第一部分　聆聽 CD 播放兩位朋友談論彼此周末活動的對話，然後回答下列問題。

CD 1
Track 21

1. One person had a good weekend. Why?
2. His friend didn't have a good weekend. Why not?

第二部分 使用過去式動詞,和你的搭檔一起完成以下對話,練習到可以不看課本就說出對話。然後和搭檔互換角色,並設計全新的對話。最後表演其中一組對話給全班觀賞。

A: Did you have a good weekend?

B: Yeah, I _____.

A: Really? That sounds like fun!

B: It _____ great! I _____.

How about you? How was your weekend?

A: I _____.

B: Did you have a good time?

A: Yes. / No. / Not really. _____

_____.

❑ **Exercise 25. 暖身活動** (表 2-6)

將 A 欄中的句子與 B 欄中的描述互相配對。

A 欄

1. I looked at the limousine.
   The movie star was waving
   out the window. _____

2. I looked at the limousine.
   The movie star waved at me. _____

B 欄

a. First I looked at the limousine.
   Then the movie star waved.

b. First the movie star began waving.
   Then I looked at the limousine.

2-6 過去簡單式與過去進行式 Simple Past and Past Progressive

過去簡單式	(a) Mary **walked** downtown yesterday. (b) I **slept** for eight hours last night.	過去簡單式用來表示「在過去時間開始並結束的動作或情況」，（如：*yesterday, last night, two days ago, in 2007*），請見例 (a) 與例 (b)。
過去進行式 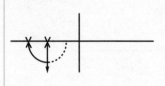	(c) I sat down at the dinner table at 6:00 P.M. yesterday. Tom came to my house at 6:10 P.M. I **was eating** dinner *when Tom came.* (d) I went to bed at 10:00. The phone rang at 11:00. I **was sleeping** *when the phone rang.*	過去進行式則表示在過去某個時間，或另一個動作發生時，「正在進行中（出現或發生中）」的動作。 如：例 (c)，吃的動作在 6 點 10 分正進行著，吃的動作「在湯姆來到時」也正進行著。 形式：**was**/**were** + **-ing**

(e) **When** *the phone rang,* I was sleeping. (f) The phone rang **while** *I was sleeping.*	**when** = 當時 **while** = 在那段時間內 例 (e) 與例 (f) 同義。

過去進行式的形式

直述句	I, She, He, It **was working**. You, We, They **were working**.		
否定句	I, She, He, It **was not** (**wasn't**) **working**. You, We, They **were not** (**weren't**) **working**.		
疑問句	**Was** I, she, he, it **working**? **Were** you, we, they **working**?		
簡答	Yes, I, she, he, it **was**. No, I, she, he, it **wasn't**.	Yes, you, we, they **were**. No, you, we, they **weren't**.	

1. At 6:00 P.M. Robert sat down at the table and began to eat. At 6:05, Robert (*eat*)
   <u>was eating</u> dinner.

2. While Robert (*eat*) _____ dinner, Ann (*come*) _____
   through the door.

3. In other words, when Ann (*come*) _____ through the door, Robert (*eat*)
   _____ dinner.

4. Robert went to bed at 10:30. At 11:00, Robert (*sleep*) _____.

5. While Robert (*sleep*) _____, his cell phone (*ring*) _____.

6. In other words, when his cell phone (*ring*) _____, Robert (*sleep*)
   _____.

7. Robert left his house at 8:00 A.M. and (*begin*) _____ to walk to class.

8. While he (*walk*) _____ to class, he (*see*) _____
   Mr. Ito.

9. When Robert (*see*) _____ Mr. Ito, he (*stand*) _____ in his
   driveway. He (*hold*) _____ a broom.

10. Mr. Ito (*wave*) _____ to Robert when he (*see*) _____ him.

☐ **Exercise 27. 文法**（表 2-6）

運用表格中的資訊，以口語或書寫的方式完成下列句子。一個子句用過去簡單式，另一個則用過去進行式。

進行中的活動	Beth	David	Lily
sit in a café	order a salad	pay a few bills	spill coffee on her lap
stand in an elevator	send a text message	run into an old friend	drop her glasses
swim in the ocean	avoid a shark	saw a dolphin	find a shipwreck

1. While Beth ___*was sitting*___ in a café, she ___*ordered*___ a salad.

2. David ___*paid*___ a few bills while he ___*was sitting*___ in a café.

3. Lily _____ coffee on her lap while she _____ in a café.

4. While Beth _____ in an elevator, she _____ a text message on her cell phone.

5. David _____ an old friend while he _____ in an elevator.

6. Lily _____ her glasses while she _____ in an elevator.

7. Beth _____ a shark while she _____ in the ocean.

8. While David _____ in the ocean, he _____ a dolphin.

9. While Lily _____ in the ocean, she _____ a shipwreck.

❑ **Exercise 28. 口說** (表 2-6)

老師將會要求兩位學生執行一項任務，在他們完成之後，另外兩位學生則要描述這項任務。只有老師的書本是打開的。

例：對學生 A 說：Write on the board.　　對學生 B 說：Open the door.

對學生 A 說：Please write your name on the board.（學生 A 在黑板上寫字）
　　　　　　　What are you doing?
　　學生 A：I'm writing on the board.
　　　老師：Good. Keep writing.

對學生 B 說：Open the door.（學生 B 開門） What did you just do?
　　學生 B：I opened the door.
對學生 A 說：Please stop writing.

對學生 C 說：Describe the two actions that just occurred, using *when*.
　　學生 C：When (_____) opened the door, (_____) was writing on the board.

對學生 D 說：Now describe the actions, using *while*.
　　學生 D：While (_____) was writing on the board, (_____) opened the door.

1. 對 A 說：Write a note to (_____).　　　對 B 說：Knock on the door.
2. 對 A 說：Read your book.　　　　　　　對 B 說：Take (_____)'s grammar book.
3. 對 A 說：Look at me.　　　　　　　　　對 B 說：Leave the room.
4. 對 A 說：Put your head on your desk.　　對 B 說：Drop your pencil.
5. 對 A 說：Look under your desk.　　　　　對 B 說：Begin doing your homework.

❑ **Exercise 29. 文法** (表 2-6)

閱讀下列各組句子，並回答問題。

1. a. Julia was eating breakfast. She heard the breaking news* report.
   b. Sara heard the breaking news report. She ate breakfast.

   問題：Who heard the news report during breakfast?

2. a. Carlo was fishing at the lake. A fish was jumping out of the water.
   b. James was fishing at the lake. A fish jumped out of the water.

   問題：Who saw a fish jump just one time?

3. a. When the sun came out, Paul walked home.
   b. When the sun came out, Vicky was walking home.

   問題：Who walked home after the sun came out?

---

breaking news 意指「電視或廣播上的即時新聞」。

Exercise 30. 閱讀 (表 2-6)

閱讀以下文章，然後再閱讀各項敘述。對的敘述圈 T；錯的則圈 F。

The First Cell Phone

The first cell phone call took place* in 1973. A man named Martin Cooper made the first call. He was working for the Motorola communications company. When Cooper placed the call, he was walking down a street in New York. People stared at him and wondered about his behavior. This was before cordless phones,** so it looked very strange.

It took another ten years before Motorola had a phone to sell to the public. That phone weighed about a pound (.45 kilogram), and it was very expensive. Now, as you know, cell phones are small enough to put in a pocket, and millions of people around the world have them.

1. A customer for Motorola made the first cell phone call.   T   F
2. Many people looked at Cooper when he was talking on the phone.   T   F
3. In the 1970s, cordless phones were very popular.   T   F
4. A few years after the first call, Motorola sold phones to the public.   T   F
5. The first cell phone was very small.   T   F

❑ **Exercise 31. 聽力** (表 2-6)

聆聽 CD 播放的各組對話；然後再聽一遍，並用聽到的字詞完成下列句子。

CD 1
Track 22 **At a checkout stand in a grocery store**

1. A: Hi. _____ what you needed?

   B: Almost everything. I _____ for sticky rice, but I

   _____ it.

   A: _____ on aisle 10, in the Asian food section.

2. A: This is the express lane. Ten items only. It _____ like you have more than

   ten. _____ count them?

   B: I _____ I _____ ten. Oh, I _____ I have more.

   Sorry.

   A: The checkout stand next to me is open.

3. A: _____ any coupons you wanted to use?

   B: I _____ a couple in my purse, but I can't find them now.

   A: What _____ they for? I might have some extras here.

   B: One _____ for eggs, and the other _____ for ice cream.

   A: I think I have those.

---

*take place = occur, happen，意指「發生」。

**cordless phones 意指「無線電話」。

❑ **Exercise 32. 文法** (表 1-1 和 2-6)

將下列各組對話中的現在進行式和過去進行式動詞劃底線。討論兩種動詞形式的使用方式，這兩種時態有什麼相似之處？

1. A: Where are Jan and Mark? Are they on vacation?
   B: Yes, they<u>'re traveling</u> in Kenya for a few weeks.

2. A: I invited Jan and Mark to my birthday party, but they didn't come.
   B: Why not?
   A: They were on vacation. They were traveling in Kenya.

3. A: What was I talking about when the phone interrupted me? I forget!
   B: You were describing the Web site you found on the Internet yesterday.

4. A: I missed the beginning of the news report. What's the announcer talking about?
   B: She's describing damage from the earthquake in Pakistan.

❑ **Exercise 33. 文法** (第 1 章和表 2-1 → 2-6)

用括弧內動詞的現在式、現在進行式、過去式或是過去進行式，完成下列句子。

第一部分

Right now Toshi and Oscar (*sit*) <u>are sitting</u> in the library. Toshi (*do*)
    1
_____ his homework, but Oscar (*study, not*) _____. He
    2   3
(*stare*) _____ out the window. Toshi (*want*) _____ to know
    4   5
what Oscar (*look*) _____ at.
    6

TOSHI: Oscar, what (*you, look*) _____ at?
    7

OSCAR: I (*watch*) _____ the skateboarder. Look at that
    8
    guy in the orange shirt. He (*turn*) _____ around
    9
    in circles on his back wheels. He's amazing!

TOSHI: It (*be*) _____ easier than it (*look*) _____.
    10   11
    I can teach you some skateboarding basics if you'd like.

OSCAR: Great! Thanks!

第二部分

Yesterday Toshi and Oscar (*sit*) <u>were sitting</u> in the library. Toshi (*do*)
    12
_____ his homework, but Oscar (*study, not*) _____. He
    13   14
(*stare*) _____ out the window. Toshi (*want*) _____ to know
    15   16
what Oscar (*look*) _____ at. Oscar (*point*) _____ to the
    17   18
skateboarder. He (*say*) _____ that he was amazing. Toshi (*offer*)
    19
_____ to teach him some skateboarding basics.
    20

Exercise 34. 暖身活動（表 2-7）

勾選 (✓) 具有以下含義的句子：

「先發生的動作」：We gathered our bags.

「後發生的動作」：The train arrived at the station.

1. _____ We gathered our bags before the train arrived at the station.
2. _____ Before the train arrived at the station, we gathered our bags.
3. _____ After we gathered our bags, the train arrived at the station.
4. _____ As soon as the train arrived at the station, we gathered our bags.
5. _____ We didn't gather our bags until the train arrived at the station.

2-7 表達過去時間的副詞子句

(a) ┌─時間副詞子句─┐ ┌─主要子句─┐ **After I finished my work,** *I went to bed.* ┌─主要子句─┐ ┌──時間副詞子句──┐ (b) *I went to bed* **after I finished my work.**	**After I finished my work** = 時間副詞子句★ **I went to bed** = 主要子句 例 (a) 和例 (b) 同義。 時間副詞子句可放在： (1) 主要子句之前，如：例 (a)； (2) 主要子句之後，如：例 (b)。
(c) I went to bed **after** I finished my work. (d) **Before** I went to bed, I finished my work. (e) I stayed up **until** I finished my work. (f) **As soon as** I finished my work, I went to bed. (g) The phone rang **while** I was watching TV. (h) **When** the phone rang, I was watching TV.	用下列字詞引導這類時間副詞子句： *after* *before* *until* ⎱ *as soon as* ⎰ + 主詞和動詞 = 時間副詞子句 *while* *when*
	例 (e)：*until* = 到那時為止★★ 例 (f)：*as soon as* = 緊接著之後
	標點符號：當時間副詞子句置於句首時（在主要子句之前），在該子句後加逗點： 　時間副詞子句＋逗點＋主要子句 　主要子句（**不加逗點**）＋ 時間副詞子句
(i) When the phone **rang,** I **answered** it.	當 *when* 引導時間副詞子句時，時間副詞子句和主要子句中的動詞均用過去式。在這種情況下，*when* 子句中的動作先發生。 例 (i)：先：*The phone rang.* 　　　後：*I answered it.*
(j) While I **was doing** my homework, my roommate **was watching** TV.	例 (j)：當時間副詞子句與主要子句中的動作同時都在進行時，這兩個動詞可同時使用過去進行式。

★「子句」是具有一個主詞和一個動詞的句子結構。

★★*Until* 也可以用來表示在某特定時間點之前，某件事「尚未」發生，例：*I didn't* go to bed *until I* finished my work.（在完成工作前，我不睡覺。）

❏ **Exercise 35.** 文法 (表 2-7)

勾選 (✓) 所有的子句。切記：一個子句必須要有主詞和語義完整的動詞。

1. _____ applying for a visa
2. _____ while the woman was applying for a visa
3. _____ the man took passport photos
4. _____ when the man took passport photos
5. _____ as soon as he finished
6. _____ he needed to finish
7. _____ after she sent her application
8. _____ sending her application

❏ **Exercise 36.** 文法 (表 2-7)

在下列子句下劃底線，然後再決定哪一個先發生（標示 1），哪一個後發生（標示 2）。

1. a. After the taxi dropped me off, I remembered my coat in the backseat.
   b. I remembered my coat in the backseat after the taxi dropped me off.

2. a. Before I got out of the taxi, I double-checked the address.
   b. Before I double-checked the address, I got out of the taxi.

3. a. As soon as I tipped the driver, he helped me with my luggage.
   b. As soon as the driver helped me with my luggage, I tipped him.

❏ **Exercise 37.** 文法 (表 2-7)

用時間副詞子句將下列各組句子合併為一句，並討論標點符號的正確用法。

1. 先發生：I got home.

   後發生：I ate dinner.

   After _I got home, I ate dinner._

   I ate dinner after _I got home._

2. 先發生：I unplugged the coffee pot.

   後發生：I left my apartment this morning.

   Before _____

   _____ before _____

3. 先發生：I lived on a farm.

   後發生：I was seven years old.

   Until _____

   _____ until _____

4. 先發生：I heard the doorbell.

   後發生：I opened the door.

   As soon as _____

   _____ as soon as _____

5. 先發生：It began to rain.

   後發生：I stood under my umbrella.

   When _____

   _____ when _____

6. 同時間發生：I was lying in bed with the flu.

   　　　　　　My friends were swimming at the beach.

   While _____

   _____ while _____

❏ **Exercise 38. 文法** (表 2-1 → 2-7)
   用括弧內動詞的過去式或過去進行式，完成下列句子，並用括弧標示出時間副詞子句。

1. My mom called me around 5:00. My husband came home a little after that. [When he
   (*get*) __got__ home,] I (*talk*) __was talking__ to my mom on the phone.

2. I (*buy*) _____ a small gift before I (*go*) _____ to the hospital
   yesterday to visit my friend.

3. Yesterday afternoon I (*go*) _____ to visit the Lopez family. When I (*get*)
   _____ there, Mrs. Lopez (*be*) _____ in the yard. She (*plant*)
   _____ flowers. Mr. Lopez (*be*) _____ in the garage.
   He (*change*) _____ the oil on his car. The kids (*play*)
   _____ in the front yard. In other words, while Mr. Lopez (*change*)
   _____ the oil in the car, the kids (*throw*) _____
   a ball in the yard.

4. I (*hit*) _____ my thumb while I (*use*) _____ the hammer.
   Ouch! That (*hurt*) _____.

5. As soon as we (*hear*) _____ about the hurricane, we (*begin*)
   _____ to get ready for the storm.

6. It was a long walk home. Mr. Chu (*get*) _____ tired and (*stop*)
   _____ after an hour. He (*rest*) _____ until he (*feel*)
   _____ strong enough to continue.

❑ **Exercise 39. 聽力** (第 1 章和表 2-1 → 2-7)

閤上書本，聆聽 CD 播放的文章；然後再聽一遍，並用聽到的字詞完成下列句子。

Jennifer's Problem

Jennifer _____ for an insurance company. When people _____ help
with their car insurance, they _____ her. Right now it is 9:05 A.M., and Jennifer
_____ at her desk.

She _____ to work on time this morning. Yesterday Jennifer _____ late
to work because she _____ a minor auto accident. While she _____
to work, her cell phone _____. She _____ for it.

While she _____ for her phone, Jennifer _____ control of the
car. Her car _____ into a row of mailboxes beside the road and _____.
Fortunately no one was hurt in the accident.

Jennifer _____ okay, but her car _____. It _____ repairs.
Jennifer _____ very embarrassed now. She _____ a bad decision, especially
since it is illegal to talk on a cell phone and drive at the same time where she lives.

❑ **Exercise 40. 暖身活動** (表 2-8)

第一部分　回想你當初剛開始學英文時的經歷。勾選 (✓) 符合你自身狀況的敘述。

When I was a beginning learner of English, . . .

1. _____ I remained quiet when someone asked me a question.
2. _____ I checked my dictionary frequently.
3. _____ I asked people to speak very, very slowly.
4. _____ I translated sentences into my language a lot.

第二部分　看看自己勾選的句子。這些敘述是否已不符合現況？如果答案為「是」，另一種表達
此種概念的方式是使用 ***used to***。下列哪些句子符合你自身的狀況？

1. I used to remain quiet when someone asked me a question.
2. I used to check my dictionary frequently.
3. I used to ask people to speak very, very slowly.
4. I used to translate sentences into my language a lot.

2-8 表示過去的習慣：*Used To*

(a) I ***used to live*** with my parents. Now I live in my own apartment.	***used to*** 用來表示現在已經不存在的過去情況或習慣。
(b) Ann ***used to be*** afraid of dogs, but now she likes dogs.	形式：***used to*** + 動詞原形
(c) Al ***used to smoke***, but he doesn't anymore.	
(d) ***Did*** you ***used to*** live in Paris? (或 ***Did*** you ***use to*** live in Paris?)	疑問句形式：***did*** + 主詞 + ***used to*** （或 ***did*** + 主詞 + ***use to***）★
(e) I ***didn't used to*** drink coffee at breakfast, but now I always have coffee in the morning. (或 I ***didn't use to*** drink coffee.)	否定句形式：***didn't used to*** （或 ***didn't use to***）★
(f) I ***never*** ***used to*** drink coffee at breakfast, but now I always have coffee in the morning.	以上用法少見，常見的否定句形式為 *never used to*，如：例 (f)。

★在疑問句和否定句中，***used to*** 和 ***use to*** 兩種形式皆可。英文語言權威對於何者較佳並無定論。此本書兼用兩種形式。

❑ **Exercise 41. 文法**（表 2-8）

用 ***used to*** 造出意義相近的句子；部分句子為否定句，部分句子為疑問句。

1. *When I was a child, I was shy. Now I'm not shy.*

   I ___used to be___ shy, but now I'm not.

2. *When I was young, I thought that people over 40 were old.*

   I _____ that people over 40 were old.

3. *Now you live in this city. Where did you live before you came here?*

   Where _____ ?

4. *Did you work for the phone company at some time in the past?*

   _____ for the phone company?

5. *When I was younger, I slept through the night. I never woke up in the middle of the night.*

   I _____ in the middle of the night, but now I do.

   I _____ through the night, but now I don't.

6. *When I was a child, I watched cartoons on TV. I don't watch cartoons anymore. Now I watch news programs.*

   I _____ cartoons on TV, but I don't anymore.

   I _____ news programs, but now I do.

7. *How about you?*

   What _____ on TV when you were little?

❑ **Exercise 42.** 採訪：找出…的人 (表 2-8)

在教室裡走動。用各題中的字詞造一個 ***used to*** 的問句。當你找到回答 "*yes*" 的人，就將這個人的名字寫下來，然後再繼續問下一個問題。最後，與全班分享一些你的答案。

Find someone who used to . . .

1. play in the mud. → *Did you use to play in the mud?*
2. play with dolls or toy soldiers.
3. roller skate.
4. swing on a rope swing.
5. catch frogs or snakes.
6. get into trouble at school.
7. dress up in your mother's or father's clothes.

❑ **Exercise 43.** 聽力 (表 2-8)

CD 1
Track 24

used to 常常唸成 /usta/。聆聽 CD 播放的範例，然後用聽見字詞的非弱化形式，完成下列句子。

例：I used to (*usta*) ride my bike to work, but now I take the bus.
I didn't used to (*usta*) be late when I rode my bike to work.
Did you use to (*usta*) ride your bike to work?

1. I ___*used to stay*___ up past midnight, but now I often go to bed at 10:00 because I have an 8:00 class.

2. What time _____ to bed when you were a child?

3. Tom _____ tennis after work every day, but now he doesn't.

4. I _____ breakfast, but now I always have something to eat in the morning because I read that students who eat breakfast do better in school.

5. I _____ grammar, but now I do.

❑ **Exercise 44.** 檢視學習成果 (表 2-8)

校訂下列句子，訂正錯誤的動詞時態。

1. Alex used to ~~living~~ ^{live} in Cairo.

2. Junko used to worked for an investment company.

3. Margo was used to teach English, but now she works at a publishing company.

4. Where you used to live?

5. I didn't was used to get up early, but now I do.

6. Were you used to live in Singapore?

7. My family used to going to the beach every weekend, but now we don't.

第一部分　閱讀關於一位有名作家的文章，然後再閱讀文章後的敘述句。對的敘述圈 T；錯的則圈 F。

J. K. Rowling

Did you know that J. K. Rowling used to be an English language teacher before she became successful as the author of the *Harry Potter* series? She taught English to students in Portugal. She lived there from 1991 to 1994. During that time, she also worked on her first *Harry Potter* book.

After she taught in Portugal, she went back to Scotland. By then she was a single mother with a young daughter. She didn't have much money, but she didn't want to return to teaching until she completed her book. Rowling enjoyed drinking coffee, so she did much of her writing in a café while her daughter took naps. She wrote quickly, and when her daughter was three, Rowling finished *Harry Potter and the Philosopher's Stone.*★

Many publishers were not interested in her book. She doesn't remember how many rejection letters she got, maybe twelve. Finally a small publishing company, Bloomsbury, accepted it. Shortly after its publication, the book began to sell quickly, and Rowling soon became famous. Now there are seven *Harry Potter* books, and Rowling is one of the wealthiest and most successful women in the world.

1. Rowling finished the first *Harry Potter* book in 1993.　　　T　　F
2. Rowling did a lot of writing in a café.　　　T　　F
3. At first, publishers loved her work.　　　T　　F
4. Soon after her book came out, many people bought it.　　　T　　F
5. Rowling still works as a teacher.　　　T　　F

第二部分　選擇一位你感興趣的作家或歌手，並尋找關於該作家或歌手的生平資料；將其重要或有趣的事件列成清單，並運用這些資訊撰寫一個段落。謹慎校訂每個動詞。

★在美國和印度，此書名被改爲 *Harry Potter and the Sorcerer's Stone*。

第三章
未來式

□ **Exercise 1. 暖身活動** (表 3-1)

下列哪些句子表達了未來事件的含義？未來式句子的含義是否相同？

1. The train is going to leave a few minutes late today.
2. The train left a few minutes late today.
3. The train will leave a few minutes late today.

3-1 表示未來時間：*Be Going To* 和 *Will*		
未來	(a) I *am going to leave* at nine tomorrow morning. (b) I *will leave* at nine tomorrow morning.	*be going to* 和 *will* 用來表示未來時間。 例 (a) 和例 (b) 同義。 *will* 和 *be going to* 有時候表達不同的意義，表 3-5 將討論兩者間的差異。
(c) Sam *is* in his office **this morning**. (d) Ann *was* in her office **this morning** at eight, but now she's at a meeting. (e) Bob *is going to be* in his office **this morning** after his dentist appointment.		*today*、*tonight* 和 *this* + *morning*/ *afternoon*/*evening*/*week* 等均可表示現在、過去和未來時間，如：例 (c) 到例 (e)。

注意：也可以使用 *shall*（與 *I* 或 *we* 連用）來表達未來時間，但此用法不常見，且較為正式，如：*I shall* leave at nine tomorrow morning. 和 *We shall* leave at ten tomorrow morning.

CD 1
Track 25

聆聽 CD 播放的句子。如果句子表達未來時間，圈選 *yes*；如果不是，則圈 *no*。

例：你會聽到：The airport will be busy.

你要圈出：(yes) no

At the airport

1. yes no   5. yes no
2. yes no   6. yes no
3. yes no   7. yes no
4. yes no   8. yes no

□ **Exercise 3. 暖身活動** (表 3-2)

用正確的 *be* 動詞 (+ *not*) 的形式完成下列符合自身狀況的未來式句子 (*be going to*)。

1. I _____ going to sleep in* tomorrow morning.

2. Our teacher _____ going to retire next month.

3. We _____ going to have a class party next week.

4. *To a student next to you:* You _____ going to speak English tomorrow.

3-2 *Be Going To* 的形式 Forms with *Be Going To*

(a) We *are going to **be*** late.	*be going to* 之後接原形動詞，如：例 (a) 和例 (b)。
(b) She*'s going to **come*** tomorrow. 錯誤：*She's going to comes tomorrow.*	
(c) **Am** I **Is** he, she, it ⎫ *going to be* late? **Are** they, we, you ⎭	疑問句：*be* + 主詞 + *going to*
(d) I *am not* ⎫ He, She, It *is not* ⎬ *going to be* late. They, We, You *are not* ⎭	否定句：*be* + *not* + *going to*
(e) "Hurry up! We're ***gonna*** be late!"	*be going to* 常用於口語和非正式寫作中，正式寫作則少用。在非正式言談中，*going to* 有時會唸為 "gonna" /gənə/。"gonna" 通常不用於書寫形式。

*sleep in = sleep late，意指「晚起」。

❑ **Exercise 4. 文法** (表 3-1 和 3-2)

用 ***be going to*** 的形式和括弧內的字詞，完成下列句子。

1. A: What (*you, do*) ___*are you going to do*___ next?

   B: I (*pick*) _____ up a prescription at the pharmacy.

2. A: Where (*Alex, go*) _____ after work?

   B: He (*stop*) _____ at the post office and run

   some other errands.★

3. A: (*you, finish*) _____ the project soon?

   B: Yes, (*finish*) _____ it by noon today.

4. A: What (*Dr. Ahmad, talk*) _____ about in her

   lecture tonight?

   B: She (*discuss*) _____ how to reduce health-care costs.

5. A: When (*you, call*) _____ your sister?

   B: I (*call, not*) _____ her. I (*text*) _____

   _____ her.

❑ **Exercise 5. 口說：兩人一組** (表 3-1 和 3-2)

成兩人一組，輪流用 ***be going to*** 作問答練習。

例：what \ you \ do \ after class?
說話者 A：What are you going to do after class?
說話者 B：I'm going to get a bite to eat★★ after class.

例：you \ watch TV \ tonight?
說話者 A：Are you going to watch TV tonight?
說話者 B：Yes, I'm going to watch TV tonight. 或 No, I'm not going to watch TV tonight.

1. where \ you \ go \ after your last class \ today?
2. what time \ you \ wake up \ tomorrow?
3. what \ you \ have \ for breakfast \ tomorrow?
4. you \ be \ home \ this evening?
5. where \ you \ be \ next year?
6. you \ become \ famous \ some day?
7. you \ take \ a trip \ sometime next year?
8. you \ do \ something unusual \ in the near future?

★*run errands* 意指「跑腿」。

★★*get a bite to eat* 意指「隨便吃點東西」。

❑ **Exercise 6. 聽力** (表 3-1 和 3-2)

第一部分 聆聽 CD 播放對話中 ***going to*** 的弱化發音。

Looking for an apartment

A: We're going to look for an apartment to rent this weekend.

B: Are you going to look in this area?

A: No, we're going to search in an area closer to our jobs.

B: Is the rent going to be cheaper in that area?

A: Yes, apartment rents are definitely going to be cheaper.

B: Are you going to need to pay a deposit?

A: I'm sure we're going to need to pay the first and last month's rent.

第二部分 聆聽以下對話，並寫出聽到字詞的非弱化形式。

A: Where ___*are you going to*___ move to?
       1

B: We _____ look for something outside the city. We
     2

 _____ spend the weekend apartment-hunting.*
   3

A: What fees _____ need to pay?
        4

B: I think we _____ need to pay the first and last month's rent.
     5

A: _____ there _____ be other fees?
  6   7

B: There _____ probably _____ be an application fee and a
   8   9

 cleaning fee. Also, the landlord _____ probably _____ run a
       10   11

 credit check,** so we _____ need to pay for that.
       12

❑ **Exercise 7. 口說：訪談** (第 1、2 章、表 3-1 和 3-2)

在教室內走動，並用「***what*** + ***do*** +下列表達時間的字詞」作問答練習。最後，與全班分享一些同學的答案。

例：this evening

說話者 A：What are you going to do this evening?

說話者 B：I'm going to get on the Internet for a while.

1. yesterday	6. the day before yesterday
2. tomorrow	7. the day after tomorrow
3. right now	8. last week
4. every day	9. every week
5. a week from now	10. this weekend

---

*apartment-hunting 意指「尋找公寓」。

**run a credit check 意指「查詢信用記錄」。表示取得一個人的財務記錄資訊，包含其雇主的名字、收入、銀行存款以及遲繳或未繳帳單的記錄。

❑ **Exercise 8.** 口說：兩人一組 (第1、2章、表 3-1 和 3-2)

成兩人一組，發揮創意，用自己的字詞完成以下對話；該對話複習了現在簡單式、過去簡單式和 *be going to* 的各種形式（肯定、否定、疑問，和簡答）。

例：

說話者 A：I rode a skateboard to school yesterday.

說話者 B：Really? Wow! Do you ride a skateboard to school often?

說話者 A：Yes, I do. I ride a skateboard to school almost every day.
　　　　　Did you ride a skateboard to school yesterday?

說話者 B：No, I didn't. I came by helicopter.

說話者 A：Are you going to come to school by helicopter tomorrow?

說話者 B：No, I'm not. I'm going to ride a motorcycle to school tomorrow.

A: I _____ yesterday.

B: Really? Wow! _____ you _____ often?

A: Yes, I _____. I _____ almost every day.

　　_____ you _____ yesterday?

B: No, I _____. I _____.

A: Are you _____ tomorrow?

B: No, I _____. I _____ tomorrow.

❑ **Exercise 9.** 暖身活動 (表 3-3)

用 *will* 或 *won't* 完成下列句子。

1. It _____ rain tomorrow.

2. We _____ study Chart 3-3 next.

3. I _____ teach the class next week.

4. *To your teacher:* You _____ need to assign homework for tonight.

3-3 *Will* 的形式 Forms with *Will*

直述句	I, You, She, He, It, We, They **will come** tomorrow.
否定句	I, You, She, He, It, We, They **will not** (**won't**) **come** tomorrow.
疑問句	**Will** I, you, she, he, it, we, they **come** tomorrow?
簡　答	Yes, } I, you, she, he, it, we, they { **will.**★ No, } { **won't.**

縮寫式	I**'ll**　　she**'ll**　　we**'ll** you**'ll**　　he**'ll**　　they**'ll** 　　　　it**'ll**	在口語和非正式書寫中，**will** 通常會和代名詞縮寫。
	Bob + **will** = "Bob**'ll**" the teacher + **will** = "the teacher**'ll**"	在口語中，**will** 通常會和名詞縮寫，但書寫時通常不會。

★在簡答中，代名詞「不可」與助動詞合併縮寫。

正確：*Yes, I will.*
錯誤：*Yes, I'll.*

❏ **Exercise 10. 聽力**（表 3-3）

CD 1
Track 27

第一部分　聆聽 CD 播放句子中與 **will** 合併縮寫的字詞發音。

1. I'll be ready to leave soon.
2. You'll need to come.
3. He'll drive us.
4. She'll come later.
5. We'll get there a little late.
6. They'll wait for us.

第二部分　聆聽 CD 播放的句子，並寫出聽見的縮寫字詞。

1. Don't wait up for me tonight. ___I'll___ be home late.

2. I paid the bill this morning. _____ get my check in the next day or two.

3. We have the better team. _____ probably win the game.

4. Henry twisted his ankle while running down a hill. _____ probably take a break from running this week.

5. We can go to the beach tomorrow, but _____ probably be too cold to go swimming.

6. I invited some guests for dinner. _____ probably get here around seven.

7. Karen is doing volunteer work for a community health-care clinic this week. _____ be gone a lot in the evenings.

□ **Exercise 11. 聽力** (表 3-3)

第一部分 聆聽 CD 播放的句子，並注意「名詞 + *will*」縮寫形式的發音。

At the doctor's office

1. The doctor'll be with you in a few minutes.
2. Your appointment'll take about an hour.
3. Your fever'll be gone in a few days.
4. Your stitches'll disappear over the next two weeks.
5. The nurse'll schedule your tests.
6. The lab'll have the results next week.
7. The receptionist at the front desk'll set up* your next appointment.

第二部分 聆聽 CD 播放的句子，並寫出聽見字詞的非縮寫形式。

At the pharmacy

1. Your prescription ___will be___ ready in ten minutes.

2. The medicine _____ you feel a little tired.

3. The pharmacist _____ your doctor's office.

4. This cough syrup _____ your cough.

5. Two aspirin _____ enough.

6. The generic** drug _____ less.

7. This information _____ all the side effects*** for this medicine.

□ **Exercise 12. 暖身活動** (表 3-4)

下列句子中的說話者有多肯定？在各句左邊的作答線上寫下百分比：100%、90% 或是 50%。

What is going to happen to gasoline prices?

1. _____ Gas prices may rise.

2. _____ Maybe gas prices will rise.

3. _____ Gas prices will rise.

4. _____ Gas prices will probably rise.

5. _____ Gas prices are going to rise.

6. _____ Gas prices won't rise.

---

set up = schedule，意指「安排」。

**generic* 意指「無商標的藥物」。

***side effects* 意指「副作用」，通常是病人對藥物產生的負面反應。

3-4 對未來的確定程度 Certainty About the Future

100% 確定	(a) I **will be** in class tomorrow. 或 I **am going to be** in class tomorrow.	在例 (a) 中，說話者用 **will** 或 **be going to** 來表示對未來的活動有十足的把握。他在陳述關於未來的事實。
90% 確定	(b) Po **will probably be** in class tomorrow. 或 Po **is probably going to be** in class tomorrow. (c) Anna **probably won't be** in class tomorrow. 或 Anna **probably isn't going to be** in class tomorrow.	在例 (b) 中，說話者用 **probably** 來表示他頗有把握，認為 Po 明天會來上課，但無法 100% 肯定。 **probably** 的字序：★ (1) 在直述句中： 　　助動詞 + **probably**，如：例 (b)。 (2) 在否定句中： 　　**probably** + 助動詞，如：例 (c)。
50% 確定	(d) Ali **may come** to class tomorrow. 或 Ali **may not come** to class tomorrow. I don't know what he's going to do.	**may** 用來表示對未來的推測：表某事可能發生，也可能不會發生。★★ 在例 (d) 中，說話者以猜測的口吻說 Ali 可能會來上課，也可能不來。
	(e) **Maybe** Ali **will come** to class, and **maybe** he **won't**. 或 **Maybe** Ali **is going to come** to class, and **maybe** he **isn't**.	「**maybe + will / be going to**」與 **may** 同義。 例 (d) 與例 (e) 同義。 **maybe** 須置於句首。

★**probably** 為句中副詞。更多關於句中副詞在句子中位置的說明，請見第 10 頁，表 1-3。

★★更多關於助動詞 **may** 的說明，請見第 182 頁，表 7-3。

❑ **Exercise 13. 聽力**（表 3-4）

聆聽 CD 播放的句子，判斷各句中說話者的肯定程度：100%、90% 或 50%。

CD 1
Track 29 例：你會聽到：The bank will be open tomorrow.

　　　你要寫下：___100%___

My day tomorrow

　1. _____

　2. _____

　3. _____

　4. _____

　5. _____

　6. _____

❑ **Exercise 14. 文法** (表 3-4)

依照下列各情境，用 **will** 或 **be going to** 預測可能發生和可能不會發生的事。預測中需用到副詞 **probably**。

1. Antonio is late to class almost every day.
   (be on time tomorrow? be late again?)
   → *Antonio probably won't be on time tomorrow. He'll probably be late again.*

2. Rosa has a terrible cold. She feels miserable.
   (go to work tomorrow? stay home and rest?)

3. Sami didn't sleep at all last night.
   (go to bed early tonight? stay up all night again tonight?)

4. Gina loves to run, but right now she has sore knees and a sore ankle.
   (run in the marathon race this week? skip the race?)

❑ **Exercise 15. 文法** (表 3-4)

用括弧內的字詞改寫下列句子。

1. I may be late. (*maybe*)

   <u>Maybe I will be late.</u>

2. Lisa may not get here. (*maybe*)

   _____

3. Maybe you will win the contest. (*may*)

   _____

4. The plane may land early. (*maybe*)

   _____

5. Maybe Sergio won't pass the class. (*may*)

   _____

❑ **Exercise 16. 口說：訪談** (表 3-4)

在教室內走動，並詢問及回答問題。詢問兩位同學下列問題，用 **will**、**be going to** 或 **may** 回答問題，並視情況加入 **probably** 或 **maybe**。最後，與全班分享一些同學的答案。

例：What will you do after class tomorrow?
   → *I'll probably go back to my apartment.* 或 *I'm not sure. I may go to the bookstore.*

1. What will the weather be like tomorrow?
2. Where will you be tomorrow afternoon?
3. What are you going to do on your next vacation?
4. Who will be the most famous celebrity next year?
5. What will a phone look like ten years from now?
6. Think about forms of communication (like email, social websites, phone, texting, etc.).
   What do you think will be the most common form ten years from now?
7. When do you think scientists will discover a cure for cancer?

❑ **Exercise 17. 聽力** (表 3-4)

想像一下一百年後的生活會是什麼樣子？聆聽 CD 播放的句子，你同意還是反對？同意圈 *yes*；如果不同意，則圈 *no*。最後，與同學討論答案。

Predictions about the future

1. yes   no   6. yes   no
2. yes   no   7. yes   no
3. yes   no   8. yes   no
4. yes   no   9. yes   no
5. yes   no   10. yes   no

❑ **Exercise 18. 閱讀、文法與口說** (表 3-4)

第一部分 閱讀以下文章。

An Old Apartment

Ted and Amy live in an old, run-down apartment and want to move. The building is old and has a lot of problems. The ceiling leaks when it rains. The faucets drip. The toilet doesn't always flush properly. The windows don't close tightly, and heat escapes from the rooms in the winter. In the summer, it is very hot because there is no air conditioner.

Their apartment is in a dangerous part of town. Ted and Amy both take the bus to work and have to walk a long distance to the bus stop. Their apartment building doesn't have laundry facilities, so they also have to walk to a laundromat to wash their clothes. They are planning to have children in the near future, so they want a park or play area nearby for their children. A safe neighborhood is very important.

第二部分 Ted 和 Amy 在構想他們下個公寓的樣子，並列了一份想要和不想要的物品清單。用 ***will*** 或 ***won't*** 完成下列句子。

Our next apartment

1. It ___*won't*___ have leaky faucets.

2. The toilet _____ flush properly.

3. It _____ have windows that close tightly.

4. There _____ be air-conditioning for hot days.

5. It _____ be in a dangerous part of town.

6. It _____ be near a bus stop.

7. There _____ be laundry facilities in the building.

8. We _____ need to walk to a laundromat.

9. A play area _____ be nearby.

第三部分 想像你要搬新家,這個新家需具備哪六件最重要的東西 (*It will have...*)?可以分小組進行腦力激盪,然後全班一起討論各自的想法。

❏ **Exercise 19. 暖身活動** (表 3-5)

下列兩組對話中,說話者 B 在哪個對話中有「預定的計畫 (prior plan)」(亦即在說話之前已擬定的計畫)?

1. A: Oh, are you leaving?
   B: Yes. I'm going to pick up my children at school. They have dentist appointments.

2. A: Excuse me, Mrs. Jones. The nurse from your son's school is on the phone. He's got a fever and needs to go home.
   B: Okay. Please let them know I'll be there in 20 minutes.

3-5 *Be Going To* 和 *Will* 的比較

(a) She *is going to succeed* because she works hard.	當 *be going to* 和 *will* 用於表示對未來的預測時,意思相同。
(b) She *will succeed* because she works hard.	例 (a) 與例 (b) 同義。
(c) I bought some wood because I *am going to build* a bookcase for my apartment.	表示預定的計畫時(亦即說話之前已擬定好的計畫),只能用 *be going to*(不能用 *will*)。 在例 (c) 中,說話者計畫做書櫃。
(d) This chair is too heavy for you to carry alone. I*'ll help* you.	表示說話者在說話當下所做的決定時,只能用 *will*(不能用 *be going to*)。 在例 (d) 中,說話者在說話的當下決定幫忙,他先前並未有此計畫或打算。

❑ **Exercise 20. 文法** (表 3-1 → 3-5)

討論以斜體標示的動詞，判斷說話者是否在說話前就已擬定計畫 (prior plans)。如果是，圈選 *yes*；如果不是，則圈 *no*。

已擬定計畫？

1. A: Did you return Carmen's phone call?
   B: No, I forgot. Thanks for reminding me. I*'ll call* her right away.   yes   no

2. A: I*'m going to call* Martha later this evening. Do you want to talk to her too?   yes   no
   B: No, I don't think so.

3. A: Jakob is in town for a few days.
   B: Really? Great! I*'ll give* him a call. Is he staying at his Aunt Lara's?   yes   no

4. A: Alex is in town for a few days.
   B: I know. He called me yesterday. We*'re going to get* together for dinner after I get off work tonight.   yes   no

5. A: I need some fresh air. I'm going for a short walk.
   B: I*'ll come* with you.   yes   no

6. A: I*'m going to take* Hamid to the airport tomorrow morning. Do you want to come along?   yes   no
   B: Sure.

7. A: We*'re going to go* to Uncle Scott's over the break. Are you interested in coming with us?   yes   no
   B: Gee, I don't know. I*'ll think* about it. When do you need to know?

❑ **Exercise 21. 文法** (表 3-1 → 3-5)

藉由口語或書寫的方式，用 **be going to** 重述下列句子。

My trip to Thailand

1. I'm planning to be away for three weeks.
2. My husband and I are planning to stay in small towns and camp on the beach.
3. We're planning to bring a tent.
4. We're planning to celebrate our wedding anniversary there.
5. My father, who was born in Thailand, is planning to join us, but he's planning to stay in a hotel.

❑ **Exercise 22. 文法** (表 3-1 → 3-5)

用 **be going to** 或 **will** 完成下列句子，並以 **be going to** 來表達事先擬定的計畫。

1. A: Are you going by the post office today? I need to mail this letter.
   B: Yeah, I _'ll_____ mail it for you.
   A: Thanks.

2. A: Why are you carrying that package?

   B: It's for my sister. I _'m going to_ mail it to her.

3. A: Why did you buy so many eggs?

   B: I _____ make a special dessert.

4. A: I have a book for Joe from Rachel. I'm not going to see him today.

   B: Let me have it. I _____ give it to him. He's in my algebra class.

5. A: Did you apply for the job you told me about?

   B: No, I _____ take a few more classes and get more experience.

6. A: Did you know that I found an apartment on 45th Street? I'm planning to move soon.

   B: That's a nice area. I _____ help you move if you like.

   A: Great! I'd really appreciate that.

7. A: Why can't you come to the party?

   B: We _____ be with my husband's family that weekend.

8. A: I have to leave. I don't have time to finish the dishes.

   B: No problem. I _____ do them for you.

9. A: Do you want to go to the meeting together?

   B: Sure. I _____ meet you by the elevator in ten minutes.

❑ **Exercise 23. 聽力** (表 3-1 → 3-5)

CD 1
Track 31

聆聽 CD 播放的句子，並圈選「預期的」回答（a 或 b）。

1. a. Sure, I'll do it.
   b. Sure, I'm going to do it.

2. a. Yes. I'll look at laptop computers.
   b. Yes. I'm going to look at laptop computers.

3. a. Yeah, but I'll sell it. I don't need it now that I live in the city.
   b. Yeah, but I'm going to sell it. I don't need it now that I live in the city.

4. a. Uh, I'll get your coat and we can go.
   b. Uh, I'm going to get your coat and we can go.

❑ **Exercise 24. 暖身活動** (表 3-6)

用自己的字詞完成下列句子。你注意到下列動詞的時態和粗體字有什麼特點嗎？

1. **After** I _leave_ school today, I_'m going to_ _____.

2. **Before** I _come_ to school tomorrow, I _will_ _____.

3. **If** I _have_ time this weekend, I _will_ _____.

3-6 表示未來時間的副詞子句和 *If* 子句

<table>
<tr>
<td>(a) 時間副詞子句
Before I go to class tomorrow, I'm going to eat breakfast.

(b) I'm going to eat breakfast 時間副詞子句 **before I go** to class tomorrow.</td>
<td>在例 (a) 和例 (b) 中，*before I go to class tomorrow* 是表示未來的時間副詞子句。

before
after
when
as soon as ⎬ + 主詞和動詞 = 時間副詞子句
until
while</td>
</tr>
<tr>
<td>(c) *Before I* **go** *home tonight*, I'm going to stop at the market.
(d) I'm going to eat dinner at 6:00 tonight. *After I* **eat** *dinner*, I'm going to study in my room.
(e) I'll give Rita your message *when I* **see** *her*.
(f) It's raining right now. *As soon as the rain* **stops**, I'm going to walk downtown.
(g) I'll stay home *until the rain* **stops**.
(h) *While you're at school tomorrow*, I'll be at work.</td>
<td>表未來的時間副詞子句用現在簡單式，「不用」 **will** 和 **be going to**。

錯誤：*Before I will go to class, I'm going to eat breakfast.*
錯誤：*Before I am going to go to class tomorrow, I'm going to eat breakfast.*

例 (c) 到例 (h) 的句中都含有表示未來的時間副詞子句。</td>
</tr>
<tr>
<td>(i) Maybe it will rain tomorrow. *If it* **rains** *tomorrow*, I'm going to stay home.</td>
<td>在例 (i) 中，*If it rains tomorrow* 是以 **if** 引導的副詞子句。
if + 主詞和動詞 = **if** 子句。

當 **if** 子句要表達未來意義時，也是用現在簡單式，不能用 **will** 或 **be going to**。</td>
</tr>
</table>

❑ **Exercise 25. 文法** (表 3-6)

圈選正確的動詞。

1. Before *I'm going to return,* (*I return*) to my country next year, I'm going to finish my graduate degree in computer science.

2. The boss will review your work after she *will return, returns* from vacation next week.

3. I'll give you a call on my cell phone as soon as my plane *will land, lands*.

4. I don't especially like my current job, but I'm going to stay with this company until I *find, will find* something better.

5. When you *will be, are* in Australia next month, are you going to go snorkeling at the Great Barrier Reef?

6. I need to know what time the meeting starts. Please be sure to call me as soon as you *find out, will find out* anything about it.

7. If it *won't be, isn't* cold tomorrow, we'll go to the beach.
If it *is, will be* cold tomorrow, we'll go to a movie.

用各題提供的動詞完成下列句子；如果需表達未來的含義，則運用 ***be going to*** 的形式。

1. *take, read*

   I __*'m going to read*__ the textbook **before** I __*take*__ the final exam next month.

2. *return, call*

   Mr. Lee _____ his wife **as soon as** he _____

   to the hotel tonight.

3. *make, go*

   Before I _____ to my job interview tomorrow, I _____

   a list of questions I want to ask about the company.

4. *visit, take*

   We _____ Sabrina to our favorite seafood restaurant **when** she

   _____ us this weekend.

5. *keep, call*

   I _____ my cell* on **until** Lena _____.**

6. *miss, understand not*

   If Adam _____ the meeting, he _____ the next project.

7. *get, eat*

   If Eva _____ home early, we _____ dinner at 6:30.

❑ **Exercise 27. 口說：兩人一組** (表 3-6)

成兩人一組，閱讀下列句子，並用 ***if*** 造接下來的句子；要特別注意 ***if*** 子句中的動詞形式。最後，與全班分享由搭檔所提供的部分答案。

例：Maybe you'll go downtown tomorrow.
學生 A：If I **go** downtown tomorrow, I'm going to buy some new clothes.
學生 B：If I **go** downtown tomorrow, I'm going to look at laptop computers.

1. Maybe you'll have some free time tomorrow.
2. Maybe it'll rain tomorrow.
3. Maybe it won't rain tomorrow.
4. Maybe the teacher will be absent next week.

---

*cell = cell phone，意指「手機」。

以 ***until* 引導的時間副詞子句通常接在主要子句之後。
常見：I'm going to keep my cell on ***until Lena calls***.
可用但較少見：***Until Lena calls***, I'm going to keep my cell on.

角色互換。

5. Maybe you'll be tired tonight.
6. Maybe you won't be tired tonight.
7. Maybe it'll be nice tomorrow.
8. Maybe we won't have class on Monday.

❑ **Exercise 28. 文法** (表 3-6)

查閱 Sue 的計畫日誌，可以發現她有個忙碌的上午。用括弧中的時間副詞及提供的資訊造句，並運用 *be going to* 表達未來時間。

1. (after)   go to the dentist \ pick up groceries
   → *After Sue goes to the dentist, she is going to pick up groceries.*
2. (before)   go to the dentist \ pick up groceries
3. (before)   have lunch with Hiro \ pick up groceries
4. (after)   have lunch with Hiro \ pick up groceries
5. (before)   have lunch with Hiro \ take her father to his doctor's appointment

❑ **Exercise 29. 閱讀、文法與寫作** (表 3-6)

第一部分　閱讀以下文章。

The Home of the Future

What will the home of the future look like? Imagine life 50 years from now. What kinds of homes will people have? Here are some interesting possibilities.

The living room walls will have big plasma screens. Instead of pictures on the wall, the screens will show changing scenery. If walls have different scenes, people may not even want many windows. As you know, fewer windows will make it easier to heat a house.

The house will have special electronic features, and people will control them with a remote control. For example, a person can lie in bed at night and lock all the doors in his or her house with one push of a button. Before someone arrives home from work, the remote will turn on the lights, preheat the oven, and even turn on favorite music. The bathroom faucets will have a memory. They will remember the temperature a person likes, and when he or she turns on the water in the tub or shower, it will be at the correct temperature. Maybe bedroom closets will have racks that move automatically at the touch of a button. When the weather is cold, the racks will deliver clothes that keep a person warm, and on warm days, the racks will deliver clothes that keep a person cool.

Finally, homes will be more energy-efficient. Most of the heat will probably come from the sun. Of course, solar heat will be popular because it will be inexpensive.

Which ideas do you like? Which ones do you think you may see in your lifetime?

運用上頁文章中的資訊，完成下列句子。答案可能不只一個。

1. When people look at the living room walls, they _____.

2. When a person is coming home from work, the remote _____.

3. As soon as a person gets home, _____.

4. If the bathroom faucets have a memory, they _____.

5. Before a person goes to sleep, _____.

6. When a person pushes a button, the closet racks _____.

7. When the weather is cold, the closet racks _____.

8. If a home has solar heat, the cost of heating the home _____.

第三部分 想像你在五十年後能打造自己夢想中的房子，它可以是你想要的任何樣式。想想這棟房子的風格、大小、房間種類、地點等，然後以此主題句：*My dream house will have ...* 作為段落開頭，撰寫一段描述這棟房子的文字。

❏ **Exercise 30. 文法** (第 1、2 章、表 3-1 → 3-6)
用括弧內字詞的正確形式，完成下列句子。作答時要留意表達時間的詞語。

1. Before Tim (*go*) __goes__ to bed, he always (*brush*) __brushes__ his teeth.

2. Before Tim (*go*) _____ to bed later tonight, he (*email*) _____
   his girlfriend.

3. Before Tim (*go*) _____ to bed last night, he (*take*) _____ a shower.

4. While Tim (*take*) _____ a shower last night, the phone (*ring*)
   _____.

5. As soon as the phone (*ring*) _____ last night, Tim (*jump*) _____
   out of the shower to answer it.

6. As soon as Tim (*get*) _____ up tomorrow morning, he (*brush*)
   _____ his teeth.

7. Tim always (*brush*) _____ his teeth as soon as he (*get*) _____ up.

❏ **Exercise 31. 暖身活動** (表 3-7)
下列哪些句子表達未來時間？

1. I'm catching a train tonight.
2. I'm going to take the express train.
3. The trip will only take an hour.

3-7 用現在進行式表示未來時間

(a) Tim *is going to come* to the party tomorrow. (b) Tim *is coming* to the party tomorrow. (c) We*'re going to go* to a movie tonight. (d) We*'re going* to a movie tonight. (e) I*'m going to stay* home this evening. (f) I*'m staying* home this evening. (g) Ann *is going to fly* to Chicago next week. (h) Ann *is flying* to Chicago next week.	現在進行式可以用來表示未來的時間。 現在進行式用來表達「未來確定的計畫」，即「說話之前便已擬定好的計畫」。左欄每組句子意義均相同。 用現在進行式表示未來時間時，未來的含義通常是藉由未來的時間副詞（如：*tomorrow*）或上下文情境來表明。★
(i) You*'re going to laugh* when you hear this joke. (j) 錯誤：*You're laughing when you hear this joke.*	現在進行式「不用於」預測未來。 在例 (i) 中，說話者在預測一未來事件。 在例 (j) 中，使用現在進行式是不正確的，「笑」在這裡是預測將發生的事，而非已計畫好的未來事件。

★比較：現在情境：*Look! Mary's coming. Do you see her?*

　　　未來情境：*Are you planning to come to the party? Mary's coming. So is Alex.*

❑ **Exercise 32. 文法** (表 3-7)

用括弧內動詞的正確形式，完成下列對話，並視情況使用現在進行式。討論下列句子中的現在進行式所表達的是現在或未來的時間。

1. A: What (*you, do*) ___are you doing___ tomorrow afternoon?

   B: I (*go*) ___am going___ to the mall. How about you? What (*you, do*) _____ tomorrow afternoon?

   A: I (*go*) _____ to a movie with Dan. After the movie, we (*go*) _____ out to dinner. Would you like to meet us for dinner?

   B: No, thanks. I can't. I (*meet*) _____ my son for dinner.

2. A: What (*you, major*) _____ in?

   B: I (*major*) _____ in engineering.

   A: What courses (*you, take*) _____ next semester?

   B: I (*take*) _____ English, math, and physics.

3. A: Stop! Paula! What (*you, do*) _____?

   B: I (*cut*) _____ my hair, Mom.

   A: Oh dear!

Exercise 33. 聽力（表 3-7）

聆聽 CD 播放的對話，並寫出聽見的字詞。

CD 1
Track 32 **Going on vacation**

A: I _____ on vacation tomorrow.

B: Where _____ you _____?

A: To San Francisco.

B: How are you getting there? _____ you _____ or _____
your car?

A: I _____. I have to be at the airport by seven tomorrow morning.

B: Do you need a ride to the airport?

A: No, thanks. I _____ a taxi.
What about you? Are you planning to go somewhere over vacation?

B: No. I _____ here.

□ **Exercise 34.** 口說：兩人一組（表 3-7）

成兩人一組，用現在進行式，談論彼此的計畫。

例：What are your plans for this evening?
說話者 A：I'm staying home. How about you?
說話者 B：I'm going to a coffee shop to work on my paper for a while. Then I'm meeting some
friends for a movie.

What are your plans . . .

1. for the rest of today?
2. for tomorrow?
3. for this coming weekend?
4. for next month?

□ **Exercise 35.** 寫作（表 3-7）

想像你有為期一週的假期，且可以去任何想去的地方。想一個你想造訪的地點，撰寫一段描述
此趟旅程的文字，並視情況用現在進行式。

例：　　　My friend Sara and I are taking a trip to Nashville, Tennessee. Nashville is the home of
country music, and Sara loves country music. She wants to go to lots of shows. I don't know
anything about country music, but I'm looking forward to going to Nashville. We're leaving
Friday afternoon as soon as Sara gets off work. (Etc.)

段落中可能會涵蓋下列問題的答案：

1. Where are you going?
2. When are you leaving?
3. Who are you going with, or are you traveling alone?
4. How are you getting there?
5. Where are you staying?
6. Are you visiting anyone? Who?
7. How long are you staying there?
8. When are you getting back?

❏ **Exercise 36. 暖身活動**（表 3-8）

圈選所有可能完成句子的正確答案。

1. Soccer season begins _____.
   a. today   b. next week   c. yesterday

2. The mall opens _____.
   a. next Monday   b. tomorrow   c. today

3. There is a party _____.
   a. last week   b. tonight   c. next weekend

4. The baby cries _____.
   a. every night   b. tomorrow night   c. in the evenings

3-8 用現在簡單式表示未來時間

(a) My plane **arrives** at 7:35 *tomorrow evening*. (b) Tim's new job **starts** next week. (c) The semester **ends** *in two more weeks*. (d) There **is** a meeting at ten *tomorrow morning*.	當所述事件為一既定行程或時程時，可以用現在簡單式表示未來時間；但只有少數動詞可以用現在簡單式表達未來的含義，最常見的有：**arrive**、**leave**、**start**、**begin**、**end**、**finish**、**open**、**close**、**be**。
(e) 錯誤：*I wear my new suit to the wedding next week.* 正確：*I am wearing/am going to wear* my new suit to the wedding next week.	大部分的動詞都「不能」用現在簡單式表達未來時間，如：例 (e) 中，動詞 **wear** 並非敘述既定的行程或時間表上將發生的事，因此不能用現在簡單式表達未來時間。

❏ **Exercise 37. 文法**（表 3-7 和 3-8）

圈選所有可能完成句子的正確答案。

1. The concert _____ at eight tonight.
   a. begins   b. is beginning   c. is going to begin

2. I _____ seafood pasta for dinner tonight.
   a. make   b. am making   c. am going to make

3. I _____ to school tomorrow morning. I need the exercise.
   a. walk   b. am walking   c. am going to walk

4. The bus _____ at 8:15 tomorrow morning.
   a. leaves   b. is leaving   c. is going to leave

5. I _____ the championship game on TV at Jonah's house tomorrow.
   a. watch   b. am watching   c. am going to watch

6. The game _____ at 1:00 tomorrow afternoon.
   a. starts   b. is starting   c. is going to start

7. Alexa's plane _____ at 10:14 tomorrow morning.
   a. arrives
   b. is arriving
   c. is going to arrive

8. I can't pick her up tomorrow, so she _____ the airport bus into the city.
   a. takes
   b. is taking
   c. is going to take

9. Jonas _____ to several companies. He hopes to get a full-time job soon.
   a. applies
   b. is applying
   c. is going to apply

10. School _____ next Wednesday. I'm excited for vacation to begin.
   a. ends
   b. is ending
   c. is going to end

❑ **Exercise 38. 暖身活動** (表 3-9)
圈選最能表達此句子的圖片：Joanne is about to leave for work.

A 圖   B 圖

3-9 立即的未來：*Be About To* 的用法

(a) Ann's bags are packed, and she is wearing her coat. She ***is about to leave*** for the airport. (b) Shhh. The movie ***is about to begin***.	片語 ***be about to do something*** 表達「在立即的未來」將要發生的活動，通常在數分鐘或數秒鐘之內。 例 (a) 表示：Ann 在接下來幾分鐘內即將離開。 例 (b) 表示：電影在接下來幾分鐘內即將開演。

❏ **Exercise 39.** 口說（表 3-9）

用 *be about to* 描述下列圖片中即將要發生的動作。成兩人一組、分小組、或全班一起練習。

❏ **Exercise 40. 遊戲**（表 3-9）

自己想一個動作，或從以下建議清單中挑選一個動作，但不要告訴其他人。準備表演這個動作，但在你做出完整動作前，請全班同學先描述你即將要做的動作。你也可以和搭檔一起表演。

例：（學生 A 和學生 B 向彼此伸出雙手。）
可能的猜測：They are about to shake hands.

建議動作：

stand up	sneeze	pick up a pen	erase a word
open the door	fall down	close your book	look up a word
close the window	cry	write on the board	get out your wallet

❏ **Exercise 41. 暖身活動**（表 3-10）

圈選可以完成下列句子的所有正確答案。

1. Fifteen years from now, my wife and I will retire and _____ all over the world.
   - a. will travel
   - b. travel
   - c. traveling
   - d. going to travel
   - e. are traveling
   - f. traveled

2. I opened the door and _____ my friend to come in.
   - a. will invite
   - b. invite
   - c. inviting
   - d. am going to invite
   - e. am inviting
   - f. invited

3-10 平行結構中的動詞用法 Parallel Verbs

(a) Jim $\overbrace{\textit{makes}}^{動詞}$ his bed $\overbrace{and}^{and}$ $\overbrace{\textit{cleans}}^{動詞}$ up his room every morning. (b) Anita **called** and **told** me about her new job.	同一主詞若有兩個動詞時，通常用 **and** 連結。此時，這兩個動詞為平行結構中的動詞： 　　動詞 + **and** + 動詞 　　*makes and cleans* = 平行結構中的動詞
(c) Ann **is cooking** dinner and (is) **talking** on the phone at the same time. (d) I **will stay** home and (will) **study** tonight. (e) I **am going to stay** home and (am going to) **study** tonight.	當兩個動詞時態相同，且由 **and** 連接時，不需重複助動詞 (helping verb/auxiliary verb)。

❏ **Exercise 42. 文法**（表 3-10）

用括弧內動詞的正確形式，完成下列句子。

1. When I (*walk*) __*walked*__ into the living room yesterday, Grandpa (*read*)
   _____ a newspaper and (*listen*) _____ to music.

2. Helen will graduate soon. She (*move*) _____ to New York and (*look*)
   _____ for a job after she (*graduate*) _____ .

3. Every day my neighbor (*call*) _____ me on the phone and (*complain*)
   _____ about the weather.

4. Look at Erin. She (*cry*) _____ and (*laugh*) _____ at the
   same time! I wonder if she is happy or sad?

5. I'm beat.* I can't wait to get home. After I (*get*) _____ home, I (*take*)
   _____ a hot bath and (*go*) _____ to bed.

6. While Paul (*carry*) _____ brushes and paint and (*climb*)
   _____ a ladder, a bee (*land*) _____ on his
   arm and (*sting*) _____ him. Paul (*drop*) _____ the paint and
   (*spill*) _____ it all over the ground.

❏ **Exercise 43. 文法**（第1 → 3章）
用括弧內動詞的正確形式，完成下列句子。

1. I usually (*ride*) __*ride*__ my bike to work in the morning, but it (*rain*)
   _____ when I left my house early this morning, so I (*take*)
   _____ the bus. After I (*get*) _____ to work, I (*find*) _____
   out** that I had left my briefcase on the bus.

2. A: Are you going to take the kids to the amusement park tomorrow morning?
   B: Yes. It (*open*) _____ at 10:00. If we (*leave*) _____ here at 9:30,
   we'll get there at 9:55. The kids can be the first ones in the park.

3. A: Ouch! I (*cut*) _____ my finger. It (*bleed*) _____!
   B: Put pressure on it. I (*get*) _____ some antibiotics and a bandage.
   A: Thanks.

4. A: Your phone (*ring*) _____.
   B: I (*know*) _____.
   A: (*you, want*) _____ me to get it?
   B: No.
   A: Why don't you want to answer your phone?
   B: I (*answer, not*) _____ during dinner.

---

*be beat 意指「非常疲憊」。

**find out = discover 或 learn，意指「發現；獲悉」。

5. A: Look! There (be) _____ a police car behind us. Its lights (flash)
    _____.

    B: I (know) _____. I (know) _____. I (see) _____ it.

    A: What (go) _____ on? (you, speed) _____?

    B: No, I'm not. I (drive) _____ the speed limit.

    A: Oh, look. The police car (pass) _____ us.

    B: Whew!

❏ **Exercise 44. 聽力** (第 1 → 3 章)

第一部分　用聽到的字詞完成下列句子。

CD 1
Track 33
At a Chinese restaurant

    A: Okay, let's all open our fortune cookies.

    B: What _____ yours _____?

    A: Mine says, "You _____ an unexpected gift." Great! Are you

        planning to give me a gift soon?

    B: Not that I know of. Mine says, "Your life _____ long and happy."

        Good. I _____ a long life.

    C: Mine says, "A smile _____ all communication problems." Well,

        that's good! After this, when I _____ someone,

        _____ just _____ at them.

    D: My fortune is this: "If you _____ hard, you _____ successful."

    A: Well, it _____ like all of us _____ good luck in the future!

第二部分　分小組練習，和組員們一起爲組內每位成員撰寫一張命運籤。

❏ **Exercise 45. 檢視學習成果** (第 1 → 3 章)

校訂以下段落，訂正錯誤的動詞時態。

My Cousin Pablo

    I want to tell you about Pablo. He ^is my cousin. He comes here four years ago. Before he

came here, he study statistics in Chile. He leaves Chile and move here. He went to New York

and stay there for three years. He graduated from New York University. Now he study at this

school. After he finish his master's degree, he return to Chile.

❑ **Exercise 46. 寫作** (第 3 章)

假設你有預知未來的能力，挑選一位認識的人（同學、老師、家人、朋友），並以一段文字預言其未來的生活。內容要涵蓋一些有趣或特別的細節。

例：

My Son's Future

My son is 15 years old now. In the future, he will have a happy and successful life. After he finishes high school, he will go to college. He really loves to study math. He also loves to build bridges out of toothpicks. He will study engineering, and he will specialize in bridge building. He likes to travel, so he will get a job with an international company and build bridges around the world. He will also work in poor villages, and his bridges will connect rural areas. This will make people's lives better. I will be very proud of him.

第四章
現在完成式與過去完成式

❑ **Exercise 1. 暖身活動**（表 4-1）

你知道下列動詞的過去分詞形式嗎？完成以下表格。第 1-4 項和第 5-8 項的過去分詞有何差異？

原形	過去式	過去分詞
1. stay	stayed	*stayed*
2. work	worked	*worked*
3. help	helped	_____
4. visit	visited	_____
5. go	went	*gone*
6. begin	began	*begun*
7. write	wrote	_____
8. see	saw	_____

1. 一段時間
2. 動作均開始於過去
3. 時態以動作結束（算）時間為準

4-1 過去分詞 Past Participle

	原形	過去式	過去分詞	
規則動詞	finish stop wait	finished stopped waited	**finished** **stopped** **waited**	**過去分詞**是動詞重要的形式之一（請見第 31 頁，表 2-3）。 過去分詞用於「現在完成式」與「過去完成式」。★ 規則變化的動詞，過去分詞與過去式相同：字尾皆為 **-ed**。
不規則動詞	see make put	saw made put	**seen** **made** **put**	不規則變化的動詞表，請見第 32 頁，表 2-4，或第 432-433 頁。

★過去分詞也用於被動語態，請見第 10 章。

寫出聽見的字詞。

CD 1
Track 34

例：你會聽到：go   went   gone

你要寫下：go   went   _gone_

原形	過去式	過去分詞		原形	過去式	過去分詞
1. call	called	_____	6.	come	came	_____
2. speak	spoke	_____	7.	eat	ate	_____
3. do	did	_____	8.	cut	cut	_____
4. know	knew	_____	9.	read	read	_____
5. meet	met	_____	10.	be	was/were	_____

❏ **Exercise 3. 文法** (表 2-3、2-4 和 4-1)

寫出下列動詞的過去分詞，製作一個屬於自己的表格。

原形	過去式	過去分詞		原形	過去式	過去分詞
1. finish	finished	_finished_	6.	hear	heard	_____
2. have	had	_____	7.	study	studied	_____
3. think	thought	_____	8.	die	died	_____
4. teach	taught	_____	9.	buy	bought	_____
5. live	lived	_____	10.	start	started	_____

❏ **Exercise 4. 暖身活動** (表 4-2)

判斷下列哪一句（a 或 b）符合該題情境句的語義。

1. It's 10:00 A.M. Layla has been at the bus stop since 9:50.

    a. She is still there.

    b. The bus picked her up.

2. Toshi has lived in the same apartment for 30 years.

    a. After 30 years, he moved somewhere else.

    b. He still lives there.

4-2 *Since* 和 *For* 用於現在完成式

此刻 早上十點 （圖）	(a) I**'ve been** in class **since** ten o'clock *this morning*. (b) We **have known** Ben **for** ten years. We met him ten years ago. We still know him today. We are friends. { for + 一段時間 since | 過去時間 S + P.T.	當現在完成式與 **since** 或 **for** 連用時，表達某情境開始於過去，並持續到現在。 在例 (a) 中，課堂於十點開始，且說話當下，我還在上課。 錯誤：*I am in class since ten o'clock this morning*.
(c)　　　　　I **have** 　　　　　You **have** She, He, It **has**　　} **been** here for one hour. 　　　　　We **have** 經歷 　　　　They **have**		直述句：**have/has** + 過去分詞 縮寫形式：*I've*、*You've*、*He's*、*She's*、*It's*、*We've*、*They've*。

Since

(d) I **have been** here { **since** eight o'clock. **since** Tuesday. **since** 2009 **since** yesterday. **since** last month.		**since** 後面接一「特定的時間點」：如：時、日、月、年等。 **since** 表示動作開始於過去的某特定時間點，並且持續到現在。
(e)　正確：I **have lived** here since May.* "I have been living here since May". 　　正確：I **have been** here since May. (f)　錯誤：*I am living here since May*. (g)　錯誤：*I live here since May*. (h)　錯誤：*I lived here since May*. (i)　錯誤：*I was here since May*.		留意下列有誤的句子： 例 (f)：不該用現在進行式。 例 (g)：不該用現在簡單式。 例 (h) 和例 (i)：不該用過去簡單式。
主要子句 （現在完成式）　　　　SINCE 子句 　　　　　　　　（過去簡單式）動作起始時間 (j) I **have lived** here　　　since I **was** a child. (k) Al **has met** many people　since he **came** here.		**since** 也可引導時間副詞子句（即 **since** 之後可接主詞和動詞）。 注意例句中的主要子句是用現在完成式，**since** 子句是用過去簡單式。

For

(l) I **have been** here { **for** ten minutes. **for** two hours. **for** five days. **for** about three weeks. **for** almost six months. **for** many years. **for** a long time.		**for** 後面接「一段時間」：2 分鐘、3 小時、4 天、5 週等。 注意：若表時間的名詞為複數形（幾小時、幾天、幾個禮拜等），則用 **for** 表達時間，而非 **since**。

*另一種正確的說法：*I have been living* here since May. 現在完成進行式的詳述，請見表 4-6。

❏ **Exercise 5.** 文法 (表 4-2)

用 *since* 或 *for* 完成下列句子。

Amy has been here . . .

1. ___*for*___ two months.
2. ___*since*___ September.
3. _____ yesterday.
4. _____ the term started.
5. _____ a couple of hours.
6. _____ fifteen minutes.

The Smiths have been married . . .

7. _____ two years.
8. _____ last May.
9. _____ five days.
10. _____ a long time.

Ms. Ellis has worked as a substitute teacher . . .

11. _____ school began.
12. _____ last year.
13. _____ 2008.
14. _____ about a year.
15. _____ September.
16. _____ a long time.

I've known about Sonia's engagement . . .

17. _____ almost four months.
18. _____ the beginning of the year.
19. _____ the first of January.
20. _____ yesterday.

❏ **Exercise 6.** 文法 (表 4-2)

根據自身情況完成下列句子。

1. I've been in this building . . . .
   - since ___*nine o'clock this morning*___.
   - for ___*27 minutes*___.

2. We've been in class . . . .
   - since _____.
   - for _____.

3. I've been in this city . . . .
   - since _____.
   - for _____.

4. I've had an ID★ card . . . .
   - since _____.
   - for _____.

5. I've had this book . . . .
   - since _____.
   - for _____.

★*ID* = identification，意指「身分證」。

❑ **Exercise 7. 文法**（表 4-2）

用下列動詞的現在完成式，完成下列句子。

Since 1995, Theresa, a talk-show host, . . .

1. work   _____ *has worked* _____ for a TV station in London.

2. interview _____ hundreds of guests.

3. meet   _____ many famous people.

4. find   _____ out about their lives.

5. make   _____ friends with celebrities.

6. became   _____ a celebrity herself.

7. sign   _____ lots of autographs.

8. shake   _____ hands with thousands of people.

9. write   _____ two books about how to interview people.

10. think   _____ a lot about the best ways to help people feel
              comfortable on her show.

❑ **Exercise 8. 口說**（表 4-2）

老師將會問一個問題，兩位學生要回答此問題。說話者 A 要用 *since* 回答，而說話者 B 要根據說話者 A 提供的資訊用 *for* 回答。只有老師的書是打開的。

例：
問說話者 A：How long have you been in this room?
　說話者 A：I've been in this room **since** (10:00).
問說話者 B：How long has (*Student A*) been in this room?
　說話者 B：She/He has been in this room **for** (15 minutes).

1. How long have you known me?
2. How long have you been up* today?
3. Where do you live? How long have you lived there?
4. Who has a cell phone? How long have you had your phone?
5. Who has a bike? How long have you had it?
6. How long have you been in this building today?
7. Who is wearing something new? What is new? How long have you had it/them?
8. Who is married? How long have you been married?

---

*be up 意指「起床」。

用括弧內字詞的正確形式，完成下列句子，並用括弧標示出 *since* 子句。

1. I (*know*) ___have known___ Mark Miller [ever since* we (*be*) ___were___ in college.]

2. Pedro (*change*) ___has changed___ his major three times since he (*start*)
   ___started___ school.

3. Ever since I (*be*) ___was___ a child, I (*be*) ___have been___ afraid of snakes.

4. I can't wait to get home to my own bed. I (*sleep, not*) ___haven't slept___ well since
   I (*leave*) ___left___ home three days ago.

5. Ever since Pete (*meet*) ___met___ Nicole, he (*think, not*) ___hasn't thought___
   about anything or anyone else. He's in love.

6. Otto (*have*) ___has had (有P.P)___ a lot of problems with his car ever since he (*buy*)
   ___bought___ it. It's a lemon.**

7. A: What (*you, eat*) ___have you eaten___ since you (*get*) ___got___
   up this morning?

   B: So far, I (*eat*) ___have eaten___ a banana and some yogurt.***

❏ **Exercise 10. 暖身活動：兩人一組** (表 4-3)

成兩人一組。學生 A 從下表中挑選一個詞語，並依照自身情況造句，然後將該句子改為問句詢問學生 B，學生 B 再依自身情況回答。

climbed a tree	heard bedtime stories	ridden a tricycle
flown a kite	played in the dirt	slept with a stuffed animal

學生 A：Since my childhood, I haven't _____.
　　　　Since your childhood, have you _____?

學生 B：Yes, I have. 或 No, I haven't.

have → 一般動詞 < 有 吃
　　 → 使役動詞 + O < V̄ 主動　p.p 被動

---

*ever since 與 since 同義。

**a lemon 意指「一輛問題層出不窮的車子」。

***「so far + 現在完成式」用於表示始於過去，並持續到現在的情況。

4-3 否定句、問句和簡答形式

否定句

(a) I *have not* (*haven't*) *seen* Tom since lunch.	否定句：*have/has* + *not* + 過去分詞
(b) Ann *has not* (*hasn't*) *eaten* for several hours.	否定句縮寫：*have* + *not* = *haven't* *has* + *not* = *hasn't*

問句

(c) *Have you seen Tom?*	疑問句：*have/has* + 主詞 + 過去分詞
(d) *Has Ann eaten?*	
(e) How long *have you lived* here?	
(f) — Have you *ever* met a famous person? — No, I've *never* met a famous person. Haven't you eaten your lunch? Yes, I have. 吃過了 No, I haven't 沒吃	在例 (f) 中，*ever* = in your lifetime，表示從你出生到現在。含有 *ever* 的問句常使用現在完成式。 當回答含有 *ever* 的問句時，說話者常使用 *never*。*never* 也常與現在完成式一起使用。 例 (f) 的答覆中，說話者的意思是：「沒有，從出生到現在我還沒有遇過名人。」

簡答

(g) — Have you seen Tom? — *Yes, I have.* 或 *No, I haven't.*	簡答：*have/haven't* 或 *has/hasn't*
(h) — Has Ann eaten lunch? — *Yes, she has.* 或 *No, she hasn't.*	注意：簡答中，助動詞不可和代名詞縮寫。 錯誤：*Yes, I've.* 或 *Yes, he's.*

❑ **Exercise 11. 文法** (表 4-3)

用括弧內動詞的現在完成式，完成下列對話。

1. A: (*you, eat, ever*) ___Have you ever eaten___ an insect?

   B: No, I ___haven't___. I (*eat, never*) ___have never___ eaten an insect.

2. A: (*you, stay, ever*) ___Have you ever stayed___ in a room on the top floor of a hotel?

   B: Yes, I ___have___. I (*stay*) ___have stayed___ in a room on the top floor of a hotel a few times.

3. A: (*you, meet, ever*) ___Have you ever meet___ a movie star?

   B: No, I ___haven't___. I (*meet, never*) ___have never meet___ a movie star.

4. A: (*Ted, travel, ever*) ___Has Ted ever traveled___ overseas?

   B: Yes, he ___has___. He (*travel*) ___has traveled___ to several countries on business.

5. A: (*Lara, be, ever*) _Has Lara ever been_ in Mexico?

   B: No, she _hasn't_ . She (*be, never*) _has never been_ in any
   Spanish-speaking countries.

❑ Exercise 12. 聽力 (表 2-3、2-4 和 4-3)

CD 1
Track 35

聆聽 CD 播放的句子及其後問句的開頭，然後用第一句裡動詞的過去分詞，完成下列問句。你
曾做過下列事情嗎？圈選 *yes* 或 *no*。

例：你會聽到：I saw a two-headed frog once. Have you ever . . . ?
　　你要寫下：Have you ever ___seen___ a two-headed frog?　　　　　yes　(no)

1. Have you ever _____ a two-headed snake?　　　yes　no

2. Have you ever _____ in a small plane?　　　yes　no

3. Have you ever _____ in a limousine?　　　yes　no

4. Have you ever _____ volunteer work?　　　yes　no

5. Have you ever _____ a shirt?　　　yes　no

6. Have you ever _____ a scary experience on an airplane?　　　yes　no

7. Have you ever _____ out of a boat?　　　yes　no

8. Have you ever _____ so embarrassed that your face got hot?　　　yes　no

9. Have you ever _____ to a famous person?　　　yes　no

10. Have you ever _____ to be famous?　　　yes　no

❑ Exercise 13. 口說：訪談 (表 2-4 和 4-3)

用下列動詞的現在完成式造問句，並訪問同學。

1. you \ ever \ cut \ your own hair
2. you \ ever \ catch \ a big fish
3. you \ ever \ take care of \ an injured animal
4. you \ ever \ lose \ something very important
5. you \ ever \ sit \ on a bee
6. you \ ever \ fly \ in a private plane
7. you \ ever \ break \ your arm or your leg
8. you \ ever \ find \ something very valuable
9. you \ ever \ swim \ near a shark
10. you \ ever \ throw \ a ball \ and \ break \ a window

第一部分 成兩人一組，輪流作問答練習。用 **How long have you** 和現在完成式作為問句的開頭，並用 **since**、**for** 或 **never** 和現在完成式回答問題。

例：have a pet
學生 A：How long have you had a pet?
學生 B：I've had (*a cat, a dog, a bird, etc.*) for two years. 或
　　　　I've had (*a cat, a dog, a bird, etc.*) since my 18th birthday. 或
　　　　I've never had a pet.

1. live in (*this area*)
2. study English
3. be in this class / at this school
4. have long hair / short hair
5. have a beard / a mustache
6. wear glasses / contact lenses
7. have a roommate / a pet
8. be interested in (*a particular subject*)
9. be married

第二部分 運用訪談得來的資訊，寫一段關於搭檔的文字，可增加一些資訊，讓此段文字更有趣。參考以下段落範例，並留意斜體字的現在完成式詞語。

例：

Ellie

I'd like to tell you a little about Ellie. She *has lived* in Vancouver, Canada, *for six months*. She *has studied English for five years*. She *has been* at this school *since September*. She likes it here.

She has short hair. She *has worn* short hair *for a few years*. Of course, she doesn't have a mustache! She *has never worn* glasses, except sunglasses.

Ellie doesn't have a roommate, but she has a pet bird. She *has had* her bird *for one month*. Its name is Howie, and he likes to sing.

She is interested in biology. She *has been* interested in biology *since she was a child*. She *has never been* married. She wants to be a doctor. She wants to become a doctor before she has a family.

❏ **Exercise 15.** 暖身活動（表 4-4）
圈選可完成下列句子的正確答案（a 或 b）。

b. 1. Tyler has rented a house _____.
　　　　a. last week.　　　　b. already. 己經

a. 2. I have seen it _____.
　　　　a. recently.　　　　b. two days ago.

b 3. His parents haven't seen it _____.
　　　　a. yesterday.　　　　b. yet.　　not ~ yet 尚未 / yet = but (conj.) = however (conj.)

a. 4. I have been there _____.
　　　　a. two times.　　　　b. yesterday.

Toshi has already eaten lunch.　　　　　Eva hasn't eaten lunch yet.

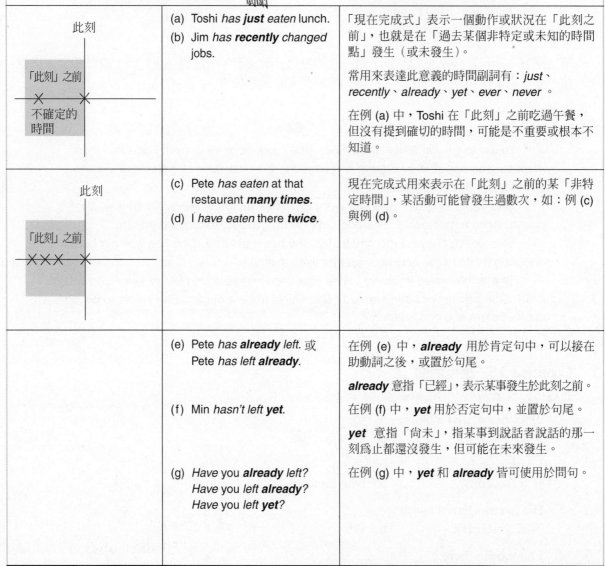

此刻 「此刻」之前 不確定的 時間	(a) Toshi *has **just** eaten* lunch. (b) Jim *has **recently** changed* jobs.	「現在完成式」表示一個動作或狀況在「此刻之前」，也就是在「過去某個非特定或未知的時間點」發生（或未發生）。 常用來表達此意義的時間副詞有：*just*、*recently*、*already*、*yet*、*ever*、*never*。 在例 (a) 中，Toshi 在「此刻」之前吃過午餐，但沒有提到確切的時間，可能是不重要或根本不知道。
此刻 「此刻」之前	(c) Pete *has eaten* at that restaurant ***many times***. (d) I *have eaten* there ***twice***.	現在完成式用來表示在「此刻」之前的某「非特定時間」，某活動可能曾發生過數次，如：例 (c) 與例 (d)。
	(e) Pete *has **already** left*. 或 Pete *has left **already***. (f) Min *hasn't left **yet***. (g) *Have you **already** left*? *Have you left **already***? *Have you left **yet***?	在例 (e) 中，***already*** 用於肯定句中，可以接在助動詞之後，或置於句尾。 ***already*** 意指「已經」，表示某事發生於此刻之前。 在例 (f) 中，***yet*** 用於否定句中，並置於句尾。 ***yet*** 意指「尚未」，指某事到說話者說話的那一刻為止都還沒發生，但可能在未來發生。 在例 (g) 中，***yet*** 和 ***already*** 皆可使用於問句。

☐ **Exercise 16.** 文法 (表 4-4)

圈選能回答該題問句的所有可能答案。分小組做練習,然後全班一起討論答案。

情境 1：
Sara is at home. At 12:00 P.M., the phone rang. It was Sara's friend from high school.
They had a long conversation, and Sara hung up the phone at 12:59. It is now 1:00.
Which sentences describe the situation?

   a. Sara has just hung up the phone.

   b. She has hung up the phone already.

   c. The phone has just rung.

   d. Sara hasn't finished her conversation yet.

   e. Sara has been on the phone since 12:00 P.M.

情境 2：
Mr. Peters is in bed. He became sick with the flu eight days ago. Mr. Peters isn't sick very
often. The last time he had the flu was one year ago. Which sentences describe the situation?

   a. Mr. Peters has been sick for a year.

   b. He hasn't gotten well yet.

   c. He has just gotten sick.

   d. He has already had the flu.

   e. He hasn't had the flu before.

情境 3：
Rob is at work. His boss, Rosa, needs a report. She sees Rob working on it at his desk.
She's in a hurry, and she's asking Rob questions. What questions is she going to ask him?

   a. Have you finished?

   b. Have you finished yet?

   c. Have you finished already?

☐ **Exercise 17.** 聽力 (表 2-4 和 4-4)

CD 1
Track 36

Richard 和 Lori 是一對新手爸媽,他們的小寶寶一星期前才剛出生。聆聽 CD 播放的句子,並
用聽見動詞的過去分詞,完成下列問句。

1. Has Richard ___*held*___ the baby a lot yet?

2. Has Lori _____ the baby a bath yet?

3. Has Richard _____ a diaper yet?

4. Has Lori _____ some pictures of the baby yet?

5. Has Richard _____ up when the baby cries yet?

6. Has Lori _____ some of the household chores yet?

7. Has Richard _____ tired during the day yet?

仔細看 Andy 的計畫日誌，並用 *yet* 和 *already* 寫出下列問句的詳答。

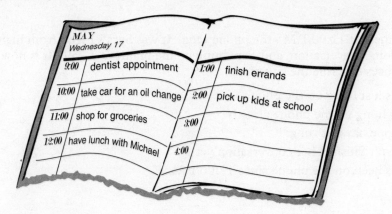

It is 11:55 A.M. right now.

1. Has Andy had his dentist appointment yet? <u>Yes, he has had his dentist</u>
   <u>appointment already.</u>

2. Has Andy picked up his kids at school yet? _____
   _____

3. Has Andy taken his car for an oil change already? _____
   _____

4. Has Andy finished his errands yet? _____
   _____

5. Has Andy shopped for groceries already? _____
   _____

6. Has Andy had lunch with Michael yet? _____

❑ **Exercise 19. 聽力**（表 4-2 → 4-4）

is 和 *has* 都可以被縮寫為 *'s*。聆聽 CD 播放的句子，並判斷縮寫的動詞是 *is* 還是 *has*。在開始前，你或許會想先確定自己是否認識這些字：*order*、*waiter*。

例：你會聽到：I have to leave. My order's taking too long.
　　你要圈出：(is)　　has

　　你會聽到：I have to leave. My order's taken too long.
　　你要圈出：is　　(has)

At a restaurant

1. is　　has　　　　3. is　　has　　　　5. is　　has

2. is　　has　　　　4. is　　has　　　　6. is　　has

Exercise 20. 聽力 （表 4-2 → 4-4）

回答下列問題，然後聆聽工作面試的內容。再聽一遍，並用聽到的字詞，完成下列句子。在開始前，你或許會想先確定自己是否認識這些字：*clinic*、*prison*、*volunteer*、*low-income*、*patient*、*challenge*。

What types of jobs can nurses have?
Which ones could be very exciting?

A job interview

Mika is a nurse. She is interviewing for a job with the manager of a hospital emergency room. He is looking at her résumé and asking her some general questions.

INTERVIEWER: It looks like _____ a lot of things since you became a
　　　　　　　　　　　　　　　　　　1
nurse.

MIKA: Yes, _____ for a medical clinic. _____
　　　　　　　　　2　　　　　　　　　　　　　　　　　　　　　　　　　3
in a prison. _____ in several area hospitals. And
　　　　　　　　　　　　　4
_____ volunteer work at a community health center for
　　　　　　5
low-income patients.

INTERVIEWER: Very good. But, let me ask you, why _____
　　　　　　　　　　　　　　　　　　　　　　　　　　　　　　　　　6
jobs so often?

MIKA: Well, I like having new challenges and different experiences.

INTERVIEWER: Why _____ for this job?
　　　　　　　　　　　　7

MIKA: Well, I'm looking for something more fast-paced,* and _____
　　　　　　　　　　　　　　　　　　　　　　　　　　　　　　　　　　　　　　8
interested in working in an E.R.** for a long time. _____
　　　　　　　　　　　　　　　　　　　　　　　　　　　　　　　　9
that this hospital provides great training for its staff, and it offers excellent

patient care.

INTERVIEWER: Thank you for coming in. I'll call you next week with our decision.

MIKA: It was good to meet you. Thank you for your time.

---

more fast-paced 意指「步調更快的」。

**E.R.* = emergency room，意指「急診室」。

閱讀以下短篇對話，並判斷誰最有可能說最後一句話，是 Pamela 還是 Jenna？

> PAMELA:　I've traveled around the world several times.
> JENNA:　I traveled around the world once.
>
> ＿＿＿＿＿：　I'm looking forward to my next trip.

4-5 過去簡單式與現在完成式的比較 Simple Past vs. Present Perfect

過去簡單式 (a) I **finished** my work *two hours ago*.	在例 (a) 中，說話者在過去的某特定時間，完成了工作 (*two hours ago*)。
現在完成式 (b) I **have** already **finished** my work.	在例 (b) 中，說話者在過去的某非特定時間，完成了工作 (*sometime before now*)。 *說話者在現在*
過去簡單式 (c) I **was** in Europe *last year/three years ago/in 2006/in 2008 and 2010/when/was ten years old*.	「過去簡單式」表示活動發生於過去的特定時間（可能不只一次），如：例 (a) 和例 (c)。
現在完成式 (d) I **have been** in Europe *many times/severa/times/a couple of times/once/(no mention of time)*.	「現在完成式」表示活動發生於過去的非特定時間（可能不只一次），如：例 (b) 和例 (d)。
過去簡單式 (e) Ann **was** in Miami *for two weeks*. ^had been	在例 (e) 中，**for** 用於表示時間，而過去簡單式表示活動開始並結束於過去。
現在完成式 (f) Bob **has been in** Miami for *two weeks/since May 1st*.	在例 (f) 中，**for** 或 **since** 用於表示時間，而現在完成式表示活動開始於過去，並持續到現在。

❑ **Exercise 22.　文法**（表 4-5）

回答下列問題，並討論斜體字動詞時態的含義。

1. All of these verbs talk about past time, but the verb in (a) is different from the other three verbs. What is the difference?
   (a) I *have had* several bicycles in my lifetime.
   (b) I *had* a red bicycle when I was in elementary school.
   (c) I *had* a blue bicycle when I was a teenager.
   (d) I *had* a green bicycle when I lived and worked in Hong Kong.

2. What are the differences in the ideas the verb tenses express?
   (e) I *had* a wonderful bicycle last year.
   (f) I *'ve had* many wonderful bicycles.

3. What are the differences in the ideas the verb tenses express?
   (g) Ann *had* a red bike for two years.
   (h) Sue *has had* a red bike for two years.

4. Who is still alive, and who is dead?
   (i) In his lifetime, Uncle Alex *had* several red bicycles.
   (j) In his lifetime, Grandpa *has had* several red bicycles.

❑ **Exercise 23. 文法** (表 4-5)

仔細看下列各個斜體動詞,該動詞是過去簡單式還是現在完成式?判斷該動詞表達的是發生在過去特定時間點,或是非特定時間點的概念,並在正確方格內打勾 (✓)。

	過去特定 時間點	過去非特定 時間點
1. Ms. Parker *has been* in Tokyo many times. → *present perfect*	☐	☑
2. Ms. Parker *was* in Tokyo last week. → *simple past*	☑	☐
3. I *'ve met* Kaye's husband. He's a nice guy.	☐	☐
4. I *met* Kaye's husband at a party last week.	☐	☐
5. Mr. White *was* in the hospital three times last month.	☐	☐
6. Mr. White *has been* in the hospital many times.	☐	☐
7. I like to travel. I *'ve been* to more than 30 foreign countries.	☐	☐
8. I *was* in Morocco in 2008.	☐	☐
9. Venita *has never been* to Morocco.	☐	☐
10. Venita *wasn't* in Morocco when I was there in 2008.	☐	☐

❑ **Exercise 24. 文法** (表 4-5)

用括弧內動詞的現在完成式或過去簡單式,完成下列句子。

1. A: Have you ever been to Singapore?

   B: Yes, I (*be*) __have__ . I (*be*) __have been__ to Singapore several times. In fact,
   I (*be*) __was__ in Singapore last year.

2. A: Are you going to finish your work before you go to bed?

   B: I (*finish, already**) __have already finished__ it. I (*finish*) __finished__ my work
   two hours ago.

3. A: Have you ever eaten at the Sunset Beach Café?

   B: Yes, I __have__ . I (*eat*) __have eaten__ there many times. In
   fact, my wife and I (*eat*) __ate__ lunch there <u>yesterday</u>.

---

*在非正式的口語英文中,***already*** 有時會搭配過去簡單式使用。在此大題中,練習將 ***already*** 與現在完成式一起搭配使用。

4. A: Do you and Erica want to go to the movie at the Galaxy Theater with us tonight?

   B: No thanks. We (*see, already*) ___have already seen___ it. We (*see*) ___saw___ it last week.

5. A: When are you going to write your report for Mr. Berg?

   B: I (*write, already*) ___have already written___ it. I (*write*) ___wrote___ it two days ago and gave it to him.

6. A: (*Antonio, have, ever*) ___Has Antonio ever had 有___ a job?

   B: Yes, he ___has___ . He (*have*) ___has had 有___ lots of part-time jobs. Last summer he (*have*) a ___had 有___ a job at his uncle's auto shop.

7. A: This is a good book. Would you like to read it when I'm finished?

   B: Thanks, but I (*read, already*) ___have already read___ it. I (*read*) ___read___ it a couple of months ago.

   ___several___

8. A: What African countries (*you, visit*) ___have you visited___ ?

   B: I (*visit*) ___have visited___ Kenya and Ethiopia. I (*visit*) ___visited___ Kenya in 2002. I (*be*) ___was___ in Ethiopia last year.

❑ **Exercise 25. 口說：兩人一組** (表 4-5)

成兩人一組，並輪流用現在完成式和過去簡單式作問答練習。最後再與全班分享搭檔的部分答案。

例：
學生 A：What countries have you been to?
學生 B：I've been to Norway and Finland.
學生 A：When were you in Norway?
學生 B：I was in Norway three years ago. How about you? What countries have you been to?
學生 A：I've never been to Norway or Finland, but I've been to . . . .

1. What countries have you been to?
   When were you in . . . ?

2. Where are some interesting places you have lived?
   When did you live in . . . ?

3. What are some interesting / unusual / scary things you have done in your lifetime?
   When did you . . . ?

4. What are some helpful things (for a friend / your family / your community) you have done in your lifetime?
   When did you . . . ?

CD 1
Track 39

聆聽 CD 播放的內容，每一題你都會聽到兩個完整句，接著是第三句的開頭；用前兩句動詞的過去分詞，完成第三句。

例：你會聽到：I eat vegetables every day. I ate vegetables for dinner last night.
　　　　　　　I have . . .
　　你要寫下：I have ___*eaten*___ vegetables every day for a long time.

1. Since Friday, I have _____ a lot of money.

2. All week, I have _____ big breakfasts.

3. Today, I have already _____ several emails.

4. I just finished dinner, and I have _____ a nice tip.

5. Since I was a teenager, I have _____ in late on weekends.

6. All my life, I have _____ very carefully.

7. Since I was little, I have _____ in the shower.

❏ **Exercise 27. 遊戲** (表 2-4 和 4-5)

分組進行。
(1) 在一張紙上寫下兩句關於自己的敘述句；一句用過去簡單式，另一句用現在完成式。
(2) 其中一句要符合自身真實狀況，另一句則與事實不符。
(3) 其他組員要猜哪一句是正確的。
(4) 當每個人都猜完後，再公布正確答案。

比賽最後以猜對次數最多的人為贏家。

例：
學生 A：I've never cooked dinner.
　　　　I saw a famous person last year.
學生 B：*You've never cooked dinner is true.*
　　　　You saw a famous person last year is false.

❏ **Exercise 28. 暖身活動** (表 4-6)

用與時間相關的訊息，完成下列句子。

1. I am sitting at my desk right now. I have been sitting at my desk since _____.

2. I am looking at my book. I have been looking at my book for _____.

4-6 現在完成進行式 Present Perfect Progressive

Al and Ann are in their car right now. They are driving home. It is now four o'clock. (a) They ***have been driving*** *since* two o'clock. (b) They ***have been driving*** *for* two hours. 　　They will be home soon.	「現在完成進行式」表示在此刻之前，某活動已進行的「時間長短」。 注意：在例 (a) 中的 ***since*** 與例 (b) 中的 ***for***，都常與現在完成進行式連用。 直述句：***have/has*** + ***been*** + ***-ing***
(c) How long ***have*** they ***been driving***?	疑問句： ***have/has*** + 主詞 + ***been*** + ***-ing***

現在進行式與現在完成進行式的比較

現在進行式 現在 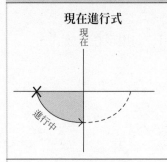 進行中	(d) Po ***is sitting*** in class right now.	「現在進行式」用來描述現在正在進行的活動，無涉於進行時間的長短，如：例 (d)。 錯誤：*Po has been sitting in class right now.*
現在完成進行式 現在 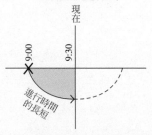 進行時間的長短	Po is sitting at his desk in class. He sat down at nine o'clock. It is now nine-thirty. (e) Po ***has been sitting*** in class *since* nine o'clock. (f) Po ***has been sitting*** in class *for* thirty minutes.	「現在完成進行式」用以表示某活動已進行的**長短**，該活動始於過去，並且持續到現在。 錯誤：*Po is sitting in class since nine o'clock.*
(g)　正確：I ***know*** Yoko. (h)　錯誤：*I am knowing Yoko.* (i)　正確：I ***have known*** Yoko *for* two years. (j)　錯誤：*I have been knowing Yoko for two years.*		注意：非動作動詞（如：*know*、*like*、*own*、*belong*）不可用於進行式的時態。★〔沒有持續性 v.〕 在例 (i) 中，因動詞是非動作動詞，所以用現在完成式與 *since* 或 *for* 連用的方式表達始於過去、並且持續到現在的情形。

★非動作動詞請見第 17 頁，表 1-6。

用括弧內動詞的現在進行式或現在完成進行式，完成下列句子。

1. I (*sit*) ___am sitting___ in the cafeteria right now. I (*sit*) ___have been sitting___ here since twelve o'clock.

2. Kate is standing at the corner. She (*wait*) ___is waiting___ for the bus. She (*wait*) ___has been waiting___ for the bus for twenty minutes.

3. Scott and Rebecca (*talk*) ___are talking___ on the phone right now. They ___have been talking___ (*talk*) on the phone for over an hour.

4. Right now we're in class. We (*do*) ___are doing___ an exercise. We (*do*) ___have been doing___ this exercise for a couple of minutes.

5. A: You look busy right now. What (*you, do*) ___are you doing___ ?
    B: I (*work*) ___am working___ on my physics experiment. It's a difficult experiment.
    A: How long (*you, work*) ___have you been working___ on it?
    B: I started planning it last January. I (*work*) ___have been working___ on it since then.

❑ **Exercise 30.** 口說 (表 4-6)

闔上書本，並回答老師的問題。

例：
老師：Where are you living?
學生 A：I'm living in an apartment on Fourth Avenue.
老師：How long have you been living there?
學生 A：I've been living there since last September.

1. Right now you are sitting in class. How long have you been sitting here?
2. When did you first begin to study English? How long have you been studying English?
3. I began to teach English in (*year*). How long have I been teaching English?
4. I began to work at this school in (*month or year*). How long have I been working here?
5. What are we doing right now? How long have we been doing it?
6. (*Student's name*), I see that you wear glasses. How long have you been wearing glasses?
7. Who drives? When did you first drive a car? How long have you been driving?
8. Who drinks coffee? How old were you when you started to drink coffee? How long have you been drinking coffee?

❑ **Exercise 31. 聽力** (表 4-2 → 4-6)

CD 1
Track 40

第一部分 在日常口語中使用現在完成式時，常會將 ***have*** 和 ***has*** 與名詞合併縮寫。聆聽 CD 播放的句子，並留意縮寫字詞的發音。

1. Jane has been out of town for two days.
2. My parents have been active in politics for 40 years.
3. My friends have moved into a new apartment.
4. I'm sorry. Your credit card has expired.
5. Bob has been traveling in Montreal since last Tuesday.
6. You're the first one here. No one else* has come yet.

第二部分 聆聽下列句子，並用聽到的字詞完成下列句子：名詞 + ***have/has***。

1. The ___*weather has*___ been warm since the beginning of April.

2. This _____ been unusually warm.

3. My _____ been living in the same house for 25 years.

4. My _____ lived in the same town all their lives.

5. You slept late. Your _____ already gotten up and made breakfast.

6. My _____ planned a going-away party for me. I'm moving back to my hometown.

7. I'm afraid your _____ been getting a little sloppy.**

8. My _____ traveled a lot. She's visited many different countries.

❑ **Exercise 32. 暖身活動** (表 4-7)

閱讀下列情境，並回答問題。

情境 1：
Roger is having trouble with math. I am helping him with his homework tonight. **I have been helping** him since 6:00.

情境 2：
Roger is moving to a new apartment. **I have helped** him move furniture several times this week.

情境 3：
I sure was busy last week. **I helped** Roger with his homework, and **I helped** him move to a new apartment.

a. In which situation does the speaker emphasize the duration or the time that something continues?
b. In which situation(s) is the speaker finished with the activity?
c. Do you think the activity in situation 1 or 2 is more recent? Why?

---

*else 爲副詞，並常在慣用詞組中與 have 和 has 一起縮寫，如：no one else、someone else、anyone else 等。

**sloppy = careless 或 messy，意指「草率的，凌亂的」。

4-7 現在完成進行式與現在完成式的比較

現在完成進行式

(a) Gina and Tarik are talking on the phone. They **have been talking** on the phone for 20 minutes.	「現在完成進行式」使用動作動詞來表達目前**正在進行的活動已持續一段時間**，如：在例 (a) 中，該談話動作在過去開始，但仍在持續進行中。

現在完成式

(b) Gina **has talked** to Tarik on the phone many times (before now). (c) 錯誤：*Gina has been talking to Tarik on the phone many times.* (d) Gina **has known** Tarik for two years. (e) 錯誤：*Gina has been knowing Tarik for two years.*	「現在完成式」表示： (1) **在過去非特定時間**所重複發生的活動，如：例 (b)。 (2) 目前「**情況**」已持續的時間，如：例 (d)，使用非動作動詞。

現在完成進行式和現在完成式

(f) I **have been living** here for six months. 或 (g) I **have lived** here for six months. (h) Ed **has been wearing** glasses since he was ten. 或 Ed **has worn** glasses since he was ten. (i) I**'ve been going** to school ever since I was five years old. 或 I**'ve gone** to school ever since I was five years old.	對某些動詞（並非全部）而言，現在完成進行式與現在完成式皆可表示活動持續的時間。 例 (f) 與例 (g) 意義上大抵相同，而且也都正確。 通常，若動詞用於表達**常態性或習慣性活動／情況所持續的時間**（每天或有規律性發生的事情），如：*live、work、teach、smoke、wear glasses、play chess、go to school、read the same newspaper every morning* 等，則皆可和上面兩種時式連用。

❑ **Exercise 33. 文法** (表 4-7)

用括弧內動詞的現在完成式或現在完成進行式，完成下列句子。有些句子適用兩種時式。

1. A: I'm tired. We (hike) ___have been hiking___ for more than an hour.
   B: Well, let's stop and rest for a while.

2. A: Is the hike to Glacier Lake difficult?
   B: No, not at all. I (hike) ___have hiked___ it many times with my kids.

3. A: Do you like it here?
   B: I (live) ___have been living / have lived___ here for only a short while. I don't know yet.

4. A: My eyes are getting tired. I (read) ___have been reading___ for two hours.
   I think I'll take a break.
   B: Good idea.

5. A: I (read) ___have read___ this same page in my chemistry book three times,
   and I still don't understand it.
   B: Maybe I can help.

6. A: Do you like the Edgewater Inn? 旅館
   B: Very much. I (stay) ___have stayed___ there at least a dozen times. It's
   my favorite hotel.

7. A: The baby's crying. Shouldn't we do something? He (cry) ___has been crying___
   for several minutes.
   B: I'll go check.

8. A: Who's your daughter's teacher for next year?
   B: I think her name is Mrs. Jackson.
   A: She's one of the best teachers at the elementary school. She (teach) ___has taught___
   ___has been teaching___ kindergarten for twenty years.

9. A: Ed (play) ___has played___ (兩者皆可) tennis for ten years, but he still doesn't have
   a good serve.
   B: Neither do I, and I (play) ___have played___ (ˋ ˋ) tennis for twenty years.

10. A: Where does Mrs. Alvarez work?
    B: At the power company. She (work) ___has worked___ (ˊ ˋ) there for fifteen
    years. She likes her job.
    A: What about her husband?
    B: He's currently unemployed, but he'll find a new job soon.
    A: What kind of experience does he have?
    B: He (work) ___has worked___ for two different accounting firms and at
    one of the bigger software companies. With his work experience, he won't have any
    trouble finding another job.

❏ **Exercise 34.** 聽力 (表 4-7)

聆聽 CD 播放的氣象預報，然後再聽一遍，並用聽見的字詞完成下列句子。在開始前，你或許會想先確定自己是否認識這些字：*hail*、*weather system*、*rough*。

Today's Weather

The weather _____ certainly _____ today. Boy,
what a day! _____ already _____ rain, wind, hail, and sun. So, what's
      3   4
in store* for tonight? As you _____ probably _____, dark clouds
                                          5   6
_____. We have a weather system moving in that is going to
              7
bring colder temperatures and high winds. _____ all week that
                                                                      8
this system is coming, and it looks like tonight is it! _____ even
                                                                          9
_____ snow down south of us, and we could get some snow here too. So hang
       10
onto your hats! We may have a rough night ahead of us.

❏ **Exercise 35.** 文法 (第 1、2、4 章)

閱讀下列各組句子。比較斜體字動詞時態，並勾選 (✓) 表達持續一段時間的句子。

1. a. _____ Rachel *is taking* English classes.

    b. _____ Nadia *has been taking* English classes for two months.

2. a. _____ Ayako *has been living* in Jerusalem for two years. She likes it there.

    b. _____ Beatriz *has lived* in Jerusalem. She's also lived in Paris. She's lived in New York
        and Tokyo. She's lived in lots of cities.

3. a. _____ Jack *has visited* his aunt and uncle many times.

    b. _____ Matt *has been visiting* his aunt and uncle for the last three days.

4. a. _____ Cyril *is talking* on the phone.

    b. _____ Cyril *talks* on the phone a lot.

    c. _____ Cyril *has been talking* to his boss on the phone for half an hour.

    d. _____ Cyril *has talked* to his boss on the phone lots of times.

5. a. _____ Mr. Woods *walks* his dog in Forest Park every day.

    b. _____ Mr. Woods *has walked* his dog in Forest Park many times.

    c. _____ Mr. Woods *walked* his dog in Forest Park five times last week.

    d. _____ Mr. Woods *is walking* his dog in Forest Park right now.

    e. _____ Mr. Woods *has been walking* his dog in Forest Park since two o'clock.

---

what's in store 意指「可預期或即將來臨的事物」。

❑ **Exercise 36. 聽力** （表 4-1 → 4-7）

CD 1
Track 42

聆聽 CD 播放的對話，並圈選最能描述該對話含義的句子（a 或 b）。

例：你會聽到： A: This movie is silly.
B: I agree. It's really dumb.

你要圈出：(a.) The couple has been watching a movie.
b. The couple finished watching a movie.

1. a. The speakers listened to the radio already.

   b. The speakers have been listening to the radio.

2. a. The man lived in Dubai a year ago.

   b. The man still lives in Dubai.

3. a. The man has called the children several times.

   b. The man called the children once.

4. a. The speakers went to a party and are still there.

   b. The speakers went to a party and have already left.

❑ **Exercise 37. 聽力與口說** （第 1 → 4 章）

第一部分　聆聽 Lara 和她母親在電話中的對話。

CD 1
Track 43 **A common illness**

LARA: Hi, Mom. I was just calling to tell you that I can't come to your birthday party this weekend. I'm afraid I'm sick.

MOM: Oh, I'm sorry to hear that.

LARA: Yeah, I got sick Wednesday night, and it's just been getting worse.

MOM: Are you going to see a doctor?

LARA: I don't know. I don't want to go to a doctor if it's not serious.

MOM: Well, what symptoms have you been having?

LARA: I've had a cough, and now I have a fever.

MOM: Have you been taking any medicine?

LARA: Just over-the-counter* stuff.

MOM: If your fever doesn't go away, I think you need to call a doctor.

LARA: Yeah, I probably will.

MOM: Well, call me tomorrow and let me know how you're doing.

LARA: Okay. I'll call you in the morning.

---

*over-the-counter 意指「成藥」，也就是不需要醫生處方箋就可以買到的藥。

104 第四章

第二部分 成兩人一組，並輪流扮演爸爸／媽媽和病人。完成以下對話，再與搭檔練習完成的對話。

可能的症狀：

a fever	chills	a sore throat
a runny nose	achiness	a stomachache
a cough	a headache	sneezing
nausea		

A: Hi, Mom/Dad. I was just calling to tell you that I can't come to _____. I'm afraid I'm sick.

B: Oh, I'm sorry to hear that.

A: Yeah, I got sick Wednesday night, and it's just been getting worse.

B: Are you going to see a doctor?

A: I don't know. I don't want to go to a doctor if it's not serious.

B: Well, what symptoms have you been having?

A: I've had _____, and now I have _____.

B: Have you been taking any medicine?

A: Just over-the-counter stuff.

B: If your _____ doesn't go away, I think you need to call a doctor.

A: Yeah, I probably will.

B: Well, call me tomorrow and let me know how you're doing.

A: Okay. I'll call you in the morning.

❑ **Exercise 38.** 文法 (第 1 章和表 4-1 → 4-7)

圈選正確的動詞，並與班上同學討論你的答案。有些句子不限一個答案。

1. I _____ the windows twice, and they still don't look clean.
   a. am washing   b. have washed   c. have been washing

2. Please tell Mira to get off the phone. She _____ for over an hour.
   a. is talking   b. has talked   c. has been talking

3. Where are you? I _____ at the mall for you to pick me up.
   a. wait   b. am waiting   c. have been waiting

4. We _____ at the Lakes Resort once. We want to go back again.
   a. stay   b. have stayed   c. have been staying

5. Where have you been? The baby _____, and I can't comfort her.
   a. cries   b. is crying   c. has been crying

回答下列問題，然後閱讀以下文章及其後敘述。正確的敘述圈 T，錯的則圈 F。

Have you heard about the problem of disappearing honeybees?
Why are honeybees important to fruit and many other crops?

Where Have the Honeybees Gone?

Honeybees have been disappearing around the world for several years now. In the United States, billions of bees have already died. Europe, Australia, and Brazil have also reported losses of honeybees. This is a serious problem because bees pollinate* crops. Without pollination, apple, orange, and other fruit trees cannot produce fruit. Other crops like nuts also need pollination. In the United States, one-third of the food supply depends on honeybees.

Scientists have a name for this problem: colony collapse disorder (CCD). Bees live in colonies or hives, and thousands of beekeepers have been finding their hives empty. A hive that once held 50,000 bees may just have a few dead or dying ones left.

There have been many theories about why this has happened; for example, disease, pests,** unnatural growing conditions, and damaged DNA.*** Scientists now think that the cause may be a combination of a virus and a fungus, but they need to do more research to find a solution to this very serious problem.

1. Honeybees have stopped disappearing.   T   F

2. Scientists expect that more bees will die.   T   F

3. Apples and other fruits depend on honeybees.   T   F

4. Bee hives have been disappearing.   T   F

5. There are only four reasons why honeybees have died.   T   F

---

*pollinate（動詞）= fertilize；pollination（名詞），意指「授粉」。

**pest 意指「害蟲」。

***DNA = deoxyribonucleic acid，意指「脫氧核糖核酸」，為動植物細胞中帶有基因信息的化學物質。

第一部分 用括弧內字詞的正確形式，完成下列句子。

My name (*be*) ___is___ Surasuk Jutukanyaprateep. I (*be*) ___am___ from
1   2

Thailand. Right now I (*study*) ___am studying___ English at this school. I (*be*)
3

___have been___ at this school since the beginning of January. I (*arrive*)
4

___arrived___ here January 2nd, and my classes (*begin*) ___began___
5   6

January 6th.

Since I (*come*) ___came___ here, I (*do*) ___have done___ many
7   8

things, and I (*meet*) ___have met___ many people. Last week, I (*go*)
9

___went___ to a party at my friend's house. I (*meet*) ___met___ some of the
10   11

other students from Thailand at the party. Of course, we (*speak*) ___spoke___ Thai, so
12

I (*practice, not*) ___didn't practice___ my English that night. There (*be*)
13

___were___ only people from Thailand at the party.
14

However, since I (*come*) ___came___ here, I (*meet*)
15

___have meet___ a lot of other people too, including people from Latin America,
16

Africa, the Middle East, and Asia. I enjoy meeting people from other countries. Now I (*know*)

___know___ people from all these places, and they (*become*) ___become___
17   18

my friends.

第二部分 將第一部分的文章作為參考範例，寫一篇有三個段落的文章來描述自己。文章中需
回答下列問題：

第一段：
1. What is your name?
2. Where are you from?
3. How long have you been here?

第二段：
4. What have you done since you came here? 或
5. What have you learned since you began studying English?

第三段：
6. Who have you met in this class? 或
7. Who have you met recently?
8. Give a little information about these people.

閱讀 Karen 的敘述，並判斷哪一個選項裡 (a 或 b) 的事件順序是正確的。

> KAREN: Jane met me for lunch. She was so happy. She had passed her driver's test.
>   a. Jane talked to Karen. Then she passed her test.
>   b. Jane passed her test. Then she talked to Karen.

4-8 過去完成式 Past Perfect

情境： *Jack left his apartment at 2:00. Sue arrived at his apartment at 2:15 and knocked on the door.* (a) <u>When Sue arrived</u>, Jack wasn't there. <u>He **had left**</u>.	當說話者在談論發生在過去不同時間的兩件事時，可以使用「過去完成式」，表示一件事情結束後，另一件事情才發生。 在例 (a) 中，有兩件事情都發生在過去：第一件是 *Jack left his apartment*，第二件是 *Sue arrived at his apartment*。 為了顯示這兩件事情的時間先後關係，我們用過去完成式 (**had left**) 表示在第二件事 (Sue arrived at his apartment) 發生之前，第一件事 (Jack left his apartment) 就已經結束了。

(b) Jack **had left** his apartment when Sue arrived.	形式：**had** = 過去分詞
(c) He**'d** left. I**'d** left. They**'d** left. Etc.	縮寫：*I/you/she/he/it/we/they* + **'d**
(d) Jack **had left** before Sue arrived. (e) Jack **left** before Sue arrived. (f) Sue **arrived** after Jack had left. (g) Sue **arrived** after Jack left.	當一個句子中使用了 **before** 和 **after**，時間順序已經很明顯了，因此毋需使用過去完成式，如：例 (e) 和 (g) 中，使用過去簡單式即可。 例 (d) 和 (e) 意義相同。 例 (f) 和 (g) 意義相同。
(h) Stella was alone in a strange city. She walked down the avenue slowly, looking in shop windows. Suddenly, she turned her head and looked behind her. Someone **had called** her name.	過去完成式在正式寫作中較為常用，如：小說。請見例 (h)。

辨認在過去的哪個動作先發生 (標示 1st)，哪個動作後發生 (標示 2nd)。

1. The tennis player **jumped** in the air for joy. She **had won** the match.

   a. ___1st___ The tennis player won the match.

   b. ___2nd___ The tennis player jumped in the air.

2. Before I went to bed, I **checked** the front door. My roommate **had** already **locked** it.

   a. ___2nd___ I checked the door.

   b. ___1st___ My roommate locked the door.

3. I **looked** for Diego, but he **had left** the building.

   a. _____ Diego left the building.

   b. _____ I looked for Diego.

4. I **laughed** when I saw my son. He **had poured** a bowl of noodles on top of his head.

   a. _____ I laughed.

   b. _____ My son poured a bowl of noodles on his head.

5. Oliver **arrived** at the theater on time, but he couldn't get in. He **had left** his ticket at home.

   a. _____ Oliver left his ticket at home.

   b. _____ Oliver arrived at the theater.

6. I **handed** Betsy the newspaper, but she didn't want it. She **had read** it during her lunch hour.

   a. _____ I handed Betsy the newspaper.

   b. _____ Betsy read the newspaper.

7. After Carl arrived in New York, he **called** his mother. He **had promised** to call her as soon as he got in.

   a. _____ Carl made a promise to his mother.

   b. _____ Carl called his mother.

CD 1
Track 44

聆聽 CD 播放的簡短對話，並圈選聽到的動詞。

例：你會聽到：A: I'll introduce you to Professor Newton at the meeting tonight.

B: You don't need to. I have already met him.

你要圈出：has （have） had

你會聽到：A: Did Jack introduce you to Professor Newton?

B: No, it wasn't necessary. I had already met him.

你要圈出：has have （had）

1. has	have	had	3. has	have	had
2. has	have	had	4. has	have	had

❏ **Exercise 44.** 檢視學習成果（第 4 章）

校訂下列句子，訂正錯誤的動詞時態。

My experience with English

1. I have been ~~studied~~ *studying* English for eight years, but I still have a lot to learn.

2. I started English classes at this school four weeks ago, and I am learning a lot of English since then.

3. I want to learn English since I am a child.

4. I have been thinking about how to improve my English skills quickly since I came here, but I hadn't found a good way.

5. Our teacher likes to give tests. We has have six tests since the beginning of the term.

6. I like learning English. When I was young, my father found an Australian girl to teach my brothers and me English, but when I move to another city, my father didn't find anyone to teach us.

7. I meet many friends in this class. I meet Abdul in the cafeteria on the first day. He was friendly and kind. We are friends since that day.

8. Abdul have been study English for three months. His English is better than mine.

第五章

發問

□ **Exercise 1. 暖身活動**（表 5-1）

圈選可完成句子的正確答案。

A: _____ you need help?

    a. Are   c. Have

    b. Do   d. Were

B: Yes, _____.

    a. I need   c. I have

    b. I'm   d. I do

5-1 Yes/No 問句和簡答 Yes/No Questions and Short Answers

Yes/No 問句	簡答（＋詳答）	
(a) **Do you like** tea?	*Yes, I do.* (I like tea.) *No, I don't.* (I don't like tea.)	**yes/no** 問句是在回答中會出現 *yes*（是）或 *no*（不是）的問句。
(b) **Did** Sue **call**?	*Yes, she did.* (Sue called.) *No, she didn't.* (Sue didn't call.)	在肯定的簡答中 (*yes*)，助動詞不得與主詞縮寫。
(c) **Have** you **met** Al?	*Yes, I have.* (I have met Al.) *No, I haven't.* (I haven't met Al.)	例 (c)：錯誤：*Yes, I've.* 例 (d)：錯誤：*Yes, it's.* 例 (e)：錯誤：*Yes, he'll.*
(d) **Is** it **raining**?	*Yes, it is.* (It's raining.) *No, it isn't.* (It isn't raining.)	簡答中的說話重音放在動詞上。
(e) **Will** Rob **be** here?	*Yes, he will.* (Rob will be here.) *No, he won't.* (Rob won't be here.)	

□ **Exercise 2. 文法**（表 5-1）

圈選正確的動詞。

A new cell phone

1. *Is, Does*   that your new cell phone? Yes, it   *is, does*.

2. *Are, Do*   you like it? Yes, I   *am, do*.

3. *Were, Did*   you buy it online? Yes, I   *was, did*.

4. *Was, Did*   it expensive? No, it   *wasn't, didn't.*

5. *Is, Does*   it ringing? Yes, it   *is, does.*

6. *Are, Do*   you going to answer it? Yes, I   *am, do.*

7. *Was, Did*   the call important? Yes, it   *was, did.*

8. *Have, Were*   you turned your phone off? No, I   *haven't, wasn't.*

9. *Will, Are*   you call me later? Yes, I   *will, are.*

❑ **Exercise 3. 文法** (表 5-1)

用括弧中的內容造 yes/no 問句，再用適當的簡答完成下列對話，避免在問句中使用否定動詞。

1. A: <u>Do you know my brother?</u>

   B: No,   <u>I don't.</u>   (I don't know your brother.)

2. A: _____

   B: No, _____ (Snakes don't have legs.)

3. A: _____

   B: Yes, _____ (Mexico is in North America.)

4. A: _____

   B: No, _____ (I won't be at home tonight.)

5. A: _____

   B: Yes, _____ (I have a bike.)★

6. A: _____

   B: Yes, _____ (Simon has left.)

7. A: _____

   B: Yes, _____ (Simon left with Kate.)

8. A: _____

   B: Yes, _____ (Acupuncture relieves pain.)

★在美式英文中，*have* 當主動詞用時，通常搭配的助動詞形式為 *do*，如：*Do you have a car?*。
在英式英文中，主動詞 *have* 則不需搭配助動詞 *do* 使用，如：*Have you a car?*。

❏ **Exercise 4.** 聽力 (表 5-1)

聆聽 CD 播放的問題，並圈選正確的回答。

例：你會聽到：Are you almost ready?
　　你要圈出：a. Yes, I was.　　b. Yes, I do.　　ⓒ Yes, I am.

Leaving for the airport

1. a. Yes, I am.　　　　b. Yes, I do.　　　　c. Yes, it does.

2. a. Yes, I did.　　　　b. Yes, I was.　　　　c. Yes, I am.

3. a. Yes, I will.　　　　b. Yes, it will.　　　　c. Yes, it did.

4. a. Yes, they are.　　　b. Yes, it did.　　　　c. Yes, it is.

5. a. Yes, I am.　　　　b. Yes, I will.　　　　c. Yes, I do.

❏ **Exercise 5.** 口說：訪談 (表 5-1)

訪問班上七位同學。用下列提供的字詞造問句，並詢問每位學生一個不一樣的問題。

1. you \ like \ animals?
2. you \ ever \ had \ a pet snake?
3. it \ be \ cold \ in this room?
4. it \ rain \ right now?
5. you \ sleep \ well last night?
6. you \ be \ tired right now?
7. you \ be \ here next year?

❏ **Exercise 6.** 聽力 (表 5-1)

在英文口語中，或許很難聽見 yes/no 問句的開頭，因為那些開頭的字詞發音常被弱化。*

第一部分　聆聽 CD 播放的常用弱化發音。

1. Is he absent?　　　→　　*Ih-ze* absent? 或 *Ze* absent?
2. Is she absent?　　　→　　*Ih-she* absent?
3. Does it work?　　　→　　*Zit* work?
4. Did it break?　　　→　　*Dih-dit* break? 或 *Dit* break?
5. Has he been sick?　→　　*Ze* been sick? 或 *A-ze* been sick?
6. Is there enough?　　→　　*Zere* enough?
7. Is that okay?　　　→　　*Zat* okay?

第二部分　用聽見的字詞，完成下列句子，並寫出非弱化的形式。

At the grocery store

1. I need to see the manager. ＿＿＿＿＿＿＿＿＿ available?

2. I need to see the manager. ＿＿＿＿＿＿＿＿＿ in the store today?

3. Here is one bag of apples. ＿＿＿＿＿＿＿＿＿ enough?

4. I need a drink of water. ＿＿＿＿＿＿＿＿＿ a drinking fountain?

5. My credit card isn't working. Hmmm. ＿＿＿＿＿＿＿＿＿ expire?

---

*亦可參閱第 21 頁，第 1 章，Exercise 33，以及第 39 頁，第 2 章，Exercise 20。

6. Where's Simon? _____ left?

7. The price seems high. _____ include the tax?

❑ **Exercise 7. 暖身活動** (表 5-2)
圈選正確的答案。各題答案或許不只一個。

1. Where did you go?
   a. To the hospital.　b. Yes, I did.　c. Outside.　　　　　d. Yesterday.

2. When is James leaving?
   a. I'm not sure.　b. Yes, he is.　c. Yes, he does.　　d. Around noon.

3. Who did you meet?
   a. Tariq did.　　b. Sasha.　c. Well, I met Sam and Mia.　d. Yes, I did.

5-2 Yes/No 問句和訊息問句 Yes/No and Information Questions

yes/no 問句：可用 yes 或 no 回答的問句
　　A: *Does Ann live in Montreal?*
　　B: *Yes, she does.* 或 *No, she doesn't.*

訊息問句：使用疑問詞詢問各種訊息的問句：**where**、**when**、**why**、**who**、**whom**、**what**、**which**、**whose**、**how**。
　　A: *Where does Ann live?*
　　B: *In Montreal.*

（疑問詞）	助動詞	主詞	主要動詞	（句子的其他部分）	
(a)	**Does**	*Ann*	**live**	in Montreal?	yes/no 問句和訊息問句有同樣的主詞—動詞詞序：
(b) Where	**does**	*Ann*	**live?**		
(c)	**Is**	*Sara*	**studying**	at the library?	助動詞 + 主詞 + 主要動詞
(d) Where	**is**	*Sara*	**studying?**		例 (a) 是 yes/no 問句。
(e)	**Will**	*you*	**graduate**	next year?	例 (b) 是訊息問句。
(f) When	**will**	*you*	**graduate?**		
(g)	**Did**	*they*	**see**	Jack?	在例 (i) 和例 (j) 中，當主要動詞 **be** 動詞為現在簡單式和過去簡單式時 (**am**、**is**、**are**、**was**、**were**)，位置和助動詞相同，放在主詞前面。
(h) Who(m)*	**did**	*they*	**see?**		
(i)	**Is**	*Heidi*		at home?	
(j) Where	**is**	*Heidi?*			
(k)		*Who*	**came**	to dinner?	當疑問詞（如：**who** 或 **what**）作為問句的主詞時，不採用一般問句的詞序，也不會用 **do** 造問句。注意例 (k) 和例 (l)。
(l)		*What*	**happened**	yesterday?	

*關於 *who(m)* 的詳述，請見表 5-4。

閱讀關於 Irina 和 Paul 的一段文字；然後用下列提供的字詞，寫出完整的問句，並圈選正確的簡答。

The Simple Life

Irina and Paul live a simple life. They have a one-room cabin on a lake in the mountains. They fish for some of their food. They also raise chickens. They pick fruit from trees and berries from bushes. They don't have electricity or TV, but they enjoy their life. They don't need a lot to be happy.

1. QUESTION: where \ Irina and Paul \ live?

   Where do Irina and Paul live?

   ANSWER: a. Yes, they do. ⓑ On a lake.

2. QUESTION: they \ live \ a simple life?

   Do they live a simple life?

   ANSWER: a. Yes, they live. b. Yes, they do.

3. QUESTION: what \ they \ pick \ from the trees?

   ANSWER: a. Fruit. b. Yes, they pick.

4. QUESTION: they \ have \ electricity?

   Do they have electricity?

   ANSWER: a. No, they don't. b. No, they don't have.

5. QUESTION: they \ enjoy \ their life?

   ANSWER: a. Yes, they do. b. Yes, they enjoy.

6. QUESTION: they \ be \ happy?

   Are they happy?

   ANSWER: a. Yes, they do. b. Yes, they are.

CD 1
Track 47

聆聽 CD 播放的對話，然後再聽一遍，並用聽到的字詞完成下列句子。

Where are Roberto and Isabel?

A: _____ Roberto and Isabel?
　　　　　　　　1

B: Yes, _____. They live around the corner from me.
　　　　　　2

A: _____ them lately?
　　　　　　　　3

B: No, _____. They're out of town.
　　　　　　　4

A: _____ to their parents? I heard Roberto's parents are ill.
　　　　　　　　5

B: Yes, _____. They went to help them.
　　　　　　6

A: _____ them soon?
　　　　　　　　7

B: Yes, _____. In fact, I'm going to pick them up at the airport.
　　　　　8

A: _____ back this weekend? I'm having a party, and I'd like
　　　　　　　　9
to invite them.

B: No, _____. They won't be back until Monday.
　　　　　　　10

❏ **Exercise 10. 暖身活動** (表 5-3)

用下表中最合適的疑問詞，完成下列句子，其中一句適用兩個疑問詞；然後將下列搭配問句的答案，填入問句後的空格中。

Why	What time	Where	When

疑問句

1. _____ do you live? ____
2. _____ are you laughing? ____
3. _____ will you get here? ____

答案

a. At noon.

b. On Fifth Street.

c. Because the joke was funny.

問句	回答	
(a) **Where** did he go?	Home.	**where** 詢問地點。
(b) **When** did he leave?	Last night. Two days ago. Monday morning. Seven-thirty.	**when** 所引導的問句可用任何表達時間的字詞回答，如：例 (b) 中的回答範例。
(c) **What time** did he leave?	Seven-thirty. Around five o'clock. A quarter past ten.	**what time** 引導的問句詢問幾點。
(d) **Why** did he leave?	Because he didn't feel well.*	**why** 詢問原因。
(e) **What** did he leave *for*? (f) **How come** he left?	**why** 也可以用慣用語 **what . . . for** 以及 **how come** 來表示，如：例 (e) 和 (f)。 注意 **how come** 的用法並不同於一般問句的詞序：主詞在動詞之前，也不用助動詞 **do**。	

*because 的用法請見第 221 頁，表 8-6；例：Because I didn't feel well 為副詞子句，而非完整句。以此例句來看，該句為問句的簡答。

❑ **Exercise 11. 文法** (表 5-3)
用說話者 A 提供的訊息造問句，完成下列對話。

1. A: I'm going downtown in a few minutes.

   B: I didn't catch that. When __*are you going downtown*__? 或

   B: I didn't catch that. Where __*are you going in a few minutes*__?

2. A: My kids are transferring to Lakeview Elementary School because it's a better school.

   B: What was that? Where _____? 或

   B: What was that? Why _____?

3. A: I will meet Taka at 10:00 at the mall.

   B: I couldn't hear you. Tell me again. What time _____? 或

   B: I couldn't hear you. Tell me again. Where _____?

4. A: Class begins at 8:15.

   B: Are you sure? When _____? 或

   B: Are you sure? What time _____?

5. A: I stayed home from work because I wanted to watch the World Cup final on TV.

   B: Huh?! Why _____? 或

   B: Huh?! What _____ for?

❏ **Exercise 12. 文法** (表 5-3)

用 *how come* 和 *what for* 改寫下列句子。

1. Why are you going?
2. Why did they come?
3. Why does he need more money?
4. Why are they going to leave?

❏ **Exercise 13. 閱讀與文法** (表 5-2 和 5-3)

閱讀以下關於 Nina 生日的文章。用下列提供的字詞造問句，可分小組或全班一起回答問題。

The Birthday Present

Tom got home late last night, around midnight. His wife, Nina, was sitting on the couch waiting for him. She was quite worried because Tom is never late.

Tomorrow is Nina's birthday. Unfortunately, Tom doesn't think she will be happy with her birthday present. Yesterday, Tom bought her a bike and he decided to ride it home from the bike shop. While he was riding down a hill, a driver came too close to him, and he landed in a ditch. Tom was okay, but the bike was ruined. Tom found a bus stop nearby and finally got home.

Tom told Nina the story, but Nina didn't care about the bike. She said she had a better present: her husband.

1. When \ Tom \ get home
2. Where \ be \ his wife
3. What \ Tom \ buy
4. Why \ be \ Tom \ late
5. What present \ Nina \ get

❏ **Exercise 14. 聽力** (表 5-2 和 5-3)

聆聽 CD 播放的問題，圈選最恰當的答案。

CD 1
Track 48

例：你會聽到：When are you leaving?
你要圈出：a. Yes, I am.　　(b.) Tomorrow.　　c. In the city.

1. a. I am too.　　b. Yesterday.　　c. Sure.
2. a. For dinner.　　b. At 6:00.　　c. At the restaurant.
3. a. Outside the mall.　　b. After lunch.　　c. Because I need a ride.
4. a. At work.　　b. Because traffic was heavy.　　c. A few hours ago.
5. a. A pair of jeans.　　b. At the store.　　c. Tomorrow.

❏ **Exercise 15. 暖身活動** (表 5-4)

將 A 欄的問句與 B 欄中的正確答案相配對。

A 欄

1. Who flew to Rome? _____
2. Who did you fly to Rome? _____
3. What did you fly to Rome? _____
4. What flew to Rome? _____

B 欄

a. A small plane flew to Rome.
b. Pablo flew to Rome.
c. I flew a small plane to Rome.
d. I flew Pablo to Rome.

5-4 以 *Who*、*Who(m)* 和 *What* 開頭的問句

問句		回答	
(a)	主詞 (S) ***Who*** came?	主詞 ***Someone*** came.	在例 (a) 中，***who*** 作爲問句的主詞 (S)。 在例 (b) 中 ***who*** (*m*) 作爲問句的受詞 (O)。 ***whom*** 於非常正式的英文中使用，在日常口語中，常以 ***who*** 代替 ***whom***： 　不常用：Whom did you see? 　　常用：Who did you see?
(b)	受詞 (O) ***Who*** (*m*) did *you* see?	主詞　　受詞 *I* saw ***someone***.	
(c)	主詞 ***What*** happened?	主詞 ***Something*** happened.	***what*** 可在問句中當主詞或受詞。 注意例 (a) 和例 (c)：若問句的主詞是 ***who*** 或 ***what*** 時，不用一般問句的詞序，也不用 ***do*** 造問句。 　正確：Who came? 　錯誤：*Who did come*?
(d)	受詞 ***What*** did *you* see?	主詞　　受詞 *I* saw ***something***.	

❑ **Exercise 16.** 文法 (表 5-4)

用 ***who***、***who*** (*m*) 和 ***what*** 造問句。如果疑問詞爲主詞，就在該字詞上方寫 S；如果是受詞，就寫 O。

問句	答句
S 1. *Who knows?*	*S* **Someone** knows.
O 2. *Who(m) did you ask?*	*O* I asked **someone**.
3. _____	**Someone** knocked on the door.
4. _____	Talya met **someone**.
5. _____	Mike learned **something**.
6. _____	**Something** changed Gina's mind.
7. _____	Gina is talking about **someone**.★
8. _____	Gina is talking about **something**.

★在非常正式的英文中，介系詞也許會出現在問句的句首：***About whom*** (非 ***who***) *is Tina talking*?。
　在日常英文中，介系詞通常不會出現在問句的句首。

❏ **Exercise 17. 文法** (表 5-4)

用 *who* 或 *what* 完成下列句子。

1. A: _____ just called?
   B: That was Antonia.

2. A: _____ do you need?
   B: A pair of scissors. I'm cutting my hair.

3. A: _____ is Jae?
   B: My stepmom.

4. A: _____ is going on?
   B: Ben's having a party.

5. A: _____ did you call?
   B: Tracy.

6. A: _____ do you need?
   B: Dr. Smith or her nurse.

❏ **Exercise 18. 口說：訪談** (表 5-4)

在教室裡走動，並用 *who* 或 *what* 為首的問句詢問同學問題。

例：_____ are you currently reading?
說話者 A：What are you currently reading?
說話者 B：A book about a cowboy.

1. _____ do you like to do in your free time?
2. _____ is your idea of the perfect vacation?
3. _____ is your best friend?
4. _____ was the most memorable event of your childhood?
5. _____ stresses you out?
6. _____ do you need that you don't have?
7. _____ would you most like to invite to dinner? Why? (*The person can be living or dead.*)

❏ **Exercise 19. 聽力** (表 5-4)

聆聽 CD 播放的對話，然後再聽一遍，並用聽見的字詞完成下列句子。

CD 1
Track 49 **A secret**

A: John told me something.

B: _____ tell you?
                $\overline{1}$

A: It's confidential. I can't tell you.

B: _____ anyone else?
                $\overline{2}$

A: He told a few other people.

B: _____ tell?
                $\overline{3}$

A: Some friends.

B: Then it's not a secret. _____ say?
                                        $\overline{4}$

A: I can't tell you.

B: _____ can't _____ me?
          $\overline{5}$ $\overline{6}$

A: Because it's about you. But don't worry. It's nothing bad.

B: Gee. Thanks a lot. That sure makes me feel better.

❑ **Exercise 20. 閱讀與口說** (表 5-4)

分小組練習，詢問組員文章中斜體字詞的字義；如果有需要，可以查字典。

例：type
學生 A：What does *type* mean?
學生 B：*Type* means *kind* or *category*.

Types of Books

There are several different *types* of books. You may be familiar with the categories of *fiction* and *nonfiction*. These are the two main types. *Fiction* includes *mysteries, romance, thrillers, science fiction,* and *horror. Nonfiction* includes *biographies, autobiographies, history,* and *travel*. There are other types, but these are some of the more common ones. Which type do you like best?

❑ **Exercise 21. 暖身活動** (表 5-5)

依據自身真實情況，回答下列問題。

1. What do you do on weekends? I . . .
2. What did you do last weekend? I . . .
3. What are you going to do this weekend? I'm going to . . .
4. What will you do the following weekend? I will . . .

5-5 *What + Do* 的形式

問句	回答	
(a) *What **does** Bob **do** every morning?*	He *goes to class.*	「***what + do***」的各種形式用於詢問與活動相關的問題。
(b) *What **did** you **do** yesterday?*	I *went downtown.*	
(c) *What **is** Anna **doing** (right now)?*	She*'s studying.*	***do*** 的形式有：*am doing*、*will do*、*are going to do*、*did* 等。
(d) *What **are** you **going to do** tomorrow?*	I *'m going to go to the beach.*	
(e) *What **do** you **want to do** tonight?*	I *want to go to a movie.*	
(f) *What <u>would</u> you **like to do** tomorrow?*	I *would like to visit Jim.*	

想要

❑ **Exercise 22. 文法** (表 5-5)

用「***what + do***」的正確形式作為問句的開頭。

1. A: _____*What are you doing*_____ right now?

   B: I'm working on my monthly report.

2. A: _____ last night?

   B: I worked on my monthly report.

3. A: _____ tomorrow?

   B: I'm going to visit my relatives.

4. A: _____ tomorrow?

   B: I want to go to the beach.

5. A: _____ this evening?

   B: I would like to go to a movie.

6. A: _____ tomorrow?

   B: I'm staying home and relaxing most of the day.

7. A: _____ in your history class every day?

   B: We listen to the teacher talk.

8. A: _____ (for a living)?*

   B: I'm a teacher.

   A: _____ your wife _____ ?

   B: She designs websites. She works for an Internet company.

❑ **Exercise 23. 口說：訪談** (表 5-5)

訪問班上同學。用下列提供的字詞和「*what* + *do*」的正確形式造問句，且不限一種動詞時態。最後與全班分享一些同學的答案。

例：tomorrow
說話者 A：What are you going to do tomorrow? / What do you want to do tomorrow? / What would you like to do tomorrow? / Etc.
說話者 B：I'm going to buy a new video game. / I want to buy a new video game. / I'd like to buy a new video game. / Etc.

1. last night
2. right now
3. next Saturday
4. this afternoon
5. tonight
6. last weekend
7. after class yesterday
8. every morning
9. since you arrived in this city
10. on weekends

❑ **Exercise 24. 暖身活動** (表 5-6)

回答下列有關冰淇淋口味的問題。

| blackberry | chocolate | coffee | lemon | strawberry |
| caramel | coconut | green tea | mint | vanilla |

1. Which ice-cream flavors are popular in your country?
2. What kind of ice cream do you like?

---

*__What do you do?__ 有特別的意義，爲用來詢問他人職業的問句：*What is your occupation, your job?*。另一種詢問方式爲：*What do you do for a living?*。

5-6 *Which* 和 *What Kind Of* 的用法

Which 選擇

(a) TOM: May I borrow a pen from you? ANN: Sure. I have two pens. This pen has black ink. That pen has red ink. **Which pen** do you want? 或 **Which one** do you want? 或 **Which** do you want?	在例 (a) 中，Ann 用 **which** 這個字（而非 **what**）發問，因為她想讓 Tom 選擇。 **which** 用在說話者提供多種可能性讓他人做選擇時，如：這個 (*this one*) 或那個 (*that one*)；這些 (*these*) 或那些 (*those*)。
(b) SUE: I like these earrings, and I like those too. BOB: **Which** (*earrings/ones*) are you going to buy? SUE: I think I'll get these.	**which** 可搭配單數名詞或複數名詞使用。
(c) JIM: Here's a photo of my daughter's class. KIM: Very nice. **Which one** is your daughter?	**which** 所詢問的對象可以是人，也可以是事物。
(d) SUE: My aunt gave me some money for my birthday. I'm going to take it with me to the mall. BOB: **What** are you going to buy with it? SUE: I haven't decided yet.	在例 (d) 中，問句並非在某特定項目群體中做選擇，所以 Bob 用疑問詞 **what**，而非 **which**。

What kind of 種類：kind、type、sort (n.)

問句	回答	
(e) **What kind of** *shoes* did you buy?	Boots. Sandals. Tennis shoes. Loafers. 矮鞋 Running shoes. High heels. 高根鞋 Etc.	**what kind of** 是用於詢問總類中某一種特定型態（種類）的資訊。 例 (e)： 總類 = shoes 特定種類 = boots 　　　　　sandals 　　　　　tennis shoes 等
(f) **What kind of** *fruit* do you like best?	Apples. Bananas. Oranges. Grapefruit. Strawberries. Etc.	例 (f)： 總類 = fruit 特定種類 = apples 　　　　　bananas 　　　　　oranges 等

☐ **Exercise 25. 文法** (表 5-6)

用 **which** 或 **what** 開頭造問句。

1. A: I have two books. *Which book / Which one / Which do you want?*

   B: That one. (I want that book.)

2. A: *What did you buy when you went shopping?*

   B: A book. (I bought a book when I went shopping.)

3. A: Could I borrow your pen for a minute?

    B: Sure. I have two. _____

    A: That one. (I would like that one.)

4. A: _____

    B: A pen. (Hassan borrowed a pen from me.)

5. A: _____

    B: Two pieces of hard candy. (I have two pieces of hard candy in my hand.) Would you like one?

    A: Yes. Thanks.

    B: _____

    A: The yellow one. (I'd like the yellow one.)

6. A: Tony and I went shopping. I got some new shoes.

    B: _____

    A: A tie. (Tony got a tie.)

7. A: Did you enjoy your trip to South America?

    B: Yes, I did. Very much.

    A: _____

    B: Peru, Brazil, and Venezuela. (I visited Peru, Brazil, and Venezuela.)★

    A: _____

    B: Peru. (I enjoyed Peru the most. I have family there.)

❑ **Exercise 26.** 口說：訪談 (表 5-6)

完成下列問句。詢問一位同學下列問題，並寫下該名同學的答案，然後再與全班分享該名同學的部分答案。

1. A: What kind of ___*shoes*___ are you wearing?

    B: Boots. *Classmate's answer:* _____

2. A: What kind of ___*meat*___ do you eat most often?

    B: Beef. *Classmate's answer:* _____

3. A: What kind of _____ do you like best?

    B: Rock 'n roll. *Classmate's answer:* _____

4. A: What kind of _____ do you like to watch?

    B: Comedy. *Classmate's answer:* _____

5. A: What kind of _____ do you like best?

    B: *Classmate's answer:* _____

★在多數情況下，***what*** country 和 ***which*** country 間的差異很小。

❑ **Exercise 27. 暖身活動** (表 5-7)

回答下列問題。

1. This is Ted's daughter. Whose daughter is that?
   a. That's Terry.   b. That's Terry's.

2. This is Ted. Who's next to him?
   a. That's Terry.   b. That's Terry's.

It's John's pen.

John's book
adj.

5-7 *Whose* 的用法

問句	回答	
(a) **Whose** (**book**) is this?	It's John's (book).	**whose** 用在詢問「所有關係★」。
(b) **Whose** (**books**) are those?	They're mine (或 my books).	注意在例 (a) 中，若聽話者很清楚句義，可以將 *whose* 後的名詞 (**book**) 省略。
(c) **Whose car** did you borrow?	I borrowed Karen's (car).	
比較		**who's** 和 **whose** 的發音相同。
(d) **Who's** that?	Mary Smith.	**who's** 為 **who is** 的縮寫。
(e) **Whose** is that?	Mary's.	**whose** 用於詢問所有關係。

★所有關係的表達方式請見第 166 頁，表 6-11，以及第 168 頁，表 6-12。

❑ **Exercise 28. 口說：兩人一組** (表 5-7)

成兩人一組。學生 B 仔細看以下照片，並試著記住圖中兩位女子的穿著，然後闔上書本。學生 A 指著第 126 頁的品項，並用 *whose* 造問句詢問學生 B。詢問四個品項之後，就互換角色。

例：
學生 A：Whose purse is that?
學生 B：It's Rita's.

Nina   Rita

❑ **Exercise 29. 聽力** (表 5-7)

聆聽 CD 播放的問題,並圈選可完成句子的正確答案。

1. Who's   Whose   3. Who's   Whose   5. Who's   Whose

2. Who's   Whose   4. Who's   Whose   6. Who's   Whose

❑ **Exercise 30. 聽力** (表 5-7)

聆聽 CD 播放的問題,並判斷說話者說的是 *whose* 還是 *who's*。

An old vacation photo

1. whose   who's   3. whose   who's   5. whose   who's

2. whose   who's   4. whose   who's   6. whose   who's

❑ **Exercise 31. 暖身活動** (表 5-8)

將 A 欄中的問句與 B 欄中的正確回答相配對。

A 欄

1. How tall is your sister? _____

2. How old is your brother? _____

3. How did you get here? _____

4. How soon do we need to go? _____

5. How well do you know Kazu? _____

B 欄

a. By bus.

b. In five minutes.

c. I don't. I only know his sister.

d. Fifteen.

e. Five feet (1.52 meters).

5-8 *How* 的用法

問句	回答	
(a) **How** did you get here?	I drove. / By car. I took a taxi. / By taxi. I took a bus. / By bus. I flew. / By plane. I took a train. / By train. I walked. / On foot.	**how** 有許多用法，其中之一就是用於詢問運輸工具（或方法）。
(b) **How old** are you? (c) **How tall** is he? (d) **How big** is your apartment? (e) **How sleepy** are you? (f) **How hungry** are you? (g) **How soon** will you be ready? (h) **How well** does he speak English? (i) **How quickly** can you get here?	Twenty-one. About six feet. It has three rooms. Very sleepy. I'm starving. In five minutes. Very well. I can get there in 30 minutes.	**how** 常和形容詞（如：*old*、*big*）及副詞（如：*well*、*quickly*）連用。 long → 長度 far → 距離 often → 頻率

❑ **Exercise 32. 閱讀與文法**（表 5-8）

閱讀以下關於 John 的文章，並回答下列問題。

Long John

　　John is 14 years old. He is very tall for his age. He is 6 foot, 6 inches (2 meters). His friends call him "Long John." People are surprised to find out that he is still a teenager. Both his parents are average height, so John's height seems unusual.

　　It causes problems for him, especially when he travels. Beds in hotels are too short, and there is never enough leg room on airplanes. He is very uncomfortable. When he can, he prefers to take a train because he can walk around and stretch his legs.

1.　How tall is John?　_____.

2.　How old is John?　_____.

3.　How well do you think he sleeps in hotels?　_____.

4.　How comfortable is he on airplanes?　_____.

5.　How does he like to travel?　_____.

Exercise 33. 文法（表 5-8）

用 *how* 造問句。

1. A: _How old is your daughter?_

   B: Ten. (My daughter is ten years old.)

2. A: How important is education?

   B: Very important. (Education is very important.)

3. A: How

   B: By bus. (I get to school by bus.)

4. A: How deep is the ocean?

   B: Very, very deep. (The ocean is very, very deep.)

5. A: How are you going to get to Buenos Aires?

   B: By plane. (I'm going to get to Buenos Aires by plane.)

6. A: How difficult was the test?

   B: Not very. (The test wasn't very difficult.)

7. A: How

   B: It's 29,029 feet high. (Mt. Everest is 29,029 feet high.)*

8. A: How did you get here?

   B: I ran. (I ran here.)

☐ **Exercise 34. 聽力**（表 5-8）

用聽到的字詞完成下列對話。

1. A: _____ are these eggs?

   B: I just bought them at the Farmers' Market, so they should be fine.

2. A: _____ were the tickets?

   B: They were 50% off.

3. A: _____ was the driver's test?

   B: Well, I didn't pass, so that gives you an idea.

4. A: _____ is the car?

   B: There's dirt on the floor. We need to vacuum it inside.

5. A: _____ is the frying pan?

   B: Don't touch it! You'll burn yourself.

6. A: _____ is the street you live on?

   B: There is a lot of traffic, so we keep the windows closed a lot.

7. A: _____ are you about interviewing for the job?

   B: Very. I already scheduled an interview with the company.

---

*29,029 英尺等於 8,848 公尺。

將 A 欄中的問句與 B 欄中最恰當的回答相配對。★

A 欄

1. How often does the earth go completely around the sun? ＿＿＿
2. How often do the summer Olympics occur? ＿＿＿
3. How often do earthquakes occur? ＿＿＿
4. How many times a year can a healthy person safely donate blood? ＿＿＿
5. How many times a day do the hands on a clock overlap? ＿＿＿

B 欄

a. About six times a year.
b. Several hundred times a day.
c. Once a year.
d. Every four years.
e. Exactly 22 times a day.

5-9 *How Often* 的用法

問句	回答	
(a) **How often** do you go shopping? 每隔一天	Every day. Once a week. About twice a week. Every other day or so.★ Three times a month.	*how often* 用來詢問頻率。
(b) **How many times a day** do you eat?	Three or four.	其他代替 *how often* 的問法：
How many times a week do you go shopping?	Two.	*how many times* { *a day* *a week* *a month* *a year*
How many times a month do you go to the post office?	Once.	
How many times a year do you take a vacation?	Once or twice.	

表達頻率的字詞	
a lot	every
occasionally 偶爾	every other
once in a while 有時	once a
not very often	twice a \ day/week/month/year
hardly ever 幾乎不 rarely	three times a
almost never scarcely	ten times a /
never	

★*Every other day* 表示「星期一有、星期二沒有、星期三有、星期四沒有⋯⋯」；以此類推，也就是「每隔一天」的意思。
Or so 意指「大概」。

＿＿＿＿＿＿＿＿＿＿
★請見解答本中的 *Trivia Answers*。

❑ **Exercise 36. 口說：兩人一組** (表 5-9)

成兩人一組，並輪流用 *how often* 或 *how many times a day/week/moth/year* 作問答練習。

例：eat lunch at the cafeteria
說話者 A：How often do you eat lunch at the cafeteria?
說話者 B：About twice a week. How about you? How often do you eat at the cafeteria?
說話者 A：I don't. I bring my own lunch.

1. check email
2. listen to podcasts
3. go out to eat
4. cook your own dinner
5. buy a toothbrush
6. go swimming
7. attend weddings
8. download music from the Internet

❑ **Exercise 37. 閱讀與聽力** (表 5-8 和 5-9)

閱讀關於 Ben 的一段文字，然後用聽到的字詞完成下列問句。

Ben's Sleeping Problem

    Ben has a problem with insomnia. He's unable to fall asleep at night very easily. He also wakes up often in the middle of the night and has trouble getting back to sleep. Right now he's talking to a nurse at a sleep disorders clinic. The nurse is asking him some general questions.

1. _____ you?

2. _____ you?

3. _____ you weigh?

4. In general, _____ you sleep at night?

5. _____ you fall asleep?

6. _____ you wake up during the night?

7. _____ you in the mornings?

8. _____ you exercise?

9. _____ you feeling right now?

10. _____ you come in for an overnight appointment?

仔細看以下地圖，並回答關於其中三個城市間飛行距離的問題。

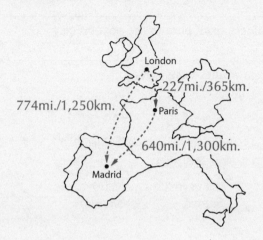

227mi./365km.

774mi./1,250km.

640mi./1,300km.

1. How far is <u>it</u> from London to Madrid?
2. How many miles is it from London to Paris?
3. How many kilometers is it from Paris to Madrid?

5-10 *How Far* 的用法	
(a) ***It is*** 489 miles ***from*** Oslo ***to*** Helsinki by air.*	最常用來表示距離的句型：
(b) ***It is*** 3,605 miles ***from*** Moscow ***to*** Beijing. ***from*** Beijing ***to*** Moscow. ***to*** Beijing ***from*** Moscow. ***to*** Moscow ***from*** Beijing.	***It is*** + 距離 + ***from/to*** + ***to/from*** 在例 (b) 中，四組含 ***from*** 和 ***to*** 的表達字詞同義。

(c) — ***How far is it*** from Mumbai to Delhi?
   — 725 miles.
(d) — ***How far do you*** live from school?
   — Four blocks.
	how far 可用於詢問有關距離的問題。

(e) ***How many miles*** is it from London to Paris? (f) ***How many kilometers*** is it to Montreal from here? (g) ***How many blocks*** is it to the post office?	其他詢問**距離**的問法： • *how many miles* • *how many kilometers* • *how many blocks*

*1 英哩等於 1.60 公里；1 公里等於 0.614 英哩。

❑   **Exercise 39. 文法**（表 5-10）
用 ***how far*** 造問句。

1. A: <u>*How far is it from Prague to Budapest?*</u>
    B: 276 miles. (It's 276 miles to Prague from Budapest.)

2. A: _____

   B: 257 kilometers. (It's 257 kilometers from Montreal to Quebec.)

3. A: _____

   B: Six blocks. (It's six blocks from here to the post office.)

4. A: _____

   B: A few miles. (I live a few miles from work.)

❑ **Exercise 40. 文法** (表 5-10)

用 *how far* 和下列提供的字詞寫出四句問句，並詢問其他同學。需使用以下句型：***How far is it from*** (___) ***to*** (___)?，並查詢正確的距離。

the sun	the moon	the earth	Mars
Venus	Jupiter	Saturn	Neptune

❑ **Exercise 41. 暖身活動** (表 5-11)

完成下列句子。用 ***How long does it take you to ...?*** 作為開頭，詢問三位同學有關他們晚間作息的相關資訊。最後，與全班分享一些答案。

1. It takes me _____ minutes to get ready for bed.

2. It takes me _____ minutes to brush my teeth.

3. It usually takes me _____ minutes/hour(s) to fall asleep.

5-11 所需時間的表示法：*It + Take* 和 *How Long* 的用法

IT + TAKE + （某人） + 時間長短 + 不定詞				*it + take* 常與時間用語和不定詞連用，來表示**時間長短**，如：例 (a) 與例 (b)。
(a) *It*	takes		20 minutes	***to cook*** rice.
(b) *It*	took	Al	two hours	***to drive*** to work.

不定詞 = *to* + 動詞原形★

在例 (a) 中，*to cook* 是不定詞。

(c) ***How long*** does it take to cook rice? Twenty minutes.	*how long* 用來詢問「時間的長短」。
(d) ***How long*** did it take Al to drive to work today? Two hours.	
(e) ***How long*** did you study last night? Four hours.	
(f) ***How long*** will you be in Hong Kong? Ten days.	

(g) ***How many days*** will you be in Hong Kong?	其他詢問**時間長短**的方法：

人 + spend ｜money / time｜ onth / Ving

how many +
- minutes
- hours
- days
- weeks
- months
- years

★請見第 346 頁，表 13-3。

❑ **Exercise 42.** 口說：兩人一組（表 5-11）

成兩人一組，並輪流用 *it* + *take* 作問答練習。最後，與全班分享一些你的答案。

1. How long does it take you to . . .
   a. eat breakfast? → *It takes me ten minutes to eat breakfast.*
   b. get to class?
   c. write a short paragraph in English?
   d. read a 300-page book?

2. Generally speaking, how long does it take to . . .
   a. fly from (*a city*) to (*a city*)?
   b. get from here to your hometown?
   c. get used to living in a foreign country?
   d. commute from (*a local place*) to (*a local place*) during rush hour?

❑ **Exercise 43.** 文法（表 5-11）

用 *how long* 造問句。

1. A: _How long did it take you to drive to Istanbul?_
   B: Five days. (It took me five days to drive to Istanbul.)

2. A: _____
   B: A week. (Mr. McNally will be in the hospital for a week.)

3. A: _____
   B: A long time. (It takes a long time to learn a second language.)

4. A: _____
   B: Six months. (I've been living here for six months.)

5. A: _____
   B: Six years. (I lived in Oman for six years.)

6. A: _____
   B: A couple of years. (I've known Mr. Pham for a couple of years.)

7. A: _____
   B: Since 2005. (He's been living in Canada since 2005.)

CD 1
Track 54

聆聽 CD 播放的問句。問句中斜體字型的動詞與疑問詞合併縮寫。從下表中選擇正確的動詞形式，並填入空格中。

does	did	is	are	will

A birthday

1. *When's* your birthday? _____

2. *When'll* your party be? _____

3. *Where'd* you decide to have it? _____

4. *Who're* you inviting? _____

5-12 口語和書寫中疑問詞的合併縮寫

僅限口語使用

is	(a) "*When's* he coming?" "*Why's* she late?"	*is*、*are*、*does*、*did*、*has*、*have* 和 *will* 在口語中常與疑問詞合併縮寫。
are	(b) "*What're* these?" "*Who're* they talking to?"	
does	(c) "*When's* the movie start?" "*Where's* he live?"	
did	(d) "*Who'd* you see?" "*What'd* you do?"	
has	(e) "*What's* she done?" "*Where's* he gone?"	
have	(f) "*How've* you been?" "*What've* I done?"	
will	(g) "*Where'll* you be?" "*When'll* they be here?"	
	(h) **What do you** → Whaddaya think? (i) **What are you** → Whaddaya thinking?	在口語英文中，**what do you** 和 **what are you** 的弱化發音為 "Whaddaya"。

書寫

is	(j) *Where's* Ed? *What's* that? *Who's* he?	只有 **where**、**what** 或 **who** 與 **is** 的合併縮寫，常用於書寫形式中，如：寄給朋友的信件或電子郵件。此類的縮寫形式在較正式的書寫中並不恰當，如：雜誌文章或參考文獻。

☐ **Exercise 45.** 聽力 (表 5-12)

聽聽下列問題中與疑問詞合併縮寫的字詞發音。

1. Where is my key?
2. Where are my keys?
3. Who are those people?
4. What is in that box?
5. What are you doing?
6. Where did Bob go last night?
7. Who will be at the party?
8. Why is the teacher absent?
9. Who is that?
10. Why did you say that?
11. Who did you talk to at the party?
12. How are we going to get to work?
13. What did you say?
14. How will you do that?

☐ **Exercise 46.** 聽力 (表 5-12)

用聽見字詞的非縮寫形式完成下列句子。

On an airplane

例：你會聽到： When's the plane land?
　　你要寫下： _____When does_____ the plane land?

1. _____ you going to sit with?

2. _____ you going to get your suitcase under the seat?

3. _____ the flight attendant just say?

4. _____ we need to put our seat belts back on?

5. _____ the plane descending?

6. _____ we going down?

7. _____ the pilot tell us what's going on?

8. _____ meet you when you land?

9. _____ our connecting flight?

10. _____ we get from the airport to our hotel?

☐ **Exercise 47.** 聽力 (表 5-12)

用聽見字詞的非縮寫形式完成下列問題。

A mother talking to her teenage daughter

1. _____ going?

2. _____ going with?

3. _____ that?

4. _____ known him?

5. _____ meet him?

6. _____ go to school?

7. _____ a good student?

8. _____ be back?

9. _____ wearing that outfit?

10. _____ giving me that look?

11. _____ asking so many questions?

Because I love you!

❑ **Exercise 48.** 聽力（表 5-12）

聆聽 CD 播放的問題，並圈選聽見字詞的正確非縮寫形式。

CD 1
Track 58

例：你會聽到：Whaddya want?
　　你要圈出：What are you　(What do you)

1. What are you　　　What do you

2. What are you　　　What do you

3. What are you　　　What do you

4. What are you　　　What do you

5. What are you　　　What do you

6. What are you　　　What do you

7. What are you　　　What do you

8. What are you　　　What do you

❑ **Exercise 49.** 暖身活動（表 5-13）

第一部分　下列各組句子皆合文法，你認為哪一句在口語英文中較為常見？

1. a. How do you spell "Hawaii?"
    b. What is the spelling for "Hawaii?"

2. a. How do you pronounce G-A-R-A-G-E?
    b. What is the pronunciation for G-A-R-A-G-E?

第二部分　下列哪兩個問句的句義相同？

1. How are you doing?
2. How's it going?
3. How do you do?

5-13 *How* 的其他問句 More Questions with *How*

問句	回答	
(a) ***How do you spell*** "coming"?	C-O-M-I-N-G.	例 (a) 的回答：拼出該字。
(b) ***How do you say*** "yes" in Japanese?	Hai.	例 (b) 的回答：說出該字。
(c) ***How do you say/pronounce*** this word?	——	例 (c) 的回答：唸出該字。
(d) ***How are you getting along?*** (e) ***How are you doing?*** (f) ***How's it going?***	Great. Fine. Okay. So-so.	例 (d)、(e)、(f) 的句意：你過得如何？一切順利嗎？有沒有什麼問題呢？ 注意：例 (f) 也可用作問候語： *Hi, Bob. How's it going?*
(g) ***How do you feel?*** ***How are you feeling?***	Terrific! Wonderful! Great! Fine. Okay. So-so. A bit under the weather. Not so good. Terrible!/Lousy./Awful!	例 (g) 用來詢問他人健康或心情狀態。
(h) ***How do you do?***	How do you do?	***How do you do?*** 常用在較正式的場合，作為說話者被介紹時，打招呼的問候語，如：例 (h)。★

★A: *Dr. Erickson, I'd like to introduce you to a friend of mine, Rick Brown. Rick, this is my biology professor, Dr. Erickson.*
 B: ***How do you do**, Mr. Brown?*
 C: ***How do you do**, Dr. Erickson? I'm pleased to meet you.*

❑ **Exercise 50. 遊戲**（表 5-13）

將全班分為兩組。闔上書本，並輪流拼出老師說的字。正確拼出最多字的組別獲勝。

例：country
老師：How do you spell "country"?
A 組：C-O-U-N-T-R-Y.
老師：Good.（如果 A 組答案有誤，另一組可以回答）

1. together
2. people
3. daughter
4. beautiful
5. foreign
6. neighbor
7. beginning
8. intelligent
9. Mississippi
10. purple
11. rained
12. different

❑ **Exercise 51. 口說** (表 5-13)

在教室裡走動，用此問句：***How do you say*** (___) ***in*** (___)? 詢問同學下列字詞在其他語言中的說法，如：日文 (Japanese)、阿拉伯文 (Arabic)、德文 (German)、法文 (French)、韓文 (Korean)等。如果有人不知道，就問另一個。

例：

說話者 A：How do you say "yes" in French?

說話者 B："Yes" in French is "oui."

1. No.
2. Thank you.
3. Okay.
4. How are you?
5. Good-bye.
6. Excuse me.

❑ **Exercise 52. 暖身活動** (表 5-14)

在以下對話中，說話者提出不少建議。劃<u>底線</u>標示他們所提的建議。

A: Let's invite the Thompsons over for dinner.

B: Good idea! How about next Sunday?

A: Let's do it sooner. What about this Saturday?

5-14 *How About* 和 *What About* 的用法

(a) A: We need one more player. B: ***How about/What about Jack?*** Let's ask him if he wants to play.	***how about*** 和 ***what about*** 的意義和用法相同，是用來提出建議或協助。
(b) A: What time should we meet? B: ***How about/What about three o'clock?***	***how about*** 和 ***what about*** 後面常接名詞（或代名詞），或動詞 *-ing* 形式（動名詞）。
(c) A: What should we do this afternoon? B: ***How about going*** to the zoo?	注意：***how about*** 和 ***what about*** 常用於非正式的口語英文，但通常不用於書寫中。
(d) A: ***What about asking*** Sally over for dinner next Sunday? B: Okay. Good idea.	
(e) A: I'm tired. ***How about you?*** B: Yes, I'm tired too.	***How about you?*** 和 ***What about you?*** 是用於詢問先前才提過的說話內容或問題。
(f) A: Are you hungry? B: No. ***What about you?*** A: I'm a little hungry.	例 (e) 中的 ***How about you?*** = ***Are you tired?*** 例 (f) 中的 ***What about you?*** = ***Are you hungry?***

❑ **Exercise 53. 文法與聽力** (表 5-14)

CD 1
Track 59

圈選最恰當的回答，然後聆聽 CD 播放的各組對話，並核對答案。

例：

說話者 A：What are you going to do over vacation?

說話者 B：I'm staying here. What about you?

說話者 A：a. Yes, I will. I have a vacation too.

　　　　ⓑ. I'm going to Jordan to visit my sister.

　　　　c. I did too.

1. A: Did you like the movie?
   B: It was okay, I guess. How about you?
   A: a. I thought it was pretty good.
      b. I'm sure.
      c. I saw it last night.

2. A: Are you going to the company party?
   B: I haven't decided yet. What about you?
   A: a. I didn't know that.
      b. Why aren't you going?
      c. I think I will.

3. A: Do you like living in this city?
   B: Sort of. How about you?
   A: a. I'm living in the city.
      b. I'm not sure. It's pretty noisy.
      c. Yes, I have been.

4. A: What are you going to have?
   B: Well, I'm not really hungry. I think I might order just a salad. How about you?
   A: a. I'll have one too.
      b. I'm eating at a restaurant.
      c. No, I'm not.

□ **Exercise 54.** 口說：兩人一組 (表 5-14)
成兩人一組。下列提供的問句常用來當作輕鬆對話或「閒聊」的開頭。學生 A 負責問問題，學生 B 負責回答。兩人說話時，不可看書，必須看著彼此。

例：What kind of books do you like to read?
學生 A：What kind of books do you like to read?
學生 B：I like biographies. How about you?
學生 A：Thrillers are my favorite.

1. How long have you been living in (*this city or country*)?
2. What are you going to do after class today?
3. What kind of movies do you like to watch?

角色互換。
4. Do you come from a large family?
5. What kind of sports do you enjoy?
6. Do you speak a lot of English outside of class?

□ **Exercise 55.** 暖身活動 (表 5-15)
「預期的」回答為何？圈選 *yes* 或 *no*。

1. You're studying English, aren't you?   yes   no

2. You're not a native speaker of English, are you?   yes   no

5-15 附加問句 Tag Questions

(a) Jill is sick, **isn't she?** (b) You didn't know, **did you?** (c) There's enough time, **isn't there?** (d) I'm not late, **am I?** (e) I'm late, **aren't I?**	附加問句是加在句尾且含有助動詞的問句。 注意：在否定的附加問句中，**I am** 會變成 **aren't I**，如：例 (e)。（也可用 *Am I not*，但該用法非常正式且罕見。）

肯定 (+)	否定 (−)	肯定的預期回答	
(d) *You know* Bill,	**don't** you?	**Yes**.	當主要動詞為肯定時，附加問句為否定，且預期回答的形式與主要動詞一致。
(e) *Marie is* from Paris,	**isn't** she?	**Yes**.	

否定 (−)	肯定 (+)	否定的預期回答	
(f) *You don't know* Tom,	**do** you?	**No**.	當主要動詞為否定時，附加問句則為肯定，且預期回答的形式與主要動詞一致。
(g) *Marie isn't* from Athens,	**is** she?	**No**.	

說話者的問題	說話者的想法
	附加問句有兩種語調：上揚與下降。語調決定附加問句傳達的意思。
(h) It will be nice tomorrow, **won't it?**	說話者使用上揚的語調來確認資訊的正確性 (make sure information is correct)。例 (h) 中：說話者有個想法，而他想確認這個想法是否正確。
(i) It will be nice tomorrow, **won't it?**	說話者使用下降的語調是為了要尋求認同 (seeking agreement)。在例 (i) 中，說話者認為明天天氣會不錯，且幾乎肯定聽話者會同意他的看法。
YES/NO 問句 (j) — Will it be nice tomorrow? — **Yes, it will.** 或 **No, it won't.**	在例 (j) 中，說話者對問題的答案沒有想法 (has no idea)，他只是希望獲得資訊。 比較例 (h)、例 (i) 與例 (j)。

❑ **Exercise 56. 聽力與文法** (表 5-15)

聆聽 CD 播放的各組句子，並回答問題。

CD 1
Track 60

1. a. You're Mrs. Rose, aren't you?
   b. Are you Mrs. Rose?

   QUESTION: In which sentence is the speaker checking to see if her information is correct?

2. a. Do you take cream with your coffee?
   b. You take cream with your coffee, don't you?

   QUESTION: In which sentence does the speaker have no idea?

3. a. You don't want to leave, do you?
   b. Do you want to leave?

   QUESTION: In which sentence is the speaker looking for agreement?

CD 1
Track 61

用正確的動詞完成附加問句，然後聆聽 CD 播放的問句，並核對答案。

1. 現在簡單式

   a. You *like* strong coffee, ___don't___ you?

   b. David *goes* to Ames High School, _____ he?

   c. Leila and Sara *live* on Tree Road, _____ they?

   d. Jane *has* the keys to the storeroom, _____ she?

   e. Jane*'s* in her office, _____ she?

   f. You*'re* a member of this class, _____ you?

   g. Oleg *doesn't* have a car, _____ he?

   h. Lisa *isn't* from around here, _____ she?

   i. I*'m* in trouble, _____ I?

2. 過去簡單式

   a. Paul *went* to Indonesia, _____ he?

   b. You *didn't talk* to the boss, _____ you?

   c. Ted's parents *weren't* at home, _____ they?

   d. That *was* Pat's idea, _____ it?

3. 現在進行式、*Be Going To*，以及過去進行式

   a. You*'re studying* hard, _____ you?

   b. Greg *isn't working* at the bank, _____ he?

   c. It *isn't going to rain* today, _____ it?

   d. Michelle and Yoko *were helping*, _____ they?

   e. He *wasn't listening*, _____ he?

4. 現在完成式

   a. It *has been* warmer than usual, _____ it?

   b. You*'ve had* a lot of homework, _____ you?

   c. We *haven't spent* much time together, _____ we?

   d. Fatima *has started* her new job, _____ she?

   e. Bruno *hasn't finished* his sales report yet, _____ he?

   f. Steve's *had to leave* early, _____ he?

Exercise 58. 口說：兩人一組 (表 5-15)

成兩人一組。依據實際情況造句，並詢問你的搭檔。切記，如果你的搭檔在附加問句前說了肯定句，預期的回答應該是 yes；相反地，如果你的搭檔在附加問句前說了否定句，預期的回答則為 no。

1. The weather is _____ today, isn't it?

2. This book costs _____, doesn't it?

3. I'm _____, aren't I?

4. The classroom isn't _____, is it?

5. Our grammar homework wasn't _____,was it?

6. Tomorrow will be _____, won't it?

❏ **Exercise 59. 聽力** (表 5-15)

聆聽 CD 播出的附加問句，並圈選「預期的」回答。

CD 1
Track 62

Checking in at a hotel

例：你會聽到： Our room's ready, isn't it?

你要圈出： (yes)　　no

1. yes	no		6. yes	no
2. yes	no		7. yes	no
3. yes	no		8. yes	no
4. yes	no		9. yes	no
5. yes	no		10. yes	no

❏ **Exercise 60. 檢視學習成果** (第 5 章)

校訂下列句子，訂正錯誤的問句結構。

1. Who you saw? → *Who did you see?*

2. Where I buy subway tickets?

3. Whose is that backpack?

4. What kind of tea you like best?

5. It's freezing out and you're not wearing gloves, aren't you?

6. Who you studied with at school?

7. She is going to work this weekend, doesn't she?

8. How long take to get to the airport from here?

9. How much height your father have?

10. It's midnight. Why you so late? Why you forget to call?

CD 1
Track 63

第一部分　聆聽 CD 播放的問題，並圈選正確的答案。

例：你會聽到：　How often do you brush your teeth?
　　你要圈出：　ⓐ. Three times a day.
　　　　　　　　b. Yes, I do.
　　　　　　　　c. In the evening.

1.　a. I love it.
　　b. Jazz and rock.
　　c. The radio.

2.　a. I was really tired.
　　b. At 7:30.
　　c. A package.

3.　a. A little sick.
　　b. No, I'm not.
　　c. Howard's fine.

4.　a. Two miles.
　　b. Three blocks.
　　c. Ten minutes.

5.　a. Amy is.
　　b. Amy's.
　　c. That is Amy.

6.　a. Next week.
　　b. A few days ago.
　　c. On Fifth Street.

第二部分　聆聽 CD 播放的對話，圈選最適合用來完成各組對話的句子。

7.　a. My wallet.
　　b. At the box office.
　　c. I think so.

8.　a. It usually comes by noon.
　　b. By truck.
　　c. One time a day.

9.　a. Yes, I am.
　　b. My company is moving to another city.
　　c. I loved my job.

10.　a. It's great.
　　b. I'm a construction supervisor.
　　c. We're doing really well.

❏ **Exercise 62. 聽力與口說：兩人一組**（第 5 章）

CD 1
Track 64

聆聽 CD 播放的對話。然後兩人一組，輪流扮演收銀員和顧客的角色。運用菜單裡的項目完成下列句子，並練習對話。

burger	chicken strips	soft drinks: *cola, lemon soda, iced tea*
cheeseburger	fish burger	milkshakes: *vanilla, strawberry, chocolate*
double cheeseburger	veggie burger	*(small, medium, large)*
fries	salad	

Ordering at a fast-food restaurant

CASHIER:　So, what'll it be?

CUSTOMER:　I'll have a _____ .

CASHIER:　Would you like fries or a salad with your burger?

CUSTOMER:　I'll have (a) _____ .

CASHIER:　What size?

CUSTOMER:　_____ .

CASHIER:　Anything to drink?

CUSTOMER:　I'll have a _____ .

CASHIER:　Size?

CUSTOMER: _____.

CASHIER: Okay. So that's _____

_____.

CUSTOMER: About how long'll it take?

CASHIER: We're pretty crowded right now. Probably 10 minutes or so. That'll be $6.50.
Your number's on the receipt. I'll call the number when your order's ready.

CUSTOMER: Thanks.

❑ **Exercise 63. 閱讀與寫作**（第 1 → 5 章）

第一部分 閱讀以下童話故事，並回答故事後的問題。

The Frog Prince

Once upon a time, there was a king with three unmarried daughters. One day while the
king was thinking about his daughters' futures, he had an idea. He thought, "I'm going to drop
three jewels among the young men in the village center. The men who find* the jewels will
become my daughters' husbands." He announced his plan to all of the people of his kingdom.

The next day, the king took an emerald, a ruby, and a diamond into the village. He walked
among the young men and dropped the jewels. A handsome man picked up the emerald. Then
a wealthy prince found the ruby. But a frog hopped toward the diamond and took it. He said
to the king, "I am the Frog Prince. I claim your third daughter as my wife."

When the king told Trina, his third daughter, about the Frog Prince, she refused to marry
him. She hid from her friends and grew sadder every day. Meanwhile, her two sisters had
grand weddings.

---

*在此句中使用現在簡單式是因為故事裡一字不改地引述了國王說的每個字。注意此篇故事中引號（" . . ."）的使用。更多關於
引號的用法，請見第 387 頁，表 14-8。

Eventually, Trina ran away and went to live in the woods, but she was very lonely and unhappy. One day Trina went swimming in a lake. Trina became tired in the cold water and decided to give up. She didn't want to live anymore. As she was drowning, the frog suddenly appeared and pushed Trina to the shore.

"Why did you save my life, Frog?"

"Because you are very young, and you have a lot to live for."

"No, I don't," said the princess. "I am the most miserable person in the world."

"Let's talk about it," said the frog. Trina and the Frog Prince sat together for hours and hours. Frog listened and understood. He told her about his own unhappiness and loneliness. They shared their deepest feelings with each other.

One day while they were sitting near the lake, Trina felt great affection for the frog. She bent down and kissed him on his forehead. Suddenly the frog turned into a man! He took Trina in his arms and said, "You saved me with your kiss. An evil wizard changed me from a prince into a frog. I needed to find the love of a woman with a truly good heart to set me free.★ You looked inside me and found the real me."

Trina and the prince returned to the castle and got married. Her two sisters, she discovered, were very unhappy because their husbands treated them poorly. But Trina and her Frog Prince lived happily ever after.

問題：

1. What did the king want for his daughters?
2. Why did a frog claim Trina for his wife?
3. What did Trina do to escape the marriage?
4. Where did she meet the frog again?
5. Why did she kiss the frog?
6. What did an evil wizard do to the frog?
7. What kind of lives did her sisters have?
8. What kind of life did Trina and the Frog Prince have?

第二部分 用下列提供的其中一個題目，寫一篇以 *Once upon a time* 為開頭的故事。

題目：

1. 再讀一遍這篇故事，然後用自己的話重述。寫一到兩段的文字，寫的時候不要看原故事。

2. 寫一篇自己所熟悉的童話故事，也許是一篇在自己國家文化中廣為人知的故事。

3. 和同學一起編寫故事。每位同學一次寫一到兩句：由一位同學開始寫，然後再傳給另一位同學；這位同學寫一到兩句後，再把這張紙傳下去，直到班上所有同學都為這篇故事添寫了一個部分或直到這篇故事的結局出現。將這篇故事印製給全班每個人，然後全班一起作校訂。全班同學亦可考慮為這篇作品作一些加強美感的設計，然後把它製作成小書出版。

---

*★set me free 意指「釋放我」或是「讓我重獲自由」。

第六章
名詞與代名詞

❑ **Exercise 1. 檢視已知**（第 6 章）

此練習將預習此章中會使用到的文法詞彙。辨別下列句子中斜體字的詞性：名詞、形容詞、介系詞或代名詞。

1. Miki is a *student* at my school.   _____noun_____

2. *She* is from Kyoto, Japan.   _____pronoun_____

3. Kyoto is south *of* Tokyo.   _____preposition_____

4. It is a *beautiful* city.   _____adjective_____

5. This summer *I* am going there with Miki.   _____

6. I am looking forward to this *trip*.   _____

7. My parents are *happy* for me.   _____

8. I will stay *with* Miki's family.   _____

9. They have a *small* hotel.   _____

10. *It* is near a popular park.   _____

11. The park has lovely *gardens*.   _____

12. Miki has shown me postcards *of* them.   _____

❑ **Exercise 2. 暖身活動**（表 6-1）

在單數名詞前的空格中寫下 **one**，在複數名詞前的空格中寫下 **two**。

1. _____ trips   4. _____ way

2. _____ vacation   5. _____ cities

3. _____ classes   6. _____ knives

6-1 名詞的複數形 Plural Forms of Nouns

單數	複數	
(a) one bird one street one rose	two **birds** two **streets** two **roses**	在大多數名詞的字尾加 **-s**，即可改為複數形。
(b) one dish one match one class one box	two **dishes** two **matches** two **classes** two **boxes**	名詞字尾是 **-sh**、**-ch**、**-ss**、**-x** 時，複數形在字尾加 **-es**。
(c) one baby one city	two **babies** two **cities**	若名詞字尾是子音字母 ＋ **-y**，則將 **-y** 改成 **-i**，再加上 **-es**，如：例 (c)。
(d) one toy one key	two **toys** two **keys**	若名詞字尾是母音字母 ＋ **-y**，則只需在字尾加 **-s**，如：例 (d)。
(e) one knife one shelf	two **knives** two **shelves**	若名詞字尾是 **-fe** 或 **-f** 時，將字尾改成 **-ves**，即可改為複數形。 （例外：beliefs、chiefs、roofs、cuffs、cliffs。） *wolves*
(f) one tomato one zoo one zero	two **tomatoes** two **zoos** two **zeroes/zeros**	名詞字尾是 **-o** 時，加上 **-es** 或 **-s**，即成複數形。 **-oes:** tomatoes, potatoes, heroes, echoes **-os:** zoos, radios, studios, pianos, solos, sopranos, photos, autos, videos **-oes** 或 **-os:** zeroes/zeros、volcanoes/volcanos、tornadoes/tornados、mosquitoes/mosquitos
(g) one child one foot one goose one man one mouse one tooth one woman ————	two **children** two **feet** two **geese** two **men** two **mice** two **teeth** two **women** two **people**	有些名詞的複數形為不規則變化。 注意：people 的單數形泛指 person、woman、man、child。 例如：one man and one child = two people。（也可以是 two persons。）
(h) one deer one fish one sheep	two **deer** two **fish** two **sheep**	有些名詞的單複數同形。
(i) one bacterium one crisis	two **bacteria** two **crises**	英文中來自其他語言的外來字，通常會有特殊的複數形。

❑ **Exercise 3. 文法** (表 6-1)

寫出下列提供字詞的正確單複數形。

1. one chair   two ＿＿＿＿＿＿＿＿＿＿＿＿

2. a ＿＿＿＿＿＿＿＿   a lot of windows

3. one wish   several ＿＿＿＿＿＿＿＿＿＿＿

4. a _____   two dishes

5. a tax   a lot of _____taxes_____

6. one boy   two _____

7. a hobby (n.) 嗜好 habit 習慣   several ____hobbies_____

8. one leaf   two _____leaves_____

9. a _____   two halves

10. a belief   many _____

11. one wolf   two _____

12. a radio   several _____

13. one _____   a lot of sheep

14. one _____   two feet

❏   **Exercise 4. 文法** (表 6-1)
    在正確的類別標題下，寫出各名詞的複數形。括弧內的數字為各類別名詞的總數。注意：*fish*
    和 *thief* 可以有兩種歸類。

✓butterfly	child	hero	mouse	thief
baby	city	library	✓museum	tomato
boy	fish	✓man	potato	woman
✓bean	girl	mosquito	sandwich	zoo

人 (8)	食物 (5)	人們補捉的事物 (5)	人們參觀的地方 (4)
men	beans	butterflies	museums

Exercise 5. 檢視學習成果 (表 6-1)

校訂以下報紙廣告，視情況將單數名詞更正為複數；共有八個錯誤。

ON SALE (while supply last)

shirt   jean   pant   dress

Outfit and shoe for babys 50% off

Exercise 6. 暖身活動：聽力 (表 6-2)

聆聽 CD 播放的名詞，聽到複數字尾，圈 *yes*；如果不是，圈 *no*。

CD 2
Track 1

例：你會聽到：books
你要圈出：(yes)   no
你會聽到：class
你要圈出：yes   (no)

1. yes	no	3. yes	no	5. yes	no
2. yes	no	4. yes	no	6. yes	no

6-2 字尾 *-s/-es* 的發音 Pronunciation of Final *-s/-es*

字尾 *-s/-es* 有三種不同的發音：/s/、/z/ 和 /əz/。

(a)	seats maps lakes	= seat/s/ = map/s/ = lake/s/	在無聲音之後的字尾 *-s* 發音為 /s/。在例 (a) 中，/s/ 的音如同 "bus" 字尾 "s" 的發音。 無聲音★的例子：/t/、/p/、/k/。
(b)	seeds stars holes laws	= seed/z/ = star/z/ = hole/z/ = law/z/	在有聲音之後的字尾 *-s* 發音為 /z/。在例 (b) 中，/z/ 的音如同 "buzz" 字尾 "z" 的發音。 有聲音★的例子：/d/、/r/、/l/、/m/、/b/ 及全部的母音。
(c)	dishes matches classes sizes pages judges	= dish/əz/ = match/əz/ = class/əz/ = size/əz/ = page/əz/ = judge/əz/	在 *-sh*、*-ch*、*-s*、*-z*、*-ge/-dge* 等字母之後的字尾 *-s/-es* 發音為 /əz/。在例 (c) 中，/əz/ 會讓單字增加一個音節。

*更多無聲音和有聲音的相關資訊，請見第 39 頁，表 2-5。

Exercise 7. 聽力（表 6-2）

聆聽 CD 播放的字詞，並圈選聽到的尾音：/s/、/z/ 或 /əz/。

CD 2
Track 2

1. pants	/s/	/z/	/əz/		4. pens	/s/	/z/	/əz/
2. cars	/s/	/z/	/əz/		5. wish**es**	/s/	/z/	/əz/
3. box**es**	/s/	/z/	/əz/		6. lakes	/s/	/z/	/əz/

❑ **Exercise 8. 聽力**（表 6-2）

聆聽 CD 播放的各組字詞，並判斷兩字的尾音是否相同。

CD 2
Track 3

例：你會聽到：　maps　　streets
　　你要圈出：　(same)　　different

　　你會聽到：　knives　　forks
　　你要圈出：　same　　(different)

1. same	different		5. same	different
2. same	different		6. same	different
3. same	different		7. same	different
4. same	different		8. same	different

❑ **Exercise 9. 聽力與發音**（表 6-2）

聆聽 CD 播放的字詞，並寫出聽到的尾音：/s/、/z/ 或 /əz/；練習這些字詞的發音。

CD 2
Track 4

1. names = name/z/	4. boats = boat/　/	7. lips = lip/　/
2. clocks = clock/s/	5. eyelashes = eyelash/　/	8. bridges = bridge/　/
3. eyes = eye/　/	6. ways = way/　/	9. cars = car/　/

❑ **Exercise 10. 聽力**（表 6-2）

聆聽 CD 播放的句子，並圈選聽到的字詞。

CD 2
Track 5

| 1. size | sizes | 3. fax | faxes | 5. glass | glasses |
| 2. fax | faxes | 4. price | prices | 6. prize | prizes |

❑ **Exercise 11. 暖身活動**（表 6-3）

第一部分　分小組進行。針對下列指示，列出清單。

1. 列出人們在旅行時，會隨身攜帶的必需品。
2. 列出你在空閒時會從事的活動。
3. 列出你人生中的重要人物。

第二部分　閱讀剛剛列出的清單，並運用下列資訊造句。最後，與全班分享一些你造的句子。

1. People need to take _____ with them when they travel.
2. I _____ when I have free time.
3. _____ have been important in my life.

1. In which sentence did you write verbs?
2. In which two sentences did you write nouns?
3. In which sentence did you write subjects?
4. In which sentence did you write objects?

6-3 主詞、動詞和受詞 Subjects, Verbs, and Objects

(a) The **sun** (名詞) **shines**. (動詞)	英文句子的基本組成是主詞 (s) 加動詞 (v)。 主詞必須是**名詞**。在例 (a) 中，**sun** 是名詞；是動詞 **shines** 的主詞。	
(b) **Plants** (名詞) **grow**. (動詞)		
(c) **Plants** (名詞) **need** (動詞) **water**. (名詞)	有時動詞後面會接受詞 (o)。 動詞的受詞是**名詞**。在例 (c) 中，**water** 作為動詞 **need** 的受詞。	
(d) **Bob** (名詞) **is reading** (動詞) **a book**. (名詞)		

❑ **Exercise 12. 文法** (表 6-3)

用正確的主詞、動詞和受詞完成下列圖表。

1. The carpenter built a table.

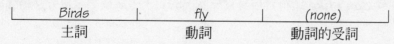

The carpenter	built	a table
主詞	動詞	動詞的受詞

2. Birds fly.

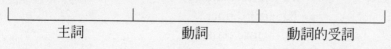

Birds	fly	(none)
主詞	動詞	動詞的受詞

3. Cows eat grass.

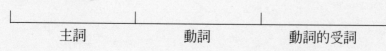

主詞	動詞	動詞的受詞

4. The actor sang.

主詞	動詞	動詞的受詞

5. The actor sang a song.

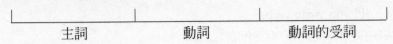

|　　　主詞　　　|　　　動詞　　　|　　動詞的受詞　　|

6. Accidents happen frequently.

|　　　主詞　　　|　　　動詞　　　|　　動詞的受詞　　|

7. The accident injured a woman.

|　　　主詞　　　|　　　動詞　　　|　　動詞的受詞　　|

❑ **Exercise 13. 文法** (表 6-2 和 6-3)
如果下列句子中的斜體字為名詞，圈 N；如果是動詞，圈 V。

1. People *smile* when they're happy.	N	Ⓥ
2. Maryam has a nice *smile* when she's happy.	Ⓝ	V
3. Please don't sign your *name* in pencil.	N	V
4. People often *name* their children after relatives.	N	V
5. Airplanes *land* on runways at the airport.	N	V
6. The *land* across the street from our house is vacant.	N	V
7. People usually *store* milk in the refrigerator.	N	V
8. We went to the *store* to buy some milk.	N	V
9. I took the express *train* from New York to Washington, D.C., last week.	N	V
10. Lindsey *trains* horses as a hobby.	N	V

❑ **Exercise 14. 暖身活動：兩人一組** (表 6-4)
成兩人一組；用 **like** 或 **don't like** 造符合自身實際狀況的句子，然後與全班分享搭檔的部分答案。

I like/don't like to do my homework . . .

1. at the library.
2. at the kitchen table.
3. in my bedroom.
4. on my bed.
5. with a friend.
6. in the evening.
7. on weekends.
8. after dinner.
9. before class.
10. during class.

6-4 介系詞的受詞 Objects of Prepositions

主詞 動詞 受詞 介系詞 介系詞的受詞 (a) Ann put her books **on** the **desk**. （名詞） 主詞 動詞 介系詞 介系詞的受詞 (b) A leaf fell **to** the **ground**. （名詞）	英文的句子中常有介系詞片語，如：例 (a)，**on the desk** 就是一個介系詞片語。 介系詞片語由「介系詞」(PREP) 和「介系詞的受詞」(O of PREP) 組成；介系詞的受詞必須是「名詞」。

介系詞參考表

about	before	despite	of	to
above	behind	down	off	toward(s)
across	below	during	on	under
after	beneath 在旁邊	for	out	until
against	beside = by = next to	from	over	up
along	besides 此外	in	since	upon
among	between	into	through	with
around	beyond	like	throughout	within
at	by	near	till	without

❑ **Exercise 15. 文法**（表 6-4）

勾選 (✓) 介系詞片語，並劃底線標示出在下列詞組中作爲介系詞受詞的名詞。

1. __✓__ across the <u>street</u>   5. _____ next to the phone

2. _____ in a minute   6. _____ doing work

3. _____ daily   7. _____ in a few hours

4. _____ down the hill   8. _____ from my parents

❑ **Exercise 16. 文法**（表 6-3 和 6-4）

勾選 (✓) 有介系詞受詞的句子，並辨別介系詞（以 P 標示）和介系詞受詞（以 Obj. of P 標示）。

1. a. _____ Emily waited quietly.

                           P   Obj. of P

   b. __✓__ Emily waited quietly for her mother.

                            P Obj. of P

   c. __✓__ Emily's mother was talking to a friend.

2. a. _____ Kimiko saw a picture on the wall.

   b. _____ Kimiko recognized the people.

   c. _____ Kimiko looked at the picture closely.

3. a. _____ Annika lost her ring yesterday.

   b. _____ Annika lost her ring in the sand.

   c. _____ Annika lost her ring in the sand at the beach.

4. a. _____ A talkative woman sat with her husband.

   b. _____ We were at a meeting.

   c. _____ She talked to her husband the entire time.

❏ **Exercise 17. 口說** (表 6-4)
用下列提供的片語造完整句，複習地方介系詞。邊唸句子，邊以動作演示句中介系詞的意義。
成兩人一組、小組或全班一起練習。

例：across the room
→ *I'm walking across the room.* 或 *I'm looking across the room.*

1. above the door
2. against the wall
3. toward(s) the door
4. between two pages of my book
5. in the room
6. into the room
7. on my desk
8. at my desk
9. below the window
10. beside my book
11. near the door
12. far from the door
13. off my desk
14. out the window
15. behind me
16. through the door

❏ **Exercise 18. 遊戲：知識問答比賽** (表 6-4)
分小組比賽，不看地圖回答下列問題。回答完所有問題後，再對照地圖檢查答案。* 答對最多題
的組別獲勝。

1. Name a country directly under Russia.
2. Name the country directly above Germany.
3. What river flows through London?
4. What is a country near Haiti?
5. Name a country next to Vietnam.
6. Name a city far from Sydney, Australia.
7. What is the country between Austria and Switzerland?
8. Name the city within Rome, Italy.
9. Name two countries that have a river between them.
10. Name a country that is across from Saudi Arabia.

---

*請見解答本中的 *Trivia Answers*。

Exercise 19. 閱讀 (表 6-4)

閱讀以下文章，然後回答下列問題。

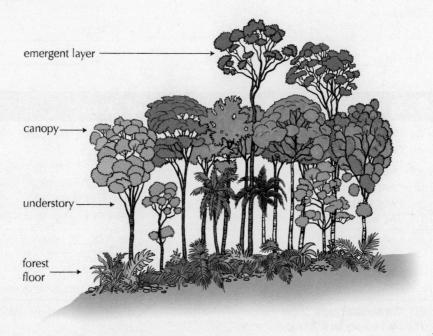

emergent layer

canopy

understory

forest
floor

The Habitats of a Rainforest

Rainforests have different areas where animals live. These areas are called *habitats*. Scientists have given names to the four main habitats or layers of a rainforest.

Some animals live in the tops of giant trees. The tops of these trees are much higher than the other trees, so this layer is called the *emergent* layer*. Many birds and insects live there.

Under the emergent layer is the *canopy*. The canopy is the upper part of the trees. It is thick with leaves and vines, and it forms an umbrella over the rainforest. Most of the animals in the rainforest live in the canopy.

The next layer is the *understory*. The understory is above the ground and under the leaves. In the understory, it is very dark and cool. It gets only 2–5% of the sunlight that the canopy gets. The understory has the most insects of the four layers, and a lot of snakes and frogs also live there.

Finally, there is the *forest floor*. On the surface of this floor are fallen leaves, branches, and other debris.** In general, the largest animals in the rainforest live in this layer. Common animals in this habitat are tigers and gorillas.

1. Name two types of animals that live in the tops of giant trees.
2. Where is the understory?
3. Where do you think most mosquitoes live?
4. What are some differences between the emergent layer and the forest floor?

---

*emergent 意指「顯露出的植物」，在植物學中，這代表一株植物比周圍所有的植物高，好比森林中一棵高大的樹木。

**debris 意指「動植物殘骸」，好比泥土。

□ **Exercise 20. 暖身活動** (表 6-5)

用與自身情況相關的資訊，完成下列句子。

I was born . . .

1. in _____ (*month*).   3. on _____ (*weekday*).

2. on _____ (*date*).   4. at _____ (*time*).

6-5 表示時間的介系詞 Prepositions of Time

in	(a) Please be on time ***in*** the future. (b) I usually watch TV ***in*** the evening. (c) I was born ***in*** October. (d) I was born ***in*** 1995. (e) I was born ***in*** the 20th century. (f) The weather is hot ***in*** (the) summer.	*in* 可與過去 (*the past*)、現在 (*the present*)、未來 (*the future*)★ 連用。 *in* 可與早上 (*the morning*)、下午 (*the afternoon*) 和傍晚 (*the evening*) 等詞語連用。 *in* 可與<u>月份</u> (*month*)、<u>年份</u> (*year*)、<u>世紀</u> (*century*)、<u>季節</u> (*season*) 連用。
on	(g) I was born ***on*** October 31st, 1995. (h) I went to a movie ***on*** Thursday. (i) I have class ***on*** Thursday morning(s).	*on* 可與<u>日期</u> (*date*) 連用。 *on* 可與平日的某一天 (*weekday*) 連用。 *on* 可與平日的某一<u>早晨</u>、下午或傍晚 (*weekday morning/afternoon/evening*) 連用。
at	(j) We sleep at night. I was asleep ***at*** midnight. (k) I fell asleep ***at*** 9:30 (*nine-thirty*). (l) He's busy ***at*** the moment. Can I take a message?	*at* 可與中午 (*noon*)、夜晚 (*night*)、午夜 (*midnight*) 連用。 *at* 可與幾點幾分 ("clock time") 連用。 *at* 可與此刻 (*the moment*)、當前時間 (*the present time*)、現在 (*present*) 連用。

★在英式英文中也可以用 *in future*（如：*Please be on time in future.*）。

□ **Exercise 21. 文法** (表 6-5)

用 *in*、*at* 或 *on* 完成含有表達時間字詞的句子。

Studious Stan has college classes . . .

1. __in__ the morning.   6. __on__ Saturdays. (every Saturdays)

2. __in__ the afternoon.   7. __on__ Saturday mornings.

3. __in__ the evening.   8. __at__ noon.

4. __at__ night.   9. __at__ midnight.

5. __on__ weekdays.

Unlucky Lisa has a birthday every four years. She was born . . .

10. __on__ February 29th.   13. __in__ 2000.

11. __on__ February 29th, 2000.   14. __in__ February 2000.

12. __in__ February.   15. __in__ the winter.

Cool Carlos is a fashion designer. He's thinking about clothing designs . . .

16. __at__ the moment.

17. __at__ the present time.

18. __at__ the past.

□ **Exercise 22. 口說：訪談** (表 6-5)

用適當的介系詞完成下列問句，並分別詢問七位同學一個問題。

1. What do you like to do _____ the evening?

2. What do you usually do _____ night before bed?

3. What do you like to do _____ Saturday mornings?

4. What did you do _____ January 1st of this year?

5. What were you doing _____ January 1st, 2000 (the beginning of the new millennium)?

6. How do you spend your free time _____ January?

7. What will you do with your English skills _____ the future?

□ **Exercise 23. 暖身活動** (表 6-6)

勾選 (✓) 所有合文法的句子。

1. a. _____ I left Athens in 2005.

   b. _____ I left in 2005 Athens.

   c. _____ In 2005, I left Athens.

2. a. _____ Lee sold his car yesterday.

   b. _____ Yesterday Lee sold his car.

   c. _____ Lee sold yesterday his car.

6-6 詞序：地點和時間 Word Order: Place and Time

(a)	S V PLACE TIME Ann moved *to Paris* *in 2008.* We went *to a movie* *yesterday.*	在典型的英文句子中，「地點」(place) 出現在「時間」(time) 之前，如：例 (a)。 錯誤：*Ann moved in 2008 to Paris.*	
(b)	S V O P T We bought a house in Miami in 2005.	S-V-O-P-T = 主詞 (Subject)-動詞 (Verb)-受詞 (Object)-地點 (Place)-時間 (Time) （基本英語句構）	
(c) (d)	TIME S V PLACE *In 2008,* Ann moved to Paris. *Yesterday* we went to a movie.	表達時間的字詞亦可置於句首，如：例 (c) 和例 (d)。 置於句首的時間片語之後常加逗號，如：例 (c)。	

□ **Exercise 24. 文法** (表 6-6)

將各題提供的字詞重組為詞序正確的句子。

1. to Paris \ next month

   Monique's company is going to transfer her ___to Paris next month___.

2. last week \ through Turkey

   William began a bike trip _____.

3. at his uncle's bakery \ Alexi \ on Saturday mornings \ works

 <u>Alexi works at his uncle's bakery on Saturday mornings</u>   .

4. arrived \ in the early morning \ at the airport \ my plane

_____ .

❑ **Exercise 25. 暖身活動** (表 6-7)

如有必要，在空格中填入字尾 **-s**；如果不需要，就寫 **Ø**。

1. Lions roar _____ .

2. A lion roar _____ .

3. Lions and tigers roar _____ .

4. A tiger in the jungle roar _____ .

5. Tigers in the jungle roar _____ .

6. Tigers in jungles roar _____ .

6-7 主詞與動詞的一致性 Subject-Verb Agreement

單數　　　　單數 (a) The *sun*　　 shine**s**. 複數　　複數 (b) *Bird***s**　 sing.	單數主詞搭配單數動詞，如：例 (a)。 複數主詞搭配複數動詞，如：例 (b)。 注意：動詞 + **-s** = 單數（如：*shines*） 　　　名詞 + **-s** = 複數（如：*birds*）
單數　　　　單數 (c) *My brother*　　 **lives**　 in Jakarta. 複數　　　　　　複數 (d) *My brother* **and** *sister*　　 **live**　 in Jakarta.	由 **and** 連接的兩個主詞要搭配複數動詞，如：例 (d)。
(e) The **glasses** over there under the window by the sink **are** clean. (f) The **information** in those magazines about Vietnamese culture and customs **is** very interesting.	有時主詞與動詞之間會置入片語，這些片語並不會影響到主詞與動詞的一致。
v　　　 s (g) *There* **is** a **book** on the desk. 　　　　　 v　　　 s (h) *There* **are** some **books** on the desk.	「**there** + **be** 動詞 + 主詞」表示某物存在於某處，這時動詞的單複數要與 **be** 動詞之後的名詞一致。
(i) **Every student is** sitting down. (j) **Everybody/Everyone hopes** for peace.	**every** 是單數形的字，只與單數名詞搭配。 錯誤：*Every students* . . . 與 **every** 連用的主詞要搭配單數動詞，如：例 (i) 和例 (j)。
(k) **People** in my country **are** friendly.	**people** 是複數名詞，故搭配複數動詞。

分小組練習。用下表中動詞的正確形式，完成下列句子。另外，請用母語討論用來描述不同動物聲音的字詞。

bark	chirp	hiss	meow	roar

What sounds do these animals make?

1. A dog _____.

2. Dogs _____.

3. Lions in the wild _____.

4. Lions, tigers, and leopards _____.

5. Every snake _____.

6. A bird _____.

7. Cats _____.

8. Sea lions on a beach _____.

9. A lizard _____.

10. Baby chickens _____.

☐ **Exercise 27.** 文法 (表 6-7)

辨別主詞 (S) 和動詞 (V)，並劃底線作標示。另外，更正主詞與動詞不一致的錯誤。

1. The <u>students</u> in this class <u>speaks</u> English very well.

2. My aunt and uncle speak Spanish. → *OK (no error).*

3. Every students in my class speak English well.

4. There are five student from Korea in Mr. Ahmad's class.

5. There's a vacant apartment in my building.

6. Does people in your neighborhood know each other?

7. The neighbors in the apartment next to mine is very friendly and helpful.

☐ **Exercise 28.** 聽力 (表 6-2 和 6-7)

CD 2
Track 6

聆聽 CD 播放的文章，然後再聽一遍，並視情況加上字尾 **-s**。在開始前，你可以先確定自己是否認識這些字：*sweat、fur、paw、flap、mud*。

How Some Animals Stay Cool

How do animal ____ stay cool in hot weather? Many animal ____ don't sweat like
　　　　　　　1　　　　　　　　　　　　　　　　　　　2
human ____, so they have other way ____ to cool themselves.
　　　　3　　　　　　　　　　4

Dog ____, for example, have a lot of fur ____ and can become very hot. They stay ____
　　　5　　　　　　　　　　　　　　　　　6　　　　　　　　　　　　　　7
cool mainly by panting. By the way, if you don't know what *panting* means, this is the sound of

panting.

Cat ____ lick ____ their paw ____ and chest ____. When their fur ____ is wet, they
   8   9   10   11   12
become cooler.

Elephant ____ have very large ear ____. When they are hot, they can flap their huge
         13   14
ear ____. The flapping ear ____ act ____ like a fan and it cool ____ them. Elephant ____ also
 15   16   17   18   19
like to roll in the mud ____ to stay cool.
                   20

❑ **Exercise 29. 暖身活動** (表 6-8)
回想一下你的第一位老師，並從下表中挑選字詞來形容那位老師。

young	friendly	serious
middle-aged	unfriendly	patient
elderly	fun	impatient

6-8 修飾名詞的形容詞

(a) Bob is reading a 形容詞 名詞 ***good*** book.	修飾名詞的字稱作「形容詞」。 在例 (a) 中，***good*** 是形容詞，在此修飾 book。
(b) The ***tall*** woman wore a ***new*** dress. (c) The ***short*** woman wore an ***old*** dress. (d) The ***young*** woman wore a ***short*** dress.	我們說形容詞「修飾」名詞；「修飾」表示「稍微改變」，由於形容詞提供更多有關名詞的資訊，使得名詞的意義有所變化。
(e) Roses are ***beautiful*** flowers. 錯誤：*Roses are beautifuls flowers.*	形容詞沒有單複數之分，因此「沒有」複數形。
(f) He wore a ***white*** shirt. 錯誤：*He wore a shirt white.* (g) Roses are ***beautiful***. (h) His shirt was ***white***.	<u>形容詞的位置通常緊接在名詞之前</u>，如：例 (f)。 形容詞也可以接在當主要動詞用的 ***be*** 動詞之後，如：例 (g) 和例 (h)。

❑ **Exercise 30. 文法** (表 6-8)
勾選 (✓) 含有形容詞的詞組，並劃<u>底線</u>標示出形容詞。

1.   ✓ a <u>scary</u> story
2. ____ on Tuesday
3. ____ going to a famous place
4. ____ a small, dark, smelly room
5. ____ quickly and then slowly
6. ____ long or short hair

❑ **Exercise 31. 文法** (表 6-8)
從各題提供的三個形容詞中選出兩個形容詞，再加到句子裡。

例：hard, heavy, strong   A man lifted the box.
    → A strong man lifted the heavy box.

1. beautiful, safe, red   Roses are flowers.
2. empty, wet, hot   The waiter poured coffee into my cup.
3. fresh, clear, hungry   Mrs. Fields gave the kids a snack.
4. dirty, modern, delicious   After our dinner, Frank helped me with the dishes.

❑ **Exercise 32. 文法** (表 6-8)

分小組練習。

第一部分　在下表中加入自己發想的名詞 (noun)、形容詞 (adjective) 和介系詞 (preposition)，但不可以先去看第二部分。

1. an adjective _____old_____   6. an adjective _____

2. a person's name _____   7. an adjective _____

3. a plural noun _____   8. a preposition of place _____

4. a plural noun _____   9. an adjective _____

5. a singular noun _____   10. a plural noun _____

第二部分　用剛剛添加到第一部分的字詞，完成下列句子（有些句子聽起來或許會有些奇怪或好笑）；然後，對著另外一組或是全班同學大聲唸出完成的文章。

One day a/an _____old_____ girl was walking in the city. Her name was
                        1

_____. She was carrying a package for her grandmother. It contained some
           2

_____, some _____, and a/an _____, among other
           3   4   5

things.

    As she was walking down the street, a/an _____ thief stole her package.
                                                        6

The _____ girl pulled out her cell phone and called the police, who caught the
           7

thief _____ a nearby building and returned her package to her. She took it
           8

immediately to her _____ grandmother, who was glad to get the package
                              9

because she really needed some new _____.
                                              10

❑ **Exercise 33. 暖身活動** (表 6-9)

將 *chicken* 與下表中的字作結合。

✓fresh	hot	✓legs	recipe	soup

1. _____chicken legs_____   4. _____

2. _____fresh chicken_____   5. _____

3. _____

6-9 名詞作為形容詞的用法

(a) I have a **flower** garden. (b) The **shoe** store also sells socks.	名詞有時也可以作形容詞用，例如：**flower** 通常作名詞用，但在例 (a) 中，**flower** 作為修飾 **garden** 的形容詞。
(c) 錯誤： a flowers garden (d) 錯誤： the shoes store	當名詞作形容詞使用時，只用單數形，「無」複數形。

❏ **Exercise 34. 文法** (表 6-9)

辨別名詞 (N)，並劃<u>底線</u>作標示；將第一句裡其中一個名詞用作第二句的形容詞。

1. This <u>book</u> is about <u>grammar</u>. It's a __*grammar book*★_____.

2. My garden has vegetables. It's a __vegetable garden_____.

3. The soup has beans. It's _____.

4. I read a lot of articles in magazines. I read a lot of __magazines   articles_____.

5. The factory makes toys. It's a _____.

6. The villages are in the mountains. They are __mountain   villages_____.

7. The lesson was about art. It was an _____.

8. Flags fly from poles. Many government buildings have __flag   poles_____.

❏ **Exercise 35. 文法** (表 6-9)

視情況於斜體名詞後加上字尾 **-s**；如果同意該敘述，圈 *yes*；如果不同意，圈 *no*。

1. One day, *computer* programs will make it possible for computers to think.   yes   no

2. *Computer* make life more stressful.   yes   no

3. *Airplane* trips are enjoyable nowadays.   yes   no

4. *Airplane* don't have enough legroom.   yes   no

5. *Bicycle* are better than cars for getting around in a crowded city.   yes   no

6. It's fun to watch *bicycle* races like the *Tour de France* on TV.   yes   no

7. *Vegetable* soups are delicious.   yes   no

8. Fresh *vegetable* are my favorite food.   yes   no

---

*當某一個名詞用來修飾另一名詞時，說話的重音通常落在第一個名詞：**a grammar** book。

□ **Exercise 36. 聽力與口說** (表 6-1 → 6-9)

CD 2
Track 7

第一部分 聆聽 CD 中播放兩位朋友談論找公寓的對話。

第二部分 你可以選用下表中的字詞完成屬於自己的對話，並上台表演給全班看。注意：此對話和第一部分的對話會有些許不同。

air-conditioning	an elevator	near a bus stop	a studio
a balcony	an exercise room	near a freeway	a two-bedroom
close to my job	a laundry room	parking	a walk-up

A: I'm looking for a new place to live.

B: How come?

A: _____ . I need _____ .

B: I just helped a friend find one. I can help you. What else do you want?

A: I want _____ . Also, I _____

I don't want _____ .

B: Anything else?

A: _____ would be nice.

B: That's expensive.

A: I guess I'm dreaming.

□ **Exercise 37. 暖身活動** (表 6-10)

閱讀以下對話，注意斜體的人稱代名詞；判斷其為當主詞或受詞用的代名詞 (subject or object pronoun)。

A: Did *you* hear? Ivan quit his job.
   1

B: *I* know. I don't understand *him*. Between *you* and *me*, I think it's a bad decision.
   2   3   4   5

1. *you*　　　　　subject　　object

2. *I*　　　　　　subject　　object

3. *him*　　　　　subject　　object

4. *you*　　　　　subject　　object

5. *me*　　　　　subject　　object

		I	II	III
主		I; we	you×2	he; she; it; they
受		me; us	you×2	him; her; it; them
所有	pron.	mine ours	yours	his; hers; its; theirs
	adj.	my our	yours	his; hers; its; their
反身		myself ourselves	yourself yourselves	himself itself herself themselves

名詞與代名詞 **163**

人稱代名詞

作為主詞的代名詞：	*I*	*we*	*you*	*he*、*she*、*it*	*they*
作為受詞的代名詞：	*me*	*us*	*you*	*him*、*her*、*it*	*them*

主詞 (a) **Kate** is married. **She** has two children.	代名詞用來代替前面已提的名詞。 在例 (a) 中，**she** 是代名詞，指的是 **Kate**。 在例 (b) 中，**her** 是代名詞，指的也是 **Kate**。
受詞 (b) **Kate** is my friend. I know **her** well.	例 (a) 中的 **she** 為「作主詞用的代名詞」；例 (b) 中的 **her** 為「作受詞用的代名詞」。
(c) Mike has **a new blue bike**. He bought **it** yesterday.	代名詞可以單指一個名詞（如：**Kate**），也可以表示名詞片語。 在例 (c) 中，**it** 所指的是整個名詞片語 **a new blue bike**。
主詞 (d) *Eric and I* are good friends.	代名詞與 **and** 連用的原則： 若代名詞為主詞的一部分，選用作為主詞的代名詞，如：例 (d)。
受詞 (e) Ann met *Eric and me* at the museum.	若代名詞為受詞的一部分，選用作為受詞的代名詞，如：例 (e) 與例 (f)。
介系詞的受詞 (f) Ann walked between *Eric and me*.	錯誤：*Eric and me are good friends.* 錯誤：*Ann met Eric and I at the museum.*

單數代名詞：	*I*	*me*	*you*	*he*、*she*、*it*	*him*、*her*
複數代名詞：	*we*	*us*	*you*	*they*	*them*

(g) **Mike** is in class. **He** is taking a test.	singular（單數）= one；plural（複數）= more than one。
(h) The **students** are in class. **They** are taking a test.	單複數代名詞分別用來指單複數名詞，如：左欄的例子。
(i) **Kate and Tom** are married. **They** have two children.	

❏ **Exercise 38. 文法**（表 6-10）

寫出**粗體**代名詞所指的名詞。

1. The apples were rotten, so the children didn't eat **them** even though **they** were really hungry.

   a. them = _____apples_____

   b. they = _____children_____

2. Do bees sleep at night? Or do **they** work in the hive all night long? You never see **them** after dark. What do **they** do after night falls?

   a. they = _____bees_____

   b. them = _____bees_____

   c. they = _____bees_____

3. Table tennis began in England in the late 1800s. Today **it** is an international sport. My brother and I played **it** a lot when we were teenagers. I beat **him** sometimes, but **he** was a better player and usually won.

a. it = <u>table tennis</u>

b. it = <u>table tennis</u>

c. him = <u>my brother</u>

d. he = <u>my brother</u>

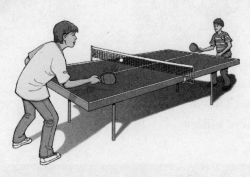

❑ **Exercise 39.** 文法 (表 6-10)

圈選正確的斜體字。

1. Toshi ate dinner with *I, me.*

2. Toshi ate dinner with Mariko and *I, me.*

3. *I, me* had dinner with Toshi last night.

4. Jay drove Eva and *I, me* to the store. He waited for *we, us* in the car.

5. A: I want to get tickets for the soccer game.

   B: You'd better get *it, them* right away. *It, They   is, are* selling fast.

❑ **Exercise 40.** 文法 (表 6-10)

用 *she*、*he*、*it*、*her*、*him*、*they* 或 *them* 完成下列句子。

1. I have a grammar book. <u>It</u> is black.

2. Brian borrowed my books. _____ returned _____ yesterday.

3. Sonya is wearing some new earrings. _____ look good on _____ .

4. Don't look directly at the sun. Don't look at _____ directly even if you are wearing sunglasses. The intensity of its light can injure your eyes.

5. Recently, I read about "micromachines." _____ are machines that are smaller than a grain of sand. One scientist called _____ "the greatest scientific invention of our time."

□ **Exercise 41. 暖身活動** (表 6-11)

將下列片語與其所描述的圖片配對。

A 圖

B 圖

Tom and Mary's father

Tom's and Mary's fathers

1. _____ the teacher's office

2. _____ the teachers' office

6-11 名詞的所有格 Possessive Nouns

單數：(a) I know the **student's** name. 複數：(b) I know the **students'** names. 複數：(c) I know the **children's** names.	名詞字尾加上所有格符號 (') 和 **-s**，即形成所有格。
單數	(d) the student → the **student's** name 　　my baby → my **baby's** name 　　a man → a **man's** name (e) James → **James'/James's** name	單數名詞所有格： 名詞 + 所有格符號 (') + **-s** 以 **-s** 結尾的單數名詞有兩種所有格形式，如：*James'* 或 *James's* 皆可。
複數	(f) the students → the **students'** names 　　my babies → my **babies'** names (g) men → **men's** names 　　the children → the **children's** names	複數名詞所有格： 名詞 + **-s** + 所有格符號 (') 不規則的複數名詞所有格： 名詞 + 所有格符號 (') + **-s** (不規則的複數名詞是指不以 **-s** 結尾的複數名詞，如：*children*、*men*、*people*、*women*，請見表 6-1。)
比較： (h) **Tom's** here. (i) **Tom's** brother is here.	在例 (h) 中，**Tom's** 不是名詞所有格，而是非正式寫作中 *Tom is* 的縮寫。 在例 (i) 中，**Tom's** 是名詞所有格。

□ **Exercise 42. 文法** (表 6-11)

判斷斜體字的含義為一個 (one) 或一個以上 (more than one)。

1. The teacher answered the *student's* questions.   (one)   more than one

2. The teacher answered the *students'* questions.   one   more than one

3. Our *daughters'* bedroom is next to our room.   one   more than one

4. Our *son's* room is downstairs.   one   more than one

5. *Men's* clothing is on sale at the department store.   one   more than one

6. This looks like a *woman's* shirt.   one   more than one

❏ Exercise 43. 文法 (表 6-11)

仔細看 Nelson 的家譜，並用正確的所有格形式完成下列句子。

Nelson 的家譜

Ella + Ned

Lisa + Sam   Howard + Monica

William

1. _____Ned's_____ wife is Ella.

2. _____ husband is Sam.

3. Howard is _____ brother.

4. Howard is _____ husband.

5. _____ grandmother is Ella.

6. _____ parents are Sam and Lisa.

7. Ella and _____ grandson is William.

8. Howard and Monica are _____ aunt and uncle.

❏ Exercise 44. 遊戲：知識問答比賽 (表 6-11)

分小組比賽。使用各題名詞的正確所有格形式來完成句子，並判斷該項資訊是否正確。答對最多題的組別獲勝。★

1. earth   The _____ surface is about 70% water.   T   F

2. elephant   An _____ skin is pink and wrinkled.   T   F

3. man   Pat is a _____ name.   T   F

4. woman   Pat is a _____ name.   T   F

5. women   The area for language is larger in _____ brains.   T   F

6. Men   _____ brains are bigger than women's brains.   T   F

7. person   A _____ eyes blink more if he/she is nervous.   T   F

8. People   _____ voices always get lower as they age.   T   F

❏ Exercise 45. 暖身活動 (表 6-12)

勾選 (✓) 所有合文法的答案。

Whose camera is this?

1. ____ It's my camera.   5. ____ It's your camera.

2. ____ It's mine.   6. ____ It's your's.

3. ____ It's my.   7. ____ It's theirs.

4. ____ It's yours.   8. ____ It's their camera.

---

*請見解答本中的 *Trivia Answers*。

6-12 所有格代名詞與形容詞 Possessive Pronouns and Adjectives

This pen belongs to me. (a) It's **mine.** (b) It is **my** pen.	例 (a) 與例 (b) 同義，都表「擁有」。 **mine** 是「所有格代名詞」，**my** 是「所有格形容詞」。

所有格代名詞	所有格形容詞	「所有格代名詞」只能單獨使用，後面不加名詞。
(c) I have **mine.**	I have **my** pen.	「所有格形容詞」後面必須接名詞。
(d) You have **yours.**	You have **your** pen.	
(e) She has **hers.**	She has **her** pen.	錯誤：*I have mine pen.*
(f) He has **his.**	He has **his** pen.	錯誤：*I have my.*
(g) We have **ours.**	We have **our** pens.	
(h) You have **yours.**	You have **your** pen.	
(i) They have **theirs.**	They have **their** pens.	
(j) ——	I have a book. **Its** cover is black.	

its 和 **it's** 的比較： (k) Sue gave me a book. I don't remember **its** title. (l) Sue gave me a book. **It's** a novel.	在例 (k) 中，**its**（「不含」所有格符號）是所有格形容詞，在句中修飾 *title* 這個名詞。 在例 (l) 中，**it's**（含所有格符號）則是 it + is 的縮寫。

their、**there** 和 **they're** 的比較： (m) The students have **their** books. (n) My books are over **there**. (o) Where are the students? **They're** in class.	**their**、**there** 和 **they're** 的發音相同，但意義不同。 　**their** = 所有格形容詞，如：例 (m) 　**there** = 表示地點的副詞，如：例 (n) 　**they're** = they are 的縮寫，如：例 (o)

❑ **Exercise 46. 文法**（表 6-12）

圈選可完成句子的正確答案。

1. Alice called (her,) hers friend.

2. Hasan wrote a letter to his, he's mother.

3. It's, Its normal for a dog to chase it's, its tail.

4. The bird cleaned its, it's feathers with its, it's beak.

5. Paula had to drive my car to work. Hers, Her had a flat tire.

6. Junko fell off her bike and broke hers, her arm.

7. Anastasia is a good friend of me, mine.★

8. I met a friend of you, yours yesterday.

9. A: Excuse me. Is this my, mine pen or your, yours?

   B: This one is my, mine. Your, Yours is on your, yours desk.

★*A friend of* + 所有格代名詞（如：*a friend of mine*）是常見的表達用語。

10. a. Adam and Amanda are married. *They, Them* live in an apartment building.
 b. *Their, There, They're* apartment is on the fifth floor.
 c. We live in the same building. *Our, Ours* apartment has one bedroom, but *their, theirs* has two.
 d. *Their, There, They're* sitting *their, there, they're* now because *their, there, they're* waiting for a visit from *their, there, they're* son.

❑ **Exercise 47. 暖身活動** (表 6-13)

分小組進行；使用鏡子以演示下列句子的句意，並在其他同學表演動作時，輪流唸出句子。

1. I am looking at myself.
2. You are looking at yourself.
3. You are looking at yourselves.
4. He is looking at himself.
5. They are looking at themselves.
6. She is looking at herself.
7. We are looking at ourselves.

6-13 反身代名詞 Reflexive Pronouns

myself	(a) *I saw **myself** in the mirror.*	反身代名詞的字尾是 **-self** / **-selves**，用在主詞（如：*I*）和受詞（如：*myself*）指同一人的情況下。
yourself	(b) *You*（單數）*saw **yourself**.*	
herself	(c) *She saw **herself**.*	錯誤：*I saw me in the mirror.*
himself	(d) *He saw **himself**.*	
itself	(e) *It*（如：the kitten）*saw **itself**.*	
ourselves	(f) *We saw **ourselves**.*	
yourselves	(g) *You*（複數）*saw **yourselves**.*	
themselves	(h) *They saw **themselves**.*	

(i) *Greg lives **by himself**.*	**by** + 反身代名詞 = alone
(j) *I sat **by myself** on the park bench.*	在例 (i) 中，Greg 一人獨居，沒有家人或室友同住。
(k) *I **enjoyed myself** at the fair.*	某些動詞（如：*enjoy*）後面常接反身代名詞，見下表所列。

含反身代名詞的常見表達字詞

believe in yourself	help yourself	pinch yourself	tell yourself
blame yourself	hurt yourself	be proud of yourself	work for yourself
cut yourself	give yourself (something)	take care of yourself	wish yourself (luck)
enjoy yourself	introduce yourself	talk to yourself	
feel sorry for yourself	kill yourself	teach yourself	

❏ **Exercise 48. 文法** (表 6-13)

用反身代名詞完成下列句子。

1. Are you okay, Heidi? Did you hurt ___*yourself*___?

2. Leo taught _____ to play the piano. He never had a teacher.

3. Do you ever talk to _____? Most people talk to

   _____ sometimes.

4. A newborn baby can't take care of _____.

5. It is important for all of us to have confidence in our own abilities. We need to believe in

   _____.

6. Isabel always wishes _____ good luck before a big test.

7. Kazu, there's plenty of food on the table. Please help _____.

8. I couldn't believe my good luck! I had to pinch _____ to make sure I

   wasn't dreaming.

❏ **Exercise 49. 聽力** (表 6-13)

聆聽 CD 播放的句子，並用反身代名詞完成句子。

CD 2
Track 8

例：你會聽到：The accident was my fault. I caused it. I was responsible. In other words, I
　　　　　　　blamed . . .

　　你要寫下： ___*myself*___

1. _____   4. _____

2. _____   5. _____

3. _____   6. _____

❏ **Exercise 50. 口說：訪談** (表 6-13)

訪問班上六位同學，詢問每人一個不一樣的問題。最後，與全班同學分享一些他們的答案。

1. In this town, what is a good way to enjoy yourself?
2. How do people introduce themselves in your country? What do they say?
3. Have you ever wished yourself good luck? When or why?
4. Have you ever felt sorry for yourself? Or, have you ever felt proud of yourself? If so, why?
5. When athletes talk to themselves before an important event, what do you imagine they say?
6. In your country, at what age does a person usually begin living by himself or herself?

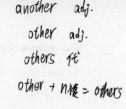

❏ **Exercise 51. 暖身活動** (表 6-14)

選擇符合描述的圖片。

One flower is red. Another is yellow. The other is pink.

A 圖　　　　　　　　　　　　B 圖

6-14 *Other* 的單數形：*Another* 和 *The Other* 的比較

Another

(a) There is a large bowl of apples on the table. Paul is going to eat one apple. If he is still hungry after that, he can eat *another* apple. There are many apples to choose from.	**another** 表示「同類物品中，除已提過的那些之外，再取出一個。」 **another** = *an* + *other* 寫成一個字。

The Other

(b) There are two apples on the table. Paul is going to eat one of them. Sara is going to eat **the other** apple.	**the other** 表示「一定數目的同類物品中，剩下的最後一個。」
(c) Paul ate one apple. Then he ate { *another* apple. / *another* one. / *another*.	**another** 和 **the other** 可以作為形容詞，放在名詞（如：*apple*）或 *one* 之前。 **another** 和 **the other** 也可以單獨使用，作為代名詞。
(d) Paul ate one apple. Sara ate { *the other* apple. / *the other* one. / *the other*.	

❏ **Exercise 52. 文法** (表 6-14)
用 *another* 或 *the other*，完成下列句子。

1. There are two birds in Picture A. One is an eagle. ___The other___ is a chicken.

A 圖　　　　　　　　　　　　　　　B 圖

2. There are three birds in Picture B. One is an eagle.
   a. ____another____ one is a chicken.
   b. ____the other____ bird is a crow.

3. There are many kinds of birds in the world. One kind is an eagle.
   a. ____another____ kind is a chicken.
   b. ____still another____ kind is a crow.
   c. ____still another____ kind is a sea gull.
   d. What is the name of ____another____ kind of bird in the world?

4. It rained yesterday, and from the look of those dark clouds, we're going to have _____ rainstorm today.

5. Nicole and Michelle are identical twins. The best way to tell them apart is by looking at their ears. One of them has pierced ears, and ____the other____ doesn't.

6. France borders several countries. One is Spain. _____ is Italy.

❏ **Exercise 53. 暖身活動** (表 6-15)
將下列句子與正確的圖片配對。

A 圖　　　　　　　　　　　　　　　B 圖

1. _____ Some are red. Others are yellow.
2. _____ Some are red. The others are yellow.

Other(s)

There are many apples in Paul's kitchen. Paul is holding one apple.	***other***(*s*)（沒有 ***the***）表示「同類物品中，除了已提過的那些外，再取出幾個。」
(a) There are ***other*** *apples* in a bowl. （形容詞）+（名詞）	***other*** 作為形容詞（不加 ***-s***），後面可接複數名詞（如：*apples*）或 *ones*。
(b) There are ***other*** *ones* on a plate. （形容詞）+ *ones*	***others*** 是複數形的代名詞（加 ***-s***），後面不接名詞。在例 (c) 中，***others*** = ***other apples***。
(c) There are ***others*** on a chair. （代名詞）	

The Other(s)

There are four apples on the table. Paul is going to take one of them.	***the other***(*s*) 表示「一定數目的同類物品中，剩下的最後幾個」。
(d) Sara is going to take ***the other*** *apples*. （形容詞）+（名詞）	***the other*** 作為形容詞（不加 ***-s***），放在名詞或 *ones* 之前，如：例 (d) 和例 (e)。
(e) Sara is going to take ***the other*** *ones*. （形容詞）+ *ones*	***the others*** 是複數形的代名詞（加 ***-s***），後面不接名詞。在例 (f) 中，***the others*** = ***the other apples***。
(f) Sara is going to take ***the others***. （代名詞）	

Exercise 54. 文法 (表 6-14 和 6-15)

表演下列動作。

1. 握住兩隻筆，並用 *other* 的形式描述第二隻筆。
   → *I'm holding two pens. One is mine, and the other belongs to Ahmed.*
2. 握住三隻筆，並用 *other* 的形式描述第二隻和第三隻筆。
3. 舉起兩隻手，一隻手是你的右手；請用 *other* 的形式介紹你的左手。
4. 舉起你的右手。五根手指之一是你的大姆指 (thumb)，用 *other* 的形式分別介紹你的食指 (index finger)、中指 (middle finger)、無名指 (ring finger)，然後才是你右手的最後一根手指頭—小指 (little finger)。

❑ **Exercise 55. 文法** (表 6-15)

用 *other*(s) 或 *the other*(s) 完成下列句子。

1. There are many kinds of animals in the world. The elephant is one kind. Some
   ___*others*___ are tigers, horses, and bears.

2. There are many kinds of animals in the world. The elephant is one kind. Some
   ___other___ kinds are tigers, horses, and bears.

3. There are three colors in the Italian flag. One of the colors is red.
   _____ are green and white.

4. There are three colors in the Italian flag. One of the colors is red.
   ___the other___ colors are green and white.

5. Many people like to get up very early in the morning. _____ like to
   sleep until noon.

6. There are many kinds of geometric figures. Some are circles. ___other___
   figures are squares. Still ___others___ are rectangular.

7. There are four geometric figures in the above drawing. One is a square.
   _____ figures are a rectangle, a circle, and a triangle.

8. Of the four geometric figures in the drawing, only the circle has curved lines.
   ___The others___ have straight lines.

第一部分　閱讀以下文章，並回答下列問題。

Calming Yourself

When was the last time you felt nervous or anxious? Were you able to calm yourself? There are a variety of techniques that people use to calm themselves. Here are three that many people have found helpful.

One way that people relax is by imagining a peaceful place, such as a tropical beach. Thinking about the warm water, cool breezes, and steady sounds of the ocean waves helps people calm themselves. Another popular method is deep breathing. Inhaling deeply and then slowly exhaling is an easy way for people to slow their heart rate and relax their body. Still other people find exercise helpful. Some people benefit from a slow activity like a 20-minute walk. Others prefer activities that make them tired, like running or swimming.

How about you? How do you calm yourself when you feel nervous? Do any of these methods help you, or do you do other things to relax?

1. What are three ways people relax when they are nervous? (Use **one** and **another** in your answer.)
2. Why do some people choose activities like running and swimming as a way to relax?
3. Imagine you are trying to relax by thinking of a peaceful place. What place would you think of?
4. How do you relax when you are nervous?

第二部分　閱讀一名學生寫的段落文字，該生敘述自己感到緊張時的放鬆方式。

How I Calm Down

Sometimes I feel nervous, especially when I have to give a speech. My body begins to shake, and I realize that I have to calm myself down. This is the technique I use: I imagine myself in a peaceful place. My favorite place in the world is the sea. I imagine myself on the water. I am floating. I feel the warm water around me. The sounds around me are very relaxing. I only hear the waves and maybe a few birds. I don't think about the past or the future. I can feel my heart rate decrease a little, and my body slowly starts to calm down.

第三部分　遵照提供的範例，寫一段關於自己緊張時如何放鬆的文字；請提供放鬆方式及其效果的明確細節。

Sometimes I feel nervous, especially when I have to _____ . My _____ and I realize that I have to calm myself down. This is the technique I use: _____ .

6-16 *Other* 形式總整理 Summary of Forms of *Other*

	形容詞	代名詞	注意：***others***（***other*** + 字尾 ***-s***）只作複數代名詞使用。
單數	another apple	another	
複數	other apples	other**s**	
單數	the other apple	the other	
複數	the other apples	the other**s**	

❑ **Exercise 57. 文法**（表 6-15 和 6-16）

用 *other* 的正確形式完成下列句子：*another*、*other*、*others*、*the other*、*the others*。

1. Juan has only two suits, a blue one and a gray one. His wife wants him to buy
   ___*another*___ one.

2. Juan has two suits. One is blue, and _____ is gray.

3. Some suits are blue. _____ are gray.

4. Some jackets have zippers. _____ jackets have buttons.

5. Some people keep dogs as pets. _____ have cats. Still
   _____ people have fish or birds as pets.

6. My boyfriend gave me a ring. I tried to put it on my ring finger, but it didn't fit. So I had
   to put it on _____ finger.

7. People have two thumbs. One is on the right hand. _____ is on the
   left hand.

8. Sometimes when I'm thirsty, I'll have a glass of water, but often one glass isn't enough, so
   I'll have _____ one.

9. There are five letters in the word *fresh*. One of the letters is a vowel. _____
   are consonants.

10. Smith is a common last name in English. _____ common names are
    Johnson, Jones, Miller, Anderson, Moore, and Brown.

❑ **Exercise 58. 聽力**（表 6-15 和 6-16）

CD 2
Track 9

聆聽 CD 播放的各組對話，並圈選正確的敘述（a 或 b）。

1. a. The speaker was looking at two jackets.
   b. The speaker was looking at several jackets.

2. a. The speakers have only two favorite colors.
   b. The speakers have more than two favorite colors.

3. a. There are several roads the speakers can take.
   b. There are two roads the speakers can take.

4. a. There are only two ways to get downtown.
   b. There are more than two ways to get downtown.

5. a. The speaker had more than four pets.
   b. The speaker had only four pets.

□ **Exercise 59. 聽力** （表 6-15 和 6-16）

CD 2
Track 10

聆聽 CD 中關於處理寂寞情緒的對話，並用聽到的字詞完成下列句子。

A: What do you do when you're feeling lonely?

B: I go someplace where I can be around _____ people. Even if they are strangers, I feel better when there are _____ around me. How about you?

A: That doesn't work for me. For example, if I'm feeling lonely and I go to a movie by myself, I look at all _____ people who are there with their friends and family, and I start to feel even lonelier. So I try to find _____ things to do to keep myself busy. When I'm busy, I don't feel lonely.

□ **Exercise 60. 檢視學習成果** （第 6 章）

校訂下列句子，訂正錯誤的名詞、代名詞、形容詞和主詞與動詞不一致之處。

               wishes
1. Jimmy had three ~~wish~~ for his birthday.

2. I had some black beans soup for lunch.

3. The windows in our classroom is dirty.

4. People in Brazil speaks Portuguese.

5. Are around 8,600 types of birds in the world.

6. My mother and father work in Milan. Their teacher's.

7. Today many womens are carpenter, pilot, and doctor.

8. Is a new student in our class. Have you met her?

9. There are two pool at the park. The smaller one is for childs. The another is for adults.

10. The highways in my country are excellents.

11. I don't like my apartment. Its in a bad neighborhood. Is a lot of crime. I'm going to move to other neighborhood.

第七章
情態助動詞

❑ **Exercise 1. 暖身活動** (表 7-1)

勾選 (✓) 合文法的句子。

1. __✓__ I can speak English well.
2. ____ He cans speaks English well.
3. ____ She can to speak English well.
4. __✓__ Our neighbors can speak some English.
5. ____ My parents can't speaking English at all.

7-1 情態助動詞的形式 The Form of Modal Auxiliaries

下表所列之動詞稱爲「情態助動詞」，用來幫助動詞表達以下各種意義，如：能力、應允、可能性、必須性等。大部分的情態助動詞都有一種以上的含意。

助動詞 + 原形動詞

can	(a)	Olga **can speak** English.
could	(b)	He **couldn't come** to class.
may	(c)	It **may rain** tomorrow.
might	(d)	It **might rain** tomorrow.
should	(e)	Mary **should study** harder.
had better	(f)	I **had better study** tonight.
must	(g)	Billy! You **must listen** to me!
will	(h)	I **will be** in class tomorrow.
would	(i)	**Would** you please **close** the door?

can、could、may、might、should、had better、must、will 及 would 後面接原形動詞。

• 這些情態助動詞後面不接 **to**：
  錯誤：*Olga can to speak English.*

• 主要動詞結尾不可加 **-s**：
  錯誤：*Olga can speaks English.*

• 主要動詞不可爲過去式：
  錯誤：*Olga can spoke English.* *I had better = I'd better*

• 主要動詞結尾不可加 **-ing**：
  錯誤：*Olga can speaking English.*

助動詞 + to + 原形動詞

have to	(j)	I **have to study** tonight.
have got to	(k)	I **have got to study** tonight.
be able to	(l)	Kate **is able to study** harder.
ought to	(m)	Kate **ought to study** harder.

「**to** + 原形動詞」可與下列助動詞連用：
have to、*have got to*、*be able to* 和 *ought to*。

應該

Exercise 2. 文法 （表 7-1）

運用此句型：*Leo _____ tonight.* 和下列提供的動詞 + ***come*** 造句，並視情況加 ***to***。

例： can → *Leo can come tonight.*

1. may
2. should
3. ought
4. will not
5. could not

6. might
7. had better
8. has
9. has got
10. is not able

❏ Exercise 3. 聽力 （表 7-1）

CD 2
Track 11

聆聽 CD 播放的句子，並視情況加 ***to***；如果<u>不需要加</u> ***to***，則寫 **Ø**。注意：***to*** 或許會聽起來像 "ta"。

1. I have _*to*_ go downtown tomorrow.　　　Mom cooks dinner (in the kitchen)

2. You must _Ø_ fasten your seat belt.

3. Could you please _____ open the window?

4. May I _____ borrow your eraser?

5. I'm not able _____ sign the contract today.

6. Today is the deadline. You must _____ sign it!

7. I have got _____ go to the post office this afternoon.

8. Shouldn't you _____ save some of your money for emergencies?

9. I feel bad for Elena. She has _____ have more surgery.

10. Alexa! Stop! You must not _____ run into the street!

❏ Exercise 4. 暖身活動 （表 7-2）

圈選最適合用來完成下列句子的答案，並與同學討論。

1. A newborn baby *can / can't* roll over.
2. A baby of four months *can / can't* smile.
3. A newborn baby *is able to / isn't able to* see black and white shapes.
4. A baby of six months *is able to / isn't able to* see colors.
5. When I was nine months old, I *could / couldn't* crawl.
6. When I was nine months old, I *could / couldn't* walk.

7-2 表示能力：*Can* 與 *Could*

(a) Bob *can play* the piano. (b) You *can buy* a screwdriver at a hardware store. (c) I *can meet* you at Ted's tomorrow afternoon.	*can* 意指現在或未來的能力。
(d) I $\left\{\begin{array}{l}\textbf{\textit{can't}}\\ \textbf{\textit{cannot}}\\ \textbf{\textit{can not}}\end{array}\right\}$ understand that sentence.	*can* 的否定形式：*can't*、*cannot* 或 *can not*。
(e) I *can go*. (f) I *can't go*. Do you speak Chinese?（禮貌）	在口語英文中，*can* 通常為非重音，唸作 /kən/ = "kun"。 *can't* 應以加重音的方式發音，其尾音為喉塞音★，唸作 /kæn?/。喉塞音在口語英文中用以取代 /t/。即便是以英語為母語的人士，有時也難以分辨 *can* 與 *can't* 之間的區別，而須跟說話者作確認。
(g) Our son *could walk* when he was one year old.	*can* 的過去式：*could*。
(h) He *couldn't walk* when he was six months old.	*could* 的否定形式：*couldn't* 或 *could not*。
(i) He *can read*. (j) He *is able to read*. (k) She *could read*. (l) She *was able to read*.	*be able to* 也可以用來表達能力。 例 (i) 和 (j) 同義。 例 (k) 和 (l) 同義。

*喉塞音 (glottal stop) 是在表達否定用語 "unh-uh" 時會聽到的音。發此音時，空氣會被位於喉嚨後面的聲門阻擋，其音標為 /?/。

❏ **Exercise 5. 文法** (表 7-2)

第一部分 用 *can* 或 *can't* 完成下列句子。

1. A dog ___can___ swim, but it ___can't___ fly.

2. A frog ___can___ live both on land and in water, but a cat ___can't___ .

3. A bilingual person ___can't___ speak three languages, but a trilingual person
   雙語的
   ___can___ .

4. People with a Ph.D. degree ___can___ use "Dr." in front of their name, but people
   with a master's degree ___can't___ .

第二部分 用 *be able to* 改寫第一部分的句子。

❏ **Exercise 6. 口說：訪談** (表 7-2)

訪問同學，並詢問每人一個不一樣的問題；如果答案是 yes，便繼續問括弧內的問題。最後，與全班分享一些你的答案。

Can you . . .

1. speak more than two languages? (Which ones?)
2. play chess? (How long have you played?)
3. fold a piece of paper in half more than six times? (Can you show me?)
4. draw well — for example, draw a picture of me? (Can you do it now?)

Are you able to . . .

5. write clearly with both your right and left hands?
   (Can you show me?)
6. pat the top of your head with one hand and rub your
   stomach in a circle with the other hand at the same time?
   (Can you show me?)
7. drive a stick-shift car? (When did you learn?)
8. play a musical instrument? (Which one?)

❏ **Exercise 7. 聽力** (表 7-2)

CD 2
Track 12

聆聽 CD 播放的對話，你會聽到 *can* 和 *can't* 的弱化發音，請寫下聽到的字詞。

In the classroom

A: I _____ this math assignment.
$\quad$ 1

B: I _____ you with that.
$\quad$ 2

A: Really? _____ this problem to me?
$\quad$ 3

B: Well, we _____ out the answer unless we do this part first.
$\quad$ 4

A: Okay! But it's so hard.

B: Yeah, but I know you _____ it. Just go slowly.
$\quad$ 5

A: Class is almost over. _____ me after school today to finish this?
$\quad$ 6

B: Well, I _____ you right after school, but how about at 5:00?
$\quad$ 7

A: Great!

❏ **Exercise 8. 口說** (表 7-2)

用 *could／couldn't／be able to／not be able to* 以及自己的話，完成下列句子。

例：A year ago I _____, but now I can.
$\quad$ → *A year ago I couldn't speak English, but now I can.*

1. When I was a child, I _____, but now I can.
2. When I was six, I _____, but I wasn't able to do that
   when I was three.
3. Five years ago, I _____, but now I can't.
4. In the past, I _____, but now I am.

勾選 (✓) 下列各組中同義的句子。

A 組

1. _____ Maybe it will be hot tomorrow.

2. _____ It might be hot tomorrow.

3. _____ It may be hot tomorrow.

B 組

4. _____ You can have dessert, now.

5. _____ You may have dessert, now.

C 組

6. _____ She can't stay up late.

7. _____ She might not stay up late.

7-3 表示可能性：*May*、*Might* 與 *Maybe*；表示應允：*May* 與 *Can*

(a) It **may rain** tomorrow. (b) It **might rain** tomorrow. (c) — Why isn't John in class? 　　 — I don't know. He { **may** / **might** } be sick today.	**may** 和 **might** 表示現在或未來的「可能性」，兩者同義。例 (a) 和例 (b) 在意思上並無差別。
(d) It **may not rain** tomorrow. (e) It **might not rain** tomorrow.	否定形式：**may not** 與 **might not** （**may** 和 **might** 不可與 **not** 縮寫。）
(f) **Maybe** it will rain tomorrow. 比較： (g) **Maybe** John is sick.（副詞） (h) John **may be** sick.（動詞） *副詞不影響對話的句意*	在例 (f) 和例 (g) 中，**maybe**（一個字）是副詞，置於句首，意指「或許」(possibly)。 錯誤：*It will maybe rain tomorrow.* 在例 (h) 中，**may be**（兩個字）為動詞形式：助動詞 **may** + 主要動詞 **be**。 例 (g) 與例 (h) 同義。 錯誤：*John maybe sick.*
(i) Yes, children, you **may have** a cookie after dinner. (j) Okay, kids, you **can have** a cookie after dinner.	**may** 也用於表示「允許」，如：例 (i)。 **can** 也常用於表示「允許」，如：例 (j)。 注意：例 (i) 與例 (j) 同義，但 **may** 比 **can** 正式。
(k) You **may not have** a cookie. 　　 You **can't have** a cookie.	**may not** 與 **cannot** (**can't**) 用來表示反對 （如同說 no）。

Exercise 10. 文法 (表 7-3)

用 *can*、*may* 或 *might* 完成下列句子，並辨別情態助動詞表達的意思：「可能性」
(possibility) 或「許可」(permission)。

In a courtroom for a speeding ticket

1. No one speaks without the judge's permission. You ___may / can___ not speak until the judge asks you a question. *Meaning:* ___permission___

2. The judge _____ reduce your fine for your speeding ticket, or she _____ not. It depends. *Meaning:* _____

3. You _____ not argue with the judge. If you argue, you will get a fine. *Meaning:* _____

4. You have a strong case, but I'm not sure if you will convince the judge. You _____ win or you _____ lose. *Meaning:* _____

Exercise 11. 文法 (表 7-3)

用括弧內的字詞改寫下列句子。

1. It may snow tonight.
   (might) It might snow tonight
   (Maybe) Maybe it will snow tonight

2. You might need to wear your boots.
   (may) You may need to wear your boots
   (Maybe) Maybe you will need to wear your boots

3. Maybe there will be a blizzard.
   (may) There may be a blizzard.
   (might) There might be a blizzard.

there is
there are } 那裡有

成兩人一組、分小組或全班一起練習用 *may*、*might* 和 *maybe*，回答下列問題；每題的答案至少要用到三種表達可能性的情態助動詞。

例：What are you going to do tomorrow?
→ *I don't know. I **may** go downtown.* 或 *I **might** go to the laundromat.*
***Maybe** I'll study all day. Who knows?*

1. What are you going to do tomorrow night?
2. What's the weather going to be like tomorrow?
3. What is our teacher going to do tonight?
4. (_____) isn't in class today. Where is he/she?
5. What is your occupation going to be ten years from now?

❑ **Exercise 13. 聽力** (表 7-2 和 7-3)

CD 2
Track 13

聆聽 CD 中即將播出含 *can*、*may* 或 *might* 的句子，判斷說話者表達的是「能力」(ability)、「可能性」(possibility) 或「許可」(permission)。

例：你會聽到：A: Where's Victor?
B: I don't know. He may be sick.

你要圈出：ability ⟮possibility⟯ permission

1.	ability	possibility	permission	4. ability	possibility	permission
2.	ability	possibility	permission	5. ability	possibility	permission
3.	ability	possibility	permission			

❑ **Exercise 14. 暖身活動** (表 7-4)

下列哪一句表達的是過去的能力 (past ability)、現在的可能性 (present possibility) 或未來的可能性 (future possibility)？

A soccer game

1. There is five minutes left and the score is 3–3. Our team could win.
2. The goalie is on the ground. He could be hurt.
3. Our team didn't win. We couldn't score another goal.

7-4 用 *Could* 表示可能性

(a) — How was the movie? ***Could** you **understand** the English?* — Not very well. *I **could** only **understand** it with the help of <u>subtitles</u>.* 字幕	*could* 可表示「過去的能力」，如：例 (a)★ *could* 還可以表示「可能性」。 在例 (b) 中，***He could be sick*** 相當於 He *may/might* be sick，亦如同 *It is possible that he is sick*。
(b) — Why isn't Greg in class? — I don't know. *He **could be** sick.*	在例 (b) 中，*could* 表示「現在的」可能性。
(c) Look at those dark clouds. *It **could start** raining* any minute.	在例 (c) 中，*could* 表示「未來的」可能性。

★亦可參見表 7-2。

❑ **Exercise 15.** 文法 (表 7-2 和 7-4)

下列句子中的 *could* 表達的是過去、現在還是未來時間？而代表的意義是能力或是可能性？

句子	過去	現在	未來	能力	可能性
1. I *could be* home late tonight. Don't wait for me for dinner.			✗		✗
2. Thirty years ago, when he was a small child, David *could speak* Swahili fluently. Now he's forgotten a lot of it.					
3. A: Where's Alicia? B: I don't know. She *could be* at the mall.					
4. When I was a child, I *could climb* trees, but now I'm too old.					
5. Let's leave for the airport now. Yuki's plane *could arrive* early, and we want to be there when she arrives.					
6. A: What's that on the carpet? B: I don't know. It looks like a bug. Or it *could be* a piece of fuzz.					

❑ **Exercise 16.** 口說 (表 7-4)

成兩人一組、分小組或全班一起練習用 *could*，爲下列各情境提供合理的解決方案。

例：Tim has to go to work early tomorrow. His car is completely out of gas. His bicycle is broken.
  → *He could take the bus to work.*
  → *He could get a friend to take him to a gas station to get gas.*
  → *He could try to fix his bike.*
  → *He could get up very early and walk to work.*
    Etc.

1. Lisa walked to school today. Now she wants to go home. It's raining hard. She doesn't have an umbrella, and she's wearing sandals.

2. Joe and Joan want to get some exercise. They have a date to play tennis this morning, but the tennis court is covered with snow.

3. Roberto just bought a new camera. He has it at home now. He has the instruction manual. It is written in Japanese. He can't read Japanese. He doesn't know how to operate the camera.

4. Albert likes to travel around the world. He is 22 years old. Today he is alone in Paris. He needs to eat, and he needs to find a place to stay overnight. But while he was asleep on the train last night, someone stole his wallet. He has no money.

❏ **Exercise 17. 聽力**（表 7-3 和 7-4）

聆聽 CD 中一對夫妻的對話；再聽一遍，用聽到的字詞完成下列句子。

CD 2
Track 14

In a home office

A: Look at this cord. Do you know what it's for?

B: I don't know. We have so many cords around here with all our electronic equipment. It
_____ for the printer, I guess.
1

A: No, I checked. The printer isn't missing a cord.

B: It _____ for one of the kid's toys.
2

A: Yeah, I _____. But they don't have many electronic toys.
3

B: I have an idea. It _____ for the cell phone. You know — the one I
4
had before this one.

A: I bet that's it. We _____ probably throw this out.
5

B: Well, let's be sure before we do that.

❏ **Exercise 18. 暖身活動**（表 7-5）

勾選 (✓) 下列含義相同的句子。

1. _____ May I use your cell phone?

2. _____ Can I use your cell phone?

3. _____ Could I use your cell phone?

7-5 禮貌請求的問句：*May I, Could I, Can I*

禮貌請求的問句	可能的回答	
(a) ***May I*** please borrow your pen? (b) ***Could I*** please borrow your pen? (c) ***Can I*** please borrow your pen?	Yes. Yes. Of course. Yes. Certainly. Of course. Certainly. Sure.（非正式） Okay.（非正式） Uh-huh（意思是「可以」） I'm sorry, but I need to use it myself.	***may I***、***could I****和 ***can I*** 用於禮貌的問句，目的在於請求對方的允許或同意。例 (a)、(b) 和 (c) 基本上同義。 注意：***can I*** 不如 ***may I*** 和 ***could I*** 正式。
(d) ***Can I*** borrow your pen, *please*? (e) ***Can I*** borrow your pen?		***please*** 可置於問句末尾，如：例 (d)。 問句中的 ***please*** 可省略，如：例 (e)。

*在禮貌請求的問句中，***could***「不是」***can*** 的過去式。

❑ **Exercise 19. 文法**（表 7-5）

用 ***may I***、***could I*** 或 ***can I*** 及下表中的動詞，完成下列各組電話對話。注意：各組對話中的說話者 B 代表來電者。

> ask   help   leave   speak/talk   take

1. A: Hello?

   B: Hello. Is Ahmed there?

   A: Yes, he is.

   B: _____ to him?

   A: Just a minute. I'll get him.

2. A: Hello. Mr. Black's office.

   B: _____ to Mr. Black?

   A: _____ who is calling?

   B: Susan Abbott.

   A: Just a moment, Ms. Abbott. I'll transfer you.

3. A: Hello?

   B: Hi. This is Bob. _____ to Pedro?

   A: Sure. Hold on.

4. A: Good afternoon. Dr. Wu's office. _____ you?

   B: Yes. I have an appointment that I need to change.

   A: Just a minute, please. I'll transfer you to our appointment desk.

5. A: Hello?

   B: Hello. _____ to Emily?

   A: She's not at home right now. _____ a message?

   B: No, thanks. I'll call later.

6. A: Hello?

   B: Hello. _____ to Maria?

   A: She's not here right now.

   B: Oh. _____ a message?

   A: Sure. Just let me get a pen.

❏ **Exercise 20. 口說：兩人一組** (表 7-5)

成兩人一組，詢問及回答禮貌請求的問句。用 *may I*、*could I* 或 *can I* 作為問句開頭，編寫可以表演給全班觀賞的對話。

例：(A), you want to see (B)'s grammar book for a minute.
說話者 A：May/Could/Can I (please) see your grammar book for a minute?
說話者 B：Of course./Sure./Etc.
說話者 A：Thank you./Thanks. I forgot to bring mine to class today.

1. (A), you want to see (B)'s dictionary for a minute.

2. (A), you are at a restaurant. (B) is your server. You have finished your meal. You want the check.

3. (B), you run into (A) on the street. (A) is carrying some heavy packages. What are you going to say to him/her?

4. (A), you are speaking to (B), who is one of your teachers. You want to leave class early today.

5. (B), you are in a store with your good friend (A). The groceries cost more than you expected. You don't have enough money. What are you going to say to your friend?

❏ **Exercise 21. 暖身活動** (表 7-6)

勾選合文法的問句；以下哪兩句問句比其他句子還要有禮貌？

In the kitchen

1. _____ Will you help me with the dishes?

2. _____ Would you load the dishwasher?

3. _____ May you load the dishwasher?

4. _____ Can you unload the dishwasher?

5. _____ Could you unload the dishwasher?

7-6 禮貌請求的問句：*Would You, Could You, Will You, Can You*

禮貌請求的問句	可能的回答	
(a) ***Would you*** please open the door? (b) ***Could you*** please open the door? (c) ***Will you*** please open the door? (d) ***Can you*** please open the door?	Yes. Yes. Of course. Certainly. I'd be happy to. Of course. I'd be glad to. Sure.（非正式） Okay.（非正式） Uh-huh.（意思是「可以」） I'm sorry. I'd like to help, but my hands are full.	***would you***、***could you***、***will you*** 和 ***can you*** 用於作禮貌性的請求，其目的在請求對方幫忙或合作。 例 (a)、(b)、(c) 和 (d) 基本上同義。 一般認為用 *would* 和 *could* 比用 *will* 和 *can* 更有禮貌。
		注意：禮貌請求的問句中，若主詞為 ***you***，不可用 ***may***。 錯誤：*May you please open the door?*

❑ **Exercise 22. 文法**（表 7-6）

用 ***you*** 為下列各題情境造兩句問句。

1. You're in a room and it's getting very hot.

   正式的：___*Would you please open the window?*___

   非正式的：___*Can you turn on the air-conditioner?*___

2. You're trying to listen to the news on TV, but your friends are talking too loud, and you can't hear it.

   正式的：_____

   非正式的：_____

3. You're in a restaurant. You are about to pay and notice the bill is more than it should be. The server has made a mistake.

   正式的：_____

   非正式的：_____

❑ **Exercise 23. 口說：兩人一組**（表 7-5 和 7-6）

成兩人一組，依照下列提供的一個（或更多）的情境編寫對話，並在其他同學面前表演該對話。

例：You're in a restaurant. You want the server to refill your coffee cup.
   You catch the server's eye and raise your hand slightly. He approaches your table and says: "Yes? What can I do for you?"

學生 A：Yes? What can I do for you?
學生 B：Could I please have some more coffee?

學生 A：Of course. Right away. Could I get you anything else?
學生 B：No thanks. Oh, on second thought, yes. Would you bring some cream too?
學生 A：Certainly.
學生 B：Thanks.

1. You've been waiting in a long line at a busy bakery. Finally, it's your turn. The clerk turns toward you and says: "Next!"

2. You are at work. You feel sick and you have a slight fever. You really want to go home. You see your boss, Mr. Jenkins, passing by your desk. You say: "Mr. Jenkins, could I speak with you for a minute?"

3. The person next to you on the plane has finished reading his newspaper. You would like to read it. He also has a bag on the floor that is in your space. You would like him to move it. You say: "Excuse me."

❑ **Exercise 24. 暖身活動**（表 7-7）

你的朋友 Paula 頭痛得屬害，你會給她什麼樣的建議？勾選 (✓) 下列你同意的句子。

1. _____ You *should* lie down.
2. _____ You *should* take some medicine.
3. _____ You *ought to* call the doctor.
4. _____ You *should* go to the emergency room.
5. _____ You *ought to* put an ice-pack on your forehead.

7-7 表示建議：*Should* 與 *Ought to*

(a) My clothes are dirty. I { *should* / *ought to* } wash them.	*should* 和 *ought to* 同義，意指：「這是個好主意、好建議」。
(b) 錯誤：I should ~~to~~ wash them. (c) 錯誤：I ought washing them. 　　　　　　^to	形式：*should* + 原形動詞（不加 *to*） 　　　　*ought* + *to* + 原形動詞
(d) You need your sleep. You *should not* (*shouldn't*) stay up late.	否定句：*should* + *not* = *shouldn't* （*ought to* 通常不用於否定句。）
(e) A: I'm going to be late for the bus. 　　　What *should I do*? 　B: Run!	問句：*should* + 主詞 + 主要動詞 （*ought to* 通常不用於問句。）
(f) A: I'm tired today. 　B: You *should*/*ought to* go home and take a nap. 　　　　　　　　　　　　　　　小睡一下 (g) A: I'm tired today. 　B: *Maybe* you *should*/*ought to* go home and take a nap. burn the mid-night oil 熬夜	*maybe* 與 *should*/*ought to* 連用可以「緩和」提出建議的語氣。 比較： 例 (f)：說話者 B 提出勸告的語氣頗為堅定，他清楚地表示回家小睡是個好主意，可以解決說話者 A 的困境。 例 (g)：說話者 B 提出建議，表示回家小睡可能可以解決說話者 A 的困境。

❏ **Exercise 25. 口說：兩人一組** (表 7-7)

成兩人一組，學生 A 說出問題，學生 B 用 **should** 或 **ought to** 提供建議；如果你認爲適當，也可以用 **maybe** 來緩和提出建議的語氣。

例：I'm sleepy.
學生 A：I'm sleepy.
學生 B：(Maybe) You should/ought to drink a cup of tea.

1. I can't fall asleep at night.
2. I have a sore throat.
3. I have the hiccups.
4. I sat on my friend's sunglasses. Now the frames are bent.

角色互換。

5. I'm starving.*
6. I dropped my sister's camera, and now it doesn't work.
7. Someone stole my lunch from the refrigerator in the staff lounge at work.
8. I bought some shoes that don't fit. Now my feet hurt.

❏ **Exercise 26. 暖身活動** (表 7-8)

Marco 弄丟他的護照了。以下爲一些建議，勾選 (✓) 你同意的，並判斷哪些建議看起來較嚴肅或迫切。

1. _____ He *had better* go to the embassy.
2. _____ He *should* wait and see if someone returns it.
3. _____ He *had better* report it to the police.
4. _____ He *should* ask a friend to help him look for it.

7-8 表示建議：*Had Better*

(a) My clothes are dirty. I $\begin{cases} \textbf{\textit{should}} \\ \textbf{\textit{ought to}} \\ \textbf{\textit{had better}} \end{cases}$ *wash* them.	**had better** 與 should 和 ought to 基本上同義，意指：「這是個好主意、好建議」。 *fine* 罩單
(b) You're driving too fast! You**'d better** *slow* down.	**had better** 比 should 或 ought to 更有急迫感；通常隱含對可能發生之不良後果的警告，在例 (b) 中，說話者表示若不放慢速度，可能遭致惡果，例如：被開罰單或發生車禍。
(c) You**'d better not** *eat* that meat. It looks spoiled.	否定形式：**had better not**
(d) I**'d better** *send* my boss an email right away.	在會話中，**had** 常縮寫爲 **'d**。

---

*starving（非正式英文）意指「快餓壞了」。

❏ **Exercise 27. 文法** (表 7-8)

成兩人一組、分小組或是全班一起練習用 ***had better*** 給予建議。假如沒有遵照建議，可能會有哪些後果？

1. I haven't paid my electric bill.
   → *You'd better pay it by tomorrow. If you don't pay it, the electric company will turn off the power.*

2. Joe oversleeps a lot. This week he has been late to work three times. His boss is very unhappy about that.

3. I don't feel good right now. I think I'm coming down with something.★

4. I can't remember if I locked the front door when I left for work.

5. My ankle really hurts. I think I've sprained it.

6. I can't find my credit card, and I've looked everywhere.

❏ **Exercise 28. 檢視學習成果** (第 7 章)

校訂下列句子，訂正錯誤的動詞形式。

1. You ~~will~~ ^{had} better not be late.

2. Anna shouldn't ^{wear} wears shorts ^{to} ~~to~~ work.

3. I should ~~to~~ go to the post office today.

4. I ought ^{to pay} ~~paying~~ my bills today.

5. You'd ~~had~~ better ~~to~~ call the doctor today.

6. You ^{shouldn't} ~~don't should~~ stay up too late tonight.

7. You ^{had} better not ~~leaving~~ ^{leave} your key in the door.

8. Mr. Lim is having a surprise party for his wife. He ought ^{tell} told people soon.

❏ **Exercise 29. 口說** (表 7-7 和 7-8)

分小組練習，用 ***should***、***ought to*** 和 ***had better*** 給予建議。組長陳述問題，其他組員則提供建議。下列各題應分別選出不同組長。

例：
組長：I study, but I don't understand my physics class. It's the middle of the term, and I'm failing the course. I need a science course in order to graduate. What should I do?★★
說話者 A：You**'d better** get a tutor right away.
說話者 B：You **should** make an appointment with your teacher and see if you can get some extra help.
說話者 C：Maybe you **ought to** drop your physics course and take a different science course next term.

★慣用語 *come down with something* 意指「生病，像是感冒或流感」。

★★*should*（不像 *ought to* 或 *had better*）常用在尋求建議的疑問句中，而 *should*、*ought to* 或 *had better* 則適用於答句，如：
   A: *My houseplants always die. What **should** I do?*
   B: *You'd better get a book on plants. You **should** try to find out why they die. Maybe you **ought to** look on the Internet and see if you can find some information.*

1. I forgot my dad's birthday yesterday. I feel terrible about it. What should I do?

2. I just discovered that I made dinner plans for tonight with two different people. I'm supposed to meet my parents at one restaurant at 7:00, and I'm supposed to meet my boss at a different restaurant across town at 8:00. What should I do?

3. Samira accidentally left the grocery store with an item she didn't pay for. Her young daughter put it in Samira's shopping bag, but she didn't see it. What should Samira do?

4. I borrowed Karen's favorite book of poetry. It was special to her. A note on the inside cover said "To Karen." The author's signature was under it. Now I can't find the book. I think I lost it. What should I do?

❏ **Exercise 30.** 暖身活動 (表 7-9)
下列哪些與撰寫履歷表相關的敘述，符合你們國家的現況？勾選 (✓) 相符的敘述，然後判斷哪些句子在書寫中較常見，而哪些則在口語中較常見。

Writing a résumé
1. _____ You must list all your previous employers.
2. _____ You have to provide references.
3. _____ You have got to include personal information, for example, whether you are married or not.

7-9 表示必須：*Have to, Have Got to, Must*

(a) I have a very important test tomorrow. I { **have to** / **have got to** / **must** } *study* tonight.	**have to**、**have got to** 與 **must** 基本上同義，皆表「必須」的意思。
(b) I'd like to go with you to the movie this evening, but I can't. I **have to go** to a meeting. (c) Bye now! I **'ve got to go**. My wife's waiting for me. I'll call you later. (d) All passengers **must present** their passports at 海關 customs upon arrival. (e) Tommy, you **must hold** onto the railing when you go down the stairs.	在日常口語和書寫中，**have to** 比 **must** 更常用。 **have got to** 通常只用於非正式口語中，如：例 (c)。 **must** 通常用於書面指示語或規定條文中，如：例 (d)。成人對小孩說話時也會使用，如：例 (e)。must 的語氣聽起來非常強硬。
(f) **Do** we **have to bring** pencils to the test? (g) Why **did** he **have to leave** so early?	疑問句：問句中通常用 **have to**，而非 **must** 或 **have got to**，該問句與 **do** 的變化形連用。
(h) I **had to** *study* last night.	**have to**、**have got to** 與 **must**（表「必須」）的「過去式」為 **had to**。
(i) I **have to** ("hafta") *go* downtown today. (j) Rita **has to** ("hasta") *go* to the bank. (k) I've **got to** ("gotta") *study* tonight.	注意：**have to**、**has to** 和 **have got to** 的發音常被弱化，如：例 (i) 到例 (k)。

❏ **Exercise 31. 口說** (表 7-7 和 7-9)

成兩人一組、分小組或全班一起回答下列問題。

1. What are some things you *have to do* today? tomorrow? every day?
2. What is something you *had to do* yesterday?
3. What is something you*'ve got to do* soon?
4. What is something you*'ve got to do* after class today or later tonight?
5. What is something a driver *must do,* according to the law?
6. What is something a driver *should always do* to be a safe driver?
7. What are some things a person *should do* to stay healthy?
8. What are some things a person *must do* to stay alive?

❏ **Exercise 32. 聽力** (表 7-9)

CD 2
Track 15

用聽到的字詞完成下列句子。在開始前，你可以先確定自己是否認識這些字：*apply*、*applicable*、*legal*、*nickname*、*previous*、*employer*。

EMPLOYMENT APPLICATION

Applications are considered for all positions without regard to race, color, religion, sex, national origin, age, marital or veteran status, or in the presence of a non-related medical condition or handicap.

Donna	N/A	Frost	May 4, 2011
First Name	Middle Initial	Last Name	Date

1443 Maple Ridge Heights			555-545-5454
Address			Phone #

Happyville	PA	05055	123-000-7890
City	State	Zip Code	Social Security #

Filling out a job application

1. The application _____ be complete. You shouldn't skip any parts. If a section doesn't fit your situation, you can write N/A (not applicable).

2. _____ type it, but your writing _____ be easy to read.

3. _____ use your full legal name, not your nickname.

4. _____ list the names and places of your previous employers.

5. _____ list your education, beginning with either high school or college.

6. _____ always _____ apply in person. Sometimes you can do it online.

7. _____ write some things, like the same telephone number, twice. You can write "same as above."

8. All spelling _____ be correct.

閱讀以下文章，然後給予建議。

A Family Problem

Mr. and Mrs. Hill don't know what to do about their 15-year-old son, Mark. He's very intelligent but has no interest in learning. His grades are getting worse, and he won't do any homework. Sometimes he skips school and spends the day at the mall.

His older sister Kathy is a good student, and she never causes any problems at home. Kathy hasn't missed a day of school all year. Mark's parents keep asking him why he can't be more like Kathy. Mark is jealous of Kathy and picks fights* with her.

All Mark does when he's home is stay in his room and listen to loud music. He often refuses to eat meals with his family. He argues with his parents, his room is a mess, and he won't** help around the house.

This family needs advice. Tell them what changes they should make. What should they do? What shouldn't they do?

給予建議時，下列各字詞至少要用一次：

should	ought to
shouldn't	have to/has to
have got to/has got to	must
had better	

❏ **Exercise 34. 暖身活動**（表 7-10）

哪一句（a 或 b）可讓以下的句子表達出完整的語義？

We have lots of time.

    a. You must not drive so fast!

    b. You don't have to drive so fast.

7-10 表示不必：*Do Not Have to*；表示禁止：*Must Not*

(a) I finished all of my homework this afternoon. I ***don't have to study*** tonight. (b) Tomorrow is a holiday. Mary ***doesn't have to go*** to class.	***don't/doesn't have to*** 表示「某事並非必要」。
(c) Bus passengers ***must not talk*** to the driver. (d) Children, you ***must not play*** with matches!	***must not*** 表示禁止。（即不可做這件事！）
(e) You ***mustn't play*** with matches.	***must*** + ***not*** = ***mustn't***.（注意：第一個 t 不發音。）

---

*pick a fight 意指「挑起爭端」。

**won't 在句中用以表達「拒絕」，如：He refuses to help around the house.

用 ***don't have to***、***doesn't have to*** 或 ***must not*** 完成下列句子。

1. You ___must not___ drive when you are tired. It's dangerous.

2. I live only a few blocks from my office. I ___don't have to___ drive to work.

3. Liz finally got a car, so now she drives to work. She ___doesn't have to___ take the bus.

4. Mr. Murphy is very wealthy. He ___doesn't have to___ work for a living.

5. You ___must not___ tell Daddy about the birthday party. We want it to be a surprise.

6. A: Did Professor Acosta give an assignment?

   B: Yes, she assigned Chapters 4 and 6, but we ___don't have to___ read Chapter 5.

7. A: Listen carefully, Kristen. If a stranger offers you a ride, you ___must not___ get in the car. Never get in a car with a stranger. Do you understand?

   B: Yes, Mom.

❑ **Exercise 36.** 暖身活動（表 7-11）

閱讀以下情境及其後的推論句；判斷哪些推論句似乎較合邏輯，並視情況解釋你的答案。

情境：Mr. Ellis is a high school gym teacher. He usually wears gym clothes to work. Today he is wearing a suit and tie.

1. He must have an important meeting.
2. He must be rich.
3. He must need new clothes.
4. He must want to make a good impression on someone.
5. His gym clothes must not be clean.

7-11 作合邏輯的推論：*Must*

(a)	A: Nancy is yawning. B: She *must be* sleepy.	在例 (a) 中，說話者 B 正在作合理推測，而其根據則是 Nancy 打呵欠的事實。他能猜想到的「最合理推論」是 Nancy 想睡了，因此用 *must* 表示他的邏輯推論。
(b) (c)	合邏輯的推論：Amy plays tennis every day. She *must like* to play tennis. 必須：If you want to get into the movie theater, you *must buy* a ticket.	比較：*must* 可表示： ・合邏輯的推論，如：例 (b)。 ・必須，如：例 (c)。
(d) (e)	否定的合邏輯推論：Eric ate everything on his plate except the pickle. He *must not like* pickles. 禁止：There are sharks in the ocean near our hotel. We *must not go* swimming there.	比較：*must not* 可表示： ・否定的合邏輯推論，如：例 (d)。 ・禁止，如：例 (e)。

❑ **Exercise 37. 文法** (表 7-11)

用 *must* 或 *must not* 完成下列對話。

1. A: Did you offer our guests something to eat?

   B: Yes, but they didn't want anything. They __must not__ be hungry yet.

2. A: You haven't eaten since breakfast? That was hours ago. You __must__ be hungry.

   B: I am.

3. A: Gregory has already had four glasses of water, and now he's having another.

   B: He _____ be really thirsty.

4. A: I offered Holly something to drink, but she doesn't want anything.

   B: She _____ be thirsty.

5. A: The dog won't eat.

   B: He _____ feel well.

6. A: Brian has watery eyes and has been coughing and sneezing.

   B: Poor guy. He _____ have a cold.

7. A: Erica's really smart. She always gets above 95 percent on her math tests.

   B: I'm sure she's pretty bright, but she _____ also study a lot.

8. A: Listen. Someone is jumping on the floor above us.

   B: It _____ be Sam. Sometimes he does exercises in his apartment.

❑ **Exercise 38. 文法** (表 7-11)

用 ***must*** 為下列情境作出合邏輯的推論。

1. Alima is crying. → *She must be unhappy.*
2. Mrs. Chu has a big smile on her face.
3. Samantha is shivering.
4. Olga watches ten movies a week.
5. James is sweating.
6. Toshi can lift one end of a compact car by himself.

❑ **Exercise 39. 口說** (表 7-11)

用 ***must*** 或 ***must not***，加上可完成句子的提示字詞，和／或自己的話，作出合邏輯的推論。

1. I am at Cyril's apartment door. I've knocked on the door and have rung the doorbell several times. Nobody has answered the door. *be at home? be out somewhere?*
   → *Cyril must not be at home. He must be out somewhere.*

2. Jennifer reads all the time. She sits in a quiet corner and reads even when people come to visit her. *love books? like books better than people? like to talk to people?*

3. Lara has a full academic schedule, plays on the volleyball team, has the lead in the school play, is a volunteer at the hospital, takes piano lessons, and has a part-time job at an ice-cream store. *be busy all the time? have a lot of spare time? be a hard worker?*

4. Simon gets on the Internet every day as soon as he gets home from work. He stays at his computer until he goes to bed. *be a computer addict? have a happy home life? have a lot of friends?*

❑ **Exercise 40. 文法** (表 7-9 和 7-11)

用 ***must***、***have to*** 或 ***had to***，以及括弧內動詞的正確形式，完成下列句子。

At work

A: Your eyes are red. You (*be*) _____ really tired.
                                       1

B: Yeah, I (*stay*) _____ up all night working on a project.
                             2

A: Did you finish?

B: No, I (*work*) _____ on it later today, but I have a million other
                             3

things to do.

A: You (*be*) _____ really busy.
                     4

B: I am!

Exercise 41. 暖身活動 (表 7-12)

用下表中正確的字詞完成下列問句；表中有兩個字不適用任一問題。

can't	couldn't	do	does	will	wouldn't

1. You can work this weekend, _____ you?

2. He won't be late, _____ he?

3. We'd like you to stay, _____ we?

4. They don't have to leave, _____ they?

*句子為肯定，附加問句：否定
句子為否定，附加問句：肯定

7-12 含有情態助動詞的附加問句 Tag Questions with Modal Auxiliaries

(a) You *can* come, **can't you**? (b) She *won't* tell, **will she**? (c) He *should* help, **shouldn't he**? (d) They *couldn't* do it, **could they**? (e) We *would like* to help, **wouldn't we**?	附加問句常含有下列情態助動詞：**can**、**will**、**should**、**could** 和 **would**。★
(f) They *have to* leave, **don't they**? (g) They *don't have to* leave, **do they**? (h) He *has to* leave, **doesn't he**? (i) He *doesn't have to* leave, **does he**? (j) You *had to* leave, **didn't you**? (k) You *didn't have to* leave, **did you**?	附加問句裡常用到 **have to**、**has to** 和 **had to**。 注意：在例 (f) 到 (k) 的附加問句中，會用到助動詞 **do** 的形式。

★更多關於附加問句的用法，請見第 140 頁，表 5-15。

❏ **Exercise 42. 文法** (表 7-12)

完成下列附加問句。

1. You can answer these questions, _____ you?

2. Melinda won't tell anyone our secret, _____ she?

3. Alice would like to come with us, _____ she?

4. I don't have to do more chores, _____ I?

5. Steven shouldn't come to the meeting, _____ he?

6. Flies can fly upside down, _____ they?

7. You would rather have your own apartment, _____ you?

8. Jill has to renew her driver's license, _____ she?

9. If you want to catch your bus, you should leave now, _____ you?

10. Ms. Baxter will be here tomorrow, _____ she?

11. You couldn't hear me, _____ you?

12. We have to be at the doctor's early tomorrow, _____ we?

❑ **Exercise 43. 暖身活動** (表 7-13)
閱讀下列各組句子，判斷各組說話者是誰及可能的情境。

A 組
1. Show me your driver's license.
2. Take it out of your wallet, please.
3. Step out of the car.

B 組
1. Open your mouth.
2. Stick out your tongue.
3. Say "ahhh."
4. Let me take a closer look.
5. Don't bite me!

祈使句：通常祈使句不帶主詞

7-13 下命令：祈使句

命令： (a) Captain: **Open** the door! 　　Soldier: Yes, sir!	祈使句用來下達命令、提出禮貌請求和給予指示。表示命令與請求的區別在於說話者的語氣與是否用了 **please** 這個字。
請求： (b) Teacher: **Open** the door, please. 　　Student: Sure.	在請求句中，**please** 可置於句首或句尾： 　Open the door, please. 　Please open the door.
指示： (c) Barbara: Could you tell me how to get to the post office? 　　Stranger: Certainly. **Walk** two blocks down this street. **Turn** left and **walk** three more blocks. It's on the right-hand side of the street.	
(d) **Close** the window. (e) Please **sit** down. (f) **Be** quiet! (g) **Don't walk** on the grass. (h) Please **don't wait** for me. (i) **Don't be** late.	祈使句的動詞要用原形。在例 (d) 中，句中可推知的主詞為 **you**（表說話者與之交談的對象）：Close the window = You close the window。 否定句形式： **Don't** + 原形動詞

□ **Exercise 44.** 口說（表 7-13）

第一部分 成兩人一組或分小組，閱讀以下煮飯的步驟，並將它們以合乎邏輯的順序排列 (1-9)。

1. Measure the rice. _____
2. Cook for 20 minutes. _____
3. Pour water into a pan. _____
4. Bring the water to a boil. _____
5. Put the rice in the pan. _____
6. Don't burn yourself. _____
7. Set the timer. _____
8. Turn off the heat. _____
9. Take the pan off the stove. _____

第二部分 寫出烹煮某樣簡單食物的說明文字，並與全班同學分享這份食譜。

□ **Exercise 45.** 聽力（表 7-13）

第一部分 聆聽 CD 中數字遊戲的步驟，並寫下聽到的動詞。
在開始前，你可以先確定自己是否認識這些字：*add*、*subtract*、*multiply*、*double*。

CD 2
Track 16

遊戲的步驟：

1. _____ down the number of the month you were born. For example,

   _____ the number 2 if you were born in February.

   _____ 3 if you were born in March, etc.

2. _____ the number.

3. _____ 5 to it.

4. _____ it by 50.

5. _____ your age.

6. _____ 250.

第二部分 現在遵循第一部分的步驟，完成此遊戲。在最後得到的數字中，右邊數來的前兩位數將會是你的年齡，而左邊數來第一位或前二位數字將會是你出生的月份。

第一部分　閱讀以下文章，並刪去不適用於自己國家的工作面試建議；然後，再將建議增加到 10 個。

How to Make a Good Impression in a Job Interview

　　Do you want to know how to make a good impression when you interview for a job? Here are some suggestions for you to consider.

1. Dress appropriately for the company. Flip-flops and shorts, for example, are usually not appropriate.
2. Be sure to arrive early. Employers like punctual workers.
3. Bring extra copies of your résumé and references. There may be more than one interviewer.
4. Make eye contact with the interviewer. It shows confidence.
5. Don't chew gum during the interview.
6. Research the company before you go. That way you can show your knowledge and interest in the company.

　　If you follow these suggestions, you will have a better chance of making a good impression when you go for a job interview.

第二部分　寫一篇含有三個段落的文章。可運用第一部分的主題，或提供概略性的建議給想要⋯⋯的人們。

1. improve their health.
2. get good grades.
3. improve their English.
4. find a job.
5. get a good night's sleep.
6. protect the environment by recycling.

使用下列範例。
I. Introductory paragraph: *Do you want to . . . ? Here are some suggestions for you to consider.*
II. Middle paragraph: (List the suggestions and add details.)
III. Final paragraph: *If you follow these suggestions, you will . . . .*

❑ **Exercise 47. 暖身活動** (表 7-14)

勾選 (✓) 提出建議的句子。

1. _____ Why do bears hibernate?
2. _____ I have a day off. Why don't we
   take the kids to the zoo?
3. _____ Let's go see the bears at the zoo.

7-14 提出建議：*Let's* 與 *Why Don't*	
(a) — It's hot today. ***Let's*** go to the beach. — Okay. Good idea. (b) — It's hot today. ***Why don't we*** go to the beach? — Okay. Good idea.	***Let's*** 和 ***Why don't we*** 用於建議你和另一個人去做某些活動。 例 (a) 與例 (b) 同義。 ***Let's*** = let us
(c) — I'm tired. — ***Why don't you*** take a nap? — That's a good idea. I think I will.	在例 (c) 中，***Why don't you*** 用來提出友善的提議或建議。

❑ **Exercise 48. 口說** (表 7-14)

用 ***Let's*** 或 ***Why don't we*** 作為給予建議的開頭用語。

1. Where should we go for dinner tonight?
2. Who should we ask to join us for dinner tonight?
3. What time should we meet at the restaurant?
4. Where should we go afterwards?

❑ **Exercise 49. 口說** (表 7-14)

分小組練習。組長負責陳述問題，其他組員則用 ***Why don't you*** 開頭，給予建議。

1. I'm freezing.
2. I'm feeling dizzy.
3. I feel like doing something interesting and fun this weekend. Any ideas?
4. I need to get more exercise, but I get bored with indoor activities. Any suggestions?
5. I haven't done my assignment for Professor Lopez. It will take me a couple of hours, and class starts in an hour. What am I going to do?
6. I've lost the key to my apartment, so I can't get in. My roommate is at the library. What am I going to do?
7. My friend and I had an argument, and now we aren't talking to each other. I've had some time to think about it, and I'm sorry for what I said. I miss her friendship. What should I do?

❏ **Exercise 50. 聽力** (表 7-14)

CD 2
Track 17

聆聽 CD 中一對情侶談及如何安排夜晚活動的對話；再聽一次，並將下列各提議正確排序 (1-3)。

建議：

1. go to a restaurant _____

2. go dancing _____

3. go to a movie _____

❏ **Exercise 51. 暖身活動** (表 7-15)

勾選 (✓) 符合自身情況的敘述。

1. _____ I prefer fruit to vegetables.

2. _____ I like raw vegetables better than cooked.

3. _____ I would rather eat vegetables than meat.

7-15 表示偏好：*Prefer, Like . . . Better, Would Rather*

(a) I **prefer** apples **to** oranges. (b) I **prefer** watching TV **to** studying.	**prefer** + 名詞 + **to** + 名詞 **prefer** + 動詞 *-ing* + **to** + 動詞 *-ing*
(c) I **like** apples **better than** oranges. (d) I **like** watching TV **better than** studying.	**like** + 名詞 + **better than** + 名詞 **like** + 動詞 *-ing* + **better than** + 動詞 *-ing*
(e) Ann **would rather have** an apple than an orange. (f) 錯誤：*Ann would rather has an apple.* (g) I'd rather visit a big city **than live** there. (h) 錯誤：*I'd rather visit a big city than to live there.* 錯誤：*I'd rather visit a big city than living there.*	**would rather** 後面直接加原形動詞（如：*have*、*visit*、*live*），如：例 (e)。 **than** 後面也要直接加原形動詞，如：例 (g)。
(i) **I'd/You'd/She'd/He'd/We'd/They'd** rather have an apple.	**would** 的縮寫 = **'d**
(j) **Would you rather** have an apple **or** an orange?	在例 (j) 中，禮貌問句中的 **would rather** 後面可接 **or**，以提供對方其他選擇。

❏ **Exercise 52. 文法** (表 7-15)

用 **than** 或 **to** 完成下列句子。

1. When I'm hot and thirsty, I **prefer** cold drinks __*to*__ hot drinks.

2. When I'm hot and thirsty, I **like** cold drinks **better** __*than*__ hot drinks.

3. When I'm hot and thirsty, I'd **rather have** a cold drink __*than*__ a hot drink.

4. I **prefer** tea _____ coffee.

5. I **like** tea **better** _____ coffee.

6. **I'd rather** drink tea _____ coffee.

7. When I choose a book, **I prefer** nonfiction _____ fiction.

8. **I like** folk music **better** _____ rock and roll.

9. My parents **would rather work** _____ retire. They enjoy their jobs.

10. Do you **like** spring **better** _____ fall?

11. **I prefer visiting** my friends in the evening _____ watching TV by myself.

12. **I would rather read** a book in the evening _____ visit with friends.

❑ **Exercise 53.** 口說：兩人一組（表 7-15）
　成兩人一組，並輪流作問答練習；務必以完整句回答問題。

例：Which do you prefer: apples or oranges?★
　→ *I prefer oranges to apples.*

Which do you like better: bananas or strawberries?
→ *I like bananas better than strawberries.*

Which would you rather have right now: an apple or a banana?
→ *I'd rather have a banana.*

1. Which do you like better: rice or potatoes?
2. Which do you prefer: peas or corn?
3. Which would you rather have for dinner tonight: fish or chicken?
4. Name two sports. Which do you like better?
5. Name two movies. Which one would you rather see?
6. What kind of music would you rather listen to: rock or classical?
7. Name two vegetables. Which do you prefer?
8. Name two TV programs. Which do you like better?

❑ **Exercise 54.** 口說：訪談（表 7-15）
　訪問你的同學，並用 ***would rather . . . than*** 回答問題。

Would you rather . . .
1. live in an apartment or in a house?★★ Why?
2. be an author or an artist? Why?
3. drive a fast car or fly a small plane? Why?
4. be rich and unlucky in love or poor and lucky in love? Why?
5. surf the Internet or watch TV? Why?
6. have a big family or a small family? Why?
7. be a bird or a fish? Why?
8. spend your free time with other people or be by yourself? Why?

★唸出後面例句中第一個選擇時，用上揚語調；唸第二個選擇用下降語調 ，如：*Which do you prefer, apples or oranges?*

★★在 ***than*** 之後可以重複使用介系詞，但不是必要。
　　正確：*I'd rather live in an apartment **than in a house**.*
　　正確：*I'd rather live in an apartment **than a house**.*

圈選可完成下列句子的正確答案。

例：A: My cat won't eat.
　　B: You _____ call the vet.
　　　　a. will　　　　(b.) had better　　　　c. may

1.　A: Does this pen belong to you?
　　B: No. It _____ be Susan's. She was sitting at that desk.
　　　　a. had better　　　　b. will　　　　c. must

2.　A: Let's go to a movie this evening.
　　B: That sounds like fun, but I can't. I _____ finish a report before I go to bed tonight.
　　　　a. have got to　　　　b. would rather　　　　c. ought to

3.　A: Hey, Pietro. What's up* with Ken? Is he upset about something?
　　B: He's angry because you recommended Ann instead of him for the promotion. You
　　　_____ sit down with him and explain your reasons. At least that's what I think.
　　　　a. should　　　　b. will　　　　c. can

4.　A: Does Omar want to go with us to the film festival tonight?
　　B: No. He _____ go to a wrestling match than the film festival.
　　　　a. could　　　　b. would rather　　　　c. prefers

5.　A: I did it! I did it! I got my driver's license!
　　B: Congratulations, Michelle. I'm really proud of you.
　　A: Thanks, Dad. Now _____ I have the car tonight? Please, please?
　　B: No. You're not ready for that quite yet.
　　　　a. will　　　　b. should　　　　c. may

6.　A: I just tripped on your carpet and almost fell. It's loose right by the door. You _____ fix
　　　it before someone gets hurt.
　　B: Yes, Uncle Ben. I should. I will. I'm sorry. Are you all right?
　　　　a. can　　　　b. ought to　　　　c. may

7.　A: Are you going to the conference in Atlanta next month?
　　B: I _____ . It's sort of iffy** right now. I've applied for travel money, but who knows what
　　　my supervisor will do.
　　　　a. will　　　　b. have to　　　　c. might

8.　A: What shall we do after the meeting this evening?
　　B: _____ pick Jan up and all go out to dinner together.
　　　　a. Why don't　　　　b. Let's　　　　c. Should

9.　A: What shall we do after that?
　　B: _____ we go back to my place for dessert.
　　　　a. Why don't　　　　b. Let's　　　　c. Should

---

*What's up? = What's going on?，意指「發生什麼事了？」或「怎麼了？」

**iffy = uncertain; doubtful，意指「不確定的」。

10. A: Have you seen my denim jacket? I _____ find it.
    B: Look in the hall closet.
       a. may not   b. won't   c. can't

11. A: Bye, Mom. I'm going to go play soccer with my friends.
    B: Wait a minute, young man! You _____ do your chores first.
       a. had better not   b. have to   c. would rather

12. A: Do you think that Scott will quit his job?
    B: I don't know. He _____. He's very angry. We'll just have to wait and see.
       a. must   b. may   c. will

13. A: The hotel provides towels, you know. You _____ pack a towel in your suitcase.
    B: This is my bathrobe, not a towel.
       a. don't have to   b. must not   c. couldn't

14. A: Did you climb to the top of the Statue of Liberty when you were in New York?
    B: No, I didn't. My knee was very sore, and I _____ climb all those stairs.
       a. might not   b. couldn't   c. must not

15. A: Rick, _____ work for me this evening? I'll take your shift tomorrow.
    B: Sure. I was going to ask you to work for me tomorrow anyway.
       a. should you   b. could you   c. do you have to

16. A: What are you children doing? Stop! You _____ play with sharp knives.
    B: Why not?
       a. must not   b. couldn't   c. don't have to

17. A: Don't wait for me. I _____ late.
    B: Okay.
       a. maybe   b. can be   c. may be

18. A: The Bensons are giving their daughter a new skateboard for her birthday.
    B: They _____ give her a helmet, too. She does some dangerous things on a skateboard.
       a. had better   b. can't   c. would rather

第八章

連接詞

❑ **Exercise 1. 暖身活動** (表 8-1)

勾選 (✓) 下列正確使用標點符號的句子。

1. _____ I ate an apple, and an orange.
2. _____ I ate an apple and an orange.
3. _____ I ate an apple, an orange, and a banana.
4. _____ I ate an apple, Nina ate a peach.
5. _____ I ate an apple, and Nina ate a peach.

(手寫筆記)
Conj.
對等 → 子句可單獨存在
　and so
　or neither
　but
從屬 → ⋯不⋯
　because
　when
　if

; = , + and

8-1 連接詞 *And* 的用法

連接句中的字詞

(a) 不加逗點：I saw a cat **and** a mouse. (b) 加逗點：I saw a cat, a mouse, **and** a dog.	當 **and** 在句中只連接「兩個字」(或片語)時，「不需加逗點」，如：例 (a)。 當 **and** 連接「三個或三個以上」的詞彙時，則要「加逗點」，如：例 (b)。★

連接兩個句子

(c) 加逗點：I saw a cat, **and** you saw a mouse.	當 **and** 連接兩個完整句 (亦稱「獨立」子句) 時，通常用「逗點」隔開，如：例 (c)。
(d) 句點：I saw a cat. You saw a mouse. (e) 錯誤：*I saw a cat, you saw a mouse.*	在不以 **and** 連接的情形下，兩個完整句子由「句點」分開，而非逗點，如：例 (d)。★★ 完整句子是以大寫字母開頭，注意例 (d) 中的第一個字母 *You* 是大寫。

★在連續三個或三個以上的項目中，**and** 之前的逗點可省略。
　亦正確：*I saw a cat, a mouse and a dog.*
★★在英式英文中，"period" (句點) 稱作 "full stop"。

將 ***and*** 所連接的字詞劃<u>底線</u>，並標明其詞性（名詞、動詞、形容詞）；視情況在正確的位置加逗點。

              noun + *noun*
1. My mom puts <u>milk</u> and <u>sugar</u> in her tea. → (*no commas needed*)

             noun + *noun* + *noun*
2. My mom puts <u>milk</u>**,** <u>sugar</u>**,** and <u>lemon</u> in her tea. → (*commas needed*)

3. The river is wide and deep.

4. The river is wide deep and dangerous.

5. The teenage girls at the slumber* party played music ate pizza and told ghost stories.

6. The teenage girls played music and ate pizza.

7. My mom dad sister and grandfather came to the party to see my son and daughter celebrate their fourth birthday.

8. When he wanted to entertain the children, my husband mooed like a cow roared like a lion and barked like a dog.

❏ **Exercise 3. 口說與寫作：訪談** (表 8-1)

訪問班上一位同學，同時做筆記；然後用 ***and*** 寫成完整的句子。最後，與全班同學分享一些答案。

What are . . .
1. your three favorite sports?
2. three adjectives that describe the weather today?
3. four cities that you would like to visit?
4. two characteristics that describe this city or town?
5. five things you did this morning?
6. three things you are afraid of?
7. two or more things that make you happy?
8. three or more adjectives that describe the people in your country?
9. the five most important qualities of a good parent?

---

*slumber = sleep，意指「睡眠」；在睡衣派對 (slumber party) 上，朋友們聚在一起過夜。

Exercise 4. 文法 (表 8-1)

在正確的位置加上逗點及句點，並視情況將字母改爲大寫。

1. The rain fell. The wind blew.

2. The rain fell, and the wind blew.★

3. I talked he listened.

4. I talked to Ryan about his school grades and he listened to me carefully.

5. The five most common words in English are *the and of to* and *a*.

6. The man asked a question the woman answered it.

7. The man asked a question and the woman answered it.

8. Rome is an Italian city it has a mild climate and many interesting attractions.

9. You should visit Rome its climate is mild and there are many interesting attractions.

❑ **Exercise 5. 暖身活動** (表 8-2)

用自己的話完成符合自身狀況的句子。

1. When I'm not sure of the meaning of a word in English, I _____

_____ or _____ .

2. Sometimes I don't understand native speakers of English, but I _____

_____ .

8-2 連接詞 *But* 和 *Or* 的用法

(a) I *went* to bed *but couldn't* sleep.	***and***、***but*** 和 ***or*** 都稱爲「對等連接詞」★。
(b) Is a lemon *sweet or sour*?	***but*** 和 ***or*** 的用法與 ***and*** 相同，都是在句子中連接對等詞彙。
(c) Did you order *coffee, tea, or milk*?	若連接的詞彙爲三個或三個以上，就需加逗點，如：例 (c)。
I dropped the vase. = 句子 *It didn't break.* = 句子	當 ***but*** 或 ***or*** 連接兩個完整（獨立的）句子時，常會加逗點，如：例 (d) 和 (e)。
(d) I dropped the vase, ***but*** it didn't break.	除非是正式的寫作，不然連接詞也可以置於句首。
(e) Do we have class on Monday, ***or*** is Monday a holiday?	亦正確：I dropped the vase. But it didn't break. I saw a cat. And you saw a mouse.

★當 ***and*** 連接兩個很短的獨立子句時，逗點有時亦可省略。

此句亦無誤：*The rain fell **and** the wind blew.*（沒有逗點）

在較長的句子中，逗點可幫助閱讀也很常見。

Exercise 6. 文法 (表 8-1 和 8-2)

用 ***and***、***but*** 或 ***or*** 完成下列句子，並視情況在正確的位置加上逗點。

1. I washed my shirt, __*but*__ it didn't get clean.

2. Would you like some water __*or*__ some fruit juice?

3. I bought some paper, a birthday card, __*and*__ some envelopes.

4. The flight attendants served dinner __, *but*__ I didn't eat it.

5. I was hungry __*but*__ didn't eat on the plane. The food didn't look appetizing.

6. I washed my face, brushed my teeth __, *and*__ combed my hair.

7. Golf __*and*__ tennis are popular sports.

8. Sara is a good tennis player __, *but*__ she's never played golf.

9. Which would you prefer? Would you like to play tennis __*or*__ golf Saturday?

10. Who made the call? Did Bob call you __, *or*__ did you call Bob?

❑ **Exercise 7.** 文法 (表 8-1 和 8-2)

在正確的位置加上逗點或句點，並視情況將字母改為大寫。

Electronic devices★ on airplanes

1. Laptops are electronic devices. ¢ell phones are electronic devices.

2. Laptops and portable DVD players are electronic devices but flashlights aren't.

3. Passengers can't use these electronic devices during takeoffs and landings they can use them the rest of the flight.

4. During takeoffs and landings, airlines don't allow passengers to use laptops DVD players electronic readers or PDAs.★★

5. The devices may cause problems with the navigation system and they may cause problems with the communication system.

❑ **Exercise 8.** 暖身活動 (表 8-3)

將 A 欄句子及能與該欄組成合理語義的 B 欄項目配對。

A 欄	**B 欄**
1. I was tired, so I _____.	a. didn't sleep
2. I was tired, but I _____.	b. slept

★*device* 意指「設備，裝置」，通常為有特定用途的用電物品或電子類產品。

★★*PDA* = personal digital assistant，意指「個人數位助理」，為一種掌上型電腦。

8-3 連接詞 *So* 的用法

(a) The room was dark**,** *so* I turned on a light.	*so* 可作爲連接詞，前面要加逗點，如：例 (a)。它可連接兩個獨立子句，用以表示「結果」： 原因：*The room was dark.* 結果：*I turned on a light.*
(b) 比較： The room was dark**,** *but* I didn't turn on a light.	*but* 通常表示意料之外的結果，如：例 (b)。

❑ **Exercise 9. 文法** (表 8-2 和 8-3)
用 **so** 或 **but** 完成下列句子。

1. It began to rain, __so__ I opened my umbrella.

2. It began to rain, __but__ I didn't open my umbrella.

3. I didn't have an umbrella, _____ I got wet.

4. I didn't have an umbrella, _____ I didn't get wet because I was wearing my raincoat.

5. The water was cold, _____ I went swimming anyway.

6. The water was cold, _____ I didn't go swimming.

7. Scott's directions to his apartment weren't clear, _____ Sonia got lost.

8. The directions weren't clear, _____ I found Scott's apartment anyway.

9. My friend lied to me, _____ I still like and trust her.

10. My friend lied to me, _____ I don't trust her anymore.

❑ **Exercise 10. 文法** (表 8-1 → 8-3)
在正確的位置加上逗點或句點，並視情況將字母改爲大寫。

Surprising animal facts:

1. Some tarantulas* can go two and a half years without food. when they eat, they like grasshoppers beetles small spiders and sometimes small lizards.

2. A female elephant is pregnant for approximately twenty months and almost always has only one baby a young elephant stays close to its mother for the first ten years of its life.

---

tarantula 意指「塔蘭托毒蛛」或「狼蛛」。

3. Dolphins sleep with one eye open they need to be conscious or awake in order to breathe if they fall asleep when they are breathing, they will drown so they sleep with half their brain awake and one eye open.

❑ **Exercise 11.** 聽力與文法 (表 8-1 → 8-3)

CD 2
Track 18

聆聽 CD 播放的文章，然後在正確的位置加上逗點或句點，並視情況將字母改為大寫。再聽一遍播放內容，並檢查答案。在開始前，你可以先確定自己是否認識這些字：*blinker*、*do a good deed*、*motioned*、*wave someone on*。

Paying It Forward*

(1)　　A few days ago, a friend and I were driving from Benton Harbor to Chicago.

(2)　　We didn't have any delays for the first hour but we ran into some highway construction

(3)　near Chicago the traffic wasn't moving my friend and I sat and waited we talked about

(4)　our jobs our families and the terrible traffic slowly it started to move

(5)　　we noticed a black sports car on the shoulder its right blinker was blinking the driver

(6)　obviously wanted to get back into traffic car after car passed without letting him in I

(7)　decided to do a good deed so I motioned for him to get in line ahead of me he waved

(8)　thanks and I waved back at him

(9)　　all the cars had to stop at a toll booth a short way down the road I held out my

(10)　money to pay my toll but the toll-taker just smiled and waved me on she told me that the

(11)　man in the black sports car had already paid my toll wasn't that a nice way of saying

(12)　thank you?

*paying it forward 意指「在別人為你做了件好事後，你也為別人做件好事」；舉例來講，想像你站在一處咖啡攤前，等著要買杯咖啡，排在前面的人在和你聊天時，幫你付了咖啡錢；然後，你也幫下一個人付咖啡錢。這樣的行為就是 *paying it forward*。*paying it forward* 的語義與 *paying it back*（償還負債或盡義務）正好相反。

❏ **Exercise 12. 暖身活動** (表 8-4)
用符合自身實際狀況的敍述，完成下列句子。

1. I like ___fish___, but ___my sister___ doesn't.

2. I don't like _____, but _____ does.

3. I've seen _____, but _____ hasn't.

4. I'm not _____, but _____ is.

8-4 *But* 之後的助動詞用法

(a) I **don't like** coffee, **but** my husband **does**.	**but** 後面連接的句子中，通常會以助動詞代替主要的動詞片語，且其時態和人稱會與主要動詞相同。
(b) I **like** tea, **but** my husband **doesn't**.	
(c) I **won't be** here tomorrow, **but** Sue **will**.	在例 (a) 中，**does** = *likes coffee*
(d) I'**ve seen** that movie, **but** Joe **hasn't**.	在下列例句中要注意：
(e) He **isn't** here, **but** she **is**.*	否定句 + **but** + 肯定句
	肯定句 + **but** + 否定句

*接在 **but** 和 **and** 之後的句尾動詞，不與代名詞合併縮寫。
正確：... *but she is.*
錯誤：... *but she's.*

❏ **Exercise 13. 文法** (表 8-4)
第一部分 用正確的否定助動詞，完成下列句子。

1. Alan reads a lot of books, but his brother ___doesn't___.

2. Alan reads a lot of books, but his brothers ___don't___.

3. Alan is reading a book, but his brother ___isn't___.

4. Alan is reading a book, but his brothers _____.

5. Alan read a book last week, but his brother(s) ___didn't___.

6. Alan has read a book recently, but his brother _____.

7. Alan has read a book recently, but his brothers ___haven't___.

8. Alan is going to read a book soon, but his brother _____.

9. Alan is going to read a book soon, but his brothers ___aren't___.

10. Alan will read a book soon, but his brother(s) ___won't___.

第二部分 用正確的肯定助動詞，完成下列句子。

1. Nicole doesn't eat red meat, but her sister ___does___.

2. Nicole doesn't eat red meat, but her sisters ___do___.

3. Nicole isn't eating red meat, but her sister _____.

4. Nicole isn't eating red meat, but her sisters _____.

5. Nicole didn't eat red meat last night, but her sister(s) _____.

6. Nicole hasn't eaten red meat recently, but her sister _____.

7. Nicole hasn't eaten red meat recently, but her sisters _____.

8. Nicole isn't going to eat red meat soon, but her sister _____.

9. Nicole isn't going to eat red meat soon, but her sisters _____.

10. Nicole won't eat red meat soon, but her sister(s) _____.

❏ **Exercise 14. 口說** (表 8-4)
用恰當的助動詞，完成符合班上同學實際狀況的句子。你可以訪問他們，以獲得更多資訊。

1. _____Kira_____ has long hair, but _____Yuki doesn't_____.

2. _____ isn't hungry right now, but _____.

3. _____ lives nearby, but _____.

4. _____ can speak (*a language*) _____, but _____.

5. _____ plays a musical instrument, but _____.

6. _____ wasn't here last year, but _____.

7. _____ will be at home tonight, but _____.

8. _____ doesn't wear a ring, but _____.

9. _____ didn't study here last year, but _____.

10. _____ has lived here for a long time, but _____.

❏ **Exercise 15. 聽力** (表 8-4)
用恰當的助動詞，完成下列句子。

CD 2
Track 19

A strong storm

例：你會聽到：My husband saw a tree fall, but I . . .
　　你要寫下：___*didn't*___.

1. _____.　　5. _____.

2. _____.　　6. _____.

3. _____.　　7. _____.

4. _____.　　8. _____.

將下列各句與正確的圖片相配對。注意：其中一張圖無法與任一句子配對。

A 圖　　　　　　　　　B 圖　　　　　　　　　C 圖

1. _____ Alice has a motorcycle, and her husband does too.

2. _____ Alice has a motorcycle, and so does her husband.

3. _____ Alice doesn't have a motorcycle, and her husband doesn't either.

4. _____ Alice doesn't have a motorcycle, and neither does her husband.

8-5　*And + Too, So, Either, Neither* 的用法

(a) Sue works, *and* **Tom does too.**　 　　主詞 + 助動詞 + *too*	在肯定句中，「助動詞 + *too*」或「*so* + 助動詞」可用於 *and* 之後。
(b) Sue works, *and* **so does Tom.**　 　　*so* + 助動詞 + 主詞	例 (a) 與例 (b) 同義。 詞序： 　主詞 + 助動詞 + *too* 　*so* + 助動詞 + 主詞
(c) Ann doesn't work, *and* **Joe doesn't either.** 　　主詞 + 助動詞 + *EITHER*	「助動詞 + *either*」或「*neither* + 助動詞」要與否定句一起使用。
(d) Ann doesn't work, *and* **neither does Joe.** 　　*NEITHER* + 助動詞 + 主詞	例 (c) 與例 (d) 同義。 詞序： 　主詞 + 助動詞 + *either* 　*neither* + 助動詞 + 主詞 注意：*neither* 要與肯定助動詞連用。
(e) — I'm hungry. 　　— *I am too. / So am I.* (f) — I don't eat meat. 　　— *I don't either. / Neither do I.*	當兩人對話時，通常不會用 *and*。
(g) — I'm hungry. 　　— *Me too.*（非正式） (h) — I don't eat meat. 　　— *Me (n)either.*（非正式）	*me too*、*me either* 和 *me neither* 常用於非正式的口語英文中。

Exercise 17. 文法 (表 8-5)

用下列各題提供的字詞，完成句子。要特別注意詞序。

| Omar | James | Marco | Ivan |

1. a. too   Marco has a mustache, and   *James does too*   .

   b. so   Marco has a mustache, and _____.

2. a. either   Omar doesn't have a mustache, and _____.

   b. neither   Omar doesn't have a mustache, and _____.

3. a. too   Marco is wearing a hat, and _____.

   b. so   Marco is wearing a hat, and _____.

4. a. either   Ivan isn't wearing a hat, and _____.

   b. neither   Ivan isn't wearing a hat, and _____.

❑ **Exercise 18. 文法** (表 8-5)

第一部分 用正確的肯定助動詞，完成下列句子。

1. Andy walks to work, and his roommate ___*does*___ too.

2. Andy walks to work, and his roommates _____*do*_____ too.

3. Andy is walking to work, and his roommate _____ too.

4. Andy is walking to work, and his roommates _____*are*_____ too.

5. Andy walked to work last week, and his roommate(s) _____ too.

6. Andy has walked to work recently, and so _____*has*_____ his roommate.

7. Andy has walked to work recently, and so _____ his roommates.

8. Andy is going to walk to work tomorrow, and so _____*is*_____ his roommate.

9. Andy is going to walk to work tomorrow, and so _____ his roommates.

10. Andy will walk to work tomorrow, and so _____*will*_____ his roommate(s).

第二部分　用正確的否定助動詞，完成下列句子。

1. Karen doesn't watch TV, and her sister ___doesn't___ either.

2. Karen doesn't watch TV, and her sisters _____ either.

3. Karen isn't watching TV, and her sister _____ either.

4. Karen isn't watching TV, and her sisters _____ either.

5. Karen didn't watch TV last night, and her sister(s) _____ either.

6. Karen hasn't watched TV recently, and neither _____ her sister.

7. Karen hasn't watched TV recently, and neither _____ her sisters.

8. Karen isn't going to watch TV tomorrow, neither _____ her sister.

9. Karen isn't going to watch TV tomorrow, and neither _____ her sisters.

10. Karen won't watch TV tomorrow, and neither _____ her sister(s).

❏ **Exercise 19. 口說與寫作** (表 8-5)

分小組練習；用 *too*、*so*、*either* 或 *neither* 完成符合實際狀況的句子。你可以去搜尋能正確作答的相關資料。

1. Haiti is a small country, and ___Cuba is too_____.

2. Japan produces rice, and _____.

3. Turkey has had many strong earthquakes, and _____.

4. Iceland doesn't grow coffee, and _____.

5. Most Canadian children will learn more than one language, and _____

_____.

6. Norway joined the United Nations in 1945, and _____.

7. Argentina doesn't lie on the equator, and _____.

8. Somalia lies on the Indian Ocean, and _____.

9. Monaco has never* hosted the Olympic Games, and _____.

10. South Korea had a Nobel Prize winner in 2000, and _____.

---

*加上 *never* 即可成爲否定句，例：The teacher is *never* late, and *neither* am I. 或 I'm *not either*.

❑ **Exercise 20. 口說：兩人一組** (表 8-5)

成兩人一組；說話者 A 說出各題中的句子，說話者 B 則用 *so* 或 *neither* 附和說話者 A。

例：I'm confused.
說話者 A（書打開）：I'm confused.
說話者 B（書闔上）：So am I.

1. I studied last night.
2. I study grammar every day.
3. I'd like a cup of coffee.
4. I'm not hungry.
5. I've never seen a vampire.
6. Running is an aerobic activity.
7. Snakes don't have legs.
8. Coffee contains caffeine.

角色互換。

9. I overslept this morning.
10. I don't like mushrooms.
11. Swimming is an Olympic sport.
12. Denmark doesn't have any volcanoes.
13. I've never touched a crocodile.
14. Chickens lay eggs.
15. Elephants can swim.
16. I'd rather go to (*name of a place*) than (*name of a place*).

❑ **Exercise 21. 聽力與口說** (表 8-5)

 如果你不同意別人的陳述，可使用下列的答覆方式。

CD 2
Track 20

第一部分 聆聽 CD 播出的範例；聽的同時，請留意 4-6 題中說話者 B 表達反對意見時的句子重音。

想獲得更多資訊：

1. A: I'm going to drop this class.
   B: **You are? Why? What's the matter?**

2. A: My laptop doesn't have enough memory for this application.
   B: **Really? Are you sure?**

3. A: I can read Braille.
   B: **You can? How did you learn to do that?**

表達反對的意見：

4. A: I love this weather.
   B: **I don't.**

5. A: I didn't like the movie.
   B: **I did!**

6. A: I'm excited about graduation.
   B: **I'm not.**

第二部分 成兩人一組；學生 A 說陳述句，學生 B 發問以獲得更多資訊。兩人輪流陳述下列句子。

1. I'm feeling tired.
2. I don't like grammar.
3. I've seen a ghost.
4. I didn't eat breakfast this morning.
5. I haven't slept well all week.
6. I'm going to leave class early.

第三部分 現在輪流針對下列陳述句，表達反對意見。

7. I believe in ghosts.
8. I didn't study hard for the last test.
9. I'm going to exercise for an hour today.
10. I like strawberries.
11. I haven't worked very hard this week.
12. I don't enjoy birthdays.

❑ **Exercise 22. 口說** (表 8-4 和 8-5)
根據班上同學的實際狀況，用 **and**、**but** 和恰當的助動詞造句。你可以訪問他們，以獲得更多的資訊。

1. _____Kunio_____ lives in an apartment, and _____Boris does too_____.

2. _____Ellen_____ is wearing jeans, but _____Ricardo isn't_____.

3. _____ is absent today, but _____.

4. _____ didn't live here last year, and _____ either.

5. _____ can cook, and _____ too.

6. _____ has a baseball cap, and _____ too.

7. _____ doesn't have a motorcycle, and _____ either.

8. _____ doesn't have a pet, but _____.

9. _____ will get up early tomorrow, but _____.

10. _____ has studied English for more than a year, and _____ too.

❑ **Exercise 23. 暖身活動** (表 8-6)
圈選能完成合理句子的答案。

Because Roger felt tired, _____.

   a. he took a nap.   c. he went to bed early.

   b. he didn't take a nap.   d. he didn't go to bed early.

8-6 連接詞 *Because* 的用法

(a) He drank water *because* he was thirsty.	*because* 表示原因，提供解釋。他爲何要喝水呢？原因：他口渴。
(b) 主要子句：*He drank water.*	主要子句是完整句子： *He drank water* = 完整句子
(c) 副詞子句：*because he was thirsty*	副詞子句「不是」完整的句子： *because he was thirsty* =「非」完整句子 *because* 引導副詞子句： *because* + 主詞 + 動詞 = 副詞子句
(d) <u>主要子句</u>　　　<u>副詞子句</u> He drank water *because* he was thirsty. 　　　（不加逗點） (e) <u>副詞子句</u>　　　<u>主要子句</u> *Because* he was thirsty, he drank water. 　　　（加逗點）	副詞子句需依附主要子句，如：例 (d) 和例 (e)。 在例 (d) 中，主要子句 + 無逗點 + 副詞子句 在例 (e) 中，副詞子句 + 逗點 + 主要子句 例 (d) 和例 (e) 意義完全一樣。
(f) 錯誤的寫法： He drank water. *Because* he was thirsty.	例 (f) 在英文書寫中是錯誤的，因爲 *Because he was thirsty* 不是一個可單獨存在、以大寫字母開頭及以句點結尾的句子，它必須如例 (d) 和例 (e) 一樣，依附主要子句存在。
(g) 正確的口語： — Why did he drink some water? — **Because he was thirsty.**	在口語英文中，副詞子句可作爲問句的簡答，如：例 (g)。

❑ **Exercise 24. 文法** (表 8-6)

運用 *because*，以兩種不同順序合併下列各組句子；注意標點符號的使用。

1. We didn't have class. \ The teacher was absent.
   → *We didn't have class because the teacher was absent.*
   → *Because the teacher was absent, we didn't have class.*

2. The children were hungry. \ There was no food in the house.

3. The bridge is closed. \ We can't get across the river.

4. My car didn't start. \ The battery was dead.

5. Talya and Patti laughed hard. \ The joke was very funny.

❑ **Exercise 25. 文法** (表 8-6)

在正確的位置加上句點或逗點，並視情況將字母改爲大寫。

1. Jimmy is very young. ~~b~~ᴮecause he is afraid of the dark, he likes to have a light on in his bedroom at night.

2. Mr. El-Sayed had a bad cold because he was not feeling well he stayed home from the office.

3. Judy went to bed early because she was tired she likes to get at least eight hours of sleep a night.

4. Frank put his head in his hands he was angry and upset because he had lost a lot of work on his computer.

❑ **Exercise 26. 文法** (表 8-3 和 8-6)
將各題改寫爲與原句同義的句子，並在正確的位置加上逗點。

第一部分 用 *so* 改寫下列句子。

1. Wendy lost her job because she never showed up for work on time.
   → *Wendy never showed up for work on time,* so she lost her job.

2. I opened the window because the room was hot.

3. Because it was raining, I stayed indoors.

第二部分 用 *because* 改寫下列句子。

4. Jason was hungry, so he ate.
   → *Because Jason was hungry,* he ate. 或 *Jason ate because he was hungry.*

5. The water in the river is polluted, so we shouldn't go swimming there.

6. My alarm clock didn't go off,⋆ so I was late for my job interview.

❑ **Exercise 27. 文法** (表 8-1 → 8-6)
在正確的位置加上逗點或句點，並視情況將字母改爲大寫。不要更改其他字詞或詞序。

1. Jim was hot. ^H/ke sat in the shade.

2. Jim was hot and tired so he sat in the shade.

3. Jim was hot tired and thirsty.

4. Because he was hot Jim sat in the shade.

5. Because they were hot and thirsty Jim and Susan sat in the shade and drank iced-tea.

6. Jim and Susan sat in the shade and drank iced-tea because they were hot and thirsty.

7. Jim sat in the shade drank iced-tea and fanned himself with his cap because he was hot tired and thirsty.

8. Because Jim was hot he stayed under the shade of the tree but Susan went back to work.

⋆*go off* = ring，意指「響起」。

□ **Exercise 28. 聽力** (表 8-1 → 8-6)

聆聽 CD 播放的文章,在正確的位置加上逗點或句點,然後視情況將字母改為大寫。最後,再聽一遍播放內容,並檢查答案。

Understanding the Scientific Term *Matter*

The word *matter* is a chemical term. M̷atter is anything that has weight this book your finger water a rock air and the moon are all examples of matter heat and radio waves are not matter because they do not have weight happiness dreams and fears have no weight and are not matter.

□ **Exercise 29. 暖身活動** (表 8-7)

下列哪個句子的結果(以斜體字標示)與你所預期的相反?

1. Even though I didn't eat dinner last night, *I wasn't hungry this morning.*
2. Because I didn't eat dinner last night, *I was hungry this morning.*
3. Although I didn't eat dinner last night, *I wasn't hungry this morning.*

8-7 連接詞 *Even Though* 和 *Although* 的用法	
(a) **Even though** I was hungry, I did not eat. I did not eat **even though** I was hungry. (b) **Although** I was hungry, I did not eat. I did not eat **although** I was hungry.	**even though** 和 **although** 用以引導副詞子句。 例 (a) 和例 (b) 同義: I was hungry, but I did not eat.
比較: (c) **Because** I was hungry, I ate. (d) **Even though** I was hungry, I did not eat.	**because** 用在表示預期的結果,如:例 (c)。 **even though** 和 **although** 則表示意料外或相反的結果,如:例 (d)。

□ **Exercise 30. 文法** (表 8-7)

用各題提供的字詞,完成下列句子。

1. *is, isn't*

   a. Because Dan is sick, he _____ going to work.

   b. Although Dan is sick, he _____ going to work.

   c. Even though Dan is sick, he _____ going to work.

2. *went, didn't go*

   a. Even though it was late, we _____ home.

   b. Although it was late, we _____ home.

   c. Because it was late, we _____ home.

❏ **Exercise 31. 文法** (表 8-7)

用 *even though* 或 *because* 完成下列句子。

1. _____Even though_____ the weather is cold, Rick isn't wearing a coat.

2. _____Because_____ the weather is cold, Ben is wearing a coat.

3. _____ Jane was sad, she smiled.

4. _____ Jane was sad, she cried.

5. _____ it was cold outside, we went swimming in the lake.

6. _____ our friends live on an island, it isn't easy to get there by car.

7. People ask Kelly to sing at weddings _____ she has a good voice.

8. _____ I'm training for the Olympics, I biked up the mountain _____ it was starting to snow.

9. George sings loudly _____ he can't carry a tune.

❏ **Exercise 32. 文法** (表 8-6 和 8-7)

圈選最適當的答案，完成句子。

1. Even though the test was fairly easy, most of the class _____.
   a. failed
   b. passed
   c. did pretty well

2. Jack hadn't heard or read about the bank robbery even though _____.
   a. he was the robber
   b. it was on the front page of every newspaper
   c. he was out of town when it occurred

3. Although _____, she finished the race in first place.
   a. Miki was full of energy and strength
   b. Miki was leading all the way
   c. Miki was far behind in the beginning

4. We can see the light from an airplane at night before we can hear the plane because ____.

    a. light travels faster than sound

    b. airplanes travel at high speeds

    c. our eyes work better than our ears at night

5. My partner and I worked all day and late into the evening. Even though ____, we stopped at our favorite restaurant before we went home.

    a. we were very hungry

    b. we had finished our report

    c. we were very tired

6. In the mountains, melting snow in the spring runs downhill into rivers. The water carries soil and rocks. In the spring, mountain rivers become muddy rather than clear because ____.

    a. mountain tops are covered with snow

    b. the water from melting snow brings soil and rocks to the river

    c. ice is frozen water

❑ **Exercise 33.** 聽力 (表 8-6 和 8-7)

CD 2
Track 22

聆聽 CD 播放的內容，圈選最適當的答案，完成句子。

例：你會聽到：Because there was a sale at the mall, . . .

    你要圈出：a. it wasn't busy.

           ⓑ there were a lot of shoppers.

           c. prices were very high.

1. a. they were under some mail.

    b. my roommate helped me look for them.

    c. I never found them.

2. a. the rain had stopped.

    b. a storm was coming.

    c. the weather was nice.

3. a. he was sick.

    b. he had graduated already.

    c. he was happy for me.

4. a. I mailed it.

    b. I decided not to mail it.

    c. I sent it to a friend.

5. a. the coaches celebrated afterwards.

    b. the fans cheered loudly.

    c. the players didn't seem very excited.

用 *because* 或 *even though* 所組成的完整句答題。成兩人一組、分小組或全班一起練習。

例： Last night you were tired. Did you go to bed early?
  → *Yes, I went to bed early because I was tired.* 或
  → *Yes, because I was tired, I went to bed before nine.* 或
  → *No, I didn't go to bed early even though I was really sleepy.* 或
  → *No, even though I was really tired, I didn't go to bed until after midnight.*

1. Last night you were tired. Did you stay up late?
2. Vegetables are good for you. Do you eat a lot of them?
3. Space exploration is exciting. Would you like to be an astronaut?
4. What are the winters like here? Do you like living here in the winter?
5. (*A recent movie*) has had good reviews. Do you want to see it?
6. Are you a good artist? Will you draw a picture of me on the board?
7. Where does your family live? Are you going to visit them over the next holiday?

❏ **Exercise 35. 閱讀與文法**（第 8 章）

第一部分　閱讀以下文章。

The Importance of Water

What is the most common substance on earth? It isn't wood, iron, or sand. The most common substance on earth is water. Every living thing contains water. For example, a person's body is about 67 percent water, a bird's is about 75 percent water, and most fruit contains about 90 percent water.

In addition, 70 percent of the earth's surface is water. Besides being in lakes, rivers, and oceans, water is in the ground and in the air. However, most of the water in the world is saltwater. Only 3 percent of the earth's water is <u>fresh</u>, and just one percent of that is available for human use. The rest is saltwater, and people can't drink it or grow food with it.

Water is essential to life, but human beings often poison it with chemicals from industry and farming. When people pollute water, the quality of all life — plant life, animal life, and human life — suffers. Life cannot exist without fresh water, so it is essential that people take care of this important natural resource.

第二部分　用 *because*、*although*、*even though* 或 *so* 完成下列句子。

1. _____Because_____ 70 percent of the earth's surface is water and water is in every living thing, it is the most common substance on earth.

2. _____Although_____ 70 percent of the earth's surface is water, only 3 percent is fresh.

3. _____Although_____ water is everywhere, not much is available for human use.

4. Chemicals pollute water, _____so_____ it is important to keep them out of the water supply.

5. _____Because_____ water is essential to human life, people need to take care of it.

6. Water is essential to human life, _____so_____ people need to take care of it.

Exercise 36. 檢視學習成果（第 8 章）

校訂下列句子；訂正句構上的錯誤，並注意標點符號的使用。

1. Even though I was sick, ~~but~~ I went to work.

2. Gold silver and copper. They are metals.

3. The children crowded around the teacher. Because he was doing a magic trick.

4. I had a cup of coffee, and so does my friend.

5. My roommate didn't go. Neither I went either.

6. Even I was exhausted, I didn't stop working until after midnight.

7. Although I like chocolate, but I can't eat it because I'm allergic to it.

8. I like to eat raw eggs for breakfast and everybody else in my family too.

9. A hardware store sells tools and nails and plumbing supplies and paint.

10. Most insects have wings, spiders do not.

❑ **Exercise 37.** 寫作（第 8 章）

遵照下列步驟，針對你有興趣的動物，寫一篇文章：

1. 挑選一種你想深入瞭解的動物。

   提示： If you are doing your research on the Internet, type in "interesting facts about _____ ."

2. 根據你找到的資訊作筆記，如以下從某一網站擷取的資訊。

   筆記範例：

   Giraffes
   → have long necks (6 feet or 1.8 meters)
   → can reach tops of trees
   → need very little sleep (20 minutes to two hours out of 24 hours)
   → eat about 140 pounds of food a day
   → can go for weeks without drinking water
   → get a lot of water from the plants they eat
   → can grab and hold onto objects with their tongues
   → don't have vocal cords
   → can communicate with one another
     (but humans can't hear them)

3. 根據取得的事實寫下句子；用 *and*、*but*、*or*、*so*、*because*、*although* 以及 *even though* 合併一些你對該動物的想法。

例句：

Giraffes

→ Giraffes have long necks, so they can reach the tops of trees.
→ Although they eat about 140 pounds of food a day, they can go for weeks without drinking water.
→ Even though giraffes don't have vocal cords, they can communicate with one another.
→ Giraffes can communicate, but people can't hear their communication.

4. 把句子組合成段落。

段落範例：

Interesting Facts About Giraffes

Giraffes are interesting animals. They have long necks, *so* they can reach the tops of trees. They eat flowers, fruit, climbing plants, *and* the twigs and leaves from trees. *Although* they eat about 140 pounds of food a day, they can go for weeks without drinking water. They get a lot of water from the plants they eat too. They have very long tongues *and* these tongues are useful. *Because* they are so long, they can grab objects with them. *Even though* giraffes don't have vocal cords, they can communicate, *but* people can't hear their communication.

第九章
比較

as long as 只要 conj.

as soon as ─…就 conj. (when)

☐ **Exercise 1. 暖身活動** (表 9-1)
比較線段 (line) 的長度。

1. Line D is as long as Line ＿＿＿＿ .
2. Line A isn't as long as Line ＿＿＿＿ .
3. Line E is almost as long as Line ＿＿＿＿ .

Line A ＿＿＿＿＿＿＿＿＿＿＿＿＿
Line B ＿＿＿＿＿＿＿＿＿＿＿＿＿＿
Line C ＿＿＿＿＿＿＿＿
Line D ＿＿＿＿＿＿
Line E ＿＿＿＿＿

9-1 用 *As ... As* 造比較句

(a) Tina is 21 years old. Sam is also 21. Tina is **as old as** Sam (is). (b) Mike came **as quickly as** he could.	*as ... as* 用於表示所比較的兩部分，在某方面相同時。 例 (a)：*as* ＋ 形容詞 ＋ *as* 例 (b)：*as* ＋ 副詞 ＋ *as*
(c) Ted is 20. Tina is 21. Ted is **not as old as** Tina. (d) Ted is **not quite as** old as Tina. (e) Amy is 5. She is **not nearly as** old as Tina.	否定形式：**not as ... as**。★ **quite** 和 **nearly** 通常用在否定句中。 例 (d)：**not quite as ... as** ＝ 些微差異 例 (e)：**not nearly as ... as** ＝ 差異很大
(f) Sam is **just as** old as Tina. (g) Ted is **nearly/almost** as old as Tina. （幾乎）	*as ... as* 常用的修飾詞是 *just*（意指「正好」）和 *nearly/almost*。

Tina
21

Sam
21

Ted
20

Amy
5

★另一種寫法：**not so ... as**，如：*Ted is **not so** old **as** Tina.*

用 *just as*、*almost as/not quite as* 或 *not nearly as*，完成下列句子。

第一部分 比較玻璃杯內水滿的程度。

1. Glass 4 is ___almost as/not quite as___ full as Glass 2.

2. Glass 3 is ___not nearly as___ full as Glass 2.

3. Glass 1 is ___just as___ full as Glass 2.

第二部分 比較下列盒子的大小。

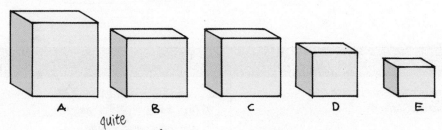

4. Box B is ___not ~~almost~~ quite as___ big as Box A.

5. Box E is ___not nearly as___ big as Box A.

6. Box C is ___just as___ big as Box B.

7. Box E is ___almost as___ big as Box D.

□ **Exercise 3. 文法** (表 9-1)

依照自己的看法，用 *as ... as* 和下表中的字詞，完成下列句子；視情況使用否定動詞。

a housefly / an ant	good health / money
a lake / an ocean	honey / sugar
a lemon / a watermelon	monkeys / people
a lion / a tiger	reading a book / listening to music
a shower / a bath	the sun / the moon

1. _An ant isn't as_ _____ big as ___ _a housefly_ _____ .

2. _A lion is as_ _____ dangerous and wild as ___ _a tiger_ _____ .

3. _____ large as _____ .

4. _____ sweet as _____ .

5. _____ important as _____ .

6. _____ quiet as _____ .

7. _____ hot as _____ .

8. _____ good at climbing trees as _____ .

9. _____ relaxing as _____ .

CD 2
Track 23

❑ **Exercise 4.** 聽力 （表 9-1）

聆聽 CD，用聽到的字詞完成下列句子。

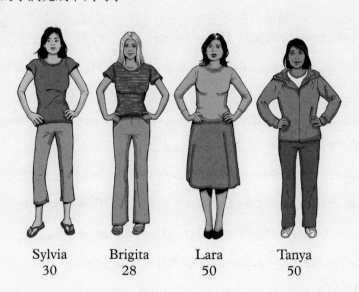

Sylvia   Brigita   Lara   Tanya
30   28   50   50

例：你會聽到：Brigita isn't as old as Lara.
你要寫下： ___ _isn't as old as_ ___

1. Lara _____ Tanya.

2. Sylvia _____ Lara.

3. Sylvia and Brigita _____ Tanya.

4. Brigita _____ Sylvia.

5. Brigita _____ Sylvia.

Exercise 5. 遊戲 (表 9-1)

在許多慣用語中常用到 *as . . . as*；而這些用語通常應用在口語上，而不是在書寫上。用提供的字詞完成下列句子，並檢視有多少是你所熟悉的。分組比賽，答對最多題的組別獲勝。

✓a bear	a cat	a hornet	a mule	an ox
a bird	a feather	a kite	a rock	the hills

ox

mule

1. When will dinner be ready? I'm **as** hungry **as** ___a bear___ .

2. Did Toshi really lift that heavy box all by himself? He must be **as** strong **as** ___an ox___ .

3. It was a lovely summer day. School was out, and there was nothing in particular that I had to do. I felt **as** free **as** ___a bird___ .

4. Marco won't change his mind. He's **as** stubborn **as** ___a mule___ .

5. How can anyone expect me to sleep in this bed? It's **as** hard **as** ___a rock___ .

6. Of course I've heard that joke before! It's **as** old **as** ___the hills___ .

7. Why are you walking back and forth? What's the matter? You're **as** nervous **as** ___a cat___ .

8. Thanks for offering to help, but I can carry the box alone. It looks heavy, but it isn't. It's **as** light **as** ___a feather___ .

9. When Erica received the good news, she felt **as** high **as** ___a kite___ .

10. A: Was he angry?

    B: You'd better believe it! He was **as** mad **as** ___a hornet___ .

hornet

❏ **Exercise 6. 暖身活動** (表 9-2)

比較以下三人的特徵。

David   Paolo   Matt

1. Paolo looks younger than _____ .

2. Matt looks younger than _____ .

3. _____ looks the youngest of all.

9-2 比較級和最高級 Comparative and Superlative

(a) "A" is **older than** "B."	比較級用在比較「這個」和「那個」或「這些」和「那些」。
(b) "A" and "B" are **older than** "C" and "D."	形式：字尾加 **-er** 或在形容詞前面加 **more**（請見表 9-3）。
(c) Ed is **more generous than** his brother.	注意：比較級<u>後面要接</u> **than**。
(d) "A," "B," "C," and "D" are sisters. "A" is **the oldest** of all four sisters.	最高級用在比較總體的一部分和所有剩下的其他部分。
(e) A woman in Turkey claims to be **the oldest person** in the world.	形式：加 **-est** 或加 **most**（各種形式變化，請見表 9-3）。
(f) Ed is **the most generous person** in his family.	注意：最高級的前面要加 **the**。

❏ **Exercise 7. 遊戲** (表 9-2)

分組比賽；判斷下列句子是正確的 (T) 還是錯誤的 (F)。答對最多題的組別獲勝。

1. Canada is larger than France.	Ⓣ	F
2. Russia and Canada are the largest countries in the world.	Ⓣ	F
3. The South Pole is generally colder than the North Pole.	Ⓣ	F
4. The Pacific Ocean is the coldest ocean in the world.	T	Ⓕ
5. The Mediterranean Sea is the biggest sea of all.	T	F
6. In general, Libya is hotter than Mexico.	T	F
7. Africa is larger than Asia.	T	F
8. Argentina has the highest and lowest points in South America.	Ⓣ	F
9. The nearest continent to Antarctica is Australia.	T	Ⓕ
10. The longest country in the world is Chile.	Ⓣ	F

❏ **Exercise 8. 聽力** (表 9-1 和 9-2)

CD 2
Track 24

聆聽 CD 播放的句子，如果你認同，圈 *yes*；不認同，圈 *no*。在開始前，你可以先確定自己是否認識這些字：*talkative*、*cooked*、*tasty*、*raw*。

1. yes　　no

2. yes　　no

3. yes　　no

4. yes　　no

5. yes　　no

6. yes　　no

7. yes　　no

8. yes　　no

❏ **Exercise 9. 暖身活動** (表 9-3)

比較下列三種筆跡範例。

A: *The meeting shines at eight!*

B: *The meeting suites at eight*

C: *The meeting starts at eight!*

1.　__C__ is neater than __A (or B)__ .

2.　____ is messier than _____ .

3.　____ is more readable than _____ .

4.　____ is better than _____ .

5.　____ is the best.

6.　____ is the worst.

7.　____ wrote more carefully than _____ .

9-3 形容詞與副詞的比較級和最高級形式

		比較級	最高級	
單音節形容詞	old wise	older wiser	the oldest the wisest	大部分單音節形容詞的比較級：字尾加 **-er**；最高級：字尾加 **-est**。
雙音節形容詞	famous pleasant	more famous more pleasant	the most famous the most pleasant	雙音節形容詞的比較級前面加 **more**；最高級前面加 **most**。
	clever gentle friendly	cleverer more clever gentler more gentle friendlier more friendly	the cleverest the most clever the gentlest the most gentle the friendliest the most friendly	有些雙音節形容詞可以在字尾加 **-er/-est** 或在前面加 **more/most**，如：*able*、*angry*、*clever*、*common*、*cruel*、*friendly*、*gentle*、*handsome*、*narrow*、*pleasant*、*polite*、*quiet*、*simple*、*sour*。
	busy pretty	busier prettier	the busiest the prettiest	雙音節形容詞字尾是 **-y** 時，將 **-y** 改成 **-i** 後，在比較級字尾加 **-er**；在最高級字尾加 **-est**。
三個（含）以上音節的形容詞	important fascinating	more important more fascinating	the most important the most fascinating	多音節形容詞用 **more** 形成比較級；用 **most** 形成最高級。
不規則形容詞	good bad	better worse	the best the worst	**good** 和 **bad** 的比較級和最高級為不規則變化。
字尾是 -ly 的副詞	carefully slowly	more carefully more slowly	the most carefully the most slowly	以 **-ly** 結尾的副詞，其比較級和最高級形式通常在前面加 **more** 和 **most**。★
單音節副詞	fast hard	faster harder	the fastest the hardest	單音節副詞通常在字尾加 **-er** 和 **-est**。
不規則副詞	well badly far	better worse farther/further （距離）（程度）	the best the worst the farthest/furthest	**farther** 和 **further** 都用來比較物理上的距離，如：*I walked farther than my friend did.* 或 *I walked further than my friend did.*。**further** 也有「附加的；更多的」之意，例：*I need further information.*。 注意：**farther** 不可用來表達「附加的；更多的」。

*例外：**early** 是形容詞也是副詞。比較級和最高級形式：*earlier*、*earliest*。

❏ **Exercise 10. 文法** (表 9-2 和 9-3)
寫出下列形容詞和副詞的比較級和最高級。

1. high _higher, the highest_
2. good _____
3. lazy _____
4. hot★ _hotter_
5. neat★ _____
6. late★ 稍后 最近、最新
   later latest
7. happy _____

8. dangerous _____
9. slowly _____
10. common _____
11. friendly _____
12. careful _____
13. bad _____
14. far _____

❏ **Exercise 11. 文法** (表 9-2 和 9-3)
用下表中形容詞的正確比較級 (*more/-er*)，完成下列句子。

clean	dangerous	funny	✓sweet
confusing	dark	pretty	wet

1. Oranges are ___sweeter___ than lemons.

2. I heard some polite laughter when I told my jokes, but everyone laughed loudly when Janet told hers. Her jokes are always much ___funnier___ than mine.

3. Many more people die in car accidents than in plane accidents. Statistics show that driving your own car is ___more dangerous___ than flying in an airplane.

4. Professor Sato speaks clearly, but I have trouble understanding Professor Larson's lectures. Her lectures are much ___more confusing___ than Professor Sato's.

5. Is there a storm coming? The sky looks ___darker___ than it __did__ an hour ago.

6. That tablecloth has some stains on it. Take this one. It's ___cleanner___.

7. We're having another beautiful sunrise. It looks like an orange fireball. The sky is even ___prettier___ than yesterday.

8. If a cat and a duck are out in the rain, the cat will get much ___wetter___ than the duck. The water will just roll off the duck's feathers, but it will soak into the cat's hair.

★拼字規則：
• 當單音節的形容詞字尾為「一個母音字母 + 一個子音字母」時，需重複字尾子音字母，並加上 *-er/-est*，如：*sad*、*sadder*、*saddest*。
• 當形容詞字尾為「兩個母音字母 + 一個子音字母」時，「不需」重複字尾子音字母，如：*cool*、*cooler*、*coolest*。
• 當形容詞字尾為 *-e* 時，「不需」重複字尾子音字母，如：*wide*、*wider*、*widest*。

❑ **Exercise 12. 聽力** (表 9-3)

CD 2
Track 25

聆聽 CD 播放的句子，並圈選聽到的字詞。

例：你會聽到：I am the shortest person in our family.

你要圈出：short   shorter   (shortest)

My family

1. young   younger   youngest

2. tall   taller   tallest

3. happy   happier   happiest

4. happy   happier   happiest

5. old   older   oldest

6. funny   funnier   funniest

7. hard   harder   hardest

8. hard   harder   hardest

❑ **Exercise 13. 文法** (表 9-3)

圈選可完成下列句子的正確答案。

1. Ron and his friend went jogging. Ron ran two miles, but his friend got tired after one mile. Ron ran _____ than his friend did.
   (a.) farther   (b.) further

2. If you have any _____ questions, don't hesitate to ask.
   a. farther   b. further

3. I gave my old computer to my younger sister because I had no _____ use for it.
   a. farther   b. further

4. Paris is _____ north than Tokyo.
   a. farther   b. further

5. I like my new apartment, but it is _____ away from school than my old apartment was.
   a. farther   b. further

6. Thank you for your help, but I'll be fine now. I don't want to cause you any _____ trouble.
   a. farther   b. further

7. Which is _____ from here: the subway or the train station?
   a. farther   b. further

❏ **Exercise 14. 口說：兩人一組** (表 9-2 和 9-3)

成兩人一組；用 *more/-er* 和下表中的形容詞造比較級的句子，然後再與全班分享一些你的答案。

beautiful	enjoyable	light	soft
cheap	expensive	relaxing	stressful
deep	fast	shallow	thick
easy	heavy	short	thin

1. traveling by air \ traveling by train
   → *Traveling by air is faster than traveling by train.*
   → *Traveling by air is more stressful than traveling by train.*
     Etc.
2. a pool \ a lake
3. an elephant's neck \ a giraffe's neck
4. taking a trip \ staying home
5. iron \ wood
6. going to the doctor \ going to the dentist
7. gold \ silver
8. rubber \ wood
9. an emerald \ a diamond
10. a feather \ a blade of grass

❏ **Exercise 15. 聽力** (表 9-1 → 9-3)

聆聽 CD 播放的句子，並圈選句義相近的敘述（a 或 b）。

CD 2
Track 26

例：你會聽到：I need help! Please come as soon as possible.
    你要圈出：ⓐ Please come quickly.
              b. Please come when you have time.

1. a. Business is better this year.
   b. Business is worse this year.

2. a. Steven is a very friendly person.
   b. Steven is an unfriendly person.

3. a. The test was difficult for Sam.
   b. The test wasn't so difficult for Sam.

4. a. We can go farther.
   b. We can't go farther.

5. a. Jon made a very good decision.
   b. Jon made a very bad decision.

6. a. I'm going to drive faster.
   b. I'm not going to drive faster.

7. a. Your work was careful.
   b. Your work was not careful.

8. a. I am full.
   b. I would like more to eat.

9. a. My drive and my flight take
      the same amount of time.
   b. My drive takes more time.

用你知道的人名完成與實際狀況相符的句子。

1. I'm older than _____ is.

2. I live nearer to/farther from school than _____ does.

3. I got to class earlier/later than _____ did.

4. _____'s hair is longer/shorter than mine.

9-4 比較級的用法

(a) I'm older *than **my brother*** (is). (b) I'm older *than **he** is.* 主格 (c) I'm older *than **him***. （非正式）	在正式英文中，***than*** 後面通常會接主格代名詞，如：例 (b) 中的 *he*。 但在日常、口語和非正式英文中，***than*** 後面則會用受格代名詞，如：例 (c) 中的 *him*。
(d) He works harder *than **I do***. (e) I arrived earlier *than **they did***.	通常 ***than*** 後面的主詞會接助動詞。 例 (d)：*than I do = than I work*。
(f) ***Ann's*** hair is longer *than **Kate's***. (g) ***Jack's*** apartment is smaller *than **mine***.	***than*** 後面可以接名詞所有格（如：*Kate's*）或所有格代名詞（如：*mine*）。

❏ **Exercise 17. 文法** (表 9-4)

用代名詞完成下列句子。

1. My sister is only six. She's much younger than __*I am* OR (informally) *me*__.

2. Peggy is thirteen, and she feels sad. She thinks most of the other girls in school are far more popular than __*she (is)*__.

3. The kids can't lift that heavy box, but Mr. El-Sayid can. He's stronger than __*they (are)*__.

4. Jared isn't a very good speller. I can spell much better than __*he (can)*__.

5. I was on time. Carlo was late. I got there earlier than __*he (did)*__.

6. Mariko is out of shape. I can run a lot faster and farther than __*she (can)*__.

7. Isabel's classes are difficult, but my classes are easy. Isabel's classes are more difficult than __*my classes / mine*__. My classes are easier than __*her classes / hers*__.

8. Our neighbor's house is very large. Our house is much smaller than __*theirs*__. Their house is larger than __*ours*__.

❑ **Exercise 18. 暖身活動** (表 9-5)

如果你同意下列敘述，圈 *yes*；如果不同意，圈 *no*。

1. I enjoy very cold weather.	yes no
2. It's cooler today than yesterday.	yes no
3. It's much warmer today than yesterday.	yes no
4. It's a little hotter today than yesterday.	yes no

9-5 比較級的修飾

(a) Tom is **very old**. (b) Ann drives **very** carefully.	**very** 常用來修飾形容詞，如：例 (a)，和副詞，如：例 (b)。
(c) 錯誤：*Tom is very older than I am.* 錯誤：*Ann drives very more carefully than she used to.*	**very** 「不」用來修飾形容詞和副詞的比較級。
(d) Tom is **much/a lot/far** older than I am. (e) Ann drives **much/a lot/far** more carefully than she used to.	反之，**much**、**a lot** 或 **far** 則用來修飾形容詞和副詞的比較級，如：例 (d) 與例 (e)。 still
(f) Ben is **a little** (**bit**) older than I am 或（非正式用法）me.	另一個常見的修飾語為 **a little/a little bit**，如：例 (f)。

❑ **Exercise 19. 文法** (表 9-5)

在下列句子中加上 **very**、**much**、**a lot** 或 **far**。

1. It's hot today. → *It's **very** hot today.*
2. It's hotter today than yesterday. → *It's **much/a lot/far** hotter today than yesterday.*
3. An airplane is fast.
4. Taking an airplane is faster than driving.
5. Learning a second language is difficult for many people.
6. Learning a second language is more difficult than learning chemistry formulas.
7. You can live more inexpensively in student housing than in a rented apartment.
8. You can live inexpensively in student housing.

❑ **Exercise 20. 暖身活動** (表 9-6)

用自己的話完成下列句子。

1. Compare the cost of two cars:

   (*A/An*) _____ is more expensive than (*a/an*) _____.

2. Compare the cost of two kinds of fruit:

   _____ are less expensive than _____.

3. Compare the cost of two kinds of shoes (boots, sandals, tennis shoes, flip-flops, etc.):

   _____ are not as expensive as _____.

4. Compare the cost of two kinds of heat: (gas, electric, solar, wood, coal, etc.):

_____ heat is not as cheap as _____ heat.

9-6 用 *Less . . . Than* 與 *Not As . . . As* 表示比較級

雙音節或多音節： (a) A pen is *less expensive than* a book. (b) A pen is *not as expensive as* a book.	*less* 或 *not as . . . as* 用來表達 *-er/more* 的反義。 例 (a) 與例 (b) 同義。
	less 和 *not as . . . as* 可與**雙音節**或**多音節**的形容詞和副詞連用。
單音節： (c) A pen is *not as large as* a book. 錯誤：*A pen is less large than a book.*	只有 *not as . . . as* 可與**單音節**的形容詞或副詞連用，如：例 (c)，*less* 則「不行」。

❑ **Exercise 21. 文法** (表 9-6)

圈選可完成下列句子的正確答案。

1. My nephew is _____ old _____ my niece.
   a. less . . . than   b. not as . . . as

2. My nephew is _____ hard-working _____ my niece.
   a. less . . . than   b. not as . . . as

3. A bee is _____ big _____ a bird.
   a. less . . . than   b. not as . . . as

4. My brother is _____ interested in computers _____ I am.
   a. less . . . than   b. not as . . . as

5. Some students are _____ serious about their schoolwork _____ others.
   a. less . . . than   b. not as . . . as

6. I am _____ good at repairing things _____ Diane is.
   a. less . . . than   b. not as . . . as

❑ **Exercise 22. 遊戲** (表 9-1 → 9-6)

分組比賽；用 (*not*) *as . . . as*、*less* 和 *more/-er* 比較下列提供的項目。你們可以想到多少個比較級的句子呢？能寫出最多正確句子的組別即可獲勝。

例：trees and flowers (*big, colorful, useful, etc.*)
   → *Trees are bigger than flowers.*
   → *Flowers are usually more colorful than trees.*
   → *Flowers are less useful than trees.*
   → *Flowers aren't as tall as trees.*

1. the sun and the moon
2. teenagers and adults
3. two restaurants in this area
4. two famous people in the world

❏ **Exercise 23. 聽力** (表 9-1 → 9-6)

CD 2
Track 27

聆聽 CD 播放的句子及其後的敘述，敘述如果正確，圈 T；敘述如果有錯，圈 F。

例：France \ Brazil
你會聽到：a. France isn't as large as Brazil.
你要圈出：　Ⓣ　　F

你會聽到：b. France is bigger than Brazil.
你要圈出：　T　　Ⓕ

1.　a sidewalk \ a road
　　a. T　F
　　b. T　F

2.　a hill \ a mountain
　　a. T　F
　　b. T　F

3.　a mountain path \ a mountain peak
　　a. T　F
　　b. T　F

4.　toes \ fingers
　　a. T　F
　　b. T　F
　　c. T　F

5.　basic math \ algebra
　　a. T　F
　　b. T　F
　　c. T　F
　　d. T　F

❏ **Exercise 24. 遊戲：知識問答比賽** (表 9-7)

比較馬尼拉、西雅圖以及新加坡三座城市；哪兩個城市在 12 月的降雨量較多？★

_____ and _____ have more rain

than _____ in December.

9-7 _More_ 和名詞的連用	
(a) Would you like some **_more coffee_**? (b) Not everyone is here. I expect **_more people_** to come later.	在例 (a) 中，**_coffee_** 是名詞，當 **_more_** 和名詞連用時，通常作「更多的」解，此時不需用 **_than_**。
(c) There are **_more people_** in China **_than_** there are in the United States.	**_more_** 和名詞連用時，也可以加上 **_than_**，造出較完整的比較句。
(d) Do you have enough coffee, or would you like some **_more_**?	當句義清楚時，也可以省略名詞，只用 **_more_** 表示。

★請見解答本中的 _Trivia Answers_。

❑ **Exercise 25. 遊戲：知識問答比賽** (表 9-7)

分組比賽；用下列提供的資訊，寫出符合事實的句子。完成最多正確句子的組別獲勝。*

1. more kinds of mammals: South Africa \ Kenya
   → *Kenya has more kinds of mammals than South Africa.*
2. more volcanoes: Indonesia \ Japan
3. more moons: Saturn \ Venus
4. more people: Saõ Paulo, Brazil \ New York City
5. more islands: Greece \ Finland
6. more mountains: Switzerland \ Nepal
7. more sugar (per 100 grams): an apple \ a banana
8. more fat (per 100 grams): the dark meat of a chicken \ the white meat of a chicken

❑ **Exercise 26. 文法** (表 9-2、9-3 和 9-7)

首先，將下表中的名詞劃底線；然後再用 ***-er/more*** 搭配下表中的字詞，完成下列句子。

doctors	information	responsible
happily	mistakes	responsibly
happiness	responsibilities	✓traffic
happy		

1. A city has ___more traffic___ than a small town.
2. There is ___more information___ available on the Internet today than there was one year ago.
3. I used to be sad, but now I'm a lot ___happier___ about my life than I used to be.
4. Unhappy roommates can live together ___more happily___ if they learn to respect each other's differences.
5. Maggie's had a miserable year. I hope she finds ___more happiness___ in the future.
6. I made ___more mistakes___ on the last test than I did on the first one, so I got a worse grade.
7. My daughter Layla is trustworthy and mature. She behaves much ___responsibly___ than my nephew Jakob.
8. A twelve-year-old has ___more responsibilites___ at home and in school than an eight-year-old.
9. My son is ___more responsible___ about doing his homework than his older sister is.
10. Health care in rural areas is poor. We need ___more doctors___ to treat people in rural areas.

❏ **Exercise 27. 暖身活動** (表 9-8)

如果同意下列敘述，圈 *yes*；如果不同意，圈 *no*。

1. The grammar in this book is getting harder and harder.　　　　　　yes　　　no

2. The assignments in this class are getting longer and longer.　　　yes　　　no

3. My English is getting better and better.　　　　　　　　　　　　yes　　　no

---

9-8 重複比較級的用法

(a) Because he was afraid, he walked **faster and faster**.	重複比較級，通常含有程度上漸漸增加的意思，如：密度、特質或數量的增加。
(b) Life in the modern world is getting **more and more complicated**.	

❏ **Exercise 28. 文法** (表 9-8)

用下表中字詞的重複比較級，完成下列句子。

big	✓fast	hard	loud	warm
discouraged	good	long	tired	wet

1. When I get excited, my heart beats ___faster and faster___.

2. When you blow up a balloon, it gets _____.

3. Brian's health is improving. It's getting _____ every day.

4. As the ambulance came closer to us, the siren became _____.

5. The line of people waiting to get into the theater got _____ _____ until it went around the building.

6. Thank goodness winter is over. The weather is getting _____ _____ with each passing day.

7. I've been looking for a job for a month and still haven't been able to find one. I'm getting _____.

8. The rain started as soon as I left my office. As I walked to the bus stop, it rained _____, and I got _____.

9. I started to row the boat across the lake, but my arms got _____ _____, so I turned back.

Exercise 29. 暖身活動 (表 9-9)

你同意以下看法嗎？為什麼？

> If you pay more money for something, you will get better quality. In other words, the more expensive something is, the better the quality will be.

9-9 雙重比較級

(a) ***The harder*** you study, ***the more*** you will learn. (b) ***The more*** she studied, ***the more*** she learned. (c) ***The warmer*** the weather (is), ***the better*** I like it.	雙重比較級有兩個部分，都以 ***the*** 為首，如例句所示。第二部分的比較是第一部份比較的「**結果**」。 在例 (a) 中，如果你認真讀書，「結果」是你將學到更多。
(d) — Should we ask Jenny and Jim to the party too? — Why not? ***The more, the merrier.*** (e) — When should we leave? — ***The sooner, the better.***	***the more, the merrier*** 和 ***the sooner, the better*** 是兩組常見的表達字詞。 在例 (d) 中：派對上有愈多人愈好。 在例 (e) 中：我們愈快離開愈好。

❑ **Exercise 30. 文法** (表 9-9)

第一部分 用雙重比較級 (***the more/-er . . . the more/-er***) 和各題中的斜體字，完成下列句子。

1. If the fruit is *fresh*, it tastes *good*.

   _____The fresher_____ the fruit (is), _____the better_____ it tastes.

2. We got *close* to the fire. We felt *warm*.

   _____The closer_____ we got to the fire, _____the warmer_____ we felt.

3. If a knife is *sharp*, it is *easy* to cut something with.

   _____The sharper_____ a knife (is), _____the easier_____ it is to cut something.

4. The party got *noisy* next door. I got *angry*.

   _____The noiser_____ it got, _____the angrier_____ I got.

5. If a flamingo eats a lot of *shrimp*, it becomes very *pink*.

   The _____more shrimps_____ a flamingo eats,

   the _____pinker_____ it gets.

SHRIMP, ALL YOU CAN EAT

用雙重比較級 (***the more/-er . . . the more/-er***) 和斜體字，合併下列各組句子。

6. She drove *fast*. \ I became *nervous*.

Rosa offered to take me to the airport, and I was grateful. But we got a late start, so she began to drive faster. → ***The** faster she drove, **the** more nervous I became.*

7. He *thought* about his family. \ He became *homesick*.

Pierre tried to concentrate on his studies, but he kept thinking about his family and home. →

8. The sky grew *dark*. \ We ran *fast* to reach the house.

A storm was threatening. →

❏ **Exercise 31. 暖身活動** (表 9-10)

用自己的想法完成下列句子。

1. _____ is the most expensive city I have ever visited.

2. _____ is one of the most expensive cities in the world.

3. _____ is one of the least expensive cities in the world.

9-10 最高級的用法

(a) Tokyo is one of **the largest cities in the world**.	最高級的典型用法：
(b) David is **the most generous person I have ever known**.	在例 (a) 中：最高級 + **in** 地點 (**the world**、**this class**、**my family**、**the corporation** 等等)
(c) I have three books. These two are quite good, but this one is the **best** (book) **of all**.	在例 (b) 中：最高級 + 形容詞子句★
	在例 (c) 中：最高級 + **of all**
(d) I took four final exams. The final in accounting was **the least difficult** of all.	**the least** 是 **the most** 的反義詞。
(e) Ali is **one of** the best **students** in this class.	注意 **one of** 的句型：
(f) **One of** the best **students** in this class **is** Ali.	**one of** + 複數名詞（+ 單數動詞）
(g) I've **never** taken a **harder** test.	**never** + 比較級 = 最高級
(h) I've **never** taken a **hard** test. 否定+比較=最高級	例 (g) 表示「這是我有史以來參加過最難的一次考試。」(It was the hardest test I've ever taken.) 比較例 (g) 和例 (h)。

★更多關於形容詞子句的用法，請見第 12 章。

❏ **Exercise 32. 文法** (表 9-10)

用斜體字的最高級和恰當的介系詞 ***in*** 或 ***of***，完成下列句子。

1. Kyle is *lazy*. He is ___the laziest___ student ___in___ the class.

2. Mike and Julie were *nervous*, but Amanda was _the most nervous of_ all.

3. Costa Rica is *beautiful*. It is one of _the most beautiful_ countries _in_ the world.

4. Scott got a *bad* score on the test. It was one of _the worst_ scores _in_ the class.

5. Neptune is *far* from the sun. Is it _the farthest_ planet from the sun _in_ our solar system?

6. There are a lot of *good* cooks in my family, but my mom is _the best_ cook _of_ all.

7. My grandfather is very *old*. He is _the oldest_ person _in_ the town where he lives.

8. That chair in the corner is *comfortable*. It is _the most comfortable_ chair _in_ the room.

9. Everyone who ran in the race was *exhausted*, but I was _the most exhausted of_ all.

❑ **Exercise 33. 文法** (表 9-10)

用下表中字詞的最高級完成下列句子。

> big bird   long river in South America
> two great natural dangers   popular forms of entertainment
> ✓deep ocean   three common street names
> high mountains on earth

1. The Pacific is _the deepest ocean_ in the world.

2. _____ are in the Himalayan Range in Asia.

3. Most birds are small, but not the flightless North African ostrich. It is
_____ in the world.

4. _____ to ships are fog and icebergs.

5. One of _____ throughout the world is movies.

6. _____ in the United States are Park, Washington, and Maple.

7. _____ is the Amazon.

❏ **Exercise 34. 文法**（表 9-10）

用斜體字詞的最高級完成下列句子。

1. I have had many *good experiences.* Of those, my vacation to Honduras was one of
   _____ I have ever had.

2. Ayako has had many *nice times,* but her birthday party was one of _____
   _____ she has ever had.

3. I've taken many *difficult courses,* but statistics is one of _____
   _____ I've ever taken.

4. I've made some *bad mistakes* in my life, but lending money to my cousin was one of
   _____ I've ever made.

5. We've seen many *beautiful buildings* in the world, but the Taj Mahal is one of _____
   _____ I've ever seen.

6. The *final exam* I took was pretty *easy.* In fact, it was one of _____
   _____ I've ever taken.

❏ **Exercise 35. 口說：兩人一組**（表 9-10）

成兩人一組，輪流做問答練習；請運用最高級回答問題，並特別注意 *one of* 後面是加複數名詞。

例：
說話者 A：You have known many interesting people. Who is one of them?
說話者 B：*One of* **the most interesting people** I've ever known *is* (____)。或
　　　　　(____) *is one of* **the most interesting people** I've ever known.

1. There are many beautiful countries in the world. What is one of them?
2. There are many famous people in the world. Who is one of them?
3. You've probably seen many good movies. What is one of them?
4. You've probably done many interesting things in your life. What is one of them?
5. Think of some happy days in your life. What was one of them?
6. There are a lot of interesting animals in the world. What is one of them?
7. You have probably had many good experiences. What is one of them?
8. You probably know several funny people. Who is one of them?

❏ **Exercise 36. 文法與聽力**（表 9-10）

第一部分　圈選與各題句子意義最接近的敘述（a 或 b）。

1. I've never been on a bumpier plane ride.
   a. The flight was bumpy.　　　　b. The flight wasn't bumpy.

2. I've never tasted hot chili peppers.
   a. The peppers are hot.　　　　b. I haven't eaten hot chili peppers.

3. The house has never looked cleaner.
   a. The house looks clean.   b. The house doesn't look clean.

4. We've never visited a more beautiful city.
   a. The city was beautiful.   b. The city wasn't beautiful.

第二部分　聆聽 CD 播放的下列句子，圈選與聽見句子意義最接近的敘述（a 或 b）。

5. a. His jokes are funny.   b. His jokes aren't funny.

6. a. It tastes great.   b. It doesn't taste very good.

7. a. The mattress is hard.   b. I haven't slept on hard mattresses.

8. a. The movie was scary.   b. I haven't watched scary movies.

❏ **Exercise 37.** 口說：訪談 （表 9-10）

用下列各題提供的字詞及最高級造問句，然後再訪問班上同學。最後，與全班分享一些同學的答案。

1. what \ bad movie \ you have ever seen
   → *What is the worst movie you have ever seen?*
2. what \ interesting sport to watch \ on TV
3. what \ crowded city \ you have ever visited
4. where \ good restaurant to eat \ around here
5. what \ fun place to visit \ in this area
6. who \ kind person \ you know
7. what \ important thing \ in life
8. what \ serious problem \ in the world
9. who \ most interesting person \ in the news right now

❏ **Exercise 38.** 遊戲 （表 9-1 → 9-10）

分組比賽；用斜體字比較下列各題列出的事物，並用 **as . . . as**、比較級 (**-er/more**) 和最高級 (**-est/most**) 寫出句子。寫出最多正確句子的組別即可獲勝。

例：streets in this city: *wide / narrow / busy / dangerous*
   → *First Avenue is **wider** than Market Street.*
   → *Second Avenue is **nearly as wide as** First Avenue.*
   → *First Avenue is **narrower** than Interstate Highway 70.*
   → ***The busiest** street is Main Street.*
   → *Main Street is **busier** than Market Street.*
   → ***The most dangerous street** in the city is Olive Boulevard.*

1. a lemon, a grapefruit, and an orange: *sweet / sour / large / small*
2. a kitten, a cheetah, and a lion: *weak / powerful / wild / gentle / fast*
3. boxing, soccer, and golf: *dangerous / safe / exciting / boring*
4. the food at (*three places in this city where you have eaten*): *delicious / appetizing / inexpensive / good / bad*

❑ **Exercise 39.** 文法 (表 9-1 → 9-10)
用括弧內字詞的任一正確形式，完成下列句子；此外，應視情況加上其他字詞。有些題目的答案也許不只一個。

1. Lead is a very heavy metal. It is (*heavy*) _heavier than_ gold or silver. It is one of (*heavy*) _the heaviest_ metals _of_ all.

2. Mrs. Cook didn't ask the children to clean up the kitchen. It was (*easy*) _easier_ for her to do it herself _than_ to nag them to do it.

3. A car has two (*wheels*) _more wheels than_ a bicycle.

4. Crocodiles and alligators are different. The snout of a crocodile is (*long*) _longer_ and (*narrow*) _narrower_ than an alligator's snout. An alligator has a (*wide*) _wider_ upper jaw than a crocodile.

5. Although both jobs are important, being a teacher requires (*education*) _more education_ being a bus driver.

6. The Great Wall of China is (*long*) _the longest_ structure that has ever been built.

7. Hannah Anderson is one of (*friendly*) _the friendliest_ and (*delightful*) _the most delightful_ people I've ever met.

8. One of (*famous*) _the most famous_ volcanoes _in_ the world is Mount Etna in Sicily.

9. It's possible that the volcanic explosion of Krakatoa near Java in 1883 was (*loud*) _the loudest_ noise _in_ recorded history. People heard it 2,760 miles/4,441 kilometers away.

10. (hard) _____The harder_____ I tried, (impossible) _____the more impossible_____
the math problem seemed.

11. World Cup Soccer is (big) _____the biggest_____ sporting event ___in___ the world.
It is viewed on TV by (people) _____more people than_____ any other event in sports.

12. When the temperature stays below freezing for a long period of time, the Eiffel Tower
becomes six inches or fifteen centimeters (short) _____shorter_____.

13. Young people have (high) _____the highest_____ rate of automobile accidents
___of___ all drivers.

14. You'd better buy the tickets for the show soon. (long) _____the longer_____,
you wait, (difficult) _____the more difficult_____ it will be for you to get
good seats.

15. No animals can travel (fast) _____faster than_____ birds. Birds are (fast)
_____the fastest_____ animals of all.

16. (great) _____The greatest_____ variety of birds ___in___ a single area can be
found in the rainforests of Southeast Asia and India.

❑ **Exercise 40. 暖身活動** (表 9-11)
運算下列數學題*，然後完成句子。

問題 A：2 + 2 =
問題 B：$\sqrt{900} + 20 =$
問題 C：3 × 127 =
問題 D：2 + 3 =
問題 E：127 × 3 =

1. Problem _____ and Problem _____ have *the same* answers.

2. Problem _____ and Problem _____ have *similar* answers.

3. Problem _____ and Problem _____ have *different* answers.

4. The answer to Problem _____ is *the same as* the answer to Problem _____.

5. The answers to Problem _____ and Problem _____ are *similar*.

6. The answers to Problem _____ Problem _____ are *different*.

7. Problem _____ has *the same answer as* Problem _____.

8. Problem _____ is *like* Problem _____.

9. Problem _____ and Problem _____ are *alike*.

*數學題的答案請見解答本中的 *Trivia Answers*。

9-11 *The Same, Similar, Different, Like, Alike* 的用法

(a) John and Mary have <u>the same</u> **books**.	**the same**、**similar** 和 **different** 都作形容詞用。
(b) John and Mary have **similar books**.	注意：**same** 之前一定要有 **the**。
(c) John and Mary have **different books**.	
(d) Their books are **the same**.	
(e) Their books are **similar**.	
(f) Their books are **different**.	
(g) This book is **the same as** that one.	注意：**the same** 之後接 **as**；
(h) This book is **similar to** that one.	**similar** 之後接 **to**；
(i) This book is **different from** that one.	**different** 之後接 **from**。★
(j) She is **the same age as** my mother. My shoes are **the same size as** yours.	名詞可以放在 **the same** 和 **as** 中間，如：例 (j)。
(k) My pen **is like** your pen. (l) My pen **and** your pen **are alike**.	注意例 (k) 和例 (l)： 名詞 + **be like** + 名詞 名詞 **and** 名詞 + **be alike**
(m) She **looks like** her sister. It **looks like** rain. It **sounds like** thunder. This material **feels like** silk. That **smells like** gas. This chemical **tastes like** salt. Stop **acting like** a fool. He **seems like** a nice guy.	除了 **be** 動詞外，**like** 也可接在某些動詞後，特別是感官動詞。 注意例 (m) 中的句子。
(n) The twins **look** <u>alike</u>. We **think alike**. Most four-year-olds **act alike**. My sister and I **talk alike**. The little boys are **dressed alike**.	除了 **be** 動詞之外，**alike** 也可以接在某些動詞後面。 注意例 (n) 中的句子。

*在非正式口語中，英文母語人士或許會在 *different* 後面使用 *than*，而不用 *from*。*from* 在正式英文中是正確的，除非該比較句是以子句結尾：*I have a different attitude now than I used to have.*

❏ **Exercise 41. 文法** (表 9-11)

用 *as*、*to*、*from* 或 Ø 完成下列句子。

1. Geese are similar ___to___ ducks. They are both large water birds.

2. But geese are not the same _____ ducks. Geese are usually larger and have longer necks.

3. Geese are different _____ ducks.

4. Geese are like _____ ducks in some ways, but geese and ducks are not exactly alike _____.

5. An orange is similar _____ a peach. They are both round, sweet, and juicy.

6. However, an orange is not the same _____ a peach.

7. An orange is different _____ a peach.

8. An orange is like _____ a peach in some ways, but they are not exactly alike _____ .

CD 2
Track 29

聆聽 CD 播放的兩篇文章，並用聽到的字詞完成下列句子。

Gold vs. Silver

Gold is similar _____ silver. They are both valuable metals that people use for
                        1

jewelry, but they aren't _____ same. Gold is not _____ same color
                          2   3

_____ silver. Gold is also different _____ silver in cost: gold is
       4   5

_____ expensive _____ silver.
       6   7

Two Zebras

Look at the two zebras in the picture. Their names are Zee and Bee. Zee looks

_____ Bee. Is Zee exactly _____ same _____ Bee? The pattern of
       8   9   10

the stripes on each zebra in the world is unique. No two zebras are exactly _____ .
                                                                              11

Even though Zee and Bee are similar _____ each other, they are different
                                      12

_____ each other in the exact pattern of their stripes.
       13

比較 **253**

❏ **Exercise 43.**　文法（表 9-11）

比較下列四張圖表，並用 *the same* (*as*)、*similar* (*to*)、*different* (*from*)、*like* 或 *alike*，
完成下列句子。

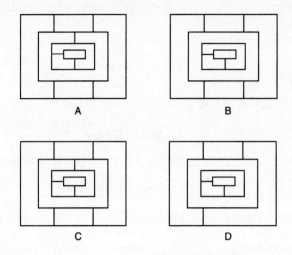

1. All of the figures are ___*similar to*___ each other.

2. Figure A is _____ Figure B.

3. Figure A and Figure B are _____ .

4. A and C are _____ .

5. A and C are _____ D.

6. C is _____ A.

7. B isn't _____ D.

❏ **Exercise 44.**　文法（表 9-11）

用 *the same* (*as*)、*similar* (*to*)、*different* (*from*)、*like* 或 *alike* 完成下列句子。有些題目
的答案也許不只一個。

1. Jennifer and Jack both come from Rapid City. In other words, they come from
    ___*the same*___ town.

2. This city is ___*the same as/similar to/like*___ my hometown. Both are quiet and
    conservative.

3. You and I don't agree. Your ideas are _____ mine.

4. Sergio never wears _____ clothes two days in a row.

5. A male mosquito is not _____ size _____ a female
    mosquito. The female is larger.

6. I'm used to stronger coffee. I think the coffee at this cafe tastes _____ dishwater!

7. *Meet* and *meat* are homonyms; in other words, they have _____ pronunciation.

8. *Flower* has _____ pronunciation _____ *flour.*

9. My twin sisters act _____, but they don't look _____.

10. Trying to get through school without studying is _____ trying to go swimming without getting wet.

❑ **Exercise 45. 閱讀**（第 9 章）

第一部分 閱讀以下文章及其後的敘述句。注意：文章中的 **he** 和 **she** 可以交換使用。

Birth Order

In your family, are you the oldest, youngest, middle, or only child? Some psychologists believe your place in the family, or your birth order, has a strong influence on your personality. Let's look at some of the personality characteristics of each child.

The oldest child has all the parents' attention when she is born. As she grows up, she may want to be the center of attention. Because she is around adults, she might act more like an adult around other children and be somewhat controlling. As the oldest, she might have to take care of the younger children, so she may be more responsible. She may want to be the leader when she is in groups.

The middle child (or children) may feel a little lost. Middle children have to share their parents' attention. They may try to be different from the oldest child. If the oldest child is "good," the second child may be "bad." However, since they need to get along with both the older and younger sibling(s), they may be the peacekeepers of the family.

The youngest child is the "baby" of the family. Other family members may see him as weaker, smaller, or more helpless. If the parents know this is their last child, they may not want the child to grow up as quickly as the other children. As a way to get attention, the youngest child may be the funniest child in the family. He may also have more freedom and turn out to be more artistic and creative.

An only child (no brothers or sisters) often grows up in an adult world. Such children may use adult language and prefer adult company. Only children may be more intelligent and serious than other children their age. They might also be more self-centered because of all the attention they get, and they might have trouble sharing with others.

Of course, these are general statements. A lot depends on how the parents raise the child, how many years are between each child, and the culture the child grows up in. How about you? Do you see any similarities to your family?

第二部分　閱讀下列敘述，並根據前一頁文章中的資訊作判斷，敘述如果正確，圈 T；敘述如果有錯，圈 F。

1. The two most similar children are the oldest and only child. T F
2. The middle child often wants to be like the oldest child. T F
3. The youngest child likes to control others. T F
4. Only children may want to spend time with adults. T F
5. All cultures share the same birth order characteristics. T F

❏ Exercise 46. 寫作（第 9 章）

第一部分　下表列出與個人特質相關的形容詞。你認識全部的字嗎？

artistic	funny	rebellious
competitive	hard-working	relaxed
controlling	immature	secretive
cooperative	loud	sensitive
creative	mature	serious
flexible	outgoing	shy

第二部分　將自己與其他家人作比較，並用下列的句型寫出句子：

句型：

1. not as . . . as
2. more . . . than
3. -er . . . than
4. the most . . .

第三部分　遵循下列步驟，寫一段文字，比較自己和一位家人的個人特質。

1. 寫一句引言：*I am different from/similar to my . . .*
2. 從上表中至少選出四項與個人特質相關的形容詞；搭配每項特質，分別寫出對應的比較級句子。
3. 寫出一些細節來說明各類比較情況。
4. 寫一到兩句的結論句。

段落範例：

My Father and I

I am different from my father in several ways. He is more hard-working than I am. He is a construction worker and has to get up at 6:00 A.M. He often doesn't get home until late in the evening. I'm a student, and I don't work as hard. Another difference is that I am funnier than he is. I like to tell jokes and make people laugh. He is serious, but he laughs at my jokes. My father was an athlete when he was my age, and he is very competitive. I don't like playing competitive sports, but we watch them together on TV. My father and I are different, but we like to spend time with each other. Our differences make our time together interesting.

校訂下列句子，訂正錯誤的比較級句型。

1. Did you notice? My shoes and your shoes are *the* ~~a~~ same.

2. Alaska is largest state in the United States.

3. A pillow is soft, more than a rock.

4. Who is most generous person in your family?

5. The harder you work, you will be more successful.

6. One of a biggest disappointment in my life was when my soccer team lost the championship.

7. My sister is very taller than me.

8. A firm mattress is so comfortable for many people than a soft mattress.

9. One of the most talkative student in the class is Frederick.

10. Professor Bennett's lectures were the confusing I have ever heard.

第十章

被動語態

❑ **Exercise 1. 暖身活動** (表 10-1 和 10-2)

圈選下列各題中能用以描述圖片的句子。答案可能不只一個。

1. a. The worm is watching the bird.
    b. The bird is watching the worm.

2. a. The bird caught the worm.
    b. The worm was caught by the bird.

3. a. The bird ate the worm.
    b. The worm was eaten.

10-1 主動句與被動句 Active Sentences and Passive Sentences

主動 (a) The mouse **ate** the cheese. 被動 (b) The cheese **was eaten** by the mouse.	例 (a) 與例 (b) 同義。
主動 	被動 
主動 　主詞　　　　　　　　　受詞 (c) *Bob*　　　mailed　**the package**. 被動 　主詞　　　　　　　*by* + 受詞 (d) **The package** was mailed　by *Bob*.	在例 (c) 中，主動句中的受詞在被動句中變成主詞。 在例 (d) 中，主動句中的主詞在被動句中作為 **by** 的受詞。

10-2 被動語態的形式 Form of the Passive

	be +	過去分詞 (past participle)	所有被動式動詞的形式： **be** 動詞 + 過去分詞
(a) Corn	**is**	**grown** by farmers.	**be** 動詞形式列舉如下：*am*、*is*、*are*、*was*、*were*、
(b) Sara	**was**	**surprised** by the news.	*has been*、*have been*、*will be* 等等。
(c) The report	**will be**	**written** by Mary.	

	主動	被動
現在簡單式	Farmers **grow** corn. ——→	Corn **is grown** by farmers.
過去簡單式	The news **surprised** Sara. ——→	Sara **was surprised** by the news.
現在進行式	Diana **is copying** the letters. ——→	The letters **are being copied** by Diana.
過去進行式	Diana **was copying** the letters. ——→	The letters **were being copied** by Diana.
現在完成式	Jack **has mailed** the letter. ——→	The letter **has been mailed** by Jack.
未來式	Mr. Lee **will plan** the meeting. ——→ Sue **is going to write** the report. ——→	The meeting **will be planned** by Mr. Lee. The report **is going to be written** by Sue.

❏ **Exercise 2. 文法** (表 10-1 和 10-2)

加上正確的 **be** 動詞形式，將主動式動詞改為被動式。被動式中須含主詞。

1. 現在簡單式

   a. The teacher *helps* **me**.   _____I_____ _____am_____ **helped** by the teacher.

   b. The teacher *helps* **Eva**.   _____Eva_____ _____is_____ **helped** by the teacher.

   c. The teacher *helps* **us**.   _____ _____ **helped** by the teacher.

2. 過去簡單式

   a. The teacher *helped* **him**.   _____ _____ **helped** by the teacher.

   b. The teacher *helped* **them**.   _____ _____ **helped** by the teacher.

3. 現在進行式

   a. The teacher *is helping* **us**.   _____ _____ **helped** by the teacher.

   b. The teacher *is helping* **her**.   _____ _____ **helped** by the teacher.

4. 過去進行式

   a. The teacher *was helping* **me**.   _____ _____ **helped** by the teacher.

   b. The teacher *was helping* **him**.   _____ _____ **helped** by the teacher.

5. 現在完成式

   a. The teacher *has helped* **Yoko**.   _____ _____ **helped** by the teacher.

   b. The teacher *has helped* **Joe**.   _____ _____ **helped** by the teacher.

6. 未來式

    a. The teacher *will help* **me**. _____ _____ **helped** by the teacher.

    b. The teacher *is going to help* **us**. _____ _____ **helped** by the teacher.

❑ **Exercise 3. 聽力** (表 10-1 和 10-2)

聆聽 CD 播放的句子，並寫下聽到的字詞和動詞字尾。再聽一遍播放內容，並檢查答案。

CD 2
Track 30 **An office building at night**

1. The janitors *clean* the building at night.

    The building __*is*__ clean __*ed*__ by the janitors at night.

2. Window washers *wash* the windows.

    The windows _____ wash ____ by window washers.

3. A window washer *is washing* a window right now.

    A window _____ wash ____ by a window washer right now.

4. The security guard *has checked* the offices.

    The offices _____ check ____ by the security guard.

5. The security guard *discovered* an open window.

    An open window _____ discover ____ by the security guard.

6. The security guard *found* an unlocked door.

    An unlocked door _____ found by the security guard.

7. The owner *will visit* the building tomorrow.

    The building _____ visit ____ by the owner tomorrow.

8. The owner *is going to announce* new parking fees.

    New parking fees _____ announce ____ by the owner.

勾選 (✓) 被動語態的句子。

At the dentist

1. _____ The dental assistant cleaned your teeth.
2. _____ Your teeth were cleaned by the dental assistant.
3. _____ The dentist is checking your teeth.
4. _____ Your teeth are being checked by the dentist.
5. _____ You have a cavity.
6. _____ You are going to need a filling.
7. _____ The filling will be done by the dentist.
8. _____ You will need to schedule another appointment.

❑ **Exercise 5.** 文法 (表 10-1 和 10-2)

在不改變時態的前提下,將下列主動語態的動詞改爲被動語態。

		be	+	過去分詞	

1. Leo *mailed* the package. — The package _*was*_ _____*mailed*_____ by Leo.

2. That company *employs* many people. — Many people _____ _____ by that company.

3. That company *has hired* Ellen. — Ellen _____ _____ by that company.

4. The secretary *is going to fax* the letter. — The letters _____ _____ by the secretary.

5. A college student *bought* my old car. — My old car _____ _____ by a college student.

6. Mrs. Adams *will do* the work. — The work _____ _____ by Mrs. Adams.

7. The doctor *was examining* the patient. — The patient _____ _____ by the doctor.

❑ **Exercise 6.** 文法 (表 10-1 和 10-2)

將下列主動語態的句子改為被動語態。

主動語態	被動語態

1. a. The news surprised Carlo.   *Carlo was surprised*   by the news.

   b. Did the news surprise you?   *Were you surprised*   by the news?

2. a. The news surprises Erin.   by the news.

   b. Does the news surprise you?   by the news?

3. a. The news will shock Greta.   by the news.

   b. Will the news shock Pat?   by the news?

4. a. Liz is signing the birthday card.   by Liz.

   b. Is Ricardo signing it?   by Ricardo?

5. a. Jill signed the card.   by Jill.

   b. Did Ryan sign it?   by Ryan?

6. a. Sami was signing it.   by Sami.

   b. Was Vicki signing it?   by Vicki?

7. a. Rob has signed it.   by Rob.

   b. Has Kazu signed it yet?   by Kazu yet?

8. a. Luis is going to sign it.   by Luis.

   b. Is Carole going to sign it?   by Carole?

❑ **Exercise 7.** 文法 (表 10-1 和 10-2)

將下列關於飯店的問題，從主動語態改為被動語態。

1. Has the maid cleaned our room yet?
   → *Has our room been cleaned by the maid yet?*

2. Does the hotel provide hair dryers?

3. Did housekeeping bring extra towels?

4. Has room service brought our meal?

5. Is the bellhop★ bringing our luggage to our room?

6. Is maintenance going to fix the air-conditioning?

7. Will the front desk upgrade★★ our room?

★*bellhop* 意指「(旅館的) 行李員」。

★★*upgrade* 意指「改善，提高」；在此句中表示「將房間升等」之意。*upgrade* 為規則變化的動詞。

❑ **Exercise 8. 暖身活動** (表 10-3)

勾選 (✓) 含有受詞的句子，並將該受詞劃底線。

1. _____ The tree fell over.
2. _____ The tree hit the truck.
3. _____ The tree fell on the truck.
4. _____ Fortunately, the driver didn't die.
5. _____ The tree didn't kill the driver.

10-3 及物動詞與不及物動詞 Transitive and Intransitive Verbs

及物動詞

	主詞	動詞	受詞
(a)	Bob	*mailed*	*the letter.*
(b)	Mr. Lee	*signed*	*the check.*
(c)	A cat	*killed*	*the bird.*

「及物動詞」是直接接受詞的動詞；受詞是名詞或代名詞。

不及物動詞

	主詞	動詞	
(d)	Something	*happened.*	
(e)	Kate	*came*	to our house.
(f)	The bird	*died.*	

「不及物動詞」後面「不可」直接加受詞。

常見的不及物動詞★

agree	die	happen	rise	stand
appear	exist	laugh	seem	stay
arrive	fall	live	sit	talk
become	flow	occur	sleep	wait
come	go	rain	sneeze	walk

及物動詞

(g) 主動：Bob *mailed* the letter.
(h) 被動：The letter *was mailed* by Bob.

只有及物動詞可用於被動句，不及物動詞則不可用於被動句。

不及物動詞

(i) 主動：Something *happened.*
(j) 被動：（沒有被動句）
(k) 錯誤：*Something was happened.*

★要確定一個動詞為及物或不及物，可以查字典。常見的及物與不及物動詞縮寫分別為 v.t. (transitive) 與 v.i. (intransitive)，有些動詞兼具及物與不及物兩種用法，如：

及物：*Students study books.*
不及物：*Students study.*

將動詞劃<u>底線</u>，並標示爲及物動詞 (v.t.) 或不及物動詞 (v.i.)。視情況將主動語態的句子改爲被動語態。

            v.i.

1. Omar <u>walked</u> to school yesterday. (*no change*)

        v.t.

2. Alexa <u>broke</u> the window. → *The window was broken by Alexa.*

3. The leaves fell to the ground.

4. I slept at my friend's house last night.

5. Many people felt an earthquake yesterday.

6. Dinosaurs existed millions of years ago.

7. I usually agree with my sister.

8. Many people die during a war.

9. Scientists will discover a cure for cancer someday.

10. Did the Italians invent spaghetti?

❏ **Exercise 10. 遊戲：知識問答比賽** (表 10-1 → 10-3)

分組比賽；將 A、B 兩欄中的資訊相配對，造出符合事實的句子；其中有些句子爲主動語態，有些則爲被動語態；視情況於句中加上 ***was/were***。答對最多題的組別獲勝。⋆ 造出來的句子需含正確的事實，且合乎文法，才算完全答對。

例：1. Alexander Eiffel **designed** the Eiffel Tower.
     2. Anwar Sadat **was shot** in 1981.

A 欄	**B 欄**
1. Alexander Eiffel _h_	a. killed in a car crash in 1997.
2. Anwar Sadat _c_	b. died in 2009.
3. Princess Diana ____	✓c. shot in 1981.
4. Marie and Pierre Curie ____	d. painted the *Mona Lisa*.
5. Oil ____	e. elected president of the United States in 1960.
6. Mahatma Gandhi and Martin Luther King Jr. ____	f. discovered in Saudi Arabia in 1938.
	g. arrested** several times for peaceful protests.
7. Michael Jackson ____	✓h. designed the Eiffel Tower.
8. Leonardo da Vinci ____	i. released from prison in 1990.
9. John F. Kennedy ____	j. discovered radium.
10. Nelson Mandela ____	

⋆請見解答本中的 *Trivia Answers*。
****arrested* 意指「逮捕；拘留」。

Exercise 11. 暖身活動（表 10-4）

根據本書前幾頁的資訊，完成下列句子。

1. This book, *Fundamentals of English Grammar,* was published by _____.

2. It was written by _____ and _____.

3. The illustrations were drawn by _____ and _____.

10-4 「*by* 片語」的用法

(a) This sweater *was made* **by my aunt.**	當被動句中的動作者為重要訊息，則以「*by* 片語」表示，如：例 (a) 中的 **by my aunt** 即為重要的訊息。
(b) My sweater *was made* in Korea. (c) Spanish *is spoken* in Colombia. (d) That house *was built* in 1940. (e) Rice *is grown* in many countries.	一般被動句中不會有「*by* 片語」，因為被動句多用於「**動作者不明**」或「**不重要**」的情形下。 在例 (b) 中，織毛衣者不詳，也根本不重要，所以此處沒有「*by* 片語」。
(f) **My aunt** is very skillful. **She** *made* this sweater. (g) A: I like your sweaters. B: Thanks. **This sweater** *was made by* my aunt. **That sweater** *was made by* my mother.	若說話者知道動作者是誰，通常會用主動句，如：例 (f)，句子的焦點是 **my aunt**。 在例 (g) 中，說話者 B 使用含有「*by* 片語」的被動句，是因為想要強調句中的主詞，即兩件毛衣。「*by* 片語」的內容添加了重要資訊。

❑ **Exercise 12. 文法**（表 10-4）

將下列主動語態的句子改為被動語態；僅在必要情況下，加上「*by* 片語」。

1. Bob Smith built that house.

   → *That house was built by Bob Smith.*

2. Someone built this house in 1904.

3. People grow rice in India.

4. Do people speak Spanish in Peru?

5. Alexander Graham Bell invented the telephone.

6. When did someone invent the first computer?

7. People sell hammers at a hardware store.

8. Has anyone ever hypnotized you?

9. Someone published *The Origin of Species* in 1859.

10. Charles Darwin wrote *The Origin of Species*.

❏ **Exercise 13. 文法** (表 10-4)
將各組句子中的被動式動詞劃<u>底線</u>，然後再回答問題。

1. a. The mail <u>is</u> usually <u>delivered</u> to Hamid's apartment around ten o'clock.
   b. The mail carrier usually delivers the mail to Hamid's apartment around ten o'clock.
   QUESTIONS: Is it important to know who delivers the mail?   → No.
   Which sentence do you think is more common? → Sentence a.

2. a. Construction workers built our school in the 1980s.
   b. Our school was built in the 1980s.

   QUESTIONS: Is it important to know who built the school?
   Which sentence do you think is more common?

3. a. That office building was designed in 1990.
   b. That office building was designed by an architect in 1990.
   c. That office building was designed by my husband in 1990.

   QUESTIONS: What additional information do the *by*-phrases provide?
   Which sentence has important information in the *by*-phrase?

4. a. *Thailand* means "land of the free."
   b. The country of Thailand has never been ruled by a foreign power.

   QUESTION: What happens to the meaning of the second sentence if there is no *by*-phrase?

❏ **Exercise 14. 文法** (表 10-1 → 10-4)
用下列各題提供的字詞，以口語或寫作的方式造句；其中有些句子為主動語態，有些則為被動語態。用過去式造句，且不能改變詞序。

A traffic stop
1. The police \ stop \ a speeding car
   → *The police stopped a speeding car.*

2. The driver \ tell \ to get out of the car \ by the police

3. The driver \ take out \ his license

4. The driver \ give \ his license \ to the police officer

5. The license \ check

6. The driver \ give \ a ticket

7. The driver \ tell \ to drive more carefully

CD 2
Track 31

用聽到的字詞完成下列句子。在開始前，你或許會想先確定自己是否認識這些字：*treated*、
bruises、*reckless*。

A bike accident

A: Did you hear about the accident outside the dorm entrance?

B: No. What _____ ?

1

A: A guy on a bike _____ by a taxi.

2

B: _____ he _____ ?

3   4

A: Yeah. Someone _____ an ambulance. He _____ to

5   6

City Hospital and _____ in the emergency room for cuts and

7

bruises.

B: What _____ to the taxi driver?

8

A: He _____ for reckless driving.

9

B: He's lucky that the bicyclist _____ .

10

❑ **Exercise 16. 文法** (表 10-1 → 10-4)

用括弧內動詞的正確形式（主動或被動語態），完成下列句子。

1. Yesterday our teacher (*arrive*) __*arrived*__ five minutes late.

2. Last night my favorite TV program (*interrupt*) _____
by breaking news.

3. That's not my coat. It (*belong*) _____ to Lara.

4. Our mail (*deliver*) _____ before noon every day.

5. The "b" in *comb* (*pronounce, not*) _____ . It is silent.

6. What (*happen*) _____ to John? Where is he?

7. When I (*arrive*) _____ at the airport yesterday, I (*meet*)
_____ by my cousin and a couple of her friends.

8. Yesterday Lee and I (*hear*) _____ about Scott's divorce. I (*surprise, not*)
_____ by the news, but Lee (*shock*)
_____ .

9. A new house (*build*) _____ next to ours next year.

10. Roberto (*write*) _____ that composition last week. This one (*write*)
_____ yesterday.

11. At the soccer game yesterday, the winning goal (*kick*) _____ by Luigi. Over 100,000 people (*attend*) _____ the soccer game.

12. A: I think American football is too violent.

    B: I (*agree*) _____ with you. I (*prefer*) _____ baseball.

13. A: When (*your bike, steal*) _____?

    B: Two days ago.

14. A: (*you, pay*) _____ your electric bill yet?

    B: No, I haven't, but I'd better pay it today. If I don't, my electricity (*shut off*) _____ by the power company.

❏ **Exercise 17. 聽力** (表 10-1 → 10-4)

CD 2
Track 32

闔上書本，聆聽 CD 播放的文章；然後再聽一遍，並用聽到的動詞完成下列句子。在開始前，你或許會想先確定自己是否認識這些字：*ancient*、*athlete*、*designed*、*wealthy*。

Swimming Pools

Swimming pools ___are___ very popular nowadays, but can you guess when swimming
₁

pools _____ first _____? _____ it 100 years ago? Five hundred
₂ ₃ ₄

years ago? A thousand years ago? Actually, ancient Romans and Greeks _____
₅

the first swimming pools. Male athletes and soldiers _____ in them for training.
₆

Believe it or not, as early as 1 B.C., a heated swimming pool _____ for
₇

a wealthy Roman. But swimming pools _____ popular until the
₈

middle of the 1800s. The city of London _____ six indoor swimming pools.
₉

Soon after, the modern Olympic games _____, and swimming races _____
₁₀ ₁₁

included in the events. After this, swimming pools _____ even more popular,
₁₂

and now they _____ all over the world.
₁₃

先閱讀下段文字，然後閱讀其後敘述句；敘述如果正確，圈 T；敘述如果有錯，圈 F。

Getting a Passport

Jerry is applying for a passport. He needs to bring proof of citizenship, two photographs, and the application to the passport office. He also needs money for the fee. He will receive his passport in the mail about three weeks after he applies for it.

1. The application process can be completed by mail.   T   F

2. Proof of citizenship must be provided.   T   F

3. A fee has to be paid.   T   F

4. Photographs should be taken before Jerry goes to the passport office.   T   F

5. The passport will be sent by mail.   T   F

10-5 被動式情態助動詞 Passive Modal Auxiliaries

主動式情態 助動詞	被動式情態助動詞 (情態助動詞 + **be** + 過去分詞)	情態助動詞常用在被動句中。
Bob *will mail* it. It *will be mailed* by Bob. Bob *can mail* it. It *can be mailed* by Bob. Bob *should mail* it. It *should be mailed* by Bob. Bob *ought to mail* it. It *ought to be mailed* by Bob. Bob *must mail* it. It *must be mailed* by Bob. Bob *has to mail* it. It *has to be mailed* by Bob. Bob *may mail* it. It *may be mailed* by Bob. Bob *might mail* it. It *might be mailed* by Bob. Bob *could mail* it. It *could be mailed* by Bob.		形式： 情態助動詞 + **be** + 過去分詞 (情態助動詞的意義和用法，請見第七章。)

❑ **Exercise 19. 文法** (表 10-5)

將主動語態的情態助動詞改為被動語態，以完成下列句子。

1. Someone must send this letter immediately.

   This letter ___*must be sent*___ immediately.

2. People should plant tomatoes in the spring.

   Tomatoes _____ in the spring.

3. People cannot control the weather.

   The weather _____.

4. Someone had to fix our car before we left for Chicago.

   Our car _____ before we left for Chicago.

5. People can reach me on my cell at 555-3815.

   I _____ on my cell at 555-3815.

6. Someone ought to wash these dirty dishes soon.

   These dirty dishes _____ soon.

7. People may cook carrots or eat them raw.

   Carrots _____ or _____ raw.

8. Be careful! If that email file has a virus, it could destroy your reports.

   Your reports _____ if that email file has a virus.

9. You must keep medicine out of the reach of children.

   Medicine _____ out of the reach of children.

❑ **Exercise 20. 閱讀** (表 10-1 → 10-5)

第一部分　先閱讀下列問題，然後再閱讀與牛仔褲有關的文章。

> Are you wearing jeans right now, or do you have a pair at home?
> If so, who were they made by?

The Origin of Jeans

Around the world, a very popular pant for men, women, and children is jeans. Did you know that jeans were created more than 100 years ago? They were invented by Levi Strauss during the California Gold Rush.

In 1853, Levi Strauss, a 24-year-old immigrant from Germany, traveled from New York to San Francisco. His brother was the owner of a store in New York and wanted to open another one in San Francisco. When Strauss arrived, a gold miner* asked him what he had to sell. Levi said he had strong canvas for tents and wagon covers. The miner told him he really needed strong pants because he couldn't find any that lasted very long.

So Levi Strauss took the canvas and designed a pair of overall pants. The miners liked them except that they were rough on the skin. Strauss exchanged the canvas for a cotton cloth from France called *serge de Nimes*. Later, the fabric was called "denim" and the pants were given the nickname "blue jeans."

Eventually, Levi Strauss & Company was formed. Strauss and tailor David Jacobs began putting rivets** in pants to make them stronger. In 1936, a red tab was added to the rear pocket. This was done so "Levis" could be more easily identified. Nowadays the company is very well known, and for many people, all jeans are known as Levis.

第二部分　以完整句回答下列問題。

1. Who was Levi Strauss?
2. Why did Strauss go to California?
3. Who were jeans first created for?
4. What is denim?
5. What two changes were later made to jeans?
6. Why were rivets put in jeans?
7. Why was a red tab added to the rear pocket?
8. Many people have a different name for blue jeans. What is it?

---

*gold miner 意指「採金礦工」。

**rivet 意指「鉚釘」，是一種固定性很強的別針，用來固定衣服的接縫。

❑ **Exercise 21. 暖身活動：知識問答比賽** (表 10-6)

你知道以下知識問答的答案嗎？* 用下表中的字詞完成下列句子。

China	monkeys	sand	spiders
Mongolia	Nepal	small spaces	whales

1. Glass is composed mainly of ＿＿＿＿＿＿＿＿＿＿＿ .

2. Dolphins are related to ＿＿＿＿＿＿＿＿＿＿ .

3. The Gobi Desert is located in two countries: ＿＿＿＿＿＿＿＿＿＿ and
   ＿＿＿＿＿＿＿＿＿＿ .

4. People with claustrophobia are frightened by ＿＿＿＿＿＿＿＿＿ .

10-6 過去分詞作爲形容詞（狀態性被動式）

	be	+	形容詞
(a)	Paul	*is*	*young.*
(b)	Paul	*is*	*tall.*
(c)	Paul	*is*	*hungry.*
	be	+	過去分詞
(d)	Paul	*is*	*married.*
(e)	Paul	*is*	*tired.*
(f)	Paul	*is*	*frightened.*

be 動詞後面可接形容詞，如：例 (a) 到例 (c)，用來描述或說明句中主詞。

be 動詞後面可接過去分詞（被動形式），如：例 (d) 到例 (f)。過去分詞和形容詞類似，用來描述或說明句中主詞。日常用語常會使用過去分詞當形容詞。

(g) Paul *is married **to*** Susan.

(h) Paul *was excited **about*** the game.

(i) Paul *will be prepared **for*** the exam.

過去分詞後面經常必須接特定的介系詞，再加受詞，例如：

例 (g) 中：***married*** 後面接 ***to***（＋ 受詞）
例 (h) 中：***excited*** 後面接 ***about***（＋ 受詞）
例 (i) 中：***prepared*** 後面接 ***for***（＋ 受詞）

「*Be* + 過去式分詞」的常見表達字詞

be acquainted (*with*)	be excited (*about*)	be opposed (*to*)
be bored (*with, by*)	be exhausted (*from*)	be pleased (*with*)
be broken	be finished (*with*)	be prepared (*for*)
be closed	be frightened (*of, by, about*)	be qualified (*for*)
be composed of	be gone (*from*)	be related (*to*)
be crowded (*with*)	be hurt	be satisfied (*with*)
be devoted (*to*)	be interested (*in*)	be scared (*of, by*)
be disappointed (*in, with*)	be involved (*in, with*)	be shut
be divorced (*from*)	be located in / south of / etc.	be spoiled
be done (*with*)	be lost	be terrified (*of, by*)
be drunk (*on*)	be made of	be tired (*of, from*)*
be engaged (*to*)	be married (*to*)	be worried (*about*)

*I'm **tired of** the cold weather. = *I've had enough cold weather. I want the weather to get warm*. 我受夠了冷天，眞希望天氣能暖和些。
I'm **tired from** working hard all day. = *I'm tired because I worked hard all day*. 辛苦地工作了整天，我覺得疲累。

*請見解答本中的 *Trivia Answers*。

圈選所有可完成句子的正確答案。

1. Roger is disappointed with _____.
   (a.) his job
   b. in the morning
   (c.) his son's grades

2. Are you related to _____?
   a. the Browns
   b. math and science
   c. me

3. Finally! We are done with _____.
   a. finished
   b. our chores
   c. our errands

4. My boss was pleased with _____.
   a. my report
   b. thank you
   c. the new contract

5. The baby birds are gone from _____.
   a. away
   b. their nest
   c. yesterday

6. Taka and JoAnne are bored with _____.
   a. their work
   b. this movie
   c. their marriage

7. Are you tired of _____?
   a. work
   b. asleep
   c. the news

❏ **Exercise 23.** 文法 (表 10-6)

用適當的介系詞完成下列句子。

Nervous Nick is . . .

1. worried _____ almost everything in life.

2. frightened _____ being around people.

3. also scared _____ snakes, lizards, and dogs.

4. terrified _____ going outside and seeing a dog.

5. exhausted _____ worrying so much.

Steady Steve is . . .

6. excited _____ waking up every morning.

7. pleased _____ his job.

8. interested _____ having a good time.

9. involved _____ many community activities.

10. satisfied _____ just about everything in his life.

用下表中動詞的現在式完成下列句子，並注意動詞後的**粗體**介系詞。

compose	interest	oppose	satisfy
finish	marry	prepare	✓scare

1. Most children __are scared__ **of** loud noises.

2. Jane _____ **in** ecology.

3. Don't clear the table yet. I _____ not _____ **with** my meal.

4. I _____ **with** my progress in English.

5. Tony _____ **to** Sonia. They have a happy marriage.

6. Roberta's parents _____ **to** her marriage. They don't like her fiancé.

7. The test is tomorrow. _____ you _____ **for** it?

8. A digital picture _____ **of** thousands of tiny dots called pixels.

❏ **Exercise 25.** 文法 (表 10-6)
用恰當的介系詞，完成下列句子。

1. Because of the sale, the mall was crowded _____ shoppers.

2. Do you think you are qualified _____ that job?

3. Mr. Ahmad loves his family very much. He is devoted _____ them.

4. My sister is married _____ a law student.

5. I'll be finished _____ my work in another minute or two.

6. The workers are opposed _____ the new health-care plan.

7. Are you acquainted _____ this writer? I can't put her books down!*

8. Janet doesn't take good care of herself. I'm worried _____ her health.

---

can't put a book down 意指無法停止閱讀一本書，因為該書是如此的激動人心或有趣。

Exercise 26. 聽力 (表 10-6)

CD 2
Track 33

聆聽 CD 所播放的句子，並寫下聽到的介系詞。

例：你會聽到：Linda loves her grandchildren. She is devoted to them.

你要寫下：___to___

1. _____   5. _____

2. _____   6. _____

3. _____   7. _____

4. _____   8. _____

❑ **Exercise 27. 文法** (表 10-6)

用下表中的詞語完成下列句子；運用現在式，並視情況加上介系詞。

be acquainted	be exhausted	be qualified
be composed	be located	be spoiled
be crowded	be made	✓be worried
be disappointed		

1. Dennis isn't doing well in school this semester. He ___is worried about___ his grades.

2. My shirt _____ cotton.

3. I live in a three-room apartment with six other people. Our apartment _____

    _____ .

4. Vietnam _____ Southeast Asia.

5. I'm going to go straight to bed tonight. It's been a hard day. I _____ .

6. The kids _____ . I had promised to take them to the

    beach today, but now we can't go because it's raining.

7. This milk doesn't taste right. I think it _____ . I'm not going to

    drink it.

8. Water _____ hydrogen and oxygen.

9. According to the job description, an applicant must have a master's degree and at least five

    years of teaching experience. Unfortunately, I _____ not _____

    that job.

10. A: Have you ever met Mrs. Novinsky?

    B: No, I _____ not _____ her.

用聽到的字詞完成下列句子。

CD 2
Track 34

例：你會聽到：My earrings are made of gold.

你要寫下：____are made of____

1. This fruit _____. I think I'd better throw it out.

2. When we got to the post office, it _____.

3. Oxford University _____ Oxford, England.

4. Haley doesn't like to ride in elevators. She's _____ small spaces.

5. What's the matter? _____ you _____?

6. Excuse me. Could you please tell me how to get to the bus station from here?

    I _____.

7. Your name is Tom Hood? _____ you _____ Mary Hood?

8. Where's my wallet? It's _____! Did someone take it?

9. Oh, no! Look at my sunglasses. I sat on them and now they _____.

10. It's starting to rain. _____ all of the windows _____?

❑ **Exercise 29. 暖身活動** (表 10-7)

將各圖片與下列三個句子相配對；其中一句無法與任一張圖配對。

A 圖   B 圖

1. The shark is terrifying. ____
2. The shark is terrified. ____
3. The swimmer is terrifying. ____
4. The swimmer is terrified. ____

10-7 分詞形容詞：動詞 + -ed 和 -ing 的比較

Art **interests** me. (a) I am **interested** in art. 錯誤：*I am interesting in art.* (b) Art is **interesting**. 錯誤：*Art is interested.* The news **surprised** Kate. (c) Kate was **surprised**. (d) The news was **surprising**.	動詞的過去分詞 (**-ed**)* 和現在分詞 (**-ing**) 可作爲形容詞使用。 在例 (a) 中：過去分詞 (**interested**) 形容人的感覺。 在例 (b) 中：現在分詞 (**interesting**) 描述引起感覺的**原因**，而引起的原因是 art。 在例 (c) 中：**surprised** 形容 Kate 的感覺。過去分詞具有被動的意義，如：*Kate was surprised **by the news***。 在例 (d) 中：引起驚訝情緒的是 **the news**。
(e) Did you hear the **surprising news**? (f) Roberto fixed the **broken window**.	如同其他形容詞，分詞形容詞出現在 **be** 動詞之後，如：例 (a) 到例 (d)；或放在名詞前面，如：例 (e) 和例 (f)。

*規則動詞的過去分詞爲動詞字尾加 **-ed**。關於不規則動詞變化，請見本書第 432-433 頁的表格。

❑ **Exercise 30. 文法** (表 10-7)

用正確的字詞，如：*girl*、*man* 或 *roller coaster*，完成下列句子。

1. The _____ is frightened.

2. The _____ is frightening.

3. The _____ is excited.

4. The _____ is exciting.

5. The _____ is thrilling.

6. The _____ is delighted.

❑ **Exercise 31. 聽力** (表 10-7)

聆聽 CD 播放的敘述句，並圈選聽到的字詞。

CD 2
Track 35

例：你會聽到：It was a frightening experience.

你要圈出：frighten　　(frightening)　　frightened

1. bore　　　　　　boring　　　　　　bored

2. shock　　　　　shocking　　　　　shocked

3. confuse　　　　confusing　　　　confused

4. embarrass　　　embarrassing　　　embarrassed

5. surprise　　　　surprising　　　　surprised

6. scare　　　　　scary*　　　　　　scared

*該字的形容詞字尾爲 **-y**，而非 **-ing**。

用斜體動詞的 **-ed**（過去分詞）或 **-ing**（現在分詞）形式，完成下列句子。

1. Talal's classes *interest* him.

   a. Talal's classes are ___interesting___.

   b. Talal is an ___interested___ student.

2. Emily is going to Australia. The idea of going on this trip *excites* her.

   a. Emily is _____ about going on this trip.

   b. She thinks it is going to be an _____ trip.

3. I like to study sea life. The subject of marine biology *fascinates* me.

   a. Marine biology is a _____ subject.

   b. I'm _____ by marine biology.

4. Mike heard some bad news. The bad news *depressed* him.

   a. Mike is very sad. In fact, he is _____.

   b. The news made Mike feel very sad. The news was _____.

5. The exploration of space *interests* me.

   a. I'm _____ in the exploration of space.

   b. The exploration of space is _____ to me.

❏ **Exercise 33. 聽力** (表 10-7)

CD 2
Track 36

聆聽 CD 播放的句子，並圈選聽到的單字。

情境：Julie 和既是同事也是朋友的 Paul，沿著公司大樓外的噴水池邊散步。突然間，她失去重心，不小心摔進水裡。

1.	embarrassed	embarrassing	6. surprised	surprising
2.	embarrassed	embarrassing	7. upset*	upsetting
3.	shocked	shocking	8. depressed	depressing
4.	shocked	shocking	9. interested	interesting
5.	surprised	surprising	10. interested	interesting

❑ **Exercise 34.** 暖身活動 (表 10-8)
下列敘述對你來說是否正確？正確的敘述，圈 *yes*；錯的敘述，圈 *no*。

Right now . . .

1. I am getting tired.   yes   no
2. I am getting hungry.   yes   no
3. I am getting confused.   yes   no

10-8 *Get* + 形容詞；*Get* + 過去分詞

Get + 形容詞	**get** 後面可以接形容詞，表達「改變」的意思——「逐漸變成」或「開始成為」。
(a) I **am getting hungry**. Let's eat. (b) Eric **got nervous** before the job interview.	在例 (a) 中，**I'm getting hungry**. ＝ 我本來不餓，但現在開始覺得餓了。
Get + 過去分詞	有時 **get** 後面也會接過去分詞，此時過去分詞的作用就像形容詞，用來補充說明句中主詞。
(c) I**'m getting tired**. Let's stop working. (d) Steve and Rita **got married** last month.	

Get + 形容詞			**Get** + 過去分詞		
get angry	get dry	get quiet	get acquainted	get drunk	get involved
get bald	get fat	get rich	get arrested	get engaged	get killed
get big	get full	get serious	get bored	get excited	get lost
get busy	get hot	get sick	get confused	get finished	get married
get close	get hungry	get sleepy	get crowded	get frightened	get scared
get cold	get interested	get thirsty	get divorced	get hurt	get sunburned
get dark	get late	get well	get done	get interested	get tired
get dirty	get nervous	get wet	get dressed	get invited	get worried
get dizzy	get old				

---

*此字不以 *-ed* 結尾。

用下表中的字完成下列句子。

bald	dirty	hurt	lost	rich
busy	✓full	late	nervous	serious

1. This food is delicious, but I can't eat any more. I'm getting ___full___.

2. This work has to be done before we leave. We'd better get _____ and stop wasting time.

3. I didn't understand Mariam's directions very well, so on the way to her house last night I got _____. I couldn't find her house.

4. It's hard to work on a car and stay clean. Paul's clothes always get _____ from all the grease and oil.

5. Tim doesn't like to fly. As soon as he sits down, his heart starts to beat quickly. He gets really _____.

6. We'd better go home. It's getting _____, and you have school tomorrow.

7. Simon wants to get _____, but he doesn't want to work. That's not very realistic.

8. If you plan to go to medical school, you need to get _____ about the time and money involved and start planning now.

9. Mr. Andersen is losing some of his hair. He's slowly getting _____.

10. Was the accident serious? Did anyone get _____?

❏ **Exercise 36. 口說：訪談** (表 10-8)
訪問班上的同學，並與全班分享一些同學的答案。

1. Have you ever gotten hurt? What happened?
2. Have you ever gotten lost? What happened?
3. When was the last time you got dizzy?
4. How long does it take you to get dressed in the morning?
5. In general, do you get sleepy during the day? When?
6. Do you ever get hungry in the middle of the night? What do you do?
7. Have you ever gotten involved with a charity? Which one?

❏ **Exercise 37. 聽力** (表 10-8)

聆聽 CD 播放的句子，並用符合前後文語義的形容詞完成句子。

CD 2
Track 37

例：你會聽到：This towel is soaking wet. Please hang it up so it will get . . .

你要寫下：___*dry*___

1. _____

2. _____

3. _____

4. _____

5. _____

6. _____

❏ **Exercise 38. 文法** (表 10-8)

用 ***get*** 的適當形式及下表中的字，完成下列句子。

angry	dressed	kill	tired
cold	dry	lost	well
crowd	hungry	marry	worry
dark	involve	✓sunburn	

1. When I stayed out in the sun too long yesterday, I ___*got sunburned*___.

2. If you're sick, stay home and take care of yourself. You won't _____ if you don't take care of yourself.

3. Alima and Hasan are engaged. They are going to _____ a year from now.

4. Sarah doesn't eat breakfast, so she always _____ by ten or ten-thirty.

5. In the winter, the sun sets early. It _____ outside by six or even earlier.

6. Put these towels back in the dryer. They didn't _____ the first time.

7. Let's stop working for a while. I'm _____. I need a break.

8. Anastasia has to move out of her apartment next week, and she hasn't found a new place to live. She's _____.

9. Toshiro was in a terrible car wreck and almost _____. He's lucky to be alive.

10. The temperature is dropping. Brrr! I'm _____. Can I borrow your sweater?

11. Sorry we're late. We took a wrong turn and _____.

280 第十章

12. Good restaurants _____ around dinner time. It's hard to find a seat because there are so many people.

13. Calm down! Take it easy! You shouldn't _____ so _____. It's not good for your blood pressure.

14. I left when Ellen and Joe began to argue. I never _____ in other people's quarrels.

15. Sam is wearing one brown sock and one blue sock today. He _____ in a hurry this morning and didn't pay attention to the color of his socks.

❑ **Exercise 39. 閱讀** (表 10-8)
閱讀以下文章及其後的敘述句。敘述如果正確，圈 T；敘述如果有錯，圈 F。

A Blended Family

Lisa and Thomas live in a blended family. They are not related to each other, but they are brother and sister. Actually, they are stepbrother and stepsister. This is how they came to be in the same family.

Lisa's mother got divorced when Lisa was a baby. Thomas' father was a widower. His wife had died seven years earlier. Lisa and Thomas' parents met five years ago at a going-away party for a friend. After a year of dating, they got engaged and a year later, they got married. Lisa and Thomas are about the same age and get along well. Theirs is a happy, blended family.

1. Lisa's mother got married. Then she got divorced.
   Then she got remarried.   T   F

2. Thomas' father got married, and then he got divorced.
   After he got divorced, he got engaged, and then he got remarried.   T   F

3. Lisa and Thomas became stepsister and stepbrother when
   their parents got remarried.   T   F

❑ **Exercise 40. 暖身活動** (表 10-9)
圈選句中符合自身情況的斜體字詞。

1. I am *used to, not used to* speaking English with native speakers.

2. I am *accustomed to, not accustomed to* speaking English without translating from my language.

3. I am *getting used to, not getting used to* English slang.

4. I am *getting accustomed to, not getting accustomed to* reading English without a dictionary.

10-9 *Be Used/Accustomed To* 和 *Get Used/Accustomed To* 的用法

(a) I *am used to* hot weather. (b) I *am accustomed to* hot weather.	例 (a) 和例 (b) 同義：對說話者而言，生活在炎熱氣候中是尋常的事，他很明白生活在天氣炎熱的地方是怎麼回事。亦即，炎熱的氣候對他而言，並不陌生或特別。
(c) I *am used to living* in a hot climate. (d) I *am accustomed to living* in a hot climate.	注意例 (c) 和例 (d)：*to*（介系詞）後面接動詞 *-ing* 形式（動名詞）。
(e) I just moved from Florida to Alaska. I have never lived in a cold climate before, but I *am getting used to (accustomed to)* the cold weather here.	在例 (e) 中，*I'm getting used to/accustomed to* = 說話者已漸漸習慣於某事物。

❑ **Exercise 41. 文法**（表 10-9）

第一部分 用 *be used to* 的肯定或否定形式，完成下列句子。

1. Juan is from Mexico. He ___is used to___ hot weather. He ___isn't used to___ cold weather.

2. Alice was born and raised in Chicago. She _____ living in a big city.

3. My hometown is New York City, but this year I'm going to school in a town with a population of 10,000. I _____ living in a small town. I _____ living in a big city.

4. We do a lot of exercises in class. We _____ doing exercises.

第二部分 用 *be accustomed to* 的肯定或否定形式，完成下列句子。

5. Spiro recently moved to Hong Kong from Greece. He ___is accustomed to___ eating Greek food. He ___isn't accustomed to___ eating Chinese food.

6. I always get up around 6:00 A.M. I _____ getting up early. I _____ sleeping late.

7. Our teacher always gives us a lot of homework. We _____ having a lot of homework every day.

8. Young schoolchildren rarely take multiple-choice tests. They _____ taking that kind of test.

❑ **Exercise 42. 聽力與口說**（表 10-9）

第一部分 用聽到的字詞完成下列問句。

CD 2
Track 38

例：你會聽到：What time are you accustomed to getting up?

你要寫下：___are you accustomed to___

1. What _____ doing in the evenings?

2. What time _____ going to bed?

3. What _____ having for breakfast?

4. _____ living in this area?

5. Do you live with someone or do you live alone? _____ that?

6. _____ speaking English every day?

7. What _____ doing on weekends?

8. What do you think about the weather here? _____ it?

第二部分　成兩人一組，輪流用第一部分的題目作問答練習。

❑ Exercise 43. 口說：訪談 (表 10-9)

用含 *be used to/accustomed to* 的問題，詢問班上同學。

例：buy \ frozen food
　　→ *Are you used to/accustomed to buying frozen food?*

1. get up \ early	6. drink \ coffee in the morning
2. sleep \ late	7. have \ dessert at night
3. eat \ breakfast	8. live \ in a big city
4. skip \ lunch	9. live \ in a small town
5. eat \ a late dinner	10. pay \ for all your expenses

❑ Exercise 44. 口說 (表 10-9)

分小組討論下列其中一個或更多主題，並列出答案清單，再與全班分享一些答案。

主題：
1. Junko is going to leave her parents' house next week. She is going to move in with two of her cousins who work in the city. Junko will be away from her home for the first time in her life. What is she going to have to get accustomed to?

2. Think of a time you traveled in or lived in a foreign country. What weren't you used to? What did you get used to? What didn't you ever get used to?

3. Think of the first day of a job you have had. What weren't you used to? What did you get used to?

❑ Exercise 45. 暖身活動 (表 10-10)

依照自身的實際情況，完成下列關於飲食偏好的句子。

1. There are some foods I liked when I was younger, but now I don't eat them. I used to eat _____, but now I don't.

2. There are some foods I didn't like when I first tried them, but now they're okay. For example, the first time I ate _____, I didn't like it, but now I'm used to eating them.

10-10 *Used To* 和 *Be Used To* 的比較

(a) I *used to **live*** in Chicago, but now I live in Tokyo. 錯誤：I *used to living* in Chicago. 錯誤：I *am used to live* in a big city.	在例 (a) 中，***used to*** 表示過去的習慣（請見第 53 頁，表 2-8），後面接**原形動詞**。
(b) I *am used to **living*** in a big city.	在例 (b) 中，***be used to*** 後面接動詞 **-ing** 形式（動名詞）。★

*注意：在 **used to**（過去的習慣）和 **be used to** 中，"d" 都不發音。

❑ **Exercise 46. 文法**（表 10-10）
用適當形式的 **be** 動詞完成下列句子；如果不需要加 **be** 動詞，則寫下 **Ø**。

1. I have lived in Malaysia for a long time. I ___am___ used to warm weather.

2. I ___Ø___ used to live in Portugal, but now I live in Spain.

3. I _____ used to sitting at this desk. I sit here every day.

4. I _____ used to sit in the back of the classroom, but now I prefer to sit in the front row.

5. When I was a child, I _____ used to play games with my friends in a big field near my house after school every day.

6. It's hard for my kids to stay inside on a cold, rainy day. They _____ used to playing outside in the big field near our house. They play there almost every day.

7. A teacher _____ used to answering questions. Students, especially good students, always have a lot of questions.

8. People _____ used to believe the world was flat.

❑ **Exercise 47. 文法**（表 10-10）
用 **used to/be used to** 及括弧內動詞的正確形式，完成下列句子。

1. Nick stays up later now than he did when he was in high school. He (*go*) ___used to go___ to bed at ten, but now he rarely gets to bed before midnight.

2. I got used to going to bed late when I was in college, but now I have a job and I need my sleep. These days I (*go*) ___am used to going___ to bed around ten-thirty.

3. I am a vegetarian. I (*eat*) _____ meat, but now I eat only meatless meals.

4. Ms. Wu has had a vegetable garden all her life. She (*grow*) _____ her own vegetables.

5. Oscar has lived in Brazil for ten years. He (*eat*) _____ Brazilian food. It's his favorite.

6. Georgio moved to Germany to open his own restaurant. He (*have*) _____ _____ a small bakery in Italy.

7. I have taken the bus to work every day for the past five years. I (*take*) _____ _____ the bus.

8. Juanita travels by train on company business. She (*go*) _____ by plane, but now it's too expensive.

❑ **Exercise 48. 暖身活動** (表 10-11)
完成下列關於航空公司乘客的句子。

1. Before getting on the plane, passengers are expected to _____.

2. After boarding the plane, passengers are supposed to _____.

3. During landing, passengers are not supposed to _____.

10-11 *Be Supposed To* 的用法

(a) Mike **is supposed to call** me tomorrow. （想法：說話者預期 Mike 明天會打電話給他。）	**be supposed to** 用在談論預期會發生的活動或事件。
(b) We **are supposed to write** a composition. （想法：老師預期學生要寫一篇作文。）	在例 (a) 中，**is supposed to** 是用於表達說話者認為 Mike 會打電話給他。說話者要求 Mike 打電話給他，而 Mike 也答應了，所以他預期 Mike 會打電話。
(c) Alice **was supposed to be** home at ten, but she didn't get in until midnight. （想法：有人預期 Alice 十點的時候會在家。）	**be supposed to** 的過去式用法通常表示預期的事件其實沒有發生，如：例 (c)。

❑ **Exercise 49. 文法** (表 10-11)
用 **be supposed to** 造出與各題語義相近的句子。

1. The teacher expects us to be on time for class.
    → *We are supposed to be on time for class.*

2. People expect the weather to be cold tomorrow.

3. People expect the plane to arrive at 6:00.

4. My boss expects me to work late tonight.

5. I expected the mail to come an hour ago, but it didn't.

☐ **Exercise 50.** 口說 (表 10-11)

用 ***be supposed to*** 造一敘述句，以摘要各個對話。成兩人一組、分小組或全班一起練習。

1. TOM'S BOSS: Mail this package.
   TOM: Yes, sir.

   → *Tom is supposed to mail a package.*

2. LENA: Call me at nine.
   ANN: Okay.

3. MS. MARTINEZ: Please make your bed before you go to school.
   JOHNNY: Okay, Mom.

4. PROF. THOMPSON: Read the test directions carefully and raise your hand if you have any
   questions.
   STUDENTS: (*no response*)

5. DR. KEMPER: You should take one pill every eight hours.
   PATIENT: Right. Anything else?
   DR. KEMPER: Drink plenty of fluids.

☐ **Exercise 51.** 聽力 (表 10-11)

CD 2
Track 39

聆聽 CD 播放的 ***be supposed to*** 句子。敘述如果正確，圈 T；敘述如果有錯，圈 F。注意：
be supposed to 中的 ***to*** 聽起來像 "ta"。

例：你會聽到：Visitors at a museum are not supposed to touch the art.

你要圈出：Ⓣ   F

1. T   F   5. T   F
2. T   F   6. T   F
3. T   F   7. T   F
4. T   F   8. T   F

☐ **Exercise 52.** 閱讀、文法與聽力 (第 10 章)

第一部分 回答下列問題，然後再閱讀關於動物園的文章。

Have you visited a zoo recently?
What was your opinion of it?
Were the animals well-taken care of?
Did they live in natural settings or in cages?

Zoos

　　Zoos are common around the world. The first zoo was established around 3,500 years ago by an Egyptian queen for her enjoyment. Five hundred years later, a Chinese emperor established a huge zoo to show his power and wealth. Later, zoos were established for the purpose of studying animals.

　　Zoos were supposed to take good care of animals, but some of the early ones were dark holes or dirty cages. At that time, people became disgusted with the poor care the animals were given. Later, these early zoos were replaced by scientific institutions. Animals were studied and kept in better conditions there. These research centers became the first modern zoos.

Because zoos want to treat animals well and encourage breeding, animals today are put in large, natural settings instead of small cages. They are fed a healthy diet and are watched carefully for any signs of disease. Most zoos have specially trained veterinarians and a hospital for their animals. Today, animals in these zoos are treated well, and zoo breeding programs have saved many different types of animals.

第二部分　圈選所有合文法的句子。

1. a. The first zoo was established around 3,500 years ago.
   b. The first zoo established around 3,500 years ago.
   c. An Egyptian queen established the first zoo.

2. a. Zoos supposed to take good care of animals.
   b. Zoos were supposed to take good care of animals.
   c. Zoos were suppose to take good care of animals.

3. a. The animals was poorly cared for in some of the early zoos.
   b. The animals were poorly cared for in some of the early zoos.
   c. The early zoos didn't take good care of the animals.

4. a. Today, animals are kept in more natural settings.
   b. Today, zoos keep animals in more natural settings.
   c. Today, more natural settings are provided for animals.

5. a. Nowadays, animals are treated better in zoos than before.
   b. Nowadays, animals are taken better care of in zoos than before.
   c. Nowadays, animals take care of in zoos than before.

第三部分　聆聽 CD 播放的文章，用聽到的動詞完成下列句子，然後回答問題。

CD 2
Track 40

Zoos

Zoos are common around the world. The first zoo ___*was*___ established around 3,500
                                                     1
years ago by an Egyptian queen for her enjoyment. Five hundred years later, a Chinese

emperor _____ a huge zoo to show his power and wealth. Later, zoos
                    2

_____ for the purpose of studying animals.
           3

　　Zoos _____ take good care of animals, but some of
                      4

the early ones were dark holes or dirty cages. At that time, people _____
                                                                                    5

disgusted with the poor care the animals _____. Later, these early
                                                        6

zoos _____ replaced by scientific institutions. Animals _____
              7   8

and _____ in better conditions there. These research centers became the first
            9

modern zoos.

Because zoos want to treat animals well and encourage breeding, animals today

_____ in large, natural settings instead of small cages. They
　　　　10

_____ a healthy diet and _____ carefully for any signs of
　　　　11　　　　　　　　　　　　　　　12

disease. Most zoos _____ specially trained veterinarians and a hospital for their
　　　　　　　　　　　13

animals. Today, animals in these zoos _____ well, and zoo breeding
　　　　　　　　　　　　　　　　　　14

programs _____ many different types of animals.
　　　　　　　　15

1. Why was the first zoo established?
2. What were some of the early zoos like?
3. What was the purpose of the first modern zoos?
4. What are zoos doing to encourage breeding?
5. Why do zoos want to encourage breeding?

❏ **Exercise 53. 檢視學習成果**（第 10 章）
校訂下列句子。

1. I ~~am~~ agree with him.

2. Something was happened.

3. This pen is belong to me.

4. I'm interesting in that subject.

5. He is marry with my cousin.

6. Mary's dog was died last week.

7. Were you surprise when you heard the news?

8. When I went downtown, I am get lost.

9. The bus was arrived ten minutes late.

10. We're not suppose to have pets in our apartment.

第一部分　閱讀以下文章，並在被動語態的動詞下劃<u>底線</u>。

My Favorite Holiday

　　(1) New Year's is the most important holiday of the year in my country. New Year's <u>is celebrated</u> for fifteen days, but my favorite day is the first day.

　　(2) The celebration actually begins at midnight. Fireworks are set off, and the streets are filled with people. Neighbors and friends greet each other and wish one another good luck for the year. The next morning, gifts are exchanged. Children are given money. It is wrapped in red envelopes because red is the color for good luck. When I was younger, this was always my favorite part of the holiday.

　　(3) On New Year's Day, everyone wears new clothes. These clothes are bought especially for the holiday. People are very polite to each other. It is considered wrong to yell, lie, or use bad language on the first day of the year. It is a custom for younger generations to visit their elders. They wish them good health and a long life.

第二部分　挑選自己喜歡的節日，並描述當天的活動。你在當天的上午、下午以及傍晚做了什麼？你最喜歡哪些活動？用一些被動語態的句子造句。

第十一章

可數／不可數名詞與冠詞

❑ **Exercise 1. 暖身活動** (表 11-1)

勾選 (✓) 你手邊有的東西。你知道有些名詞前面有 *a*，而有些名詞前卻是 *an* 的原因嗎？

1. _____ **a** pen
2. _____ **an** eraser
3. _____ **a** notebook
4. _____ **an** umbrella
5. _____ **an** interesting book
6. _____ **a** university map

冠詞：置於 n. 之前

分類 { 不定 a/an（可數 n.）
定 the（皆可）

11-1 *A* 和 *An* 的比較	
(a) I have **a** *pencil*. (b) I live in **an** *apartment*. (c) I have **a** *small apartment*. (d) I live in **an** *old building*.	*a* 和 *an* 用於單數名詞前（如：例句中的 *pencil* 和 *apartment*），意指「一個」。 若單數名詞前有形容詞修飾語（如：例句中的 *small* 和 *old*），*a* 或 *an* 則要放在形容詞之前，如：例 (c) 和例 (d)。 *a* 置於以子音字母（如：*b*、*c*、*d*、*f*、*g* 等）為首的字詞前，如：*a boy*、*a bad day*、*a cat*、*a cute baby*。 *an* 置於以母音字母（如：*a*、*e*、*i* 和 *o*）為首的字詞前，如：*an apartment*、*an angry man*、*an elephant*、*an empty room* 等。
(e) I have **an** *umbrella*. (f) I saw **an** *ugly picture*. (g) I attend **a** *university*. (h) I had **a** *unique experience*.	在以 *u* 開頭的字詞前： (1) 若 *u* 作母音發音，用 *an*： 　　如：*an umbrella*、*an uncle*、*an unusual day*。 (2) 若 *u* 作子音發音，用 *a*： 　　如：*a university*、*a unit*、*a usual event*。
(i) He will arrive in **an** *hour*. (j) New Year's Day is **a** *holiday*.	在以 *h* 開頭的字詞前： (1) 若 *h* 不發音，用 *an*： 　　如：*an hour*、*an honor*、*an honest person*。 (2) 若 *h* 有發音，用 *a*： 　　如：*a holiday*、*a hotel*、*a high grade*。

❑ **Exercise 2. 文法** (表 11-1)

在下列字詞前加上 *a* 或 *an*。

1. _a_ mistake
2. _an_ abbreviation
3. ____ dream
4. _an_ interesting dream
5. _an_ empty box
6. ____ box
7. ____ uniform
8. _an_ email
9. _an_ untrue story

10. _an_ urgent message
11. _a_ 共同 universal problem
12. _an_ unhappy child
13. _an_ hour or two
14. ____ hole in the ground
15. ____ hill
16. ____ handsome man
17. _an_ honest man
18. _an_ honor

❑ **Exercise 3. 聽力** (表 11-1)

CD 2
Track 41

聆聽 CD 播放的句子，然後判斷聽見的是 *a*、*an* 或 **Ø**（不加冠詞）。

例：你會聽到：I have a bad toothache.

你要圈出：ⓐ　　　an　　　Ø

1. a　an　Ø
2. a　an　Ø
3. a　an　Ø
4. a　an　Ø
5. a　an　Ø

6. a　an　Ø
7. a　an　Ø
8. a　an　Ø
9. a　an　Ø
10. a　an　Ø

❑ **Exercise 4. 暖身活動** (表 11-2)

圈選所有可完成句子的正確答案。

a. 1. I need one ____.
　　　　a. chair　　　b. chairs

~~ n.數、單
↑
必須冠詞

a. 2. There are two ____ in the room.
　　　　a. chairs　　　b. furniture（總稱）

a.b. 3. I found some ____ in the storage room.
　　　　a. chairs　　　b. furniture

a.b. 4. I found ____ in the storage room.
　　　　a. chairs　　　b. furniture

11-2 可數和不可數名詞 Count and Noncount Nouns

	單數	複數	
可數名詞	*a* chair *one* chair	Ø chairs *two* chairs *some* chairs	可數名詞： (1) 可以用數字計算的名詞，如：*one chair*、*two chairs*、*ten chairs* 等。 (2) 單數時，前面可加 *a* 或 *an*，如：*a chair*。 (3) 複數形以 *-s* 或 *-es* 結尾，如：*chairs*。★
不可數名詞	Ø furniture *some* furniture	Ø Ø	不可數名詞：　可加 the　不加 a/an (1) 不能用數字計算的名詞。 　錯誤：*one furniture* (2) 前面不直接加 *a* 或 *an*。 　錯誤：*a furniture* (3) 沒有複數形（不以 *-s* 結尾）。 　錯誤：*furnitures*

★ 關於 *-s/-es* 的拼字和發音，請見第 14 頁，表 1-5 及第 147 頁，表 6-1。

❏ **Exercise 5. 文法**（表 11-2）

勾選 (✓) 下列正確的句子，並訂正錯誤的句子。不可數名詞用 *some* 作訂正。

some furniture

one chair

two chairs

some chairs

1. **✓** I bought one chair for my apartment.
2. ____ I bought ~~one~~ *some* furniture for my apartment.★
3. ____ I bought four chairs for my apartment.
4. ____ I bought four furnitures for my apartment.
5. ____ I bought a chair for my apartment.
6. ____ I bought a furniture for my apartment.
7. ____ I bought some chair for my apartment.
8. ____ I bought some furnitures for my apartment.

❏ **Exercise 6. 暖身活動**（表 11-3）

將下表中的字詞，寫在正確的類別標題下。

bracelets	ideas	letters	postcards	rings	suggestions

Advice	Mail	Jewelry
_____	_____	_____
_____	_____	_____

★以下兩句皆正確：*I bought some furniture for my apartment.* 或 *I bought furniture for my apartment.*。更多關於 Ø（不加冠詞）和 *some* 的用法，請見表 11-8。

11-3 不可數名詞 Noncount Nouns

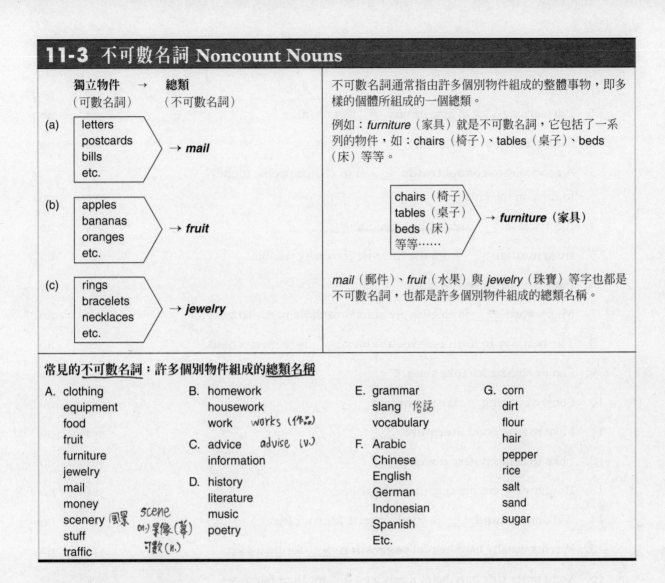

獨立物件 → 總類
（可數名詞） （不可數名詞）

(a) letters / postcards / bills / etc. → **mail**

(b) apples / bananas / oranges / etc. → **fruit**

(c) rings / bracelets / necklaces / etc. → **jewelry**

不可數名詞通常指由許多個別物件組成的整體事物，即多樣的個體所組成的一個總類。

例如：*furniture*（家具）就是不可數名詞，它包括了一系列的物件，如：chairs（椅子）、tables（桌子）、beds（床）等等。

chairs（椅子） / tables（桌子） / beds（床） / 等等…… → **furniture**（家具）

mail（郵件）、*fruit*（水果）與 *jewelry*（珠寶）等字也都是不可數名詞，也都是許多個別物件組成的總類名稱。

常見的不可數名詞：許多個別物件組成的總類名稱

A. clothing / equipment / food / fruit / furniture / jewelry / mail / money / scenery 風景 [scene (n.) 景像（幕）可數 (n.)] / stuff / traffic

B. homework / housework / work works（作品）

C. advice advise (v.) / information

D. history / literature / music / poetry

E. grammar / slang 俗話 / vocabulary

F. Arabic / Chinese / English / German / Indonesian / Spanish / Etc.

G. corn / dirt / flour / hair / pepper / rice / salt / sand / sugar

---

❑ **Exercise 7. 文法** (表 11-2 和 11-3)

用 ***a/an*** 或 ***some*** 完成下列句子，並判斷以**粗體**標示的名詞是可數 (count) 或不可數 (noncount)。

1. I often have ___*some*___ **fruit** for dessert.   count   (noncount)

2. I had ___*a*___ **banana** for dessert.   count   noncount

3. I got ___a (c)___ **letter** today.   count   noncount

4. I got ___Some (non)___ **mail** today.   count   noncount

5. Anna wears ___a (c)___ **ring** on her left hand.   count   noncount

6. Maria is wearing ___Some (non)___ **jewelry** today.   count   noncount

7. I have ___some (non.)___ **homework** to finish.   count   noncount

8. I have ___an (c)___ **assignment** to finish.   count   noncount

9. I needed ___some (non.)___ **information**.   count   noncount

10. I asked ___a (c)___ **question**.   count   noncount

❑ **Exercise 8. 文法與口說** (表 11-2 和 11-3)

視情況加上字尾 **-s/-es**；或者，在空格中填入 **Ø**，然後判斷你是否同意下列句子，並與同學討論你的答案。

1. I'm learning a lot of **grammar** _Ø_ this term.   yes   no

2. Count and noncount **noun** _s_ are easy.   yes   no

3. A good way to control **traffic** ____ is to charge people money to drive in the city.   yes   no

4. Electric **car** _s_ will replace gas **car** _s_ .   yes   no

5. **Information** ____ from the Internet is usually reliable.   yes   no

6. **Fact** _s_ are always true.   yes   no

7. Many **word** _s_ in English are similar to those in my language.   yes   no

8. The best way to learn new **vocabulary** ____ is to memorize it.   yes   no

9. I enjoy singing karaoke **song** _s_ .   yes   no

10. I enjoy listening to classical **music** ____ .   yes   no

11. I like to read good **literature** ____ .   yes   no

12. I like to read mystery **novel** _s_ .   yes   no

13. **Beach** _es_ are relaxing places to visit.   yes   no

14. Walking on **sand** ____ is good exercise for your legs.   yes   no

15. Parents usually have helpful **suggestion** _s_ for their kids.   yes   no

16. Sometimes kids have helpful **advice** _s_ for their parents.   yes   no

❑ **Exercise 9. 暖身活動** (表 11-4)

用下表中的字詞，並依照自身情況完成句子。

beauty	health	milk	pollution	traffic
coffee	honesty	money	smog	violence
happiness	juice	noise	tea	water

1. During the day, I drink _____ or _____ .

2. Two things I don't like about big cities are _____ and _____ .

3. _____ is more important than _____ .

11-4 其他不可數名詞 More Noncount Nouns

(a) 液體		固體與半固體				氣體
coffee	soup	bread	meat	chalk	paper	air
milk	tea	butter	beef	glass	soap	pollution
oil	water	cheese	chicken	gold	toothpaste	smog
		ice	fish	iron	wood	smoke

(b) 自然現象					
weather	darkness	thunder			
rain	light	lightning			
snow	sunshine				

(c) 抽象名詞★					
beauty	fun	health	ignorance	luck	selfishness
courage	generosity	help	kindness	patience	time
experience	happiness	honesty	knowledge	progress	violence

★抽象名詞只是一個概念，無外在形體，且觸碰不到。

❑ **Exercise 10. 文法** (表 11-2 → 11-4)

視情況加上字尾 **-s/-es**；如果不用加字尾，就在空格中填入 **Ø**；如有必要，可從括弧中選填正確的動詞。

1. I made some **mistake** _s___ on my algebra test.

2. In winter in Siberia, there ((is), are) **snow** _Ø___ on the ground.

3. Siberia has very cold **weather** ____ .

4. Be sure to give the new couple my best **wish** ____ .

5. I want to wish them good **luck** ____ .

6. **Silver** ____ (is, are) expensive. **Diamond** ____ (is, are) expensive too.

7. I admire Professor Yoo for her extensive **knowledge** ____ of organic farming methods.

8. Professor Yoo has a lot of good **idea** ____ and strong **opinion** ____ .

9. Teaching children to read requires **patience** ____ .

10. Doctors take care of **patient** ____ .

11. Mr. Fernandez's English is improving. He's making **progress** ____ .

12. Wood stoves are a source of **pollution** ____ in many cities.

❏ **Exercise 11.** 聽力 (表 11-2 → 11-4)

CD 2 Track 42

聆聽 CD 播放的句子,並在複數名詞字尾加上 **-s**;如果不用加字,就在空格中填入 **Ø**。

例:你會聽到:Watch out! There's ice on the sidewalk.
　　你要寫下:ice ___Ø___

1. chalk____   6. storm_____

2. soap____   7. storm_____

3. suggestion_____   8. toothpaste____

4. suggestion_____   9. stuff_____

5. gold_____   10. equipment_____

❏ **Exercise 12.** 口說 (表 11-4)

下列常用諺語都用到抽象名詞。分小組練習,各組挑選兩句諺語,並向全班解釋諺語含義。

例:Ignorance is bliss.
　　→ ***Ignorance*** *means you don't know about something.* ***Bliss*** *means happiness.*
　　　This saying means that you are happier if you don't know about a problem.

1. Honesty is the best policy.　　　4. Knowledge is power.
2. Time is money.　　　　　　　　5. Experience is the best teacher.
3. Laughter is the best medicine.

❏ **Exercise 13.** 口說 (表 11-4)

完成下列句子,每句均要給兩到四個答案;與搭檔分享你的答案,並看你們的答案有多少是相同的。注意:抽象名詞通常是不可數的。要知道名詞是可數或不可數,可以查閱字典或詢問老師。

1. Qualities I admire in a person are . . . .
2. Bad qualities people can have are . . . .
3. Some of the most important things in life are . . . .
4. Certain bad conditions exist in the world. Some of them are . . . .

❏ **Exercise 14.** 遊戲 (表 11-1 → 11-4)

分小組練習,想像你的組別置身於下頁其中一個地點,並列出你們在那裡會看見的事物。最後,與全班分享你們那一組所列出的清單。清單中項目最齊全且文法正確的組別獲勝。

例:a teacher's office
　　→ *two windows*
　　→ *a lot of grammar books*
　　→ *office equipment — a computer, a printer, a photocopy machine*
　　→ *office supplies — a stapler, paper clips, pens, pencils, a ruler*
　　→ *some pictures*
　　　etc.

Places:

a restaurant   an island
a museum   a hotel
a popular department store   an airport

❑ **Exercise 15.** 暖身活動 (表 11-5)
用 *apples* 或 *fruit* 完成下列句子。

1. I bought several _____ yesterday.

2. Do you eat a lot of _____?

3. Do you eat many _____?

4. Do you eat much _____?

5. I eat a few _____ every week.

6. I eat a little _____ for breakfast.

11-5 *Several*、*A Lot Of*、*Many/Much* 與 *A Few/A Little* 的用法

可數名詞	不可數名詞	
(a) *several* chairs	Ø	*several* 只能與可數名詞連用。
(b) *a lot of* chairs	*a lot of* furniture	*a lot of* 能與可數與不可數名詞連用。
(c) *many* chairs	*much* furniture	*many* 只能與可數名詞連用。 *much* 只能與不可數名詞連用。
(d) *a few* chairs	*a little* furniture	*a few* 只能與可數名詞連用。 *a little* 只能與不可數名詞連用。

❑ **Exercise 16.** 文法 (表 11-2 和 11-5)
勾選 (✓) 正確的句子，並訂正錯誤的句子；其中一句有拼字錯誤。

                     some / Ø
1. _____ Jakob learned ~~several~~ new vocabulary.

2. _✓_ He learned several new words.

3. _____ Takashi learned a lot of new words.

4. _____ Sonia learned a lot of new vocabulary too.

5. _____ Lydia doesn't like learning too much new vocabulary in one day.

6. _____ She can't remember too ~~much~~ new words.
                         many

7. _____ Mr. Lee assigned a few vocabulary to his class.

8. _____ He assigned a few new words.

9. _____ He explained several new vocabulary.

10. _____ There is alot of new word at this level.

11. _____ There are a lot of new vocabulary at this level.

❑ **Exercise 17.** 文法：兩人一組 (表 11-1 → 11-5)

成兩人一組，並輪流用 *how many* 或 *how much*★ 完成下列問句。視情況將名詞改爲複數形。

1. How _____ does Mr. Miller have?
   a. son   → *many sons*   d. car
   b. child → *many children*   e. stuff
   c. work   → *much work*   f. experience

2. How _____ did you buy?
   a. fruit   d. tomato
   b. vegetable   e. orange
   c. banana   f. food

3. How _____ did you have?
   a. fun   d. information
   b. help   e. fact
   c. time   f. money

❑ **Exercise 18.** 口說：訪談 (表 11-5)

訪問班上同學，並用 *how much* 或 *how many* 作爲問句的開頭。最後，與全班同學分享一些答案。

How much/How many . . .

1. pages does this book have?
2. coffee do you drink every day?
3. cups of tea do you drink every day?
4. homework do you have to do tonight?
5. assignments have you had this week?
6. provinces does Canada have?
7. countries does Africa have?
8. snow does this area get in the winter?

_____

★*much* 和 *many* 較常用於問句中，較少用於肯定句中。

❑ **Exercise 19.** 文法 (表 11-1 → 11-5)

用 **a few** 或 **a little** 以及各句中提供的名詞，完成下列句子；並視情況將名詞改爲複數形。

1. music   I feel like listening to ___*a little music*___ tonight.

2. song   We sang ___*a few songs*___ at the party.

3. help   Do you need ___a little help___ with that?

4. pepper   My grandfather doesn't use salt, but he always puts ___a little pepper___ on his eggs.

5. thing   I need to pick up ___a few things___ at the store on my way home from work tonight.

6. apple   I bought ___a few apples___ at the store.*

7. fruit   I bought ___a little fruit___ at the store.

8. advice   I need _____.

9. money   If I accept that job, I'll make ___a little___ more ___money___.

10. friend   ___A few friends___ came by last night to visit us.

11. rain   It looks like we might get ___a little rain___ today. I think I'll take my umbrella with me.

12. French   I can speak ___a little French___, but I don't know any Italian at all.

13. hour   Ron's plane will arrive in ___a few___ more ___hour___.

❑ **Exercise 20.** 暖身活動 (表 11-6)

將下列句子與圖片相配對。

A 圖   B 圖   C 圖

1. Do you need one glass or two?
2. Your glasses fit nicely.
3. A: What happened?
   B: Some neighborhood kids were playing baseball, and their ball went through the glass.

---

*I bought a few apples. 意指「我買了幾顆蘋果。」

I bought a little apple. 意指「我買了一顆小蘋果。」

11-6 兼具可數和不可數性質的名詞

很多名詞同時具有可數和不可數的性質，常見的此類名詞用法如下：

名詞	當不可數名詞使用	當可數名詞使用
glass	(a) Windows are made of **glass**.	(b) I drank **a glass** of water. (c) Janet wears **glasses** when she reads.
hair	(d) Rita has brown **hair**.	(e) There's **a hair** on my jacket.
iron	(f) **Iron** is a metal.	(g) I pressed my shirt with **an iron**.
light	(h) I opened the curtain to let in **some light**.	(i) Please turn off **the lights** (*lamps*).
paper	(j) I need **some paper** to write a note.	(k) I wrote **a paper** for Professor Lee. (l) I bought **a paper** (*a newspaper*).
time	(m) How **much time** do you need to finish your work?	(n) How **many times** have you been to Mexico?
work	(o) I have **some work** to do tonight.	(p) That painting is **a work** of art.
coffee	(q) I had **some coffee** after dinner.	(r) **Two coffees**, please.
chicken/fish	(s) I ate **some chicken/some fish**.	(t) She drew a picture of **a chicken/a fish**.
experience	(u) I haven't had **much experience** with computers. (I don't have much knowledge or skill in using computers.)	(v) I had **many** interesting **experiences** on my trip. (Many interesting events happened to me on my trip.)

❑ **Exercise 21. 文法** (表 11-6)

將第 301 頁上的句子與以下圖片相配對，並討論各句意義上的差異。

A 圖　　　　B 圖　　　　C 圖

D 圖　　　E 圖　　　　F 圖

1. That was a great meal. I ate a lot of chicken. Now I'm stuffed.* _____

2. Are you hungry? How about a little chicken for lunch? _____

3. When I was a child, we raised a lot of chickens. _____

4. I bought a few chickens so I can have fresh eggs. _____

5. There's a little chicken in your yard. _____

6. That's a big chicken over there. Who does it belong to? _____

❑ **Exercise 22. 文法** (表 11-6)
用各題提供的字詞完成下列句子，並視情況將名詞改爲複數形。必要時選填括弧內正確的字。
最後討論各句意義上的差異。

1. time   It took a lot of ___time___ to write my composition.

2. time   I really like that movie. I saw it three ___times___.

3. paper   Students in Professor Young's literature class have to write a lot of ___papers___.

4. paper   Students who take careful lecture notes can use a lot of ___paper___.

5. paper   The *New York Times* is (@, some) famous ___paper___.

6. work   Van Gogh's painting *Irises* is one of my favorite ___works___ of art.

7. work   I have a lot of ___work___ to do tomorrow at my office.

8. hair   Erin has straight ___hair___, and Mariam has curly ___hair___.

9. hair   Brian has a white cat. When I stood up from Brian's sofa, my black slacks were covered with short white ___hairs___.

10. glass   I wear ___glasses___ for reading.

11. glass   In some countries, people use ___glasses___ for their tea; in other countries, they use cups.

12. glass   Many famous paintings are covered with ___glass___ to protect them.

13. iron   ___Iron is___ (*is, are*) necessary to animal and plant life.

14. iron   ___Irons are___ (*is, are*) used to make clothes look neat.

---

*stuffed 意指「非常飽」。

15. experience   My grandfather had a lot of interesting ___experiences___ in his long career as a diplomat.

16. experience   You should apply for the job at the electronics company because you have a lot of ___experience___ in that field.

17. chicken   Joe, would you like (a, *some*) more ___some chicken___ ?

18. chicken   My grandmother raises ___chickens___ in her yard.

19. light   There (is, *are*) a lot of ___lights___ on the ceilings of the school building.

20. light   A: If you want to take a picture outside now, you'll need a flash. The ___light___ (*isn't*, aren't) good here.

B: Or, we could wait an hour. (*It*, They) will be brighter then.

❑ **Exercise 23. 暖身活動**（表 11-7）
你的廚房裡有下列哪些物品？勾選 (✓) 你擁有的物品。

1. ____ a can* of tuna

2. ____ a bag of flour

3. ____ a jar of olive oil

4. ____ a bottle of soda pop

5. ____ a box of tea bags

6. ____ a bowl of sugar

11-7 不可數名詞的計量單位

(a) I had some tea. (b) I had **two cups of** tea. (c) I ate some toast. (d) I ate **one piece of** toast.	提到不可數名詞的數量時，說話者通常會加入計量單位，如：*two cups of* 或 *one piece of*。 計量單位一般是用**容器**（如：*a cup of*、*a bowl of*）、**數量**（如：*a pound of*、*a quart of*）*或**形狀**（如：*a bar of soap*、*a sheet of paper*）來表示。

*重量單位：1 磅（pound）= 0.45 公斤（kilograms/kilos）

容積單位：1 夸脫（quart）= 0.95 公升（litres/liters）；4 夸脫 = 1 加侖（gallon）= 3.8 公升。

---

* 罐頭在美式英語中為 *a can*，英式英語中則為 *a tin*。

❑ **Exercise 24. 文法** (表 11-7)

下列名詞常用的計量單位為何？有些名詞的計量單位不止一種。

第一部分　在商店裡

bag	bottle	box	can	jar

1. a ___can/jar___ of olives

2. a ___box___ of crackers

3. a _____ of mineral water

4. a _____ of jam or jelly

5. a _____ of tuna

6. a _____ of soup

7. a _____ of sugar

8. a _____ of wine

9. a _____ of soda

10. a _____ of flour

11. a _____ of paint

12. a _____ of breakfast cereal

第二部分　在廚房裡

bowl	cup	glass	piece	slice

13. a ___cup/glass___ of green tea

14. a ___bowl___ of cereal

15. a _____ of candy

16. a _____ of bread

17. a _____ of cake

18. a _____ of orange juice

19. a _____ of soup

20. a _____ of pizza

bowl	cup	glass	piece	slice

21. a _____ of soda

22. a _____ of noodles

23. a _____ of mineral water

24. a _____ of popcorn

25. a _____ of cheese

26. a _____ of rice

27. a _____ of strawberries

28. a _____ of watermelon

watermelon

❑ **Exercise 25. 口說** (表 11-7)

你和搭檔正在幫全班籌備一個派對，你已經準備好大部分的食物了，但你還需要去商店買一些東西。遵循下列句子的引導，決定你想要買的東西。你可以用嚴肅或搞笑的方式，表演這段對話給全班看，然後班上同學會告訴你，他們是否想要參加你的派對。

注意：在開始說話前，你可以看著自己要說的台詞；但說話時，請看著你的搭檔。

Shopping list

A: So what else do we need from the store?

B: Let's see. We need a few jars of _____. We should also get a box of

_____. Oh, and a couple of bags of _____.

A: Is that it? Anything else?

B: I guess a few cans of _____ would be good.

I almost forgot. What should we do about drinks?

A: How about some bottles (or cans) of _____?

B: Good idea.

A: By the way, I thought we could serve slices of _____. How does that

sound?

B: Sure.

閱讀下列對話。為什麼說話者 A 要用 *a* 或 *the*？討論說話者 A 和 說話者 B 的想法。

對話 1

A: ***A dog*** makes a good pet.　　　B: I agree.

對話 2

A: I saw ***a dog*** in my yard　　　B: Oh?

對話 3

A: Did you feed ***the dog?***　　　B: Yes.

11-8 冠詞用法準則 Guidelines for Article Usage

泛指一般事物

單數可數名詞：*A/An*

(a) **A** *dog* makes a good pet. (b) **An** *apple* is red. (c) **A** *pencil* contains lead.	在例 (a) 中，說話者是指任何、所有、一般的狗。

複數可數名詞：Ø

(d) Ø *Dogs* make good pets. (e) Ø *Apples* are red. (f) Ø *Pencils* contain lead.	在例 (d) 中，說話者是指任何、所有、一般的狗。 注意：例 (a) 和例 (d) 同義。

不可數名詞：Ø

(g) Ø *Fruit* is good for you. (h) Ø *Coffee* contains caffeine. (i) I like Ø *music*.	在例 (g) 中，說話者是指任何、所有、一般的水果。

談論非特定的人或事物

單數可數名詞：*A/An*

(j) I saw **a** *dog* in my yard. (k) Mary ate **an** *apple*. (l) I need **a** *pencil*.	在例 (j) 中，說話者是指他看到一隻狗（不是兩隻、幾隻或很多隻），也沒有特定指哪一隻（如：你的狗、某鄰居的狗、那隻狗）。就只是所有叫做「狗」的動物裡的其中一隻而已。

複數可數名詞：*Some*

(m) I saw **some** *dogs* in my yard. (n) Mary bought **some** *apples*. (o) Bob has **some** *pencils* in his pocket.	在例 (m) 中，說話者指他看到一隻以上的狗，並未指出是特定的哪幾隻（如：你的幾隻狗、某鄰居的幾隻狗、那幾隻狗），到底確切幾隻也不重要（兩隻狗、五隻狗），他就只是要說他看到幾隻狗而已。 關於其他可與複數可數名詞連用的字詞，如：**several**、**a few** 和 **a lot of**，請見表 11-5。

不可數名詞：*Some*

(p) I bought **some** *fruit*. (q) Bob drank **some** *coffee*. (r) Would you like to listen to **some** *music*?	在例 (p) 中，說話者的意思是說他買了一些水果，確切數量（如：兩磅水果、四根香蕉、兩個蘋果）並不是說話的重點，他也沒有說是特定的水果（如：那個水果、碗裡的水果）。 關於其他可與不可數名詞連用的字詞，如：**a little** 和 **a lot of**，請見表 11-5。

說話者和聆聽者想的是<u>相同特定</u>的人或事物。

單數可數名詞：*The*

(s) Did you feed **the** dog? (t) Kay is in **the** kitchen. (u) **The** sun is shining. (v) Please close **the** door. (w) **The** president is speaking on TV tonight. (x) I had a banana and an apple. I gave **the** banana to Mary.	在例 (s) 中，說話者和聆聽者所想的是同一隻特定的狗；聽者知道說話者所講的狗，就是他們一起養、每天餵的那隻狗，說話者所講的狗一定就是這隻狗。 在例 (x) 中，當說話者第二次提到一個名詞時，會在該名詞前面加 the。 　第一次提到：*I had a banana* … 　第二次提到：*I gave the banana* … 當說話者再度提及時，聽者已經知道他所指的是「說話者」有的那根香蕉（不是 John 擁有的香蕉，也不是那個碗裡的香蕉）。

複數可數名詞：*The*

(y) Did you feed **the** dogs? (z) **The** pencils on that desk are Jim's. (aa) Please turn off **the** lights. (bb) I had some bananas and apples. I gave **the** bananas to Mary.	在例 (y) 中，說話者和聆聽者想的是一隻以上的狗，且他們想的是相同的、特定的狗。 在例 (bb) 中，**the** 用於第二次提及該事物。

不可數名詞：*The*

(cc) **The** fruit in this bowl is ripe. (dd) I can't hear you. **The** music is too loud. (ee) **The** air smells fresh today. (ff) I drank some coffee and some milk. **The** coffee was hot.	當 **the** 放在不可數名詞之前時，說話者知道或可以假設聽者熟知提及的相同特定事物。 在例 (ff) 中，**the** 用於第二次提及該事物。 注意：**a**、**an** 和 **Ø** 不能用於例 (s) 到例 (ff) 描述的情況中。

the 的使用時機

1. 前方已提的 n.　ex. I saw a bird on my way home, the bird was yellow and singing then.

2. 最高級：the + adj. 最高級 + n.

3. 序數：1st、2st、3st、… last

4. the same / only.

閱讀下列對話，並回答之後的問題。

對話 1

A: *Dogs* make good pets.　　　B: I agree.

對話 2

A: I saw *some dogs* in my yard.　　　B: Oh?

對話 3

A: Did you feed *the dogs?*　　　B: Yes.

1. In which conversation are the speakers thinking about all dogs?
2. In which conversation are the speakers talking about the same dogs?
3. In which conversation are the speakers talking about an indefinite number of dogs?

對話 4

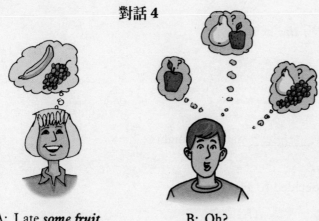

A: I ate *some fruit*.   B: Oh?

對話 5

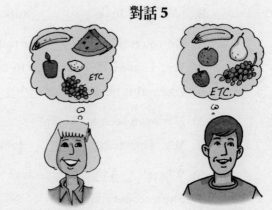

A: *Fruit* is good for you.   B: I agree.

對話 6

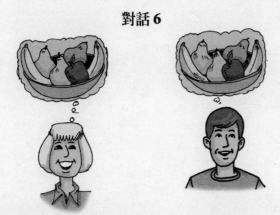

A: *The fruit* in this bowl is ripe.   B: Good.

4. In which conversation are the speakers talking about all fruit?
5. In which conversation are the speakers talking about an indefinite amount of fruit?
6. In which conversation are the speakers thinking about the same fruit?

❏ **Exercise 28. 文法** (表 11-8)

閱讀下列對話，並判斷說話者可能會用 ***the*** 或 ***a/an***。

1. A: What did you do last night?

    B: I went to ___*a*___ party.

    A: Oh? Where was it?

2. A: Did you have a good time at ___*the*___ party last night?

    B: Yes.

    A: So did I. I'm glad that you decided to go with me.

3. A: Do you have ___*a*___ car?

    B: No. But I have ___*a*___ motorcycle.

4. A: Do you need ___*the*___ car today, honey?

    B: Yes. I have a lot of errands to do. Why don't I drive you to work today?

    A: Okay. But be sure to fill ___*the*___ car up with gas sometime today.

5. A: Have you seen my keys?

    B: Yes. They're on ___*the*___ table next to ___*the*___ front door.

6. A: Where's ___*the*___ professor?

    B: She's absent today.

7. A: Is Mr. Jones ___*a*___ graduate student?

    B: No. He's ___*a*___ professor.

8. A: Would you like to go to ___*the*___ zoo this afternoon?

    B: Sure. Why not?

9. A: Does San Diego have ___*a*___ zoo?

    B: Yes. It's world famous.

10. A: Where's Dennis?

    B: He's in ___*the*___ kitchen.

11. A: Do you like your new apartment?

    B: Yes. It has ___*a*___ big kitchen.

12. A: Did you lock ___*the*___ door?

    B: Yes.

    A: Did you check ___*the*___ stove?

    B: Yes.

    A: Did you close all ___*the*___ windows downstairs?

B: Yes.

A: Did you set ___the___ alarm clock?

B: Yes.

A: Then let's turn out ___the___ lights.

B: Goodnight, dear.

A: Oh, don't forget your appointment with ___the___ doctor tomorrow.

B: Yes, dear. Goodnight.

❑ **Exercise 29.** 文法 (表 11-8)

判斷以**粗體**標示的名詞是單數、複數或是不可數，然後判斷該名詞有泛指或特定的含義。

	單數	複數	不可數	泛指	特定
1. **Birds** have feathers.		x		x	
2. A **bird** has feathers.					
3. A bird eats **worms**.					
4. A **worm** lives under the ground.					
5. Birds and worms need **water**.					
6. The **bird** is drinking water.					
7. The **birds** are drinking water.					
8. The **water** is on the ground.					

❑ **Exercise 30.** 文法 (表 11-8)

用下列提供的名詞完成句子；將 **the** 用於有特定含義的敘述句中，而不是用於泛指的敘述句。

1. flowers　　a. ___The flowers___ in that vase are beautiful.

　　　　　　　b. ___Flowers___ are beautiful.

2. mountains　a. ___A mountains___ are beautiful.

　　　　　　　b. ___The mountains___ in Switzerland are beautiful.

3. water　　　a. I don't want to go swimming today. ___The water___ is too cold.

　　　　　　　b. ___Water___ consists of hydrogen and oxygen.

4. information　a. ___The information___ in this magazine article is upsetting.

　　　　　　　b. The Internet is a widely used source of ___information___.

5. health　　　a. ___Health___ is more important than money.

　　　　　　　b. Doctors are concerned with ___the health___ of their patients.

6. men   a. ____Men____ generally have stronger muscles than

    women   ____Women____ .

         b. At the party last night, ____the men____ sat on one side of the

room, and ____the woman____ sat on the other.

7. problems   a. Everyone has ____problems____ .

         b. Irene told me about ____the problem____ she had with her car

yesterday.

8. vegetables   a. ____The vegetables____ we had for dinner last night

were overcooked.

         b. ____Vegetables____ are good for you.

❏ **Exercise 31. 閱讀** (表 11-8)

閱讀以下文章；然後用一張紙蓋住該篇文章，並完成下列句子。

Money

      In ancient times, people did not use coins for money. Instead, shells, beads, or salt were used. Around 2,600 years ago, the first metal coins were made. Today most money is made from paper. Of course, many people use plastic credit or debit cards to pay for goods. In the future, maybe we'll use only cards, and paper money won't exist.

1. In ancient times, two forms of money were _____.

2. People first made _____ 2,600 years ago.

3. Nowadays, paper is used for _____.

4. Today people can pay for goods with _____ or _____.

5. In the future, _____ may replace _____.

❏ **Exercise 32. 文法** (表 11-8)

用 *the* 或 Ø 完成下列句子，並視情況將句首字母改爲大寫。

           B

1. ____Ø____ butter is a dairy product.

2. Please pass me _____ butter.

3. _____ air is humid today.

4. When I was in Memorial Hospital, _____ nurses were wonderful.

5. I'm studying _____ grammar. I'm also studying _____ vocabulary.

6. _____ trees reduce _____ pollution by cleaning the air.

7. _____ trees in my yard are 200 years old.

Exercise 33. 文法 (表 11-8)

用 *a*/*an*、*the* 或 *some*，完成下列句子。

1. I had __a__ banana and __an__ apple. I gave __the__ banana to Mary. I ate __the__ apple.

2. I had __some__ bananas and __some__ apples. I gave __the__ bananas to Mary. I ate __the__ apples.

3. I forgot to bring my things with me to class yesterday, so I borrowed __a__ pen and __some__ paper from Joe. I returned __the__ pen, but I used __the__ paper for my homework.

4. A: What did you do last weekend?
    B: I went on __a__ picnic Saturday and saw __a__ movie Sunday.
    A: Did you have fun?
    B: __The__ picnic was fun, but __the__ movie was boring.

5. I bought __a__ bag of flour and __some__ sugar to make __some__ cookies. __The__ sugar was okay, but I had to return __the__ flour. When I opened it, I found __some__ little bugs in it. I took it back to the people at the store and showed them __the__ little bugs. They gave me __a__ new bag of flour. __The__ new bag didn't have any bugs in it.

❑ **Exercise 34. 聽力** (表 11-8)

CD 2
Track 43

聆聽 CD 播放的文章，然後再聽一遍，並寫下 *a*/*an*、*the* 或 *Ø*。在開始前，可先確定自己是否認識這些字：*roof (of your mouth)*、*nerves*、*blood vessels*、*avoid*。

Ice-Cream Headaches

Have you ever eaten something really cold like ice cream and suddenly gotten __a__ headache? This is known as _____ "ice-cream headache." About 30 percent of the population gets this type of _____ headache. Here is one theory about why _____
₁   ₂   ₃   ₄

ice-cream headaches occur. _____ roof of your mouth has a lot of nerves. When
                                    5
something cold touches these nerves, they want to warm up _____ your brain. They
                                                                    6
make _____ your blood vessels swell up (get bigger), and this causes _____ lot of pain.
        7   8
_____ ice-cream headaches generally go away after about 30–60 seconds. _____ best
        9   10
way to avoid these headaches is to keep cold food off _____ roof of your mouth.
                                                              11

❑ **Exercise 35. 文法** (表 11-8)
將 *a/an*、*the* 或 Ø 填入空格中。

1. I have __*a*___ window in my bedroom. I keep it open at night because I like fresh air.
    __*The*___ window is above my bed.

2. Kathy likes to listen to _____ music when she studies.

3. Would you please turn _____ radio down? _____ music is too loud.

4. Last week I read _____ book about _____ life of Indira Gandhi, India's only
    female prime minister, who was assassinated in 1984.

5. Let's go swimming in _____ lake today.

6. _____ water is essential to human life, but don't drink _____ water in the Flat
    River. It'll kill you! _____ pollution in that river is terrible.

7. People can drink _____ fresh water. They can't drink _____ seawater because it
    contains _____ salt.

8. Ted, pass _____ salt, please. And _____ pepper. Thanks.

9. A: How did you get here? Did you walk?
    B: No, I took _____ taxi.

10. A: Wow! What a great meal!
    B: I agree. _____ food was excellent — especially _____ fish. And _____
    service was exceptionally good. Let's leave _____ waitress a good tip.

11. A: Kids, get in _____ car, please.
    B: We can't. _____ doors are locked.

❑ **Exercise 36. 暖身活動** (表 11-9)

用 **the** 或 Ø 完成下列問句。

Would you like to see . . .

1. ___the___ Amazon River?
2. ___Ø___ Korea?
3. _____ Mexico City?
4. _____ Indian Ocean?
5. _____ Ural Mountains?

6. _____ Australia?
7. _____ Mississippi River?
8. _____ Red Sea?
9. _____ Lake Michigan?
10. _____ Mount Fuji?

11-9 定冠詞 The／零冠詞 Ø 與稱謂／名稱的連用

(a) We met **Ø** *Mr. Wang.* I know **Ø** *Doctor Smith.* **Ø** *President Rice* has been in the news.	**the**「不與」稱謂連用。 錯誤：*We met the Mr. Wang.*
(b) He lives in **Ø** *Europe.* **Ø** *Asia* is the largest continent. Have you ever been to **Ø** *Africa?*	**the**「不與」洲的名稱連用。 錯誤：*He lives in the Europe.*
(c) He lives in **Ø** *France.* **Ø** *Brazil* is a large country. Have you ever been to **Ø** *Thailand?*	大部分的國名「不與」**the** 連用。 錯誤：*He lives in the France.*
(d) He lives in **the** *United States.* **The** *Netherlands* is in Europe. Have you ever been to **the** *Philippines?*	只有少數的國名會與 **the** 連用，如：例 (d)，其他還有 *the Czech Republic*、*the United Arab Emirates*、*the Dominican Republic*。
(e) He lives in **Ø** *Paris.* **Ø** *New York* is the largest city in the United States. Have you ever been to **Ø** *Istanbul?*	**the**「不與」城市名稱連用。 錯誤：*He lives in the Paris.*
(f) **The** *Nile River* is long. They crossed **the** *Pacific Ocean.* **The** *Yellow Sea* is in Asia.	**the** 會與河流和海洋的名稱連用。
(g) Chicago is on **Ø** *Lake Michigan.* **Ø** *Lake Titicaca* lies on the border between Peru and Bolivia.	**the**「不與」湖泊名稱連用。
(h) We hiked in **the** *Alps.* **The** *Andes* are in South America.	**the** 會與山脈的名稱連用。
(i) He climbed **Ø** *Mount Everest.* **Ø** *Mount Fuji* is in Japan.	**the**「不與」個別一座山的名稱連用。

❑ **Exercise 37. 遊戲：知識問答比賽** (表 11-9)

分組比賽；用 *the* 或 Ø 完成下列句子，然後判斷該敘述是否正確。如果敘述正確，圈 T；如果有錯，圈 F。答對最多題的組別獲勝。★

1. _____ Moscow is the biggest city _____ Russia.   T   F

2. _____ Rhine River flows through _____ Germany.   T   F

3. _____ Vienna is in _____ Australia.   T   F

4. _____ Yangtze is the longest river in _____ Asia.   T   F

5. _____ Atlantic Ocean is bigger than _____ Pacific.   T   F

6. _____ Rocky Mountains are located in _____ Canada
   and _____ United States.   T   F

7. _____ Dr. Sigmund Freud is famous for his studies of astronomy.   T   F

8. _____ Lake Victoria is located in _____ Tanzania.   T   F

9. Another name for _____ Holland is _____ Netherlands.   T   F

10. _____ Swiss Alps are the tallest mountains in the world.   T   F

❑ **Exercise 38. 遊戲** (表 11-9)

分組進行；挑選世界上任一地點，可以是一個洲、一個國家、一座城市、一片海、一條河、一座山等。班上同學要以 *yes/no* 問句，試著猜出該地點。每個地點只可以問 10 個以內的問題。

例：

說話者 A：(*thinking of the Mediterranean Sea*)
說話者 B：Is it a continent?
說話者 A：No.
說話者 C：Is it hot?
說話者 A：No.
說話者 D：Is it big?
說話者 A：Yes.
以此類推……

❑ **Exercise 39. 暖身活動** (表 11-10)

用與自身狀況相關的資訊，完成下列句子。

1. I was born in _____.
   　　　　　　　　　(continent)

2. I have lived most of my life in _____.
   　　　　　　　　　　　　　　(country)

3. This term I am studying _____.

4. Two of my favorite movies are _____ and

   _____.

---

*請見解答本中的 *Trivia Answers*。

11-10 字母大寫的規則 Capitalization

大寫		
1. 句中首字	**W**e saw a movie last night. **I**t was very good.	大寫＝用大寫字母，而非小寫字母
2. 人名	I met **G**eorge **A**dams yesterday.	
3. 稱謂或頭銜	I saw **D**octor (**D**r.) Smith. There's **P**rofessor (**P**rof.) Lee.	比較 I saw a **d**octor. 和 I saw **D**octor Wilson.
4. 月份、一周七天與節日	I was born in **A**pril. Bob arrived last **M**onday. It snowed on **N**ew **Y**ear's **D**ay.	注意：季節名稱不要大寫：*spring*、*summer*、*fall/autumn*、*winter*。
5. 地名： 　城市 　州／省份 　國家 　洲 　海洋 　湖泊 　河流 　沙漠 　山脈 　學校 　企業 　街道 　建築物 　公園／動物園	He lives in **C**hicago. She was born in **C**alifornia. They are from **M**exico. Tibet is in **A**sia. They crossed the **A**tlantic **O**cean. Chicago is on **L**ake **M**ichigan. The **N**ile **R**iver flows north. The **S**ahara **D**esert is in Africa. We visited the **R**ocky **M**ountains. I go to the **U**niversity of **F**lorida. I work for the **B**oeing **C**ompany. He lives on **G**rand **A**venue. We have class in **R**itter **H**all. I went jogging in **F**orest **P**ark.	比較 She lives in a **c**ity. She lives in **N**ew **Y**ork **C**ity. 比較 They crossed a **r**iver. They crossed the **Y**ellow **R**iver. 比較 I go to a **u**niversity. I go to the **U**niversity of **T**exas. 比較 We went to a **p**ark. We went to **C**entral **P**ark.
6. 課程名稱	I'm taking **C**hemistry 101.	比較 Here's your **h**istory book. I'm taking **H**istory 101.
7. 書名、文章標題、電影名稱	*Gone with the Wind* *The Sound of the Mountain*	標題的第一個字要大寫。 標題中其他字首也要大寫，但冠詞（*the*, *a/an*）、連接詞（*and, but, or*）與短介系詞（*with*、*in*、*at* 等）除外。
8. 語言名稱與國籍	She speaks **S**panish. We discussed **J**apanese customs.	語言名稱和國籍一定要大寫。
9. 宗教名稱	**B**uddhism, **C**hristianity, **H**induism, **I**slam, and **J**udaism are major religions in the world. Talal is a **M**uslem.	宗教名稱一定要大寫。

□ **Exercise 40.** 文法 (表 11-10)
   視情況將字母改爲大寫，有些句子不用修正。

1. We're going to have a test next Ṭuesday.

2. Do you know richard smith? he is a professor at this university.

3. I know that professor smith teaches at the university of arizona.

4. Where was your mother born?

5. John is a catholic. ali is a muslem.

6. Anita speaks french. she studied in france for two years.

7. I'm taking a history course this semester.

8. I'm taking modern european history 101 this semester.

9. We went to vancouver, british columbia, for our vacation last summer.

10. Venezuela is a spanish-speaking country.

11. Canada is in north america.*

12. Canada is north of the united states.

13. The sun rises in the east.

14. The mississippi river flows south.

15. The amazon is a river in south america.

16. We went to a zoo. We went to brookfield zoo in chicago.

17. The title of this book is *fundamentals of english grammar.*

18. I enjoy studying english grammar.

19. On valentine's day (february 14th), sweethearts give each other presents.

20. I read a book called *the cat and the mouse in my aunt's house.*

---

*當 **north**、**south**、**east** 和 **west** 所指爲羅盤上的方位時，不必大寫，例：*Japan is **east** of China.*；然而，當這些字爲地理名稱的一部分時，必須要大寫，例：*Japan is in the Far **East**.*

第一部分　閱讀以下文章，並視情況將字母改為大寫。

Jane Goodall

(1) Do you recognize the name ʲane goodall? Perhaps you know her for her studies of chimpanzees. She became very famous from her work in tanzania.

(2) Jane goodall was born in england, and as a child, was fascinated by animals. Her favorite books were *the jungle book,* by rudyard kipling, and books about tarzan, a fictional character who was raised by apes.

(3) Her childhood dream was to go to africa. After high school, she worked as a secretary and a waitress to earn enough money to go there. During that time, she took evening courses in journalism and english literature. She saved every penny until she had enough money for a trip to africa.

(4) In the spring of 1957, she sailed through the red sea and southward down the african coast to mombasa in kenya. Her uncle had arranged a job for her in nairobi with a british company. When she was there, she met dr. louis leakey, a famous anthropologist. Under his guidance, she began her lifelong study of chimpanzees on the eastern shore of lake tanganyika.

(5) Jane goodall lived alone in a tent near the lake. Through months and years of patience, she won the trust of the chimps and was able to watch them closely. Her observations changed forever how we view chimpanzees — and all other animals we share the world with.

第二部分 再閱讀文章一遍，然後再閱讀下列敘述。如果敘述正確，圈 T；如果有錯，圈 F。

1. Jane Goodall was interested in animals from an early age.   T   F

2. Her parents paid for her trip to Africa.   T   F

3. She studied animals in zoos as well as chimpanzees in the wild.   T   F

4. Dr. Leakey was helpful to Jane Goodall.   T   F

5. Jane studied chimpanzees with many other people.   T   F

6. Goodall's work changed how chimpanzees look at the world.   T   F

第三部分 閱讀以下關於 Roots and Shoots（根與芽）這個組織的段落範例，然後自己寫一段與致力於幫助人們或動物組織的相關文字。注意冠詞和大小寫的正確用法，以及範例中標示斜體的冠詞。遵循下列寫作步驟：
(1) 選一個你有興趣的組織。
(2) 搜集該組織的資料；若有可能，找出該組織的網站，並記下所搜集資料的重點。那份資料須包含該組織的歷史、成立緣由、創立者以及服務宗旨。
(3) 複習表 11-10，並確定段落中的大小寫是否正確。
(4) 校訂段落中的冠詞用法。你可以請別的同學讀一遍完成的文字。

段落範例：

Roots and Shoots

Jane Goodall went to Africa to study animals. She spent 40 years observing and studying chimpanzees in Tanzania. As a result of Dr. Goodall's work, *an* organization called Roots and Shoots was formed. This organization focuses on work children and teenagers can do to help *the* local and global community. *The* idea began in 1991. *A* group of 16 teenagers met with Dr. Goodall at her home in Dar Es Salaam, Tanzania. They wanted to discuss how to help with *a* variety of problems, such as pollution, deforestation, *the* treatment of animals, and *the* future of wildlife, like Dr. Goodall's chimpanzees. Dr. Goodall was involved in *the* meetings, but *the* teenagers chose *the* service projects and did *the* work themselves. *The* first Roots and Shoots community project was *a* local one. *The* group educated villagers about better treatment of chickens at home and in *the* marketplace. Today, there are tens of thousands of members in almost 100 countries. They work to make their environment and *the* world *a* better place through community-service projects.

第十二章
形容詞子句

□ **Exercise 1. 暖身活動** (表 12-1)

勾選 (✓) 符合自身狀況的項目。

I have a friend who . . .

1. ＿＿＿ lives near me.
2. ＿＿＿ is interested in soccer.
3. ＿＿＿ likes to do exciting things.
4. ＿＿＿ is studying to be an astronaut.

12-1 形容詞子句：概述 Adjective Clauses: Introduction

形容詞	形容詞子句
「形容詞」(adjective) 用來修飾名詞，「修飾」意味「作少許改變」；亦即形容詞描述或提供有關名詞的訊息。（請見第 160 頁，表 6-8）。	「形容詞子句」(adjective clause)★ 修飾名詞，用來描述或提供有關名詞的訊息。
形容詞通常置於名詞之前。	形容詞子句置於名詞後面。
形容詞 + 名詞 (a) I met a `kind` `man`. 形容詞 + 名詞 (b) I met a `famous` `man`.	名詞 + 形容詞子句 (c) I met a `man` *who is kind to everybody*. 名詞 + 形容詞子句 (d) I met a `man` *who is a famous poet*. 名詞 + 形容詞子句 (e) I met a `man` *who lives in Chicago*.

★文法術語	
(1) **I met a man** = 獨立子句，為一完整句子。 (2) **He lives in Chicago** = 獨立子句，為一完整句子。 (3) **who lives in Chicago** = 從屬子句，不是完整句子。 (4) **I met a man who lives in Chicago** = 獨立子句 + 從屬子句，為一完整句子。	子句 (clause) 是指有主詞與動詞的句型結構。子句有兩種：獨立子句 (independent clause) 和從屬子句 (dependent clause)。 • 所謂「獨立子句」就是主要子句，可單獨存在，如：例 (1) 和例 (2)。 • 而「從屬子句」，如：例 (3)，不能單獨存在，必須依附於獨立子句，如：例 (4)。

關係代名詞 ⎨ 主格關代：關代於 adj. 子中當 S ⇒ 先 + 關 + V
受格關代：、、 ○ ⇒ 先 + 關 + S + V.

Exercise 2. 文法 (表 12-1)

勾選 (✓) 含完整句的項目。

1. _____ I know a teenager. She flies airplanes.
2. _____ I know a teenager who flies airplanes.
3. _____ A teenager who flies airplanes.
4. _____ Who flies airplanes.
5. _____ Who flies airplanes?
6. _____ I know a teenager flies airplanes.

Exercise 3. 暖身活動 (表 12-2)

用下表中的正確字詞完成句子；然後再將 ***doctor*** 後面的字劃<u>底線</u>。

| A dermatologist | An orthopedist | A pediatrician | A surgeon |

1. _____ is a doctor who performs operations.
2. _____ is a doctor that treats skin problems.
3. _____ is a doctor who treats bone injuries.
4. _____ is a doctor that treats children.

12-2 用 *Who* 和 *That* 引導形容人的形容詞子句

(a) The man is friendly.	主詞 動詞 ***He*** lives next to me. ↓ ***who*** ↓ 主詞 動詞 ***who*** lives next to me	在形容詞子句中，***who*** 和 ***that*** 當作主格代名詞，用以形容人。 在例 (a) 中，***he*** 為主格代名詞，指的是 the man。 造形容詞子句時，只需將 ***he*** 改成 ***who***。<u>***who***</u> 是主格代名詞，指的是 the man。 先 + 關 + [V.] < 主動 → ving (與時態無關) 被動 - P.P
(b) The man ***who*** *lives next to me* is friendly.		
(c) The woman is talkative.	主詞 動詞 ***She*** lives next to me. ↓ ***that*** ↓ 主詞 動詞 ***that*** lives next to me	***that*** 也是主格代名詞，可取代 ***who***，如：例 (d)。 在形容詞子句中，***who*** 和 ***that*** 當作主格代名詞用時，不可省略。 錯誤：*The woman lives next to me is talkative.* 當作主格代名詞用時，***who*** 和 ***that*** 常用於對話中；但在寫作中，則以 ***who*** 較為常用。
(d) The woman ***that*** *lives next to me* is talkative.		在例 (b) 和例 (d) 中，形容詞子句緊接在所修飾的名詞之後。 錯誤：*The woman is talkative that lives next to me.*

□ **Exercise 4.** 文法 (表 12-2)

圈選表達出該題句意的「兩個」句子。

1. The librarian who helped me with my research lives near my parents.
   a. The librarian lives near my parents.
   b. I live near my parents.
   c. The librarian helped my parents.
   d. The librarian helped me.

2. The veterinarian that took care of my daughter's goat was very gentle.
   a. The veterinarian took care of my goat.
   b. The goat was gentle.
   c. The veterinarian treated my daughter's goat.
   d. The veterinarian was gentle.

□ **Exercise 5.** 文法 (表 12-1 和 12-2)

將各題中的形容詞子句劃底線，並畫箭頭指出其所修飾的名詞。

1. The hotel clerk who gave us our room keys speaks several languages.

2. The manager that hired me has less experience than I do.

3. I like the manager that works in the office next to mine.

4. My mother is a person who wakes up every morning with a positive attitude.

5. A person who wakes up with a positive attitude every day is lucky.

□ **Exercise 6.** 文法 (表 12-1 和 12-2)

將各題的 b 句改為形容詞子句，並用 **who** 或 **that** 合併下列各組句子。

例： a. Do you know the people?   b. They live in the house on the corner.
    → *Do you know the people **who** (or **that**) live in the white house?*

1. a. The police officer was friendly.   b. She gave me directions.   *The police officer who gave me direction was friendly.*

2. a. The waiter was slow.   b. He served us dinner.   *The waiter who served us dinner was slow*

3. a. I talked to the women.   b. They walked into my office.   *I talked to the woman who walked into my office*

4. a. The man talked a lot.   b. He sat next to me on the plane.   *The man who sat next to me on the plane talked a lot.*

5. a. The people have three cars.   b. They live next to me.

   The people who live next to me have three cars.

□ **Exercise 7.** 文法 (表 12-1 和 12-2)

視情況加入 **who** 或 **that**。

1. I liked the people ^*who* sat next to us at the soccer game.

2. The man answered the phone was polite.

形容詞子句 **323**

3. People paint houses for a living are called house painters.

4. I'm uncomfortable around married couples argue all the time.

5. While I was waiting at the bus stop, I stood next to an elderly man started a conversation with me about my school.

❑ **Exercise 8. 口說** (表 12-1 和 12-2)

成兩人一組或分小組進行。依照實際狀況，完成下列句子，並與全班分享一些句子。

1. I know a man/woman who . . . .
2. I have a friend who . . . .
3. I like athletes who . . . .
4. Workers who . . . are brave.
5. People who . . . make me laugh.
6. Doctors who . . . are admirable.

❑ **Exercise 9. 暖身活動** (表 12-3)

用自己的話完成下列句子。

1. The teacher that I had for first grade was _____.

2. The first English teacher I had was _____.

3. The first English teacher who I had wasn't _____.

12-3 用形容詞子句中的受格代名詞形容人

(a) The man was friendly. [主詞 動詞 受詞] I met **him**. → **that**	形容詞子句中的代名詞當作動詞的受詞，用以形容人。 在例 (a) 中，**him** 為受格代名詞，指的是 the man。 造形容詞子句的一個方法是，將 **him** 改為 **that**。**that** 當作受格代名詞用，指的是 the man。 **that** 必須置於形容詞子句的句首。
[受詞 主詞 動詞] (b) The man **that** *I met* was friendly. (c) The man Ø *I met* was friendly.	形容詞子句中的<u>受格代名詞可以省略</u>，如：例 (c)。
(d) The man was friendly. I met [受詞 **him**. → **who** **whom**]	**him** 也可以改為 **who** 或 **whom**，如：例 (e) 和例 (f)。 **that** 當作受格代名詞用時，比 **who** 更常用於口語中；而 Ø 在口語和寫作中最為常用。 **whom** 通常只用於非常正式的寫作中。
[受詞 主詞 動詞] (e) The man **who** *I met* was friendly. (f) The man **whom** *I met* was friendly.	

□ **Exercise 10. 文法** (表 12-2 和 12-3)

勾選 (✓) 下列含受格代名詞的句子。

1. __✓__ The children who we invited to the party are from the neighborhood.

2. ____ The children that we invited to the party were excited to come.

3. ____ The children whom we invited to the party had a good time.

4. ____ The children who live next door are a lot of fun.

5. ____ Marie and Luis Escobar still keep in touch with many of the students that they met in their English class five years ago.

6. ____ People who listen to loud music on earphones can suffer gradual hearing loss.

7. ____ I know a couple who sailed around the world.

8. ____ The couple whom we had over for dinner sailed around the world.

□ **Exercise 11. 文法** (表 12-2 和 12-3)

圈選所有可完成句子的正確答案。

1. The woman _____ was interesting.
   a·b
   c·d
   a. that I met last night   c. who I met last night
   b. I met last night   d. whom I met last night

2. The man _____ was fast.
   a·c
   a. that painted our house   c. who painted our house
   b. painted our house   d. whom painted

3. The people _____ live on Elm Street.
   a·b
   c·d
   a. that Nadia is visiting   c. who Nadia is visiting
   b. Nadia is visiting   d. whom Nadia is visiting

4. The students _____ missed the quiz.
   a·c
   a. that came to class late   c. who came to class late
   b. came to class late   d. whom came to class late

□ **Exercise 12. 文法** (表 12-3)

用 *that*、*who* 或 *whom* 合併下列各組句子；將 b 句中的受格代名詞劃底線，並將 b 句改為形容詞子句。

例：a. A woman asked me for my phone number.   b. I didn't know her.

   → *A woman that/whom I didn't know asked me for my phone number.*

1. a. The couple was two hours late.   b. I invited them for dinner.

2. a. The man snored the entire flight.   b. I sat next to him on the plane.

3. a. The man tried to shoplift some groceries.   b. The police arrested him.

4. a. The chef is very experienced.   b. The company hired her.

❏ **Exercise 13.** 口說：兩人一組 (表 12-2 和 12-3)

成兩人一組，輪流將各題所提供的句子和下列主句，合併成形容詞子句。

主句：The man was helpful.

1. He gave me directions. → *The man who/that gave me directions was helpful.*
2. He answered my question.
3. I called him.
4. You recommended him.
5. He is the owner.
6. You invited him to the party.
7. He was walking with his kids.
8. I saw him in the waiting room.
9. He sold us our museum tickets.
10. He gave us a discount.

❏ **Exercise 14.** 文法 (表 12-2 和 12-3)

用 *that*、*Ø*、*who* 或 *whom* 完成下列句子；寫出所有可能的答案。

1. The man _____who that (主格)_____ married my mother is now my stepfather.

2. The man _____that, who, Ø, whom (受格)_____ my mother married is now my stepfather.

3. Do you know the boy _____who, that_____ is talking to Anita?

4. I've become good friends with several of the people _____who, whom, that, Ø_____ I met in my English class last year.

5. A woman _____who, whom, that, Ø_____ I saw in the park was holding several balloons.

6. The woman _____who, that_____ was holding several balloons was entertaining some children.

❏ **Exercise 15.** 暖身活動 (表 12-4)

閱讀以下那段關於 James 的文字，然後勾選 (✓) 你同意的句子。你注意到斜體字型的形容詞子句有些什麼特點嗎？

James is looking for a pet. He is single and a little lonely. He isn't sure what kind of pet would be best for him. He lives on a large piece of property in the country. He is gone during the day from 8:00 A.M. to 5:00 P.M. but is home on weekends. He travels about two months a year but has neighbors that can take care of a pet, as long as it isn't too big. What kind of pet should he get?

1. ____ He should get a pet *that likes to run and be outside*, like a dog.
2. ____ He needs to get a pet *which is easy to take care of*, like a fish or turtle.
3. ____ He should get an animal *that he can leave alone for a few days*, like a horse.
4. ____ He needs to get an animal *his neighbors will like*.

12-4 用形容詞子句中的代名詞形容事物

(a) The river is polluted. 主詞 It ↓ that which 動詞 flows through the town.	**who** 和 **whom** 用來指人。 **which** 用來指事物。 **that** 用來指人或事物皆可。
主詞 動詞 (b) The river **that** *flows through the town* is polluted. (c) The river **which** *flows through the town* is polluted.	在例 (a) 中，造形容詞子句時，只需將 **it** 改為 **that** 或 **which**；而 **it**、**that** 和 **which** 皆可用來指一件之前提過的事物，即 the river。 例 (b) 和例 (c) 同義，但是在口說和寫作中，例 (b) 比例 (c) 更常見。
	當 **that** 和 **which** 用作形容詞子句中的主詞時，「不可」省略。 錯誤：*The river flows through the town is polluted.*
主詞 動詞 受詞 (d) The books were expensive. I bought them. ↓ that which	**that** 或 **which** 可用作形容詞子句中的受詞，如：例 (e) 和例 (f)。 形容詞子句中的受格代名詞可以省略，如：例 (g)。 例 (e)、例 (f) 和例 (g) 同義。在口說中，**that** 和 Ø 比 **which** 常用；在寫作中，**that** 最常用，而幾乎不用 Ø。
受詞 主詞 動詞 (e) The books **that** *I bought* were expensive. (f) The books **which** *I bought* were expensive. (g) The books Ø *I bought* were expensive.	

❏ **Exercise 16. 文法** (表 12-4)

將下列形容詞子句劃底線，並畫箭頭指出其修飾的名詞。

1. I lost the scarf <u>that I borrowed from my roommate</u>.

2. The food we ate at the sidewalk café was delicious.

3. The bus that I take to school every morning is usually very crowded.

4. Pizza which is sold by the slice is a popular lunch in many cities throughout the world.

5. Piranhas are dangerous fish that can tear the flesh off an animal as large as a horse in a few minutes.

[手寫筆記]
{ This is the house
William was born in the house
This is the house | that which / in which 介 不可省 | William was born in. / William was born.
用 that
where (關副)

Tom is the boy | who that I used to take care of / of whom I used to take care.
不用 不可省略
that
who

形容詞子句 **327**

❏ **Exercise 17. 文法** (表 12-4)

將各組句子合併為一句，並寫出所有可能的形式。

    1. a. The pill made me sleepy.   b. I took it.

        → *The pill that I took made me sleepy.*
        → *The pill Ø I took made me sleepy.*
        → *The pill which I took made me sleepy.*

    2. a. The soup was too salty.   b. I had it for lunch.

    3. a. I have a class.   b. It begins at 8:00 A.M.

    4. a. The information helped me a lot.   b. I found it on the Internet.

    5. a. My daughter asked me a question.   b. I couldn't answer it.

    6. a. Where can I catch the bus?   b. It goes downtown.

❏ **Exercise 18. 文法** (表 12-3 和 12-4)

刪除形容詞子句中用法有誤的代名詞。

    1. The books I bought ~~them~~ at the bookstore were expensive.

    2. I like the shirt you wore it to class yesterday.

    3. Amanda Jones is a person I would like you to meet her.

    4. The apartment we wanted to rent it had two bedrooms.

    5. My wife and I are really enjoying the TV set that we bought it for our anniversary.

    6. The woman you met her at Aunt Barbara's house is an Olympic athlete.

    7. Ayako has a cat that it likes to catch mice.

    8. The mice that Ayako's cat catches them live in the basement.

❏ **Exercise 19. 文法** (表 12-2 → 12-4)

填入所有可連接形容詞子句和主要子句的代名詞：***that***、***who***、***which*** 或 ***whom***；若該代名詞可以省略，則填入 **Ø**。

例：The manager   [*who* / *that*]   fired Tom is a difficult person to work for.

    1. The box   [ ]   I mailed to my sister was heavy.

    2. The people   [ ]   sat in the stadium cheered for the home team.

3. The calendar [ ] hangs in Paul's office has pictures of his kids.

4. The teenagers returned the wallet [ ] they found on the sidewalk.

5. The people [ ] my brother called didn't answer their phone.

6. The tree branch [ ] was lying in the street caused problems for drivers.

❑ **Exercise 20. 聽力** (表 12-2 → 12-4)

聆聽 CD 播放的句子，每一句都包含形容詞子句。圈選聽到的代名詞，如果該句沒有主格或受格代名詞，圈 Ø。注意：在口語英文中，*that* 常常聽起來像 "thut"。

My mother's hospital stay

例：你會聽到：The doctor who treated my mother was very knowledgeable.
你要圈出：(who)   that   which   whom   Ø

1. who   that   which   whom   Ø
2. who   that   which   whom   Ø
3. who   that   which   whom   Ø
4. who   that   which   whom   Ø
5. who   that   which   whom   Ø
6. who   that   which   whom   Ø
7. who   that   which   whom   Ø
8. who   that   which   whom   Ø

❑ **Exercise 21. 口說** (表 12-1 → 12-4)

用內含適當形容詞子句的完整句，回答下列問題，並在形容詞子句所修飾的名詞前，加上定冠詞 *the*。

1. • One phone wasn't ringing.
   • The other phone was ringing.
   QUESTIONS: Which phone did Hasan answer? Which phone didn't he answer?
   → *Hasan answered **the** phone that was ringing.*
   → *He didn't answer **the** phone that wasn't ringing.*

2. • One student raised her hand in class.
   • Another student sat quietly in his seat.
   QUESTIONS: Which student asked the teacher a question? Which one didn't?

3. • One girl won the bike race.
   • The other girl lost the bike race.
   QUESTIONS: Which girl is happy? Which girl isn't happy?

4. • We ate some food from our garden.
   • We ate some food at a restaurant.
   QUESTIONS: Which food was expensive? Which food wasn't expensive?

5. • One man was sleeping.
   • Another man was listening to the radio.
   QUESTIONS: Which man heard the special report about the earthquake in China? Which one didn't?

6. • One person bought a small car.
   • Another person bought a large car.
   QUESTIONS: Which person probably spent more money than the other?

❑ **Exercise 22. 遊戲** (表 12-3 和 12-4)
分組比賽。用 *that* 或 *who* 將 A 欄和 B 欄中的字詞作正確配對，以造出完整句子。可視需要查閱字典。最先完成，且造出最多合文法句子的組別獲勝。

A 欄	**B 欄**
1. A hammer is a tool .... *that is used to pound nails.*	a. She/He leaves society and lives completely alone.
2. A comedian is someone	b. He/She tells jokes.
3. An obstetrician is a doctor	c. It forms when water boils.
4. Plastic is a chemical material	d. It is square at the bottom and has four sides that come together in a point at the top.
5. An architect is someone	e. She/He designs buildings.
6. A puzzle is a problem	f. He/She delivers babies.
7. A carnivore is an animal	✓g. It is used to pound nails.
8. Steam is a gas	h. It can be shaped and hardened to form many useful things.
9. A turtle is an animal	i. It can be difficult to solve.
10. A hermit is a person	j. It eats meat.
11. A pyramid is a structure	k. It has a hard shell and can live in water or on land.

❑ **Exercise 23. 暖身活動** (表 12-5)
閱讀下列句子；你注意到以斜體字型標示的動詞，及其前面的名詞有些什麼特點嗎？

1. I have a *friend* who *is* vegetarian. He doesn't eat any meat.
2. I have *friends* who *are* vegetarian. They don't eat any meat.

12-5 形容詞子句中動詞的單複數 Singular and Plural Verbs in Adjective Clauses

| (a) I know the **man** *who **is** sitting over there.* | 在例 (a) 中，形容詞子句中用的是單數動詞 (**is**)，因為句中的 **who** 所指的是單數名詞 **man**。 |
| (b) I know the **people** *who **are** sitting over there.* | 在例 (b) 中，形容詞子句中用的是複數動詞 (**are**)，因為句中的 **who** 所指的是複數名詞 **people**。 |

❑ **Exercise 24. 文法** (表 12-5)

圈選括弧內正確的字詞，並將決定該句動詞單複數的名詞劃底線。

1. A saw is a <u>tool</u> that ((is,) are) used to cut wood.

2. Shovels are tools that (is, (are)) used to dig holes.

3. I recently met a woman that (live, (lives)) in Montreal.

4. Most people that ((live), lives) in Montreal speak French as their first language.

5. I have a cousin who ((works), work) as a coal miner.

6. Some coal miners that (works, (work)) underground suffer from lung disease.

7. A professional athlete who (play, (plays)) tennis is called a tennis pro.

8. Professional athletes who ((play), plays) tennis for a living can make a lot of money.

9. Biographies are books which (tells, (tell)) the stories of people's lives.

10. A book that ((tells), tell) the story of a person's life is called a biography.

11. I talked to the men who (was, (were)) sitting near me.

12. The woman that ((was), were) sitting next to me at the movie was texting on her cell phone.

□ **Exercise 25. 暖身活動** (表 12-6)

用自己的話完成下列句子。

1. A person that I recently spoke to was _____.

2. A person whom I recently spoke to wasn't _____.

3. The room which we are sitting in is _____.

4. The room we are sitting in has _____.

5. The room in which we are sitting doesn't have _____.

先+關+S+V+介 ⇒ 先介+關+S+V~

12-6 形容詞子句中介系詞的用法

(a) The man was nice. I talked **to** **him**.				

形容詞子句中，**that**、**whom** 和 **which** 可作爲介系詞 (PREP) 的受詞 (OBJ)。

(b) The man **that** I talked **to** was nice.
(c) The man **Ø** I talked **to** was nice.
(d) The man **whom** I talked **to** was nice.
(e) The man **to whom** I talked was nice.

提示：形容詞子句中的受格代名詞可以省略，如：例 (c) 和例 (h)。

在非常正式的英文中，介系詞通常放在形容詞子句最前面，後面接 **whom** 或 **which**，如：例 (e) 和例 (j)。此用法在口語英文中不常見。

(f) The chair is hard. I am sitting **in** **it**.

(g) The chair **that** I am sitting **in** is hard.
(h) The chair **Ø** I am sitting **in** is hard.
(i) The chair **which** I am sitting **in** is hard.
(j) The chair **in which** I am sitting is hard.

注意：在例 (e) 和例 (j) 中，不可使用 **that** 或 **who**，且「不可」省略代名詞。

例 (b)、例 (c)、例 (d) 以及例 (e) 同義。

例 (g)、例 (h)、例 (i) 以及例 (j) 同義。

□ **Exercise 26. 文法** (表 12-6)

將 b 句改爲形容詞子句，然後合併下列各組句子；寫出子句的所有可能形式，並劃底線作標示。

1. a. The movie was funny.　　　b. We went **to** it.
   → *The movie <u>that we went</u> **to** was funny.*
   → *The movie <u>**Ø** we went</u> **to** was funny.*
   → *The movie <u>which we went</u> **to** was funny.*
   → *The movie **to** <u>which we went</u> was funny.*

2. a. The man is over there.   b. I told you **about** him.

3. a. The woman pays me a fair salary.   b. I work **for** her.

4. a. Alicia likes the family.   b. She is living **with** them.

5. a. The picture is beautiful.   b. Tom is looking **at** it.

6. a. I enjoyed the music.   b. We listened **to** it after dinner.

❏ **Exercise 27. 文法** (表 12-6)

用適當的介系詞* 完成下列句子，並以中括弧標示出形容詞子句。

1. I spoke ___to___ a person. The person [I spoke ___to___] was friendly.

2. We went ___to___ a movie. The movie we went ___to___ was very good.

3. We stayed ___in, at___ a motel. The motel we stayed ___in/at___ was clean and comfortable.

4. We listened ___to___ a new CD. I enjoyed the new CD we listened ___to___ .

5. Sally was waiting ___for___ a person. The person Sally was waiting ___for___ never came.

6. I talked ___to___ a man. The man ___to___ whom I talked was helpful.

7. I never found the book that I was looking ___for___ .

8. The interviewer wanted to know the name of the college I had graduated ___from___ .

9. Oscar likes the Canadian family ___with___ whom he is staying.

10. The man who is staring ___at___ us looks unfriendly.

11. My sister and I have the same ideas about almost everything. She is the one person ___with___ whom I almost always agree.   with 人 / in 事 / to V.

12. What's the name of the person you introduced me ___to whom___ at the restaurant last night? I've already forgotten.

13. My father is someone I've always been able to depend ___on___ when I need advice or help.

14. The person you waved ___at___ is waving back at you.

15. Your building supervisor is the person ___to___ whom you should complain if you have any problems with your apartment.

*請見附錄中單元 C 的介系詞組合表。

❑ **Exercise 28. 聽力** (表 12-1 → 12-6)

聆聽 CD 播放的句子，並圈選所有符合該句句義的敘述。

例：你會聽到：The university I want to attend is in New York.
你要圈出：(a.) I want to go to a university.
　　　　　　b. I live in New York.
　　　　　(c.) The university is in New York.

1. a. The plane is leaving Denver.
   b. I'm taking a plane.
   c. The plane leaves at 7:00 A.M.

2. a. Stores are expensive.
   b. Good vegetables are always expensive.
   c. The best vegetables are at an expensive store.

3. a. My husband made eggs.
   b. My husband made breakfast.
   c. The eggs were cold.

4. a. I sent an email.
   b. Someone wanted my bank account number.
   c. An email had my bank account number.

5. a. The hotel clerk called my wife.
   b. The speaker spoke with the hotel clerk.
   c. The hotel room is going to have a view.

❑ **Exercise 29. 閱讀與文法** (表 12-1 → 12-6)

第一部分　先回答下列問題，再閱讀以下文章，並寫出文章中斜體代名詞所指的名詞。

Have you ever visited or lived in another country?
What differences did you notice?
What customs did you like? What customs seemed strange to you?

An Exchange Student in Ecuador

　　Hiroki is from Japan. When he was sixteen, he spent four months in South America. He stayed with a family *who* lived near Quito, Ecuador. Their way of life was very different from his. At first, many things *that* they did and said seemed strange to Hiroki: their eating customs, political views, ways of showing feelings, work habits, sense of humor, and more. He felt homesick for people *who* were more similar to him in their customs and habits.

　　As time went on, Hiroki began to appreciate* the way of life *that* his host family had. Many activities *which* he did with them began to feel natural, and he developed a strong

---

appreciate 意指「體會，領會」。

friendship with them. At the beginning of his stay in Ecuador, he had noticed only the customs and habits *that* were different between his host family and himself. At the end, he appreciated
6
the many things *which* they also had in common.
7

1. who _____

2. that _____

3. who _____

4. that _____

5. which _____

6. that _____

7. which _____

第二部分　用上文中的資訊，完成下列句子。

1. One thing that Hiroki found strange _____

_____.

2. At first, he wanted to be with people _____

_____.

3. After a while, he began to better understand _____

_____.

4. At the end of his stay, he saw many things _____

_____.

❏ **Exercise 30. 暖身活動** (表 12-7)
勾選 (✓) 符合以下敘述句的句子。

We spoke with someone whose house burned down.

1. _____ Our house burned down.

2. _____ Another person's house burned down.

3. _____ Someone told us our house burned down.

4. _____ Someone told us their house burned down.

5. _____ Someone burned down their house.

12-7 形容詞子句中的 *Whose* 用法

(a) The man called the police. **His car** → **whose car** was stolen. (b) The man **whose car** *was stolen* called the police.	**whose**★ 表示「擁有」。 在例 (a) 中，造形容詞子句時，只需將 *his car* 改成 *whose car*。 在例 (b) 中，*whose car was stolen* = 形容詞子句。
(c) I know a girl. **Her brother** → **whose brother** is a movie star. (d) I know a girl **whose brother** *is a movie star.*	在例 (c) 中，造形容詞子句時，只需將 *her brother* 改成 *whose brother*。
(e) The people were friendly. We bought **their house.** → **whose house** (f) The people **whose house** *we bought* were friendly.	在例 (e) 中，造形容詞子句時，只需將 *their house* 改成 *whose house*。

*★**whose** 和 **who's** 發音相同，但意義「不同」。*
who's = **who is**，例：**Who's** (Who is) your teacher?

❏ **Exercise 31. 文法** (表 12-7)

遵循下列步驟，合併 a、b 兩句。
(1) 將 b 句中的所有格形容詞劃<u>底線</u>。
(2) 畫箭頭標出 a 句中該所有格形容詞所指的名詞。
(3) 用 **whose** 替換所有格形容詞。
(4) 將「**whose** +（接於其後的）名詞」置於箭頭所指的名詞（步驟 2 畫的）之後。
(5) 用 b 句中的其他字詞完成 **whose** 的詞組，並造出一個句子。

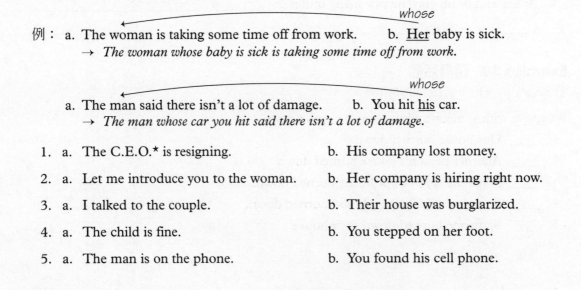

例： a. The woman is taking some time off from work.   b. <u>Her</u> baby is sick.
    → *The woman whose baby is sick is taking some time off from work.*

a. The man said there isn't a lot of damage.   b. You hit <u>his</u> car.
    → *The man whose car you hit said there isn't a lot of damage.*

1. a. The C.E.O.★ is resigning.   b. His company lost money.

2. a. Let me introduce you to the woman.   b. Her company is hiring right now.

3. a. I talked to the couple.   b. Their house was burglarized.

4. a. The child is fine.   b. You stepped on her foot.

5. a. The man is on the phone.   b. You found his cell phone.

★C.E.O. = chief executive officer 或 head of a company，意指「首席執行長」或「總裁」。

成兩人一組，輪流將 b 句改為形容詞子句，並用 ***whose*** 合併 a、b 兩句。

情境：你和朋友在派對上談論著出席該派對的賓客。

1. a. There is the man.   b. His car was stolen.
   → *There is the man whose car was stolen.*

2. a. There is the woman.   b. Her husband writes movie scripts.

3. a. Over there is the man.   b. His daughter is in my English class.

4. a. Over there is the woman.   b. You met her sister yesterday.

5. a. There is the professor.   b. I'm taking her course.

6. a. That is the man.   b. His daughter is a newscaster.

7. a. That is the girl.   b. I taught her brother.

8. a. There is the boy.   b. His mother is a famous musician.

❏ **Exercise 33. 聽力**（表 12-7）

聆聽 CD 播放的句子，並圈選聽到的字：***who's*** 或 ***whose***。

CD 2
Track 46

例：你會聽到：The neighbor who's selling her house is moving overseas.
　　你要圈出：(who's)　　　　whose

1. who's	whose	4. who's	whose
2. who's	whose	5. who's	whose
3. who's	whose	6. who's	whose

分小組練習。將 a 到 f 句改爲形容詞子句，並輪流完成各題中的句子。

1. The man _____ is an undercover police officer.
   a. His car was stolen.
      → *The man whose car was stolen*
      is an undercover police officer.
   b. He invited us to his party.
   c. His son broke our car window.
   d. His dog barks all night.
   e. He is standing out in the rain.
   f. His wife is an actress.

2. The nurse _____ is leaving for a trip across the Sahara Desert.
   a. Her picture was in the paper.
   b. Her father climbed Mount Everest.
   c. She helped me when I cut myself.
   d. She works for Dr. Lang.
   e. I found her purse.
   f. I worked with her father.

3. The book _____ is very valuable.
   a. Its pages are torn.
   b. It's on the table.
   c. Sam lost it.
   d. Its cover is missing.
   e. I gave it to you.
   f. I found.

❏ **Exercise 35. 文法** (第12章)

用所有正確的作答提示字：**who**、**that**、**Ø**、**which**、**whose** 或 **whom**，完成下列句子。

1. The people __who/that__ moved into town are Italian.

2. The lamp __that/Ø/which__ I bought downtown is beautiful but quite expensive.

3. Everyone __who /that__ came to the audition got a part in the play.

4. Ms. Rice is the teacher __who , whom , that , X__ class I enjoy most.

5. The man _____ I found in the doorway had collapsed from heat exhaustion.

6. I like the people with __whom__ I work.

7. I have a friend __whose__ father is a famous artist.

8. The camera _____ I bought takes very sharp pictures.

9. Students __who , that__ have part-time jobs have to budget their time very carefully.

10. Flying squirrels _____ live in tropical rain forests stay in the trees their entire lives without ever touching the ground.

11. The people __whose__ car I dented were a little upset.

12. The person to _____ you should send your application is the Director of Admissions.

13. Monkeys will eat almost anything __that , which , Ø__ they can find.

❏ **Exercise 36. 聽力**（第 12 章）

聆聽 CD 播放的對話，並用 *that*、*which*、*whose* 或 *Ø* 完成下列句子。

Friendly advice

A: A magazine _____ I saw at the doctor's office had an article
                ₁
   _____ you ought to read. It's about the importance of exercise in
     ₂
   dealing with stress.

B: Why do you think I should read an article _____ deals with exercise
                               ₃
   and stress?

A: If you stop and think for a minute, you can answer that question yourself. You're under a
   lot of stress, and you don't get any exercise.

B: The stress _____ I have at work doesn't bother me. It's just a normal
                ₄
   part of my job. And I don't have time to exercise.

A: Well, you should make time. Anyone _____ job is as stressful as
                             ₅
   yours should make physical exercise part of their daily routine.

❏ **Exercise 37. 文法**（第 12 章）

將下表中的敘述句改為形容詞子句，再用該子句完成下列句子；視情況省略形容詞子句中的受格代名詞。

> Their specialty is heart surgery.
> ✓James chose the color of paint for his bedroom walls.
> Its mouth was big enough to swallow a whole cow in one gulp.
> It erupted in Indonesia.
> His son was in an accident.
> They lived in the jungles of Southeast Asia.
> I slept on it in a hotel last night.

1. The color of paint   *James chose for his bedroom walls*   was an unusual shade of blue.

2. The man _____
   called an ambulance.

3. My back hurts today. The mattress _____
   was too soft.

4. A volcano _____ killed six people
   and damaged large areas of crops.

5. Doctors and nurses _____
   are some of the best-trained medical personnel in the world.

6. Originally, chickens were wild birds _____.

    At some point in time, humans learned how to raise them for food.

7. In prehistoric times, there was a dinosaur _____

    _____.

❑ **Exercise 38.** 口說：訪談 （第 12 章）

訪問班上兩位同學，分別詢問他們下列所有問題，然後與全班同學分享他們的回答，看哪些答案是最多人會講到的。

1. What is a dessert that you like? → *A dessert that I like is ice cream.*
2. What are some of the cities in the world you would like to visit?
3. What is one of the programs which you like to watch on TV?
4. What is one subject that you would like to know more about?
5. What are some sports you enjoy playing? watching on TV?
6. What is one of the best movies that you've ever seen?
7. What is one of the hardest classes you've ever taken?
8. Who is one of the people that you admire most in the world?

❑ **Exercise 39.** 遊戲 （第 12 章）

分組比賽。用含有形容詞子句的句子，回答下列問題；用最多正確句子答題的組別獲勝。

例：What are the qualities of a good friend?
    → *A good friend is someone who you can depend on in times of trouble.*
    → *A good friend is a person who accepts you as you are.*
    → *A good friend is someone you can trust with secrets.*
    → *Etc.*

1. What is your idea of the ideal roommate?
2. What are the qualities of a good neighbor?
3. What kind of people make good parents?
4. What are the qualities of a good boss and a bad boss?
5. What is your idea of the ideal school?

❑ **Exercise 40.** 檢視學習成果 （第 12 章）

校訂下列句子，訂正形容詞子句中的錯誤。

1. The book that I bought ~~it~~ at the bookstore was very expensive.

2. The woman was nice that I met yesterday.

3. I met a woman who her husband is a famous lawyer.

4. Do you know the people who lives in that house?

5. The professor teaches Chemistry 101 is very good.

6. The people who I painted their house want me to do other work for them.

7. The people who I met them at the party last night were interesting.

8. I enjoyed the music that we listened to it.

9. The apple tree is producing fruit that we planted it last year.

10. Before I came here, I didn't have the opportunity to speak to people who their native language is English.

11. One thing I need to get a new alarm clock.

12. The people who was waiting to buy tickets for the game they were happy because their team had made it to the championship.

❑ **Exercise 41. 閱讀與寫作** (第 12 章)

第一部分 閱讀以下文章，並將形容詞子句劃<u>底線</u>。

My Friend's Vegan Diet

I have a friend <u>who is a vegan</u>. As you may know, a vegan is a person who eats no animal products. When I first met him, I didn't understand the vegan diet. I thought *vegan* was another name for *vegetarian,* except that vegans didn't eat eggs. I soon found out I was wrong. The first time I cooked dinner for him, I made a vegetable dish which had a lot of cheese. Since cheese comes from cows, it's not vegan, so he had to scrape it off. I also served him bread that had milk in it and a dessert that was made with ice cream. Unfortunately, there wasn't much that he could eat that night. In the beginning, I had trouble thinking of meals which we could both enjoy. But he is a wonderful cook and showed me how to create delicious vegan meals. I don't know if I'll ever become a complete vegan, but I've learned a lot about the vegan diet and the delicious possibilities it has.

第二部分 寫一個段落，此段落是關於你認識的人及其生活中有趣和特殊的事件；試著在段落中運用一些形容詞子句。

可作爲段落文字開頭的例句：
I have a friend who . . . .
I know a person who . . . .
I've heard of a movie star who . . . .

第十三章

動名詞與不定詞

❏ **Exercise 1. 暖身活動** (表 13-1)

① S + V₁ + Ving or to V₂   ② To V / Ving ~ Vₐ + ~

勾選 (✓) 所有可完成句子，且符合你自身狀況的項目。

ex. Working late every night [is] bad for your health
                              S單   單

I enjoy . . .

1. _____ traveling.
2. _____ shopping for clothes.
3. _____ playing sports.
4. _____ watching TV commercials.
5. _____ surfing the Internet.
6. _____ learning about ancient history.

13-1 動詞 + 動名詞 Verb + Gerund

動詞 動名詞 (a) I *enjoy walking* in the park.	動名詞是動詞的 *-ing* 形式，作名詞用。 在例 (a) 中，*walking* 就是一個動名詞，作為動詞 *enjoy* 的受詞。
後面常接動名詞的動詞 enjoy (b) I *enjoy working* in my garden. finish (c) Ann *finished studying* at midnight. quit (d) David *quit smoking*. mind (e) Would you *mind opening* the window? postpone (f) I *postponed doing* my homework. put off (g) I *put off doing* my homework. keep (on) (h) *Keep (on) working*. Don't stop. consider (i) I'm *considering going* to Hawaii. think about (j) I'm *thinking about going* to Hawaii. discuss (k) They *discussed getting* a new car. talk about (l) They *talked about getting* a new car.	左列動詞都要接動名詞，這些動詞也包括片語動詞（如：*put off*）。 這些動詞後面「不」接 *to* + 原形動詞（又稱不定詞）。 錯誤：*I enjoy to walk in the park.* 錯誤：*Bob finished to study.* 錯誤：*I'm thinking to go to Hawaii.* 關於動詞 *-ing* 的拼寫規則，請見第 29 頁，表 2-2。
(m) I *considered not going* to class.	否定形式：*not* + 動名詞

❏ **Exercise 2. 文法** (表 13-1)

用下表中動詞的正確形式完成句子。

clean	hand in	sleep
close	hire	smoke
eat	pay	work

1. The Boyds own a bakery. They work seven days a week and they are very tired. They are thinking about . . .
   a. _____ fewer hours a day.
   b. _____ their shop for a few weeks and going on vacation.
   c. _____ more workers for their shop.

2. Joseph wants to live a healthier life. He made several New Year's resolutions. For example, he has quit . . .
   a. _____ cigars
   b. _____ high-fat foods.
   c. _____ until noon on weekends.

3. Martina is a procrastinator.* She puts off . . .
   a. _____ her bills.
   b. _____ her assignments to her teacher.
   c. _____ her apartment.

❑ **Exercise 3.** 文法 (表 13-1)
用動名詞完成下列句子。

1. We discussed ___going/driving___ to the ocean for our vacation.
   一家人
2. The Porters' car is too small for their growing family. They're considering
   _____ a bigger one.

3. When Martha finished _____ the floor, she dusted the furniture.

4. Beth doesn't like her job. She's talking about _____ a different job.

5. A: Are you listening to me?
   B: Yes. Keep _____. I'm listening.

6. A: Do you want to take a break?
   B: No. I'm not tired yet. Let's keep on ___working___ for another hour or so.

7. A: Would you mind _____ the window?
   B: No problem. I'm too hot too.

❑ **Exercise 4.** 聽力 (表 13-1)

CD 2
Track 48
聆聽 CD，並用聽到的字詞完成下列對話。注意：答案中含動名詞。

例：你會聽到：A: I enjoy watching sports on TV, especially soccer.
            B: Me too.
   你要寫下：___enjoy watching___

1. A: When you _____ your homework, could you help me in the kitchen?
   B: Sure.

---

*procrastinator 意指「拖延的人」。

2. A: Do you have any plans for this weekend?

   B: Henry and I _____ the dinosaur exhibit at the museum.

3. A: I didn't understand the answer. _____ it?

   B: I'd be happy to.

4. A: I'm _____ the meeting tomorrow.

   B: Really? Why? I hope you go. We need your input.

5. A: I've been working on this math problem for the last half hour, and I still don't

   understand it.

   B: Well, don't give up. _____ .

❏ **Exercise 5.** 暖身活動 (表 13-2)

用下列圖片中的活動完成句子，並與一位同學分享你的答案。你的搭檔將跟全班報告一些你的
答案。

When I'm on vacation, I like/don't like to *go* _____*ing*.

13-2 *Go* + 動詞 *-ing*

(a) **Did** you **go shopping** yesterday? (b) I **went swimming** last week. (c) Bob **hasn't gone fishing** in years.	在表達有關活動的某些常見字詞中，**go** 後面接動名詞。 注意：**go** 與動名詞之間不加 **to**。 錯誤：*Did you go to shopping?*

「**go** + 動詞 **-ing**」的常見表達字詞

go boating	go dancing	go jogging	go (window) shopping	go (water) skiing
go bowling	go fishing	go running	go sightseeing 觀光	go skydiving
go camping	go hiking	go sailing	go (ice) skating	go swimming

❑ **Exercise 6.** 口說：兩人一組（表 13-2）

成兩人一組，輪流用表 13-2 中「**go** + 動詞 **-ing**」的常見表達字詞作問答練習。

1. Patricia often goes to the beach. She spends hours in the water. What does she like to do?
   → *She likes to go swimming.*

2. Nancy and Frank like to spend the whole day on a lake with poles in their hands. What do they like to do?

3. Last summer Adam went to a national park. He slept in a tent and cooked his food over a fire. What did Adam do last summer?

4. Tim likes to go to stores and buy things. What does he like to do?

5. Laura takes good care of her health. She runs a couple of miles every day. What does Laura do every day? (*There are two possible responses.*)

6. On weekends in the winter, Fred and Jean sometimes drive to a resort in the mountains. They like to race down the side of a mountain in the snow. What do they like to do?

7. Ivan likes to take long walks in the woods. What does Ivan like to do?

8. Sonia prefers indoor sports. She goes to a place where she rolls a 13-pound ball at some wooden pins. What does Sonia often do?

9. Liz and Greg know all the latest dances. What do they probably do a lot?

10. The Taylors are going to go to a little lake near their house tomorrow. The lake is completely frozen now that it's winter. The ice is smooth. What are the Taylors going to do tomorrow?

11. Mariko and Taka live near the ocean. When there's a strong wind, they like to spend the whole day in their sailboat. What do they like to do?

12. Tourists often get on tour buses that take them to see interesting places in an area. What do tourists do on these buses?

13. Colette and Ben like to jump out of airplanes. They don't open their parachutes until the last minute. What do they like to do?

14. What do you like to do for exercise and fun?

❑ **Exercise 7.** 口說：訪談（表 13-2）

訪問班上同學，試著找出從事過下列活動的人。在開始訪談前，先用下列句子造問句。最後，與全班同學分享一些答案。

Find someone who . . .

1. has gone skydiving before. → *Have you gone skydiving before?*
2. likes to go waterskiing. → *Do you like to go waterskiing?*
3. likes to go bowling.
4. goes dancing on weekends.
5. goes jogging for exercise.
6. goes fishing in the winter.
7. goes camping in the summer.
8. likes to go snow skiing.

勾選 (✓) 符合自身狀況的句子。

1. _____ I hope to move to another town soon.
2. _____ I would like to get married in a few years.
3. _____ I intend to visit another country next year.
4. _____ I'm planning to become an English teacher.

13-3 動詞 + 不定詞 Verb + Infinitive

(a) Tom **offered to lend** me some money. (b) I've **decided to buy** a new car.	某些動詞後面接不定詞： 不定詞 = **to** + 原形動詞
(c) I've **decided not to keep** my old car.	否定形式：**not** + 不定詞

後面接不定詞的常用動詞

want	hope	decide	seem 似乎	learn (how)
need	expect	promise	appear to v̄	try
would like	plan	offer	pretend	
would love	intend	agree		(can't) afford
	mean	refuse		(can't) wait

intend to V 意圖
mean to V 穩為

❏ **Exercise 9.** 文法 (表 13-3)

try ┤ to v̄ 盡力
*   Ving 嘗試*

用下表中字詞的正確形式，完成下列句子。

be	fly to	hear	lend	visit
buy	get to	hurt	see	watch
eat	go to	leave	tell	

1. I'm planning _to fly to/to go to_ Chicago next week.

2. Hasan promised not _____ late for the wedding.

3. My husband and I would love _____ Fiji.

4. What time do you expect _____ Chicago?

5. You seem _____ in a good mood today.

6. Nadia appeared _____ asleep, but she wasn't. She was only pretending.

7. Nadia pretended _____ asleep. She pretended not _____ me when I spoke to her.

8. The Millers can't afford _____ a house.

9. My friend offered _____ me some money.

10. Tommy doesn't like broccoli. He refuses _____ it.

11. My wife and I wanted to do different things this weekend. Finally, I agreed
    _____ a movie with her Saturday, and she agreed
    _____ the football game with me on Sunday.

broccoli

12. I try _____ class on time every day.

13. I can't wait _____ my family again! It's been a long time.

14. I'm sorry. I didn't mean _____ you.

15. I learned how _____ time when I was six.

❏ **Exercise 10. 暖身活動** (表 13-4)
勾選 (✓) 可完成句子且合文法的項目。

Many children love . . .

1. _____ to eat ice cream.

2. _____ eating ice cream.

3. _____ eat ice cream.

13-4 動詞 + 動名詞或不定詞 Verb + Gerund or Infinitive

(a) It began **raining**. (b) It began **to rain**.	有些動詞後面可接動名詞，如：例 (a)，或不定詞，如：例 (b)，通常在意義上並無差別。 例 (a) 與例 (b) 同義。

後面接動名詞或不定詞的常見動詞

begin	like*	hate
start	love*	can't stand
continue		

*比較：**like** 和 **love** 後面可接動名詞或不定詞，例：*I like going/to go to movies. I love playing/to play chess.*
would like 和 *would love* 後面接不定詞，例：*I would like **to go** to a movie tonight. I'd love **to play** a game of chess right now.*

❏ **Exercise 11. 文法** (表 13-4)
圈選正確的動詞。

1. It started _____ around midnight.
   a. snow   ⓑ snowing   ⓒ to snow

2. I continued _____ even though everyone else stopped.
   a. work   b. working   c. to work

動名詞與不定詞　**347**

3. I like _____ emails from my friends.

     a. get   b. getting   c. to get

4. I would like _____ an email from my son who's away at college.

     a. get   b. getting   c. to get

5. I love _____ to baseball games.

     a. go   b. going   c. to go

6. I would love _____ to the baseball game tomorrow.

     a. go   b. going   c. to go

7. I hate _____ to pushy salespeople.

     a. talk   b. talking   c. to talk

8. I can't stand _____ in long lines.

     a. wait   b. waiting   c. to wait

❏ **Exercise 12. 口說：兩人一組** (表 13-1 → 13-4)

成兩人一組；輪流將下表中的字詞及各題提示字，合併爲表達個人好惡的完整句子。

I like	I enjoy	I hate	I don't mind
I love	I don't like	I can't stand	

1. cook
   → *I like to cook. /I like cooking. /I hate to cook. /I hate cooking. /I don't mind cooking. /*
   I don't enjoy cooking. /Etc.
2. live in this city
3. wash dishes
4. wait in airports
5. fly
6. eat food slowly
7. speak in front of a large group
8. drive in the city during rush hour
9. go to parties where I don't know anyone
10. listen to music while I'm trying to fall asleep
11. get in between two friends who are having an argument
12. travel to unusual places

❏ **Exercise 13. 文法與口說** (表 13-1 → 13-4)

用括弧內動詞的不定詞或動名詞形式，完成下列句子；然後決定你是否同意該敘述句。最後，與同學討論你的答案。

What do you do when you can't understand a native English speaker?

1. I pretend (*understand*) _____.   yes no

2. I keep on (*listen*) _____ politely.   yes no

3. I think, "I can't wait (*get*) _____ out of here!" 或   yes   no

"I can't wait for this person (*stop*) _____ talking."   yes   no

4. I say, "Would you mind (*repeat*) _____ that?"   yes   no

5. I begin (*nod*) _____ my head so I look like I understand.   yes   no

6. I start (*look*) _____ at my watch, so it appears I'm in a hurry.   yes   no

7. As soon as the person finishes (*speak*) _____,   yes   no
I say I have to leave.

❑ **Exercise 14. 文法** (表 13-1 → 13-4)
用括弧內動詞的不定詞或動名詞形式，完成下列句子。

1. We finished (*eat*) _____eating_____ around seven.

2. My roommate offered (*help*) _____to help_____ me with my English.

3. I'm considering (*move*) _____moving_____ to a new apartment.

4. Some children hate (*go*) _____to go/ going_____ to school.

5. What seems (*be*) _____to be_____ the problem?

6. I don't mind (*live*) _____living_____ with four roommates.

7. My boss refused (*give*) _____to give_____ me a raise, so I quit.   *promotion* 升官

8. That's not what I meant! I meant (*say*) _____to say_____ just the opposite.

9. Julia can't stand (*sleep*) _____to sleep / sleeping_____ in a room with all of the windows
closed.

10. Max seemed (*want*) _____to want_____ (*leave*) _____to leave_____ the
party, but he kept (*talk*) _____talking_____ anyway.

11. Sam's tomato crop always failed. Finally he quit (*try*) _____trying_____ to grow
tomatoes in his garden.

成兩人一組；輪流用「*to go/going* ＋ 地點」，完成下列句子。

例：I would like . . . .
搭檔 A：I **would like to go** to the Beach Café for dinner tonight.
搭檔 B：I **would like to go** to the movies later today.

1. I like . . . .
2. I love . . . .
3. I'd love . . . .
4. I refuse . . . .
5. I expect . . . .
6. I promised . . . .
7. I can't stand . . . .
8. I waited . . . .
9. I am thinking about . . . .
10. Are you considering . . . ?

11. I can't afford . . . .
12. Would you mind . . . ?
13. My friend and I agreed . . . .
14. I hate . . . .
15. I don't enjoy . . . .
16. My friend and I discussed . . . .
17. I've decided . . . .
18. I don't mind . . . .
19. Sometimes I put off . . . .
20. I can't wait . . . .

❏ **Exercise 16.** 文法 (表 13-1 → 13-4)

用括弧內動詞的不定詞或動名詞形式，完成下列句子。

1. I want (*relax*) _____to relax_____ tonight.

2. I want (*stay*) _____to stay_____ home and (*relax*)* _____to relax / relax_____
   tonight.

3. I want (*stay*) _____to stay_____ home, (*relax*) _____relax_____, and
   (*go*) _____go_____ to bed early tonight.

4. I enjoy (*get*) _____getting_____ up early in the morning and (*watch*)
   _____watching_____ the sunrise.

5. I enjoy (*get*) _____getting_____ up early in the morning, (*watch*)
   _____watching_____ the sunrise, and (*listen*) _____listening_____ to the birds.

6. Mr. and Mrs. Bashir are thinking about (*sell*) _____selling_____ their old house
   and (*buy*) _____buying_____ a new one.

7. Kathy plans (*move*) _____to move_____ to New York City, (*find*)
   _____find_____ a job, and (*start*) _____start_____ a new life.

---

*用 *and* 連接兩個不定詞時，可以省略 *and* 之後的 *to*。
例：I need **to stay** home and (to) **study** tonight.

8. Do you like (*go*) _____going / to go_____ out to eat and (*let*) _____ someone else do the cooking?

9. Kevin is thinking about (*quit*) _____quitting_____ his job and (*go*) _____going_____ back to school.

10. Before you leave the office tonight, would you mind (*unplug*) _____unpluging_____ the coffee pot, (*turn off*) _____turning off_____ all the lights, and (*lock*) _____locking_____ the door?

❑ **Exercise 17. 遊戲** (表 13-1 → 13-4)

分組比賽。老師負責喊題號，各組要用 ***I*** 開頭，並用該題中的提示字和任一動詞時態造句。最快造出正確句子的組別，可贏得一分，贏得最多分數的組別獲勝。

例：want \ go
　　→ *I want to go to New York City next week.*

1. plan \ go	11. postpone \ go
2. consider \ go	12. finish \ study
3. offer \ help	13. would mind \ help
4. like \ visit	14. begin \ study
5. enjoy \ read	15. think about \ go
6. intend \ get	16. quit \ try
7. can't afford \ buy	17. continue \ walk
8. seem \ be	18. learn \ speak
9. put off \ write	19. talk about \ go
10. would like \ go \ swim	20. keep \ try

介+受 → n. ← Vïng ← V.

❑ **Exercise 18. 暖身活動** (表 13-5)

表達是否同意下列敘述，並注意動詞後面的粗斜體介系詞和動名詞的用法。

I know someone who . . .

1. never *apologizes **for being*** late.	yes	no
2. is *interested **in coming*** to this country.	yes	no
3. is *worried **about losing*** his/her job.	yes	no
4. is *excited **about becoming*** a parent.	yes	no

13-5 介系詞 ＋ 動名詞 Preposition ＋ Gerund

(a) Kate *insisted **on coming*** with us. (b) We're *excited **about going*** to Tahiti. (c) I *apologized **for being*** late.	介系詞後面接動名詞，而非不定詞。 在例 (a) 中，動名詞 (coming) 接在介系詞 (on) 之後。

介系詞後面接動名詞的常用表達字詞

be afraid **of** (doing something)	be good **at**	be responsible **for**
apologize **for**	insist **on**	stop (someone) **from**
believe **in**	instead **of**	thank (someone) **for**
dream **about/of**	be interested **in**	be tired **of**
be excited **about**	look forward **to**	worry **about**/be worried **about**
feel **like**	be nervous **about**	
forgive (someone) **for**	plan **on**	

❏ **Exercise 19. 文法**（表 13-5 和附錄單元 C，表 C-2）

用「介系詞 ＋ 動名詞」和各題提示字，完成下列句子。

1. I'm looking forward ＋ go away for the weekend

   → I'm looking forward **to** *going away for the weekend.*

(手寫註記：keep / stop / protect / prevent A from B 免於...)

2. Thank you ＋ hold the door open
3. I'm worried ＋ be late for my appointment
4. Are you interested ＋ go to the beach with us
5. I apologized ＋ be late
6. Are you afraid ＋ fly in small planes
7. Are you nervous ＋ take your driver's test
8. We're excited ＋ see the soccer game
9. Tariq insisted ＋ pay the restaurant bill
10. Eva dreams ＋ become a veterinarian someday
11. I don't feel ＋ eat right now
12. Please forgive me ＋ not write sooner
13. I'm tired ＋ live with five roommates
14. I believe ＋ be honest at all times
15. Let's plan ＋ meet at the restaurant at six
16. Who's responsible ＋ clean the classroom
17. The police stopped us ＋ enter the building
18. Jake's not very good ＋ cut his own hair

❏ **Exercise 20. 口說：兩人一組**（表 13-5 和附錄單元 C，表 C-2）

成兩人一組，輪流用以下句型作問答練習：「***What*** ＋ 提示字 ＋ 介系詞 ＋ ***doing***」。

例：be looking forward
搭檔 A：What are you looking forward **to doing**?
搭檔 B：I'm looking forward **to going to a movie tonight**.

1. be interested
2. be worried
3. thank your friend
4. apologize
5. be afraid

6. be nervous
7. be excited
8. feel
9. plan
10. be tired

❑ **Exercise 21. 文法** (表 13-5 和附錄單元 C，表 C-2)
用正確的介系詞及括弧內動詞的動名詞形式，完成下列句子。

1. Carlos is nervous ___*about*___ (*meet*) ___*meeting*___ his girlfriend's parents for the first time.

2. I believe *in telling* (*tell*) _____ the truth no matter what.

3. I don't go swimming in deep water because I'm afraid ___*of*___ (*drown*) _____*drowning*_____ .

4. Every summer, I look forward ___*to*___ (*take*) ___*taking*___ a vacation with my family.

5. Do you feel ___*like*___ (*tell*) ___*telling*___ me why you're so sad?

6. My father-in-law always insists ___*on*___ (*pay*) ___*paying*___ for everything when we go out for dinner.

7. I want you to know that I'm sorry. I don't know if you can ever forgive me ___*for*___ (*cause*) ___*causing*___ you so much trouble.

8. I'm not very good ___*at*___ (*remember*) ___*remembering*___ people's names.

9. How do you stop someone ___*from*___ (*do*) ___*doing*___ something you know is wrong?

10. The kids are responsible ___*for*___ (*take*) ___*taking*___ out the garbage.

11. Monique lost her job. That's why she is afraid ___*of*___ (*have, not*) ___*not having*___ enough money to pay her rent.

12. Sheila is pregnant. She's looking forward ___*to*___ (*have*) ___*having*___ another child.

13. A: I'm not happy in my work. I often dream ___*about/of*___ (*quit*) ___*quitting*___ my job.
    B: Instead ___*of*___ (*quit*) ___*quitting*___ your job, why don't you see if you can transfer to another department?

□ **Exercise 22. 聽力** （表 13-1 → 13-5）

CD 2
Track 49

聆聽 CD 播放的對話；然後再聽一遍，並用聽到的字詞完成下列句子。

A: Have you made any vacation plans?

B: Well, I _____ home because I don't like _____.
                       1   2

   I hate _____ and _____ suitcases. But my wife
              3   4

   loves _____ and _____ a boat trip somewhere.
             5   6

A: So, what are you going to do?

B: Well, we couldn't agree, so we _____ home and
                                               7

   _____ tourists in our own town.
          8

A: Interesting. What are you planning _____?
                                                 9

B: Well, we haven't seen the new Museum of Space yet. There's also a new art exhibit

   downtown. And my wife _____ a boat trip in
                                      10

   the harbor. Actually, when we _____ about it, we
                                            11

   discovered there were lots of things to do.

A: Sounds like a great solution!

B: Yeah, we're both really _____ more of our
                                        12

   own town.

□ **Exercise 23. 暖身活動** （表 13-6）

圈選符合你自身狀況的答案。

1. I sometimes pay for things _____.
   a. by credit card   b. by check   c. in cash

2. I usually come to school _____.
   a. by bus   b. by car   c. on foot

3. My favorite way to travel long distances is _____.
   a. by plane   b. by boat   c. by train

4. I like to communicate with my family _____.
   a. by email   b. by phone   c. in person

藉由

13-6 用 *By* 和 *With* 表示事情如何完成

(a) Pat turned off the TV **by pushing** the "off" button.	「**by** + 動名詞」用來表示事情如何完成。
(b) Mary goes to work **by bus**. (c) Andrea stirred her coffee **with a spoon**.	**by** 或 **with** 後面接名詞，也用來表示事情如何完成。

BY 接「運輸工具」和「通訊方式」

by (air)plane	by subway*	by mail/email	by air
by boat	by taxi	by (tele)phone	by land
by bus	by train	by fax	by sea
by car	by foot（或 on foot）	（比較：in person）	

BY 的其他用法

by chance	by mistake	by check（比較：in cash）
by choice	by hand**	by credit card

WITH 接「工具」或「身體部位」
I cut down the tree *with an ax* (by using an ax).
I swept the floor *with a broom*.
She pointed to a spot on the map *with her finger*.

by subway 爲美式英文；*by underground*、*by tube* 爲英式英文。
by hand 通常表示事物是手工製作的，而非機器，例：*This rug was made by hand.*（這塊地毯是手工做的，而非機器。）
比較：*I touched his shoulder with my hand.*（我用手觸碰他的肩膀。）

❑ **Exercise 24. 文法**（表 13-6）

用下表中的字詞或你自己想到的字，搭配「**by** + 動名詞」，完成下列句子。

eat	smile	wag	wave
drink	stay	wash	✓write
guess	take	watch	

1. Students practice written English ___by writing___ compositions.

2. We clean our clothes _____ them in soap and water.

3. Khalid improved his English _____ a lot of TV.

4. We show other people we are happy _____.

5. We satisfy our hunger _____ something.

6. We quench our thirst _____ something.

7. I figured out what *quench* means _____.

8. Alex caught my attention _____ his arms in the air.

9. My dog shows me she is happy _____ her tail.

10. Carmen recovered from her cold _____ in bed and _____ care of herself.

□ **Exercise 25. 文法** (表 13-6)

用 *with* 和下表中的字詞，完成下列句子。

✓a broom	a pair of scissors	a spoon
a hammer	a saw	a thermometer
a needle and thread	a shovel	

1. I swept the floor ___with a broom___ .

2. I sewed a button on my shirt _____ .

3. I cut the wood _____ .

4. I took my temperature _____ .

5. I stirred cream in my coffee _____ .

6. I dug a hole in the garden _____ .

7. I nailed two pieces of wood together _____ .

8. I cut the paper _____ .

□ **Exercise 26. 文法** (表 13-6)

用 *by* 或 *with* 完成下列句子。

1. I opened the door ___with___ a key.

2. I went downtown ___by___ bus.

3. I dried the dishes _____ a dishtowel.

4. I went from Frankfurt to Vienna _____ train.

5. Ted drew a straight line _____ a ruler.

6. Rebecca tightened the screw in the corner of her eyeglasses _____ her fingernail.

7. I called Bill "Paul" _____ mistake.

8. I sent a copy of the contract _____ fax.

9. Talya protected her eyes from the sun _____ her hand.

10. My grandmother makes tablecloths _____ hand.

閱讀以下文章，並判斷是否同意下列敘述。

A White Lie

Jane gave her friend Lisa a book for her birthday. When Lisa opened it, she tried to look excited, but her husband had already given her the same book. Lisa had just finished reading it, but she thanked Jane and said she was looking forward to reading it. Lisa told a "white lie." White lies are minor or unimportant lies that a person often tells to avoid hurting someone else's feelings.

1. Telling white lies is common.   yes   no

2. It is sometimes acceptable to tell a white lie.   yes   no

3. I sometimes tell white lies.   yes   no

It is adj. (for sb) (to V ~)
虛S   真S

13-7 以動名詞作爲主詞；「It + 不定詞」的用法

(a) **Riding** horses is fun.	例 (a) 與例 (b) 同義。
(b) **It** is fun **to ride** horses.	在例 (a) 中，動名詞 (**riding**) 作爲句子的主詞。
(c) **Coming** to class on time is important.	注意：因爲動名詞是單數，句子的動詞 (**is**) 也用單數形式。★
(d) **It** is important **to come** to class on time.	在例 (b) 中，**it** 作爲句子的主詞，意指後面的不定詞片語 **to ride horses**。

★不定詞片語亦可作句子的主詞（但較爲少見），例：*To ride horses is fun.*

❑ **Exercise 28. 文法與口說：兩人一組** (表 13-7)

造出與下列各題句義相同的句子，然後判斷是否同意各題中的敘述句；同意該敘述，圈 *yes*；不同意，圈 *no*。 最後，與你的搭檔分享答案。

Living in this town

第一部分 用動名詞作爲主詞改寫下列句子。

1. It's hard to meet people here.
   → *Meeting people here is hard.*   yes   no

2. It takes time to make friends here.   yes   no

3. It is easy to get around the town.   yes   no

4. Is it expensive to live here?   yes   no

第二部分 用「*it* + 不定詞」改寫下列句子。

5. Finding things to do on weekends is hard.
   → *It's hard to find things to do on weekends.*   yes   no

6. Walking alone at night is dangerous.   yes   no

7. Exploring this town is fun.   yes   no

8. Is finding affordable housing difficult?   yes   no

訪問班上同學，詢問他們問題，然後表達你是否同意他們的答案。練習在回答時使用動名詞和不定詞。

例：
說話者 A（書本打開）：Which is easier: to make money or to spend money?
說話者 B（書本闔上）：It's easier to spend money than (it is) to make money.
說話者 A（書本打開）：I agree. Spending money is easier than making money. 或
I don't agree. I think that making money is easier than spending money.

1. Which is more fun: to visit a big city or to spend time in the countryside?

2. Which is more difficult: to write English or to read English?

3. Which is easier: to understand spoken English or to speak it?

4. Which is more expensive: to go to a movie or to go to a concert?

5. Which is more comfortable: to wear shoes or to go barefoot?

6. Which is more satisfying: to give gifts or to receive them?

7. Which is more dangerous: to ride in a car or to ride in an airplane?

8. Which is more important: to come to class on time or to get an extra hour of sleep in the morning?

❑ **Exercise 30.** 暖身活動 (表 13-8)

表達是否同意下列敘述。

In my culture . . .

1. it is common for people to shake hands when they meet.　　　　yes　　no

2. it is important for people to look one another in the eye when they are introduced.　　　　yes　　no

3. it is strange for people to kiss one another on the cheek when they meet.　　　　yes　　no

---

13-8　*It* + 不定詞：*For*（某人）的用法

(a) *You* should study hard. (b) It is important *for you* to study hard. (c) *Mary* should study hard. (d) It is important *for Mary* to study hard. (e) *We* don't have to go to the meeting. (f) It isn't necessary *for us* to go to the meeting. (g) *A dog* can't talk. (h) It is impossible *for a dog* to talk.	例 (a) 與例 (b) 同義。 注意例 (b) 的句型： *It is* + 形容詞 + *for*（某人）+ 不定詞片語

I make <u>it</u> <u>a habit</u> [to wake up at seven every morning.]
　　　　O.　　O.C.
　　　　　　　　　　　　真 O

根據提供的資訊，用 *for*（某人）和不定詞片語完成下列句子。

1. Students should do their homework.

   It's really important _____for students to do their homework_____.

2. Teachers should speak clearly.

   It's very important _____for teachers to speak clearly_____.

3. We don't have to hurry. There's plenty of time.

   It isn't necessary _____.

4. A fish can't live out of water for more than a few minutes.

   It's impossible _____for a fish to live out_____.

5. Working parents have to budget their time carefully.

   It's necessary _____.

6. A young child usually can't sit still for a long time.

   It's difficult _____for a young child to sit still_____.

7. My family spends birthdays together.

   It's traditional _____.

8. My brother would love to travel to Mars someday.

   Will it be possible _____for my brother to travel_____ to Mars someday?

9. I usually can't understand Mr. Alvarez. He talks too fast. How about you?

   Is it easy _____?

❑ **Exercise 32. 口說** (表 13-7 和 13-8)

分小組練習。用動名詞作主詞或「*it* + 不定詞」，將各題提示字和下表中的字詞合併造句。分享一些你們造的句子，並讓其他組表達是否同意你們的敘述。

boring	embarrassing	hard	impossible	scary
dangerous	exciting	illegal	interesting	waste of time
educational	fun	important	relaxing	

例：ride a bicycle
   → *Riding a bicycle is fun.* 或 *It's fun to ride a bicycle.*

1. ride a roller coaster
2. read newspapers
3. study economics
4. drive five miles over the speed limit
5. walk in a cemetery at night
6. know the meaning of every word in a dictionary
7. never tell a lie
8. visit museums

Exercise 33. 閱讀與文法 (表 13-7 和 13-8)
第一部分　閱讀以下文章。

Body Language

　　Different cultures use different body language. In some countries, when people meet one another, they offer a strong handshake and look the other person straight in the eye. In other countries, however, it is impolite to shake hands firmly, and it is equally rude to look a person in the eye.

　　How close do people stand to another person when they are speaking to each other? This varies from country to country. In the United States and Canada, people prefer standing just a little less than an arm's length from someone. But many people in the Middle East and Latin America like moving in closer during a conversation.

　　Smiling at another person is a universal, cross-cultural gesture. Although people may smile more frequently in some countries than in others, people around the world understand the meaning of a smile.

第二部分　用關於肢體語言的資訊，完成下列句子。

1. In some countries, it is important _____.

2. In some countries, _____ is impolite.

3. In my country, _____ is important.

4. In my country, it is impolite _____.

❑ **Exercise 34.** 暖身活動 (表 13-9)
勾選 (✓) 所有合文法的句子。

1. _____ I went to the store because I wanted to buy groceries.
2. _____ I went to the store in order to buy groceries.
3. _____ I went to the store to buy groceries.
4. _____ I went to the store for groceries.
5. _____ I went to the store for to buy groceries.

13-9 用 *In Order To* 和 *For* 表示目的

—*Why did you go to the post office?* (a) I went to the post office *because I wanted to mail a letter.* (b) I went to the post office *in order to* mail a letter. (c) I went to the post office *to mail* a letter.	*in order to* 用來表示「目的」，用於回答 why? 的問句。
	在例 (c) 中，*in order* 常被省略，例 (a)、例 (b) 和例 (c) 同義。
(d) I went to the post office *for* some stamps. (e) I went to the post office *to buy* some stamps. 錯誤：*I went to the post office for to buy some stamps.* 錯誤：*I went to the post office for buying some stamps.*	*for* 也可以用來表示「目的」，但它是介系詞，後面要接名詞片語，如：例 (d)。

❑ **Exercise 35. 文法** (表 13-9)

> in order | to V̄ / that + S + V ~   so | as to V̄ / that + S + V

用 (*in order*) *to* 合併 A 欄與 B 欄中的字詞，使兩組字詞成爲語義完整的句子。

例：I called the hotel desk . . .
→ *I called the hotel desk (in order) to ask for an extra pillow.*

> with | a view / an eye | to + Ving / n.

A 欄

1. I called the hotel desk __e__ .
2. I turned on the radio _____ .
3. Andy went to Egypt _____ .
4. People wear boots _____ .
5. I looked on the Internet _____ .
6. Ms. Lane stood on her tiptoes _____ .
7. The dentist moved the light closer to my face _____ .
8. I clapped my hands and yelled _____ .
9. Maria took a walk in the park _____ .
10. I offered my cousin some money _____ .

B 欄

a. keep their feet warm and dry
b. reach the top shelf
c. listen to a ball game
d. find the population of Malaysia
✓e. ask for an extra pillow
f. chase a mean dog away
g. help her pay the rent
h. get some fresh air and exercise
i. see the ancient pyramids
j. look into my mouth

❑ **Exercise 36. 文法** (表 13-9)

在句中適當位置加入 *in order*。

1. I went to the bank to cash a check. → *I went to the bank in order to cash a check.*
2. I'd like to see that movie. → (*No change. The infinitive does not express purpose.*)
3. Steve went to the hospital to visit a friend.
4. I need to go to the bank today.
5. I need to go to the bank today to deposit my paycheck.
6. On my way home, I stopped at the store to buy some shampoo.
7. Masako went to the cafeteria to eat lunch.
8. Jack and Katya have decided to get married.
9. Pedro watches TV to improve his English.
10. I didn't forget to pay my rent.
11. Donna expects to graduate next spring.
12. Jerry needs to go to the bookstore to buy school supplies.

❑ **Exercise 37. 文法** (表 13-9)

用 **to** 或 **for** 完成下列句子。

1. I went to Chicago ___*for*___ a visit.

2. I went to Chicago ___*to*___ visit my aunt and uncle.

3. I take long walks _____ relax.

4. I take long walks _____ relaxation.

5. I'm going to school _____ a good education.

6. I'm going to school _____ get a good education.

7. I sent a card to Carol _____ wish her a happy birthday.

8. Two police officers came to my apartment _____ ask me about a neighbor.

9. I looked on the Internet _____ information about Ecuador.

10. My three brothers, two sisters, and parents all came to town _____ my graduation.

effective 有效果的
efficient 有效率的

❑ **Exercise 38. 閱讀與文法** (表 13-1 → 13-9)

第一部分 閱讀以下文章。

Car Sharing

In hundreds of cities around the world, people can use a car without actually owning one. It's known as car sharing.

Car sharing works like this: people pay a fee to join a car-share organization. These organizations have cars available in different parts of a city 24 hours a day. Members make reservations for a car, and then go to one of several parking lots in the city to pick up the car. They pay an hourly or daily rate for driving it. They may also pay a charge for every mile/kilometer they drive. When they are finished, they return the car to a parking area for someone else to use.

Car sharing works well for several reasons. Some people only need to drive occasionally. Oftentimes, people only need a car for special occasions like moving items or taking long trips. Many people don't want the costs or responsibilities of owning a car. The car-share organization pays for gas, insurance, cleaning, and maintenance costs. Members also don't have to wait in line or fill out forms in order to get a car. They know a variety of cars will be available when they need one.

Car sharing also benefits the environment. People drive only when they need to, and fewer cars on the road means less traffic and air pollution. As more and more cities become interested in reducing traffic, car-share programs are becoming an effective alternative.

1. _____ is helpful to people who don't own a car.

2. People pay a fee in order _____ a car-sharing organization.

3. Car-sharing members pay an hourly or daily rate for _____ a car.

4. Sometimes people need a car _____ furniture or to _____ a trip.

5. Many people don't want the costs of _____ a car.

第三部分　回答下列問題。

1. What are three reasons that people car share?
2. What are two benefits of car sharing?
3. Does the city you live in have a form of car sharing? If yes, has it been successful? If not, why do you think there is no car-sharing program?

❑ **Exercise 39.** 暖身活動：兩人一組（表 13-10）

成兩人一組；大聲唸出以下對話，並用下表中正確的字詞，完成下列句子。

strong	heavy	strength

學生 A：Can you pick up a piano?

學生 B：No. It's too _____ for me to pick up. How about you? Can
　　　　　　　　　　　1
　　　you pick up a piano?

學生 A：No, I'm not _____ enough to pick one up. What about the
　　　　　　　　　　2
　　　class? Can we pick up a piano together?

學生 B：Maybe. We might have enough _____ to do that as a class.
　　　　　　　　　　　　　　　　3

13-10 *Too* 和 *Enough* 與不定詞的連用

too + 形容詞 + (_for_ 某人) + 不定詞 (a) That box is **_too_ heavy** **_to_ lift.** (b) A piano is **_too_ heavy** **_for_ me** **_to_ lift.** (c) That box is **_too_ heavy** **_for_ Bob** **_to_ lift.**	不定詞常接在含 **_too_** 的片語之後，而 **_too_** 的位置在形容詞之前。在說話者心中，**_too_** 的使用暗示否定的結果。 比較： *The box is too heavy. I can't lift it.* *The box is very heavy, but I can lift it.*
enough + 名詞 + 不定詞 (d) I don't have **_enough_ money** **_to_ buy** that car. (e) Did you have **_enough_ time** **_to_ finish** the test?	
形容詞 + _enough_ + 不定詞 (f) Jimmy isn't **old _enough_** **_to_ go** to school. (g) Are you **hungry _enough_** **_to_ eat** three sandwiches?	不定詞常接在含 **_enough_** 的片語之後。 **_enough_** 置於名詞前。* **_enough_** 置於形容詞後。

*__enough__ 也可以接在名詞之後，例：*I don't have* **money enough** *to buy that car.*；但在日常英文中，**_enough_** 通常放在名詞之前。

❏ **Exercise 40. 文法** (表 13-10)

根據各題的提示字，用 **_too_** 或「**_enough_** + 不定詞」完成下列句子。

1. strong/lift   I'm not <u> *strong enough to lift* </u> a refrigerator.

2. weak/lift   Most people are <u> *too weak to lift* </u> a refrigerator without help.

3. busy/answer   I was _____ the phone. I let the call go to voice mail.

4. early/get   I got to the concert _____ good seats.

5. full/hold   My suitcase is _____ _____ any more clothes.

6. large/hold   My suitcase isn't _____ all the clothes I want to take on my trip.

7. big/get   Rex is _____ into the doghouse.

8. big/hold   Julie's purse is _____ _____ her dog Pepper.

❏ **Exercise 41. 文法** (表 13-10)

合併下列各組句子。

第一部分　用 *too* 合併。

1. We can't go swimming today. It's very cold.

   → *It's **too** cold (for us) **to go** swimming today.*

2. I couldn't finish my homework last night. I was very sleepy.

3. Mike couldn't go to his aunt's housewarming party. He was very busy.

4. This jacket is very small. I can't wear it.

5. I live far from school. I can't walk there.

第二部分　用 *enough* 合併。

6. I can't reach the top shelf. I'm not that tall.

   → *I'm not tall **enough to reach** the top shelf.*

7. I can't move this furniture. I'm not that strong.

8. It's not warm today. You can't go outside without a coat.

9. I didn't stay home and miss work. I wasn't really sick, but I didn't feel good all day.

❏ **Exercise 42. 口說：兩人一組** (表 13-10)

成兩人一組；輪流用不定詞完成下列句子。

1. I'm too short . . . .

2. I'm not tall enough . . . .

3. I'm not strong enough . . . .

4. Last night I was too tired . . . .

5. Yesterday I was too busy . . . .

6. A Mercedes-Benz is too expensive . . . .

7. I don't have enough money . . . .

8. Yesterday I didn't have enough time . . . .

9. A teenager is old enough . . . but too young . . . .

10. I know enough English . . . but not enough . . . .

❏ **Exercise 43. 文法** (第 13 章)

用括弧內字詞的動名詞或不定詞形式，完成下列句子。

1. It's difficult for me (*remember*) __*to remember*__ phone numbers.

2. My cat is good at (*catch*) __*catching*__ mice.

3. I called my friend (*invite*) _____ her for dinner.

4. Fatima talked about (*go*) _____ to graduate school.

5. Sarosh found out what was happening by (*listen*) _____ carefully to everything that was said.

6. Michelle works 16 hours a day in order (*earn*) _____ enough money (*take*) _____ care of her elderly parents and her three children.

7. No matter how wonderful a trip is, it's always good (*get*) _____ back home and (*sleep*) _____ in your own bed.

8. I keep (*forget*) _____ to call my friend Jae. I'd better write myself a note.

9. Exercise is good for you. Why don't you walk up the stairs instead of (*use*) _____ the elevator?

❑ Exercise 44. 聽力 (第 13 章)

CD 2
Track 50

聆聽 CD 播放的題目，然後再聽一遍，並用聽到的字詞完成下列句子。

1. My professor goes through the lecture material too quickly. It is difficult for us _____ him. He needs _____ down and _____ us time to understand the key points.

2. _____ others about themselves and their lives is one of the secrets of _____ along with other people. If you want to make and _____ friends, it is important _____ sincerely interested in other people's lives.

3. Large bee colonies have 80,000 workers. These worker bees must visit 50 million flowers _____ one kilogram, or 2.2 pounds, of honey. It's easy _____ why "busy as a bee" is a common expression.

❑ Exercise 45. 閱讀與文法 (第 13 章)

第一部分　閱讀以下文章。

Uncle Ernesto

Have you ever had an embarrassing experience? My Uncle Ernesto did a few years ago while on a business trip in Norway.

Uncle Ernesto is a businessman from Buenos Aires, Argentina. He manufactures equipment for ships and needs to travel around the world to sell his products. Last year, he went to Norway to meet with a shipping company. While he was there, he found himself in an uncomfortable situation.

Uncle Ernesto was staying at a small hotel in Oslo. One morning, as he was getting ready to take a shower, he heard a knock at the door. He opened it, but no one was there. He stepped into the hallway. He still didn't see anyone, so he turned to go back to his room. Unfortunately, the door was locked. This was a big problem because he didn't have his key and he was wearing only a towel.

Instead of standing in the hallway like this, he decided to get help at the front desk and started walking toward the elevator. He hoped it would be empty, but it wasn't. He took a deep breath and got in. The other people in the elevator were surprised when they saw a man who was wrapped in a towel.

Uncle Ernesto thought about trying to explain his problem, but unfortunately he didn't know Norwegian. He knew a little English, so he said, "Door. Locked. No key." A businessman in the elevator nodded, but he wasn't smiling. Another man looked at Uncle Ernesto and smiled broadly.

The elevator seemed to move very slowly for Uncle Ernesto, but it finally reached the ground floor. He walked straight to the front desk and looked at the hotel manager helplessly. The hotel manager didn't have to understand any language to figure out the problem. He grabbed a key and led my uncle to the nearest elevator.

My uncle is still embarrassed about this incident. But he laughs a lot when he tells the story.

第二部分　勾選 (✓) 所有合文法的句子。

1. a. _____ Uncle Ernesto went to Norway for a business meeting.
   b. _____ Uncle Ernesto went to Norway to have a business meeting.
   c. _____ Uncle Ernesto went to Norway for having a business meeting.

2. a. _____ Is necessary for him to travel in order to sell his products.
   b. _____ To sell his products, he needs to travel.
   c. _____ In order to sell his products, he needs to travel.

3. a. _____ Instead staying in the hall, he decided to get help.
   b. _____ Instead of staying in the hall, he decided to get help.
   c. _____ Instead to stay in the hall, he decided to get help.

4. a. _____ Uncle Ernesto thought about trying to explain his problem.
   b. _____ Uncle Ernesto considered about trying to explain his problem.
   c. _____ Uncle Ernesto decided not to explain his problem.

5. a. _____ It wasn't difficult for the hotel manager figuring out the problem.
   b. _____ It wasn't difficult for the hotel manager figure out the problem.
   c. _____ It wasn't difficult for the hotel manager to figure out the problem.

□ **Exercise 46.** 寫作 (第 13 章)

閱讀以下段落範例，然後寫一段你人生中感到最爲尷尬的經歷，並在文中運用一些動名詞和不定詞。

段落範例：

My Most Embarrassing Experience

My most embarrassing experience happened at work. One morning, I was in a hurry to get to my office, so I quickly said good-bye to my wife. She knew I was planning to give an important presentation at my firm, so she wished me good luck and kissed me on the cheek. Because traffic was heavy, I got to work a few minutes after the meeting had begun. I quietly walked in and sat down. A few people looked at me strangely, but I thought it was because I was late. During my presentation, I got more stares. I began to think my presentation wasn't very good, but I continued speaking. As soon as my talk was over, I went to the restroom. When I looked in the mirror, it wasn't hard to see the problem. There was smudge of red lipstick on my cheek. I felt pretty embarrassed, but later in the day I started laughing about it and tried not to take myself so seriously.

□ **Exercise 47.** 檢視學習成果 (第 13 章)

校訂下列句子，訂正不定詞、動名詞、介系詞以及詞序等用法上的錯誤。

1. It is important ~~getting~~ *to get* an education.

2. I went to the bank for cashing a check.

3. Did you go to shopping yesterday?

4. I cut the rope by a knife.

5. I thanked my friend for drive me to the airport.

6. Is difficult to learn another language.

7. Timmy isn't enough old to get married.

8. Is easy this exercise to do.

9. Last night too tired no do my homework.

10. I've never gone to sailing, but I would like to.

11. Reading it is one of my hobbies.

12. The teenagers began to built a campfire to keep themselves warm.

13. Instead of settle down in one place, I'd like to travel around the world.

14. I enjoy to travel because you learn so much about other countries and cultures.

15. My grandmother likes to fishing.

16. Martina would like to has a big family.

第十四章

名詞子句

❑ **Exercise 1. 暖身活動** (表 14-1)

勾選 (✓) 所有合文法的句子。

n.句 → n. → S/O/C
(轉)

1. _____ How much does this book cost?

1. that + S + V ~

2. _____ I don't know.

2. wh

3. _____ How much this books costs?

3. if / whether + S + V.

4. _____ I don't know how much this book costs. *是否*

14-1 名詞子句：概述 Noun Clauses: Introduction

主詞 動詞　　　受詞 (a) I know **his address**. 　　　　　（名詞子句） 主詞 動詞　　　受詞 (b) I know **where he lives**. 　　　　　（名詞子句）	動詞後面通常會接受詞，受詞常是名詞片語。★ 在例 (a) 中，**his address** 是名詞片語； 　　　　　**his address** 作爲動詞 *know* 的受詞。 有<u>些</u>動詞後面可以接名詞子句。★ 在例 (b) 中，**where he lives** 是名詞子句； 　　　　　**where he lives** 作爲動詞 *know* 的受詞。
受詞 主詞 動詞　┌─主詞 動詞─┐ (c) I know *where he lives*.	名詞子句有自身的主詞和動詞。 在例 (c) 中，*he* 是名詞子句的主詞； 　　　　　*lives* 是名詞子句的動詞。
(d) I know *where my book is*. 　　　　　（名詞子句）	名詞子句可以用疑問詞開頭。（請見表 14-2。）
(e) I don't know *if Ed is married*. 　　　　　（名詞子句）	名詞子句也可以用 *if* 或 *whether* 開頭。（請見表 14-3。）
(f) I know *that the world is round*. 　　　　　（名詞子句）	名詞子句也可以用 *that* 開頭。（請見表 14-4。） *n.句 → S.*

*★片語 (phrase) 由一組相關字詞所組成，「不」含主詞和動詞。　[That Jack is the best student in my class] is undoubted.
　子句 (clause) 由一組相關字詞所組成，含主詞和動詞。*

[It] is undoubted [that Jack ...]
假S　　　　　　　　　真主

❑ **Exercise 2. 文法** (表 14-1)

將名詞子句劃<u>底線</u>；有些句子不含名詞子句。

1. Where are the Smiths living?

2. I don't know where the Smiths are living.

3. We don't know what city they moved to.

4. We know that they moved a month ago.

5. Are they coming back?

6. I don't know if they are coming back.

❑ **Exercise 3. 暖身活動：兩人一組**（表 14-2）

成兩人一組，輪流作問答練習，並據實回答問題。

（手寫）I wonder whether it will be fine tomorrow.

1. 學生 A：Where do I live?
   學生 B：I *know / don't know* **where you live**.

2. 學生 B：Where does our teacher live?
   學生 A：I *know / don't know* **where our teacher lives**.

3. 學生 B：In your last sentence, why is "does" missing?
   學生 A：I *know / don't know* **why "does" is missing**.

4. 學生 A：In the same sentence, why does "lives" have an "s"?
   學生 B：I *know / don't know* **why "lives" has an "s."** *（手寫）wh- 為 S → 不變* *（手寫）who broke the window? / S*

14-2 以疑問詞爲首的名詞子句 Noun Clauses That Begin with a Question Word

下列疑問詞可作爲名詞子句的前導詞：**when**、**where**、**why**、**how**、**who**、**(whom)**、**what**、**which**、**whose**。

訊息問句	名詞子句	注意左欄中的例句： 名詞子句的詞序和訊息問句「不同」。
Where **does he live**?	主詞 動詞 (a) I don't know *where **he lives***.	錯誤：*I know where does he live.* 正確：*I know where he lives.*
When **did they leave**?	主詞 動詞 (b) Do you know *when **they left***?★	
What **did she say**?	主詞 動詞 (c) Please tell me *what **she said***.	
Why **is Tom** absent?	主詞 動詞 (d) I wonder *why **Tom is** absent*.	
動詞 主詞 Who **is that boy**?	主詞 動詞 (e) Tell me *who **that boy is***.	在訊息問句中，名詞或代名詞放在 **be** 動詞後面；在名詞子句中，則放在 **be** 動詞前面，如：例 (e) 和例 (f)。
動詞 主詞 Whose pen **is this**?	主詞 動詞 (f) Do you know *whose pen **this is***?	
主詞 動詞 **Who is** in the office?	主詞 動詞 (g) I don't know **who is** in the office.	名詞子句中，介系詞片語（如：*in the office*）不可放在 **be** 動詞前面，如：例 (g) 和例 (h)。
主詞 動詞 **Whose keys are** on the counter?	主詞 動詞 (h) I wonder **whose keys are** on the counter.	
Who came to class?	主詞 動詞 (i) I don't know **who came** to class.	在例 (i) 和例 (j) 中，當疑問詞爲主詞時，訊息問句與名詞子句中的主詞和動詞順序相同。
What happened?	主詞 動詞 (j) Tell me **what happened**.	

★此句後面用問號，是因爲 *Do you know* 用於提出疑問。
　例：*Do you know when they left?*
Do you know 用於提出疑問，而 *when they left* 是名詞子句。

（手寫）wh - do/does/did → 去助 → 還原 tense   when did Judy come!
ex. Do you know when Judy came?

Exercise 4. 文法 (表 5-2 和 14-2)

判斷各題中的文字是名詞子句或訊息問句。如果是名詞子句，加上 ***I don't know***；如果是訊息問句，則將開頭字母改爲大寫，並加上問號。

			名詞子句	訊息問句
1.	a.	_I don't know_ why he left.	☒	☐
	b.	W why did he leave?	☐	☒
2.	a.	where she is living	☐	☐
	b.	where is she living	☐	☐
3.	a.	where did Nick go	☐	☐
	b.	where Nick went	☐	☐
4.	a.	what time the movie begins	☐	☐
	b.	what time does the movie begin	☐	☐
5.	a.	why is Yoko angry	☐	☐
	b.	why Yoko is angry	☐	☐

❑ **Exercise 5. 文法** (表 5-2 和 14-2)

辨別說話者 A 問句中的主詞 (S) 和動詞 (V)，並將兩者劃底線；然後再用名詞子句，完成說話者 B 的回答。

1. A: Why is fire hot?   *(V S)*
   B: I don't know _why fire is_ hot.

2. A: Where does Frank go to school?
   B: I don't know _where Frank goes_ to school.

3. A: Where did Natasha go yesterday?
   B: I don't know. Do you know _____ yesterday?

4. A: Why is Maria laughing?
   B: I don't know. Does anybody know _why Maria is laughing_ ?

5. A: How much does an electric car cost?
   B: Peter can tell you _____.

6. A: How long do elephants live?
   B: I don't know _how long elephants live_ .

7. A: When was the first wheel invented?

    B: I don't know. Do you know _____?

8. A: How many hours does a light bulb burn?

    B: I don't know exactly _how many hours does a light bulb burns_ .

9. A: Where did Emily buy her computer?

    B: I don't know _____ .

10. A: Who lives next door to Kate?

    B: I don't know _who lives next door to Kate_ next door to Kate.

11. A: Who did Julie talk to?

    B: I don't know _____ to.

12. A: Why is Mike always late?

    B: You tell me! I don't understand _why Mike is always late_ late.

❑ **Exercise 6.** 口說：兩人一組 (表 14-1 和 14-2)

成兩人一組，輪流用 *Can you tell me* 開頭，詢問對方問題。

Questions to a teacher

1. How do I pronounce this word? → *Can you tell me how I pronounce this word?*
2. What does this mean?
3. When will I get my grades?
4. What is our next assignment?
5. How soon is the next assignment due?
6. Why is this incorrect?
7. When is a good time to meet?
8. What day does the term end?
9. Why did I fail?
10. Who will teach this class next time?

Exercise 7. 文法 (表 14-2)

用名詞子句完成下列答句。

1. A: Who is that woman?
    B: I don't know <u>who that woman is</u>   .

2. A: Who is on the phone?
    B: I don't know <u>who is on the phone</u>   .

3. A: What is a lizard?
    B: I don't know   .

4. A: What is in that bag?
    B: I don't know   .

5. A: Whose car is that?
    B: I don't know   .

6. A: Whose car is in the driveway?
    B: I don't know   .

7. A: Who is Bob's doctor?
    B: I'm not sure   .

8. A: Whose ladder is this?
    B: I don't know   . Hey, Hank, do you know
       _____?

    C: It's Hiro's.

9. A: What's at the end of a rainbow?
    B: What did you say, Susie?
    A: I want to know   .

❏ **Exercise 8. 口說：兩人一組** (表 14-1 和 14-2)

成兩人一組，輪流用 ***Do you know*** 開頭，詢問對方問題。

Questions at home

1. Where is the phone?
2. Why is the front door open?
3. Who just called?
4. Whose socks are on the floor?

5. Why are all the lights on?

6. There's water all over the floor. What happened?

7. What did the plumber say about the broken pipe?

8. What is the repair going to cost?

❑ **Exercise 9.** 文法 (表 5-2 和 14-2)

用括弧中字詞的正確形式，完成下列句子。

1. A: Where (*Sophia, eat*) ___*did Sophia eat*___ lunch yesterday?

   B: I don't know where (*she, eat*) ___*she ate*___ lunch yesterday.

2. A: Do you know where (*Jason, work*) ___*Jason works*___?

   B: Who?

   A: Jason. Where (*he, work*) ___*does he work*___?

   B: I don't know.

3. A: Where (*you, see*) _____ the ad for the computer sale
   last week?

   B: I don't remember where (*I, see*) _____ it. In one of the local papers,
   I think.

4. A: How can I help you?

   B: How much (*that camera, cost*) ___*does the camera cost*___?

   A: You want to know how much (*this camera, cost*) ___*this camera costs*___, is that right?

   B: No, not that one. The one next to it.

5. A: How far (*you, can run*) _____ without stopping?

   B: I have no idea. I don't know how far (*I, can run*) _____
   without stopping. I've never tried.

6. A: Ann was out late last night, wasn't she? When (*she, get*) ___*did she get*___ in?

   B: Why do you want to know when (*she, get*) ___*she got*___ home?

   A: Just curious.

7. A: What time (*it, is*) _____?

   B: I don't know. I'll ask Sara. Sara, do you know what time (*it, is*) _____?

   C: Almost four-thirty.

8. A: Mom, why (*some people, be*) ___*are some people*___ mean to other
   people?

   B: Honey, I don't really understand why (*some people, be*) ___*some people are*___
   mean to others. It's difficult to explain.

❏ **Exercise 10. 暖身活動** (表 14-3)

勾選 (✓) 所有合文法的句子。

Is Sam at work?

1. _____ I don't know if Sam is at work.
2. _____ I don't know Sam is at work.
3. _____ I don't know if Sam is at work or not.
4. _____ I don't know whether Sam is at work.

14-3 以 *If* 或 *Whether* 爲首的名詞子句

Yes/No 問句	名詞子句	將 yes/no 問句改爲名詞子句時，常會用 *if* 引導子句。*
Is Eric at home? Does the bus stop here? Did Alice go to Chicago?	(a) I don't know **if Eric is at home**. (b) Do you know **if the bus stops here**? (c) I wonder **if Alice went to Chicago**.	
(d) I don't know **if Eric is at home or not**.		用 *if* 引導名詞子句時，句尾有時會加上 *or not*，如：例 (d)。
(e) I don't know **whether** Eric is at home (or not).		在例 (e) 中，**whether** 和 *if* 同義。

*報導句中 *if* 和 *ask* 連用的用法，請見表 14-10。

a. be → 直述 → S+be   Are you hungry?
    ex. Jack isn't sure whether you are hungry.

b. do/does/did → 去助 → 還原 tense   ①Did Tom sleep well last night?②
    ex I don't know if Tom slept well last night.

c. 其他助動詞 → 直述句 → S+助+V.   Have you seen kelly recently?
    ex Tom wants to know if you have seen kelly recently.

❏ **Exercise 11. 文法** (表 14-3)

將下列 yes/no 問句改爲名詞子句。

1. Yes/No 問句：Is Carl here today?

    名詞子句　：Can you tell me ___if/whether Carl is here today___?

2. Yes/No 問句：Will Mr. Piper be at the meeting?

    名詞子句　：Do you know ___whether Mr. Piper will be at the meeting___?

3. Yes/No 問句：Did Niko go to work yesterday?

    名詞子句　：I wonder _____.

4. Yes/No 問句：Is there going to be a windstorm tonight?

    名詞子句　：I'm not sure ___if there is going to be windstorm tonight___

5. Yes/No 問句：Do you have Yung Soo's email address?

    名詞子句　：I don't know ___whether you have Yung Soo's email address___.

❑ **Exercise 12. 文法** (表 14-3)

用 *if* 引導名詞子句，完成下列對話。

1. A: Are you tired?

   B: Why do you want to know ___*if I am*___ tired?

   A: You look tired. I'm worried about you.

2. A: Are you going to be in your office later today?

   B: What? Sorry. I didn't hear you.

   A: I need to know _____ in your office later today.

3. A: Did Tim borrow my cell phone?

   B: Who?

   A: Tim. I want to know _____ my cell phone.

4. A: Can Pete watch the kids tonight?

   B: Sorry. I wasn't listening. I was thinking about something else.

   A: Have you talked to your brother Pete? We need to know _____

   _____ the kids tonight.

5. A: Are my car keys in here?

   B: Why are you asking me? How am I supposed to know _____

   _____ in here?

   A: You're sure in a bad mood, aren't you?

6. A: Does your car have a CD player?

   B: What was that?

   A: I want to know _____.

❑ **Exercise 13.** 口說：訪談 （表 14-2 和 14-3）

用 ***Do you know*** 作為問句的開頭，訪問班上同學，並試著找出能回答問題的同學。

1. What does it cost to fly from London to Paris?
2. When was this building built?
3. How far is it from Vancouver, Canada, to Riyadh, Saudi Arabia?
4. Is Australia the smallest continent?
5. How many eyes does a bat have?
6. What is one of the longest words in English?
7. Does a chimpanzee have a good memory?
8. How old is the Great Wall of China?
9. Do all birds fly?
10. Did birds come from dinosaurs?

❑ **Exercise 14.** 口說 （表 14-2 和 14-3）

分小組練習。挑選一位有名的電影明星或名人，並用名詞子句和下列提示字，造完整句子。最後，與全班分享一些句子，並詢問是否有人知道相關資訊。

1. What do you wonder about him/her?
   a. where → *I wonder where she lives.*
   b. what
   c. if
   d. who
   e. how
   f. why

2. What do you want to ask him/her?
   a. who → *I want to ask him who his friends are.*
   b. when
   c. what
   d. whether
   e. why
   f. where

❑ **Exercise 15.** 暖身活動 （表 14-4）

勾選 (✓) 合文法的句子，想想看是否同意這些勾選的敘述。

1. _____ I think that noun clauses are hard.
2. _____ I suppose that this chapter is useful.
3. _____ I think that some of the exercises are easy.
4. _____ Is interesting this chapter I think.

14-4 以 *That* 爲首的名詞子句 Noun Clauses That Begin with *That*

主詞 動詞　　　　　　　受詞	
(a) I think **that** *Mr. Jones is a good teacher.* (b) I hope **that** *you can come to the game.* (c) Mary realizes **that** *she should study harder.* (d) I dreamed **that** *I was on the top of a mountain.*	**that** 可用來引導名詞子句。 在例 (a) 中，*that Mr. Jones is a good teacher* 是名詞子句，作爲動詞 **think** 的受詞。 表示心理活動的動詞常以「*that* 子句」作爲受詞。
(e) I think **that** *Mr. Jones is a good teacher.* (f) I think Ø *Mr. Jones is a good teacher.*	名詞子句中的 **that** 通常可以省略，特別是在口語中。 例 (e) 與例 (f) 同義。

後面接「*that* 子句」的常見動詞*

agree that	dream that	know that	realize that
assume that	feel that	learn that	remember that
believe that	forget that	notice that	say that
decide that	guess that	predict that	suppose that
discover that	hear that	prove that	think that
doubt that	hope that	read that	understand that

*更多關於後面可以接「that 子句」的動詞，請見附錄單元 A，表 A-4。

❑ **Exercise 16. 文法** (表 14-4)

在句中適當位置加入 ***that***，以標示名詞子句的開頭。

1. I think $\wedge$ most people have kind hearts.
   > *that*

2. Last night I dreamed a monster was chasing me.

3. I believe we need to protect the rain forests.

4. Did you notice Yusef wasn't in class yesterday? I hope he's okay.

5. I trust Linda. I believe what she said. I believe she told the truth.

❑ **Exercise 17. 口說：兩人一組** (表 14-4)

成兩人一組，輪流作問答練習，並於答句中使用「*that* 子句」。最後，與全班分享一些搭檔的答案。

1. What have you noticed about English grammar?
2. What have you heard in the news recently?
3. What did you dream recently?
4. What do you believe about people?
5. What can scientists prove?
6. What can't scientists prove?

❑ **Exercise 18. 暖身活動** (表 14-5)

勾選 (✓) 你同意的句子。

1. _____ I'm sure that vitamins give people more energy.

2. _____ It's true that vitamins help people live longer.

3. _____ It's a fact that vitamins help people look younger.

14-5 「*That* 子句」的其他用法 Other Uses of *That*-Clauses

(a) I'*m sure that* the bus stops here. (b) I'*m glad that* you're feeling better today. (c) I'*m sorry that* I missed class yesterday. (d) I *was disappointed that* you couldn't come.	「*that* 子句」可以接在「*be* 動詞＋形容詞」或「*be* 動詞＋過去分詞」這兩組常見表達字詞之後。 在這種情況下，省略 *that* 也無損其句意： 　*I'm sure Ø the bus stops here.*
(e) *It is true that* the world is round. (f) *It is a fact that* the world is round.	「*that* 子句」常接在下列兩組常見表達字詞之後： 　*It is true* (*that*) . . . . 　*It is a fact* (*that*) . . . .

後面接「*that* 子句」的常見表達字詞*

be afraid that	be disappointed that	be sad that	be upset that
be angry that	be glad that	be shocked that	be worried that
be aware that	be happy that	be sorry that	
be certain that	be lucky that	be sure that	It is a fact that
be convinced that	be pleased that	be surprised that	It is true that

*更多關於可以接「*that* 子句」的表達字詞，請見附錄單元 A，表 A-5。

❑ **Exercise 19. 文法** (表 14-4 和 14-5)

在句中適當位置加入 *that*。

1. A: Welcome. We're glad ⌃^{that} you could come.

   B: Thank you. I'm happy to be here.

2. A: Thank you so much for your gift.

   B: I'm pleased you like it.

3. A: I wonder why Paulo was promoted to general manager instead of Andrea.

   B: So do I. I'm surprised Andrea didn't get the job. I think she is more qualified.

4. A: Are you aware you have to pass the English test to get into the university?

   B: Yes, but I'm certain I'll do well on it.

5. Are you surprised dinosaurs lived on earth for one hundred and twenty-five million (125,000,000) years?

6. Is it true human beings have lived on earth for only four million (4,000,000) years?

❑ **Exercise 20. 口說** (表 14-4 和 14-5)

第一部分 分小組練習。看看下表中所列的健康療法，哪些是你所知悉的？哪些是你覺得有用的？如有必要，你可以查閱字典。

acupuncture	massage	naturopathy
hypnosis	meditation	yoga

第二部分 用上表中的字詞結合名詞子句，完成下列句子；與其他同學討論你的句子。

1. I believe/think _____ is useful for _____.

2. I am certain _____

3. I am not convinced _____

❑ **Exercise 21. 聽力與文法** (表 14-4 和 14-5)

CD 2
Track 51

聆聽 CD 播放的對話，然後完成下列句子。

[handwritten: Jack [said], "I want to go to the park".]
[handwritten: Jack said that he wanted to ~]
[handwritten: 人稱．時態．]

例：你會聽到：MAN: I heard Jack is in jail. I can't believe it!
WOMAN: Neither can I! The police said he robbed a house. They must have the wrong person.
你要說出：a. The man is shocked that Jack is in jail.
b. The woman is sure that the police have the wrong person.

1. a. The woman thinks that . . . .
   b. The man is glad that . . . .

[handwritten: Jack said " I have had my lunch]
[handwritten: that he had had his lunch.]

2. a. The mother is worried that . . . .
   b. Her son is sure that . . . .

3. a. The man is surprised that . . . .
   b. The woman is disappointed that . . . .

4. a. The man is happy that . . . .
   b. The woman is pleased that . . . .

5. a. The woman is afraid* that . . . .
   b. The man is sure that . . . .

---

be afraid 有時表達恐懼，
　　例：*I don't want to go near that dog. I'm afraid that it will bite me.*
be afraid 有時用於禮貌地表達遺憾，
　　例：*I'm afraid you have the wrong number.* = I'm afraid, but I think you have the wrong number.（很遺憾，我想你恐怕打錯電話了。）
　　　I'm afraid I can't come to your party. = I'm sorry, but I can't come to your party.（很遺憾，我恐怕無法參加你的派對。）

圈選所有符合對話內容的敘述句。

1. A: Did Taka remember to get food for dinner tonight?
    B: I think so.
    a. Speaker B thinks Taka got food for dinner.
    b. Speaker B is sure that Taka got food for dinner.
    c. Speaker B doesn't know for sure if Taka got food for dinner.

2. A: Is Ben marrying Tara?
    B: I hope not.
    a. Speaker B says Ben is not going to marry Tara.
    b. Speaker B doesn't know if Ben is going to marry Tara.
    c. Speaker B doesn't want Ben to marry Tara.

14-6 口語回答中，以 *So* 代替「*That* 子句」

(a) A: Is Ana from Peru? 　　B: **I think so**. (so = that Ana is from Peru)	口語英文中，**think**、**believe** 和 **hope** 之後常接 *so*，作為 yes/no 問句的回答。這種用法提供 *yes*、*no* 與 *I don't know* 等回答外的另一種選擇。
(b) A: Does Judy live in Dallas? 　　B: **I believe so**. (so = that Judy lives in Dallas)	*so* 代替了「*that* 子句」。 錯誤：*I think so that Ana is from Peru.*
(c) A: Did you pass the test? 　　B: **I hope so**. (so = that I passed the test)	
(d) A: Is Jack married? 　　B: **I *don't* think *so***./**I *don't* believe *so*.**	**think so** 和 **believe so** 的否定用法： *do not think so/do not believe so*
(e) A: Did you fail the test? 　　B: **I hope *not*.**	口語回答時，**hope** 的否定用法：*hope not*。 在例 (e) 中，*I hope not* = I hope I didn't fail the test. （我希望自己不會考不及格。） 錯誤：*I don't hope so.*
(f) A: Do you want to come with us? 　　B: Oh, I don't know. **I guess *so*.**	其他常見的口語回答： 　*I guess so. I guess not.* 　*I suppose so. I suppose not.* 注意：在口語英文中，**suppose** 常常聽起來像 "spoze"。

❏ **Exercise 23. 文法** (表 14-6)
用「*that* 子句」改寫說話者 B 的回答。

1. A: Is Karen going to be home tonight?
    B: I think so.
    → *I think that Karen is going to be home tonight.*

2. A: Are we going to have a grammar test tomorrow?
   B: I don't believe so.

3. A: Will Margo be at the conference in March?
   B: I hope so.

4. A: Can horses swim?
   B: I believe so.

5. A: Do gorillas have tails?
   B: I don't think so.

6. A: Will Janet be at Omar's wedding?
   B: I suppose so.

7. A: Will your flight be canceled because of the storms?
   B: I hope not.

❏ **Exercise 24. 口說：兩人一組** (表 14-6)
成兩人一組，輪流回答問題。如果你不確定答案，就用 *think so*；如果確定，則回答 *Yes* 或 *No*。

例：
說話者 A（書本打開）: Does this book have more than 500 pages?
說話者 B（書本闔上）: I think so./I don't think so.
　　　　　　　　　　Yes, it does./No, it doesn't.

1. Are we going to have a grammar quiz tomorrow?
2. Do spiders have noses?
3. Do spiders have eyes?
4. Is there a fire extinguisher in this room?
5. Does the word *patient* have more than one meaning?
6. Does the word *dozen* have more than one meaning?
7. Is your left foot bigger than your right foot?
8. Is there just one sun in our universe?
9. Do any English words begin with the letter "x"?
10. Do you know what a noun clause is?

❏ **Exercise 25. 暖身活動** (表 14-7)
圈出引號，並將引用句中的標點符號劃<u>底線</u>。各句的標點符號有何差異？

1. "Help!" Marcos yelled.

2. "Can someone help me?" he asked.

3. "I'm going to drop this box of jars," he said.

14-7 引用句 Quoted Speech

有時我們想引用他人的話，即一字不動地寫下說話者所說的每一個字，這種句型稱作引用句。引用句常用於不同類型的寫作中，如：報導文章、故事、小說以及學術論文等。我們在引用句上方加上引號作爲標示。

(a) **說話者所說的實際內容** Jane: Cats are fun to watch. Mike: Yes, I agree. They're graceful and playful. 　　　Do you have a cat?	(b) **引用說話者所說的話** Jane said, "Cats are fun to watch." Mike said, "Yes, I agree. They're graceful and playful. Do you have a cat?"

(c) **引用句的寫法**
1. 在動詞 *said* 後面加逗點。* ──────────────→ Jane said,
2. 加上引號。** ──────────────────────→ Jane said, "
3. 引用句的第一個字母大寫。────────────→ Jane said, "Cats
4. 寫出引用句，並在句尾加上句點。──────→ Jane said, "Cats are fun to watch.
5. 句點後再加上引號。──────────────→ Jane said, "Cats are fun to watch."

(d) Mike said, "Yes, I agree. They're graceful and playful. Do you have a cat?" (e) 錯誤：*Mike said, "Yes, I agree." "They're graceful and playful." "Do you have a cat?"*	若引用句有兩句或兩句以上，只需在整段引言的一開始和最後加上引號即可，如：例 (d)。 「不」需每個句子的前後都加引號。句末爲問號時，則和句點一樣，引號應置於問號之後。
(f) "Cats are fun to watch," Jane said. (g) "Do you have a cat?" Mike asked.	在例 (f) 中，因 ***Jane said*** 二字出現在引言之後，所以引句之後應使用逗點（非句點）。 在例 (g) 中，引句若爲問句，則句尾使用問號（非逗點）。

*除了 *say* 之外，問句前常見的動詞還有 *admit*、*announce*、*answer*、*ask*、*complain*、*explain*、*inquire*、*report*、*reply*、*shout*、*state*、*write* 等字。

**在英式英文中，引號 (quotation marks) 稱作 "inverted commas"（顛倒的逗號）。

❏ **Exercise 26. 文法** (表 14-7)

用 ***said*** 或 ***asked*** 作動詞，寫出直接引用說話者字句的句子，並注意標點符號的使用。

1. ANN: My sister is a student.
    → Ann said, "My sister is a student." 或 "My sister is a student," Ann said.

2. ANN: Is your brother a student?

3. RITA: We're hungry.

4. RITA: Are you hungry too?

5. RITA: Let's eat. The food is ready.

6. JOHN F. KENNEDY: Ask not what your country can do for you. Ask what you can do for your country.

□ **Exercise 27. 文法** (表 14-7)

以下對話為一名老師和 Roberto 最近的談話內容；練習為此段對話，標上正確的標點符號。

(TEACHER) You know sign language, don't you I asked Roberto.

(ROBERTO) Yes, I do he replied both my grandparents are deaf.

(TEACHER) I'm looking for someone who knows sign language. A deaf student is going to visit our class next Monday I said. Could you interpret for her I asked.

(ROBERTO) I'd be happy to he answered. Is she going to be a new student?

(TEACHER) Possibly I said. She's interested in seeing what we do in our English classes.

□ **Exercise 28. 閱讀與寫作** (表 14-7)

第一部分 閱讀以下故事，並將引用句劃<u>底線</u>。

The Ugly Duckling

Once upon a time, there was a mother duck. She lived on a farm and spent her days sitting on her nest of eggs. One morning, the eggs began to move and out came six little ducklings. But there was one egg that was bigger than the rest, and it didn't hatch. The mother didn't remember this egg. "I thought I had only six," she said. "But maybe I counted incorrectly."

A short time later, the seventh egg hatched. But this duckling had gray feathers, not brown like his brothers, and was quite ugly. His mother thought, "Maybe this duck isn't one of mine." He grew faster than his brothers and ate more food. He was very clumsy, and none of the other animals wanted to play with him. Much of the time he was alone.

He felt unloved by everyone, and he decided to run away from the farm. He asked other animals on the way, "Do you know of any ducklings that look like me?" But they just laughed and said, "You are the ugliest duck we have ever seen." One day, the duckling looked up and saw a group of beautiful birds overhead. They were white, with long slender necks and large wings. The duckling thought, "I want to look just like them."

He wandered alone most of the winter and finally found a comfortable bed of reeds in a pond. He thought to himself, "No one wants me. I'll just hide here for the rest of my life." There was plenty of food there, and although he was lonely, he felt a little happier.

By springtime, the duck was quite large. One morning, he saw his reflection in the water. He didn't even recognize himself. A group of swans coming back from the south saw him and flew down to the pond. "Where have you been?" they asked. "You're a swan like us." As they began to swim across the pond, a child saw them and said, "Look at the youngest swan. He's the most beautiful of all." The swan beamed with happiness, and he lived happily ever after.

第二部分 分小組練習回答問題：這個故事教了我們什麼？

第三部分 從下列主題中擇一，寫一篇含有引用句的故事。
    1. 寫一篇來自你們國家的寓言故事 (fable)★，故事裡的動物會講話。
    2. 寫一篇你年紀較小時所得知的故事。

❑ **Exercise 29. 暖身活動** (表 14-8)
    圈選正確的斜體字。

Kathy and Mark said that *we / they* didn't like *our / their* new apartment.

★寓言故事 (*fable*) 是一種傳統故事，其中常隱含啓發人生的教誨。

14-8 引用句和報導句的比較 Quoted Speech vs. Reported Speech

引用句 (a) Ann said, "**I'm** hungry." (b) Tom said, "**I need** my pen."	「引用句」= 直接重述別人所說的話，此時會用引號標示。★
報導句 (c) Ann said (that) **she was** hungry. (d) Tom said (that) **he needed** his pen.	「報導句」= 重述他人說話內容的大意，不是一字不動地重複，人稱代名詞和動詞形式可能會改變，「不」使用引號。★ 句中不一定要用到 **that**；**that** 常用於寫作，而非口語。

★引用句 (*quoted speech*) 又稱作「直接引述」(*direct speech*)，報導句 (*reported speech*) 亦可稱作「間接引述」(*indirect speech*)。

❏ **Exercise 30. 文法** (表 14-8)

將引用句的代名詞，改為報導句的代名詞。

1. Mr. Smith said, "I need help with my luggage."

    → Mr. Smith said that ___*he*___ needed help with ___*his*___ luggage.

2. Mrs. Hart said, "I am going to visit my brother."

    → Mrs. Hart said that _____ was going to visit _____ brother.

3. Sergey said to me, "I will call you."

    → Sergey said _____ would call _____.

4. Rick said to us, "I'll meet you at your house after I finish my work at my house."

    → Rick said that _____ would meet _____ at _____ house

    after _____ finished _____ work at _____ house.

❏ **Exercise 31. 暖身活動** (表 14-9)

閱讀以下對話，並仔細看該對話下方的描述句；各描述句皆正確，但你注意到各句間有何差異嗎？

JENNY: What are you doing tomorrow?
ELLA: I'm going to take my parents out to dinner.

  a. Ella said she was going to take her parents out to dinner.
  b. Ella just said she is going to take her parents out to dinner.
  c. Last week Ella said she was going to take her parents out to dinner.
  d. Ella says she is going to take her parents out to dinner.

14-9 報導句中的動詞形式 Verb Forms in Reported Speech

(a) 引用句：Joe said, "I *feel* good." (b) 報導句：Joe said (that) he *felt* good. (c) 引用句：Ken said, "I *am* happy." (d) 報導句：Ken said (that) he *was* happy.	在正式英文中，若句中的報導動詞是過去式（如：*said*），名詞子句中的動詞也會是過去式，如：例 (b) 與例 (d)。
— Ann said, "I am hungry." (e) — What did Ann just say? I didn't hear her. — She said (that) she *is* hungry. (f) — What did Ann say when she got home last night? — She said (that) she *was* hungry.	在非正式英文中，如果說話者立刻引述他人剛說過的話，名詞子句的動詞通常不會改變為過去式，如：例 (e)。 然而，若引述的時間「晚於他人說話的時間」，或是用在正式的英文中，名詞子句的動詞通常用過去式，如：例 (f)。
(g) Ann *says* (that) she *is* hungry.	若句中的報導動詞是現在式（如：*says*），名詞子句的動詞時式不需改變。

引用句	報導句 （正式英文或稍後報導）	報導句 （非正式英文或立即報導）
He said, "I *work* hard." He said, "I *am working* hard." He said, "I *worked* hard." He said, "I *have worked* hard." He said, "I *am going to work* hard." He said, "I *will work* hard." He said, "I *can work* hard."	He said he *worked* hard. He said he *was working* hard. He said he *had worked* hard. He said he *had worked* hard. He said he *was going to work* hard. He said he *would work* hard. He said he *could work* hard.	He said he *works* hard. He said he *is working* hard. He said he *worked* hard. He said he *has worked* hard. He said he *is going to work* hard. He said he *will work* hard. He said he *can work* hard.

❑ **Exercise 32. 文法**（表 14-9）

用正式的動詞形式，完成下列報導句。

1. Sonia said, "I need some help."

    → Sonia said (that) she ___*needed*___ some help.

2. Linda said, "I'm meeting David for dinner."

    → Linda said (that) she _____ David for dinner.

3. Ms. Chavez said, "I have studied in Cairo."

    → Ms. Chavez said (that) she _____ in Cairo.

4. Kazu said, "I forgot to pay my electric bill."

    → Kazu said (that) he _____ to pay his electric bill.

5. Barbara said, "I am going to fly to Hawaii for my vacation."

    → Barbara said (that) she _____ to Hawaii for her vacation.

6. I said, "I'll carry the box up the stairs."

    → I said (that) I _____ the box up the stairs.

7. Tarik said to me, "I can teach you to drive."

    → Tarik said (that) he _____ me to drive.

❏ **Exercise 33. 文法** (表 14-8 和 14-9)

將引用句改為報導句，並視情況將引用句中的動詞，改為報導句中的過去式動詞。

1. Jim said, "I'm sleepy."

   → *Jim said (that) he was sleepy.*

2. Kristina said, "I don't like chocolate."
3. Carla said, "I'm planning to take a trip with my family."
4. Ahmed said, "I have already eaten lunch."
5. Kate said, "I called my doctor."
6. Mr. Rice said, "I'm going to go to Chicago."
7. Pedro said, "I will be at your house at ten."
8. Emma said, "I can't afford to buy a new car."
9. Olivia says, "I can't afford to buy a new car."
10. Ms. Acosta said, "I want to see you in my office after your meeting with your supervisor."

❏ **Exercise 34. 暖身活動** (表 14-10)

圈選所有合文法的句子。

1. a. David asked Elena if she would marry him.
   b. David asked Elena would she marry him.
   c. David wanted to know if Elena would marry him.

2. a. Elena said she wasn't sure.
   b. Elena told she wasn't sure.
   c. Elena told David she wasn't sure.

14-10 報導句中常用動詞：*Tell, Ask, Answer/Reply*

(a) Kay *said* that* she was hungry. (b) Kay *told me* that she was hungry. (c) Kay *told Tom* that she was hungry. 錯誤：*Kay told that she was hungry.* 錯誤：*Kay told to me that she was hungry.* 錯誤：*Kay said me that she was hungry.*	引出報導句的主要動詞稱作「報導動詞」。*say* 是最常用的報導動詞**，其後通常緊接著名詞子句，如：例 (a)。 *tell* 也是常用的報導動詞，注意在例 (b) 和例 (c) 中，*told* 的後面分別緊接著 *me* 與 *Tom*。 *tell* 之後必須先接（代）名詞受詞，再接名詞子句。
(d) 引用：Ken asked me, "Are you tired?" 報導：Ken *asked* (*me*) *if* I was tired. (e) Ken *wanted to know if* I was tired. Ken *wondered if* I was tired. Ken *inquired whether or not* I was tired.	*asked* 常作為報導問句的主要動詞。 問句所改成的報導句常用 *want to know*、*wonder* 和 *inquire*。
(f) 引用：I said (to Kay), "I am not tired." 報導：I *answered/replied* that I wasn't tired.	*answer* 和 *reply* 常用來報導回答。

*that 可省略，請見表 14-8。

**其他常見的報導動詞，例：*Kay announced/commented/complained/explained/remarked/stated that she was hungry.*

名詞子句 **389**

用 *said*、*told* 或 *asked* 完成下列句子。

1. Karen ___told___ me that she would be here at one o'clock.

2. Jamal ___said___ that he was going to get here around two.

3. Sophia ___asked___ me what time I would arrive.

4. William _____ that I had a message.

5. William _____ me that someone had called me around ten-thirty.

6. I _____ William if he knew the caller's name.

7. I had a short conversation with Alice yesterday. I _____ her that I would help her move into her new apartment next week. She _____ that she would welcome the help. She _____ me if I had a truck or knew anyone who had a truck. I _____ her Dan had a truck. She _____ she would call him.

8. My uncle in Toronto called and _____ that he was organizing a surprise party for my aunt's 60th birthday. He _____ me if I could come to Toronto for the party. I _____ him that I would be happy to come. I _____ when it was. He _____ it was the last weekend in August.

❏ **Exercise 36.** 口說：兩人一組 (表 5-2、14-2、14-3 和 14-10)

成兩人一組，用正式或非正式的動詞*，寫下五個與搭檔生活或其想法相關的問題；接著訪問你的搭檔，並寫下答案；然後向全班報告一些你從搭檔的回答中，得到的相關訊息。

例：
學生 A 的問題：Where were you born?
學生 B 的回答：In Nepal.
學生 A 的報告：I asked him where he was born. He said he was born in Nepal.

學生 B 的問題：Who do you admire most in the world?
學生 A 的回答：I admire my parents.
學生 B 的報告：I asked him who he admires most in the world. He said he admires his parents the most.

---

*在日常英文口語中，母語人士有時會將正式 / 稍後報導名詞子句中的動詞改爲過去式，有時卻不會。在作如同此練習的非正式報導時，非正式 / 立即的報導或正式 / 稍後報導等兩種時態（現在式或過去式）皆可。

❑ **Exercise 37.** 文法 (表 14-8 → 14-10)

依據圖片中兩人的對話內容，用正式報導的各種時態，完成以下段落。

One day Katya and Pavel were at a restaurant. Katya picked up her menu and looked at it. Pavel left his menu on the table. Katya asked Pavel ___*what he was going to have*___. He said
_____ anything because he
            ¹

_____. He _____ already. Katya was
    ²

    ³   ⁴

surprised. She asked him why _____. He told her
                          ⁵

_____.
                          ⁶

❑ **Exercise 38.** 文法 (表 14-8 → 14-10)

將下列報導句改為引用句；只要說話者換人，就另起新的段落；特別注意代名詞、動詞形式以及詞序。

例：

報導句：This morning my mother asked me if I had gotten enough sleep last night. I told her that I was fine. I explained that I didn't need a lot of sleep. She told me that I needed to take better care of myself.

引用句：*This morning my mother said, "Did you get enough sleep last night?"*
"I'm fine," I replied. "I don't need a lot of sleep."
She said, "You need to take better care of yourself."

1. In the middle of class yesterday, my friend tapped me on the shoulder and asked me what I was doing after class. I told her that I would tell her later.

2. When I was putting on my coat, Robert asked me where I was going. I told him that I had a date with Anna. He wanted to know what we were going to do. I told him that we were going to a movie.

Exercise 39. 聽力 (表 14-8 → 14-10)

CD 2
Track 52 聆聽 CD 中播放 Roger 報告他和 Angela 的電話談話內容；然後再聽一遍，並填寫空格。

Angela called and _____ me where Bill _____.
                         1   2
I _____ her he _____ in the lunchroom. She
        3   4
_____ when he _____ back. I _____
        5   6   7
he _____ back around 2:00. I _____ her if I
              8   9
_____ something for her.
        10
She _____ that Bill had the information she _____,
              11   12
and only he _____ her. I _____ her that I
                    13   14
_____ him a message. She thanked me and hung up.
        15

❑ **Exercise 40. 閱讀** (第 14 章)

第一部分　閱讀以下文章。

The Last Lecture

In 2007, a 47-year-old computer science professor from Carnegie Mellon University was invited to give a lecture at his university. His name was Randy Pausch, and the lecture series was called "The Last Lecture." Pausch was asked to think about what wisdom he would give to people if he knew it was his last opportunity to do so. In Pausch's case, it really was his last lecture because he had cancer and wasn't expected to survive. Pausch gave an uplifting lecture called "Really Achieving Your Childhood Dreams." The lecture was recorded and put on the Internet. A reporter for the *Wall Street Journal* was also there and wrote about it. Soon millions of people around the world heard about Pausch's inspiring talk.

Here are some quotes from Randy Pausch:

To the general public:

"Proper apologies have three parts: (1) What I did was wrong. (2) I'm sorry that I hurt you. (3) How do I make it better? It's the third part that people tend to forget."

"If I could only give three words of advice, they would be 'tell the truth.' If I got three more words, I'd add 'all the time'."

"The key question to keep asking is, 'Are you spending your time on the right things?' Because time is all you have."

"We cannot change the cards we are dealt, just how we play the hand."

To his students: "Whether you think you can or can't, you're right."

To his children: "Don't try to figure out what I wanted you to become. I want you to become what you want to become."

Sadly, in 2008, Randy Pausch died. Before his death he was able to put down his thoughts in a book, appropriately called *The Last Lecture*.

第二部分 分小組練習。確定全部小組成員了解第一部分的每句引言；然後，每個人各自選擇一句，用下列一些詞組表示是否同意該句話，並列舉原因來支持你的論點。

I agree / disagree that	I think / don't think that
I believe / don't believe that	It's true that

❑ **Exercise 41.** 檢視學習成果（第 14 章）
校訂下列句子，訂正名詞子句中的錯誤。

1. My friend knows where ~~do~~ I live.

2. I don't know what is your email address?

3. I think so that Mr. Lee is out of town.

4. Can you tell me that where Victor is living now?

5. I asked my uncle what kind of movies does he like.

6. I think, that my English has improved a lot.

7. Is true that people are basically the same everywhere in the world.

8. A man came to my door last week. I didn't know who is he.

9. I want to know does Pedro have a laptop computer.

10. Sam and I talked about his classes. He told that he don't like his algebra class.

11. A woman came into the room and ask me Where is your brother?

12. I felt very relieved when the doctor said, you will be fine. It's nothing serious.

13. My mother asked me that: "When you will be home?"

附錄

文法表格補充

單元 A

現在完成式	(a) I am not hungry now. I *have* already *eaten*.	「現在完成式」表示一個動作發生在「現在之前」的非特定過去時間，如：例 (a)。
現在之前　現在		
過去完成式	(b) I was not hungry at 1:00 P.M. I *had* already *eaten*.	「過去完成式」表示動作發生在「過去某時間點前」。
下午一點之前　下午一點		在例 (b) 中，我中午吃過飯。我在下午一點時並不餓，因為我在一點之前就吃過飯了。

I laughed when I saw my son.
He *had poured* a bowl of noodles on top of his head.

A-2 過去進行式與過去完成式的比較

過去進行式	(a) I *was eating* when Bob came.	「過去進行式」表達在「過去某特定時間點正在進行」的一項活動。 在例 (a) 中，我在中午開始吃飯，而 Bob 在 12 點 10 分抵達。Bob 抵達時，我正在吃飯。
過去完成式	(b) I *had eaten* when Bob came.	「過去完成式」表達某活動在「過去某特定時間之前就已完成」。 在例 (b) 中，我在中午吃完飯。Bob 在下午 1 點抵達。在 Bob 抵達前，我已經完成吃飯的動作。

A-3 *Still* 與 *Anymore* 的用法比較

Still

(a) It was cold yesterday. **It is *still* cold** today. **We *still* need to wear** coats. (b) The mail didn't come an hour ago. **The mail *still* hasn't come.**	*still* 意指「仍然」，表示情況從過去到現在都沒改變，且用於肯定句或否定句皆可。 位置：句中*

Anymore

(c) I lived in Chicago two years ago, but then I moved to another city. **I don't live in Chicago *anymore*.**	*anymore* 意指「不再」，表示過去的情況已經改變，此時已不存在。*anymore* 和 *any longer* 意義相同，且用於否定句。 位置：句尾

*請見第 10 頁，表 1-3。句中副詞：
(1) 置於現在簡單式動詞之前，例：*We **still** need to wear coats.*
(2) 置於 *am*、*is*、*are*、*was*、*were* 之後，例：*It is **still** cold.*
(3) 置於助動詞和主要動詞之間，例：*Bob **has already arrived**.*
(4) 置於否定助動詞之前，例：*Ann **still** hasn't come.*
(5) 置於問句中的主詞之後，例：*Have **you already** seen that movie?*

A-4 其他後面接「*That* 子句」的動詞★

conclude that	guess that	pretend that	show that
demonstrate that	imagine that	recall that	suspect that
fear that	indicate that	recognize that	teach that
figure out that	observe that	regret that	
find out that	presume that	reveal that	

★更多資訊請見第 379 頁，表 14-4。

Scientists *have **concluded that*** dolphins can communicate with each other.

A-5 其他後面接「*That* 子句」的 *Be* 動詞表達字詞★

be ashamed that	be furious that	be proud that
be amazed that	be horrified that	be terrified that
be astounded that	be impressed that	be thrilled that
be delighted that	be lucky that	
be fortunate that	be positive that	

★更多資訊請見第 380 頁，表 14-5。

單元 B：片語動詞 Phrasal Verbs

注意：更多片語動詞的練習題，請見 *Fundamentals of English Grammar Workbook* 的附錄 (appendix)。

B-1 片語動詞 **Phrasal Verbs**

(a) We **put off** our trip. We'll go next month instead of this month. (*put off = postpone*)	在例 (a) 中，**put off** = 片語動詞 「片語動詞」= 動詞和介副詞 (particle) 連用，而產生特殊意義的片語。例如：*put off* 是「拖延」(postpone) 的意思。
(b) Jimmy, **put on** your coat before you go outdoors. (*put on = place clothes on one's body*)	所謂「介副詞」就是一些「陪襯的字」，使用在片語動詞中（例如：*off*、*on*、*away*、*back* 等字）。
(c) Someone left the scissors on the table. They didn't belong there. I **put** them **away**. (*put away = put something in its usual or proper place*)	注意例 (a)、(b)、(c) 和 (d) 句中的片語動詞都有 **put**，但意義各異。
(d) After I used the dictionary, I **put** it **back** on the shelf. (*put back = return something to its original place*)	
可拆開的片語動詞	有些片語動詞是**可拆開**的：即「受格名詞」可以

(e) We *put off our trip*. =（動詞 + **介副詞** + 名詞）
(f) We *put our trip off*. =（動詞 + 名詞 + **介副詞**）
(g) We *put it off*. =（動詞 + 代名詞 + **介副詞**）
	(1) 置於介副詞之後，如：例 (e)，或
	  (2) 置於動詞與介副詞之間，如：例 (f)。
	
	若一片語動詞是可拆開的，則「受格代名詞」置於動詞與介副詞之間，如：例 (g)。
	
	  錯誤：*We put off it.*

不可拆開的片語動詞	若一片語動詞是**不可拆開的**，則「名詞」或「代名詞」必須置於介副詞之後（絕不可置於介副詞之前），如：例 (h) 和例 (i)。
(h) I *ran **into** Bob*. =（動詞 + **介副詞** + 名詞） (i) I *ran **into** him*. =（動詞 + **介副詞** + 代名詞）	錯誤：*I ran Bob into.* 錯誤：*I ran him into.*
片語動詞：不及物	有些片語動詞是不及物的，其後不接受詞。
(j) The machine *broke down*. (k) Please *come in*. (l) I *fell down*.	
三個字的片語動詞	有些兩個字的片語動詞（如：*drop in*）可以改成三個字的片語動詞（如：*drop in on*）。
(m) Last night some friends **dropped in**.	在例 (m) 中，**drop in** 後面不接受詞，它是不及物的片語動詞（其後不接受詞）。
(n) Let's **drop in on** Alice this afternoon.	在例 (n) 中，**drop in on** 是三個字的片語動詞，三個字的片語動詞是及物的（後面要接受詞）。
(o) We *dropped in on **her*** last week.	在例 (o) 中，三個字的片語動詞是不可拆開的（即受詞不論是名詞或代名詞，都要置於整個片語動詞之後）。

A **ask out** = ask (someone) to go on a date

B **blow out** = extinguish (a match, a candle)

break down = stop functioning properly

break out = happen suddenly

break up = separate, end a relationship

bring back = return

bring up = (1) raise (children)
(2) mention, start to talk about

C **call back** = return a telephone call

call off = cancel

call on = ask (someone) to speak in class

call up = make a telephone call

cheer up = make happier

clean up = make neat and clean

come along (with) = accompany

come from = originate

come in = enter a room or building

come over (to) = visit the speaker's place

cross out = draw a line through

cut out (of) = remove with scissors or knife

D **dress up** = put on nice clothes

drop in (on) = visit without calling first or
without an invitation

drop out (of) = stop attending (school)

E **eat out** = eat outside of one's home

F **fall down** = fall to the ground

figure out = find the solution to a problem

fill in = complete by writing in a blank space

fill out = write information on a form

fill up = fill completely with gas, water, coffee,
etc.

find out (about) = discover information

fool around (with) = have fun while wasting
time

G **get on** = enter a bus/an airplane/a train/a
subway

get out of = leave a car, a taxi

get over = recover from an illness or a shock

get together (with) = join, meet

get through (with) = finish

get up = get out of bed in the morning

give away = donate, get rid of by giving

give back = return (something) to (someone)

give up = quit doing (something) or quit trying

go on = continue

go back (to) = return to a place

go out = not stay home

go over (to) = (1) approach
(2) visit another's home

grow up (in) = become an adult

H **hand in** = give homework, test papers, etc., to
a teacher

hand out = give (something) to this person,
then to that person, then to
another person, etc.

hang around/out (with) = spend time relaxing

hang up = (1) hang on a hanger or a hook
(2) end a telephone conversation

have on = wear

help out = assist (someone)

K **keep away (from)** = not give to

keep on = continue

L **lay off** = stop employment

leave on = (1) not turn off (a light, a machine)
(2) not take off (clothing)

look into = investigate

look over = examine carefully

look out (for) = be careful

look up = look for information in a dictionary,
a telephone directory, an
encyclopedia, etc.

P **pay back** = return borrowed money to
(someone)

pick up = lift

point out = call attention to

（接續後頁）

print out = create a paper copy from a computer

put away = put (something) in its usual or proper place

put back = return (something) to its original place

put down = stop holding or carrying

put off = postpone

put on = put clothes on one's body

put out = extinguish (stop) a fire, a cigarette

R **run into** = meet by chance

run out (of) = finish the supply of (something)

S **set out (for)** = begin a trip

shut off = stop a machine or a light, turn off

sign up (for) = put one's name on a list

show up = come, appear

sit around (with) = sit and do nothing

sit back = put one's back against a chair back

sit down = go from standing to sitting

speak up = speak louder

stand up = go from sitting to standing

start over = begin again

stay up = not go to bed

T **take back** = return

take off = (1) remove clothes from one's body (2) ascend in an airplane

take out = invite out and pay

talk over = discuss

tear down = destroy a building

tear out (of) = remove (paper) by tearing

tear up = tear into small pieces

think over = consider

throw away/out = put in the trash, discard

try on = put on clothing to see if it fits

turn around ⎫
turn back ⎬ change to the opposite direction

turn down = decrease the volume

turn off = stop a machine or a light

turn on = start a machine or a light

turn over = turn the top side to the bottom

turn up = increase the volume

W **wake up** = stop sleeping

watch out (for) = be careful

work out = solve

write down = write a note on a piece of paper

❏ **EXERCISE 1. 文法**（表 B-1 和 B-2）

將下列各句中片語動詞的第二部分劃底線。

1. I picked <u>up</u> a book and started to read.

2. The teacher called on me in class.

3. I get up early every day.

4. I feel okay now. I got over my cold last week.

5. I woke my roommate up when I got home.

6. I turned the radio on to listen to some music.

7. When I don't know how to spell a word, I look it up.

❑ **EXERCISE 2. 文法** (表 B-1 和 B-2)

勾選 (✓) 下列正確的句子；有些題目中兩個句子皆正確。

1. _____ I turned the light on.

   _____ I turned on the light.

2. _____ I ran into Mary.

   _____ I ran Mary into.

3. _____ Joe looked up the definition.

   _____ Joe looked the definition up.

4. _____ I took off my coat.

   _____ I took my coat off.

5. _____ I got in the car and left.

   _____ I got the car in and left.

6. _____ I figured out the answer.

   _____ I figured the answer out.

❑ **EXERCISE 3. 文法** (表 B-1 和 B-2)

用介副詞和代名詞 *it* 或 **them** 完成下列句子。如果片語動詞可拆開，圈 SEP；反之，圈 NONSEP。

1. I got over my cold. → I got *over it* _____.   SEP   (NONSEP)

2. I made up the story. → I made _____.   SEP   NONSEP

3. I put off my homework. → I put _____.   SEP   NONSEP

4. I wrote down the numbers. → I wrote _____.   SEP   NONSEP

5. I looked up the answer. → I looked _____.   SEP   NONSEP

6. I got on the bus. → I got _____.   SEP   NONSEP

7. I looked into the problem. → I looked _____.   SEP   NONSEP

8. I shut off the engine. → I shut _____.   SEP   NONSEP

9. I turned off the lights. → I turned _____.   SEP   NONSEP

10. I got off the subway. → I got _____.   SEP   NONSEP

注意：更多片語動詞的練習題，請見 *Fundamentals of English Grammar Workbook* 的附錄 (appendix)。

單元 C：介系詞 Prepositions

注意：更多介系詞組合的練習題，請見 *Fundamentals of English Grammar Workbook* 的附錄 (appendix)。

C-1 介系詞的組合：概述 Preposition Combinations: Introduction

形容詞 + 介系詞 (a) Ali is **absent from** class today. 　　　　動詞 + 介系詞 (b) This book **belongs to** me.	at、from、of、on 和 to 都是介系詞。 介系詞常與形容詞或動詞連用，前者如：例 (a)，後者如：例 (b)。

C-2 介系詞的組合：參考列表

A
be absent from
be accustomed to
　　add (*this*) to (*that*)
be acquainted with
　　admire (*someone*) for (*something*)
be afraid of
　　agree with (*someone*) about (*something*)
be angry at/with (*someone*) about/over (*something*)
　　apologize to (*someone*) for (*something*)
　　apply for (*something*)
　　approve of
　　argue with (*someone*) about/over (*something*)
　　arrive at (*a building/a room*)
　　arrive in (*a city/a country*)
　　ask (*someone*) about (*something*)
　　ask (*someone*) for (*something*)
be aware of

B
be bad for
　　believe in
　　belong to
be bored with/by
　　borrow (*something*) from (*someone*)

C
be clear to
　　combine with
　　compare (*this*) to/with (*that*)
　　complain to (*someone*) about (*something*)
be composed of
　　concentrate on
　　consist of
be crazy about
be crowded with
be curious about

D
　　depend on (*someone*) for (*something*)
be dependent on (*someone*) for (*something*)

be devoted to
　　die of/from
be different from
　　disagree with (*someone*) about (*something*)
be disappointed in
　　discuss (*something*) with (*someone*)
　　divide (*this*) into (*that*)
be divored from
be done with
　　dream about/of
　　dream of

E
be engaged to
be equal to
　　escape from (*a place*)
be excited about
　　excuse (*someone*) for (*something*)
　　excuse from
be exhausted from

F
be familiar with
be famous for
　　feel about
　　feel like
　　fill (*something*) with
be finished with
　　forgive (*someone*) for (*something*)
be friendly to/with
be frightened of/by
be full of

G
　　get rid of
be gone from
be good for
　　graduate from

H

    happen to
be happy about (*something*)
be happy for (*someone*)
    hear about/of (*something*) from (*someone*)
    help (*someone*) with (*something*)
    hide (*something*) from (*someone*)
    hope for
be hungry for

I

    insist on
be interested in
    introduce (*someone*) to (*someone*)
    invite (*someone*) to (*something*)
be involved in

K

be kind to
    know about

L

    laugh at
    leave for (*a place*)
    listen to
    look at
    look for
    look forward to
    look like

M

be made of
be married to
    matter to
be the matter with
    multiply (*this*) by (*that*)

N

be nervous about
be nice to

O

be opposed to

P

    pay for
be patient with
be pleased with/about
    play with
    point at
be polite to
    prefer (*this*) to (*that*)

be prepared for
    protect (*this*) from (*that*)
be proud of
    provide (*someone*) with

Q
be qualified for

R

    read about
be ready for
be related to
    rely on
be resonsible for

S
be sad about
be satisfied with
be scared of/by
    search for
    separate (*this*) from (*that*)
be similar to
    speak to/with (*someone*) about (*something*)
    stare at
    subtact (*this*) from (*that*)
be sure of/about

T

    take care of
    talk about (*something*)
    talk to/with (*someone*) about (*something*)
    tell (*someone*) about (*something*)
be terrified of/by
    thank (*someone*) for (*something*)
    think about/of
be thirsty for
be tired from
be tired of
    translate from (*onelanguage*) to (*another*)

U
be used to

W

    wait for
    wait on
    warn about/of
    wonder about
be worried about

聽力練習文字

NOTE: You may want to pause the audio after each item or in longer passages so that there is enough time to complete each task.

Chapter 1: Present Time

Exercise 1, p. 1.

SAM: Hi. My name is Sam.

LISA: Hi. I'm Lisa. It's nice to meet you.

SAM: Nice to meet you too. Where are you from?

LISA: I'm from Boston. How about you?

SAM: I'm from Quebec. So, how long have you been here?

LISA: Just one day. I still have a little jet lag.

SAM: Me too. I got in yesterday morning. So we need to ask each other about a hobby. What do you like to do in your free time?

LISA: I spend a lot of time outdoors. I love to hike. When I'm indoors, I like to surf the Internet.

SAM: Me too. I'm studying Italian right now. There are a lot of good websites for learning languages on the Internet.

LISA: I know. I found a good one for Japanese. I'm trying to learn a little. Now, when I introduce you to the group, I have to write your full name on the board. What's your last name and how do you spell it?

SAM: It's Sanchez. S-A-N-C-H-E-Z.

LISA: My last name is Paterson — with one "t": P-A-T-E-R-S-O-N.

SAM: It looks like our time is up. Thanks. It's been nice talking to you.

LISA: I enjoyed it too.

Exercise 5, p. 4.

Lunch at the Fire Station

It's 12:30, and the firefighters are waiting for their next call. They are taking their lunch break. Ben, Rita, and Jada are sitting at a table in the fire station. Their co-worker Bruno is making lunch for them. He is an excellent cook. He often makes lunch. He is fixing spicy chicken and rice. Their captain isn't eating. He is doing paperwork. He skips lunch on busy days. He works in his office and finishes his paperwork.

Exercise 6, p. 5.

1. Irene designs video games.
2. She is working on a new project.
3. She is sitting in front of her computer.
4. She spends her weekends at the office.
5. She's finishing plans for a new game.

Exercise 9, p. 6.

A problem with the printer

1. Does it need more paper?
2. Does it have enough ink?
3. Are you fixing it yourself?
4. Do you know how to fix it?
5. Do we have another printer in the office?
6. Hmmm. Is it my imagination or is it making a strange noise?

Exercise 21, p. 14.

Natural disasters: a flood

1. The weather causes some natural disasters.
2. Heavy rains sometimes create floods.
3. A big flood causes a lot of damage.
4. In towns, floods can damage buildings, homes, and roads.
5. After a flood, a town needs a lot of financial help for repairs.

Exercise 24, p. 15.

1. talks
2. fishes
3. hopes
4. teaches
5. moves
6. kisses
7. pushes
8. waits
9. mixes
10. bows
11. studies
12. buys
13. enjoys
14. tries
15. carries

Exercise 33, p. 21.

Part I.

At the doctor's office

1.	Do you	becomes	Dyou	Do you have an appointment?
2.	Does he	becomes	Dze	Does he have an appointment?
3.	Does she	becomes	Duh-she	Does she have an appointment?
4.	Do we	becomes	Duh-we	Do we have an appointment?
5.	Do they	becomes	Duh-they	Do they have an appointment?
6.	Am I	becomes	Mi	Am I late for my appointment?
7.	Is it	becomes	Zit	Is it time for my appointment?
8.	Does it	becomes	Zit	Does it hurt?

Part II.

1. Do you have pain anywhere?
2. Does it hurt anywhere else?
3. Does she have a cough or sore throat?
4. Does he have a fever?
5. Does she need lab tests?
6. Am I very sick?
7. Is it serious?
8. Does he need to make another appointment?
9. Do they want to wait in the waiting room?
10. Do we pay now or later?

Exercise 35, p. 22.

1. We have a few minutes before we need to leave. Do you want a cup of coffee?
2. We need to leave. Are you ready?
3. Look outside. Is it raining hard?
4. Do we need to take an umbrella?
5. Mr. Smith has his coat on. Is he leaving now?
6. I'm looking for the office supplies. Are they in here?

Exercise 37, p. 24.

Aerobic Exercise

Jeremy and Nancy believe exercise is important. They go to an exercise class three times a week. They like aerobic exercise.

Aerobic exercise is a special type of exercise. It increases a person's heart rate. Fast walking, running, and dancing are examples of aerobic exercise. During aerobic exercise, a person's heart beats fast. This brings more oxygen to the muscles. Muscles work longer when they have more oxygen.

Right now Jeremy and Nancy are listening to some lively music. They are doing special dance steps. They are exercising different parts of their body.

How about you? Do you like to exercise? Do your muscles get exercise every week? Do you do some type of aerobic exercise?

Chapter 2: Past Time

Exercise 4, p. 27.

1. We studied . . .
2. Mr. Green wrote a magazine article . . .
3. The sun sets . . .
4. A substitute teacher taught . . .
5. Mr. Watson drove a sports car . . .

Exercise 5, p. 28.

Part I.

1. I was in a hurry. I wasn't in a hurry.
2. They were on time. They weren't on time.
3. He was at the doctor's. He wasn't at the doctor's.
4. We were early. We weren't early.

Part II.

At a wedding

1. The bride wasn't nervous before the ceremony.
2. The groom was nervous before the ceremony.
3. His parents weren't nervous about the wedding.
4. The bride and groom were excited about their wedding.
5. The ceremony was in the evening.
6. The wedding reception wasn't after the wedding.
7. It was the next day.
8. It was at a popular hotel.
9. A lot of guests were there.
10. Some relatives from out of town weren't there.

Exercise 8, p. 30.

1. Shhh. The movie is beginning.
2. Oh, no. The elevator door is stuck. It isn't opening.
3. Here's a letter for you. I opened it accidentally.
4. I'm listening to the phone message that you already listened to.
5. Are you lying to me or telling me the truth?
6. We enjoyed the party.
7. I'm enjoying the nice weather today.
8. You look upset. What happened?

Exercise 16, p. 37.

Part I.

1.	Did you	becomes	Did-ja	Did you forget something? OR
	Did you	becomes	Did-ya	Did you forget something?
2.	Did I	becomes	Dih-di	Did I forget something? OR
	Did I	becomes	Di	Did I forget something?
3.	Did he	becomes	Dih-de	Did he forget something? OR
	Did he	becomes	De	Did he forget something?

4. Did she   becomes   Dih-she   Did she forget something?
5. Did we   becomes   Dih-we   Did we forget something?
6. Did they   becomes   Dih-they   Did they forget something?

Part II.

1. Alex hurt his finger. Did he cut it with a knife?
2. Ms. Jones doesn't have any money in her wallet. Did she spend it all yesterday?
3. Karen's parents visited. Did you meet them yesterday?
4. The Browns don't have a car anymore. Did they sell it?
5. I dropped the glass. Did I break it?
6. Ann didn't throw away her old clothes. Did she keep them?
7. John gave a book to his son. Did he read it to him?
8. You don't have your glasses. Did you lose them?
9. Mr. Jones looked for his passport in his desk drawer. Did he find it?
10. The baby is crying. Did I upset her?

Exercise 17, p. 37.

Luka wasn't home last night.

1. Did he go to a party last night?
2. Did he have a good time?
3. Did he eat a lot of food?
4. Did he drink a lot of soda?
5. Did he meet some new people?
6. Did he shake hands with them when he met them?
7. Did he dance with friends?
8. Did he sit with his friends and talk?

Exercise 19, p. 38.

A Deadly Flu

Every year, the flu kills 200,000 to 300,000 people around the world. But in 1918, a very strong flu virus killed millions of people. This flu began in 1918 and lasted until 1920. It spread around the world, and between 20 million and 100 million people died. Unlike other flu viruses that usually kill the very young and the very old, many of the victims were healthy young adults. This was unusual and made people especially afraid.

Exercise 20, p. 39.

Part I.

1. watch, watched
2. studied, studied
3. works, worked
4. decided, decided

Part II.

1. We watched a movie.
2. They studied in the morning.
3. She worked at the library.
4. They decided to leave.

Exercise 21, p. 39.

1. We agree with you.
2. We agreed with you.
3. I arrived on time.
4. The teacher explains the answers well.
5. My doctor's appointment ended late.
6. The train stopped suddenly.
7. You touched a spider!

Exercise 22, p. 40.

1. It rains in the spring . . .
2. It rained a lot . . .
3. The mail carrier walks to our house . . .
4. My friend surprised me with a birthday present . . .
5. The taxi picks up passengers at the airport . . .
6. I passed my final exam in math . . .

Exercise 23, p. 40.

1. cooked	5. started	9. added
2. served	6. dropped	10. passed
3. wanted	7. pulled	11. returned
4. asked	8. pushed	12. pointed

Exercise 24, p. 40.

A: Did you have a good weekend?
B: Yeah, I went to a waterslide park.
A: Really? That sounds like fun!
B: It was great! I loved the fast slides. How about you? How was your weekend?
A: I visited my aunt.
B: Did you have a good time?
A: Not really. She didn't like my clothes or my haircut.

Exercise 31, p. 46.

At a checkout stand in a grocery store

1. A: Hi. Did you find what you needed?
   B: Almost everything. I was looking for sticky rice, but I didn't see it.
   A: It's on aisle 10, in the Asian food section.

2. A: This is the express lane. Ten items only. It looks like you have more than ten. Did you count them?
   B: I thought I had ten. Oh, I guess I have more. Sorry.
   A: The checkout stand next to me is open.

3. A: Do you have any coupons you wanted to use?
   B: I had a couple in my purse, but I can't find them now.
   A: What were they for? I might have some extras here.
   B: One was for eggs, and the other was for ice cream.
   A: I think I have those.

Exercise 39, p. 51.

Jennifer's Problem

Jennifer works for an insurance company. When people need help with their car insurance, they call her. Right now it is 9:05 A.M., and Jennifer is sitting at her desk.

She came to work on time this morning. Yesterday Jennifer was late to work because she had a minor auto accident. While she was driving to work, her cell phone rang. She reached for it.

While she was reaching for her phone, Jennifer lost control of the car. Her car ran into a row of mailboxes beside the road and stopped. Fortunately, no one was hurt in the accident.

Jennifer is okay, but her car isn't. It needs repairs. Jennifer feels very embarrassed now. She made a bad decision, especially since it is illegal to talk on a cell phone and drive at the same time where she lives.

Exercise 43, p. 53.

1. I used to stay up past midnight, but now I often go to bed at 10:00 because I have an 8:00 class.
2. What time did you used to go to bed when you were a child?
3. Tom used to play tennis after work every day, but now he doesn't.
4. I used to skip breakfast, but now I always have something to eat in the morning because I read that students who eat breakfast do better in school.
5. I didn't used to like grammar, but now I do.

Chapter 3: Future Time

Exercise 2, p. 56.

At the airport

1. The security line will take about a half hour.
2. The plane is going to arrive at Gate 10.
3. Your flight is already an hour late.
4. Your flight will be here soon.
5. Did you print your boarding pass?
6. Are you printing my boarding pass too?
7. Are we going to have a snack on our flight?
8. We will need to buy snacks on the flight.

Exercise 6, p. 58.

Part I.

Looking for an apartment

A: We're going to look for an apartment to rent this weekend.
B: Are you going to look in this area?
A: No, we're going to search in an area closer to our jobs.
B: Is the rent going to be cheaper in that area?
A: Yes, apartment rents are definitely going to be cheaper.

B: Are you going to need to pay a deposit?
A: I'm sure we're going to need to pay the first and last month's rent.

Part II.

A: Where are you going to move to?
B: We're going to look for something outside the city. We're going to spend the weekend apartment hunting.
A: What fees are you going to need to pay?
B: I think we are going to need to pay the first and last month's rent.
A: Are there going to be other fees?
B: There is probably going to be an application fee and a cleaning fee. Also, the landlord is probably going to run a credit check, so we are going to need to pay for that.

Exercise 10, p. 60.

Part I.

1. I'll be ready to leave soon.
2. You'll need to come.
3. He'll drive us.
4. She'll come later.
5. We'll get there a little late.
6. They'll wait for us.

Part II.

1. Don't wait up for me tonight. I'll be home late.
2. I paid the bill this morning. You'll get my check in the next day or two.
3. We have the better team. We'll probably win the game.
4. Henry twisted his ankle while running down a hill. He'll probably take a break from running this week.
5. We can go to the beach tomorrow, but it'll probably be too cold to go swimming.
6. I invited some guests for dinner. They'll probably get here around seven.
7. Karen is doing volunteer work for a community health-care clinic this week. She'll be gone a lot in the evenings.

Exercise 11, p. 61.

Part I.

At the doctor's office

1. The doctor'll be with you in a few minutes.
2. Your appointment'll take about an hour.
3. Your fever'll be gone in a few days.
4. Your stitches'll disappear over the next two weeks.
5. The nurse'll schedule your tests.
6. The lab'll have the results next week.
7. The receptionist at the front desk'll set up your next appointment.

Part II.

At the pharmacy

1. Your prescription'll be ready in ten minutes.
2. The medicine'll make you feel a little tired.
3. The pharmacist'll call your doctor's office.

4. This cough syrup'll help your cough.
5. Two aspirin'll be enough.
6. The generic drug'll cost less.
7. This information'll explain all the side effects for this medicine.

Exercise 13, p. 62.

My day tomorrow

1. I'm going to go to the bank tomorrow.
2. I'll probably do other errands too.
3. I may stop at the post office.
4. I will probably pick up groceries at the store.
5. It is going to be hot.
6. Maybe I'll do my errands early.

Exercise 17, p. 64.

Predictions about the future

1. People'll have flying cars.
2. Cars'll use solar power or energy from the sun instead of gas.
3. Some people'll live underwater.
4. Some people may live in outer space.
5. Maybe creatures from outer space'll live here.
6. Children'll learn on computers in their homes, not at school.
7. Robots may clean our homes.
8. Maybe computers'll have feelings.
9. People won't die.
10. The earth'll be too crowded.

Exercise 23, p. 67.

1. Could someone please open the window?
2. Do you have plans for the weekend?
3. Do you have a car?
4. I feel sick. I need to leave.

Exercise 33, p. 73.

Going on vacation

A: I'm going on vacation tomorrow.
B: Where are you going?
A: To San Francisco.
B: How are you getting there? Are you flying or driving your car?
A: I'm flying. I have to be at the airport by seven tomorrow morning.
B: Do you need a ride to the airport?
A: No, thanks. I'm taking a taxi. What about you? Are you planning to go somewhere over vacation?
B: No. I'm staying here.

Exercise 44, p. 79.

At a Chinese restaurant

A: Okay, let's all open our fortune cookies.
B: What does yours say?
A: Mine says, "You will receive an unexpected gift." Great! Are you planning to give me a gift soon?

B: Not that I know of. Mine says, "Your life will be long and happy."
Good. I want a long life.
C: Mine says, "A smile solves all communication problems." Well, that's good! After this, when I don't understand someone, I'll just smile at them.
D: My fortune is this: "If you work hard, you will be successful."
A: Well, it looks like all of us will have good luck in the future!

Chapter 4: Present Perfect and Past Perfect

Exercise 2, p. 82.

1. call, called, called
2. speak, spoke, spoken
3. do, did, done
4. know, knew, known
5. meet, met, met
6. come, came, come
7. eat, ate, eaten
8. cut, cut, cut
9. read, read, read
10. be, was/were, been

Exercise 12, p. 88.

1. I saw a two-headed snake once. Have you ever . . . ?
2. I flew in a small plane last year. Have you ever . . . ?
3. I rode in a limousine once. Have you ever . . . ?
4. I did volunteer work last month. Have you ever . . . ?
5. I accidentally tore my shirt yesterday. Have you ever . . . ?
6. I had a scary experience on an airplane last year. Have you ever . . . ?
7. I fell out of a boat last week. Have you ever . . . ?
8. I felt very, very embarrassed once, and my face got hot. Have you ever . . . ?
9. I spoke to a famous person yesterday. Have you ever . . . ?
10. I wanted to be famous once. Have you ever . . . ?

Exercise 17, p. 91.

1. Lori holds the baby a lot.
2. Richard gives the baby a bath at the end of the day.
3. Lori changes the baby's diapers.
4. Richard has taken lots of pictures of the baby.
5. Lori wakes up when the baby cries.
6. Richard does some of the household chores.
7. Lori is tired during the day.

Exercise 19, p. 92.

At a restaurant

1. My coffee's a little cold.
2. My coffee's gotten a little cold.
3. Your order's not ready yet.
4. Wow! Our order's here already.
5. Excuse me, I think our waiter's forgotten our order.
6. Actually, your waiter's just gone home sick. I'll take care of you.

Exercise 20, p. 93.

A job interview

Mika is a nurse. She is interviewing for a job with the manager of a hospital emergency room. He is looking at her resume and asking her some general questions.

INTERVIEWER: It looks like you've done a lot of things since you became a nurse.

MIKA: Yes, I've worked for a medical clinic. I've worked in a prison. I've worked in several area hospitals. And I've done volunteer work at a community health center for low-income patients.

INTERVIEWER: Very good. But, let me ask you, why have you changed jobs so often?

MIKA: Well, I like having new challenges and different experiences.

INTERVIEWER: Why have you applied for this job?

MIKA: Well, I'm looking for something more fast-paced, and I've been interested in working in an E.R. for a long time. I've heard that this hospital provides great training for its staff, and it offers excellent patient care.

INTERVIEWER: Thank you for coming in. I'll call you next week with our decision.

MIKA: It was good to meet you. Thank you for your time.

Exercise 26, p. 97.

1. Every day, I spend some money. Yesterday, I spent some money. Since Friday, I have . . .
2. I usually make a big breakfast. Yesterday, I made a big breakfast. All week, I have . . .
3. Every day, I send emails. Yesterday I sent an email. Today I have already . . .
4. Every time I go to a restaurant, I leave a nice tip. Last night I left a nice tip. I just finished dinner, and I have . . .
5. Every weekend, I sleep in late. Last weekend, I slept in late. Since I was a teenager, I have . . .
6. I drive very carefully. On my last trip across the country, I drove very carefully. All my life, I have . . .
7. Every morning, I sing in the shower. Earlier today, I sang in the shower. Since I was little, I have . . .

Exercise 31, p. 100.

Part I.
1. Jane's been out of town for two days.
2. My parents've been active in politics for 40 years.
3. My friends've moved into a new apartment.
4. I'm sorry. Your credit card's expired.
5. Bob's been traveling in Montreal since last Tuesday.
6. You're the first one here. No one else's come yet.

Part II.
1. The weather's been warm since the beginning of April.

2. This month's been unusually warm.
3. My parents've been living in the same house for 25 years.
4. My cousins've lived in the same town all their lives.
5. You slept late. Your friend's already gotten up and made breakfast.
6. My friends've planned a going-away party for me. I'm moving back to my hometown.
7. I'm afraid your work's been getting a little sloppy.
8. My roommate's traveled a lot. She's visited many different countries.

Exercise 34, p. 103.

Today's Weather

The weather has certainly been changing today. Boy, what a day! We've already had rain, wind, hail, and sun. So, what's in store for tonight? As you have probably seen, dark clouds have been building. We have a weather system moving in that is going to bring colder temperatures and high winds. We've been saying all week that this system is coming, and it looks like tonight is it! We've even seen snow down south of us, and we could get some snow here too. So hang onto your hats! We may have a rough night ahead of us.

Exercise 36, p. 104.

1. A: What song is playing on the radio?
   B: I don't know, but it's good, isn't it?
2. A: How long have you lived in Dubai?
   B: About a year.
3. A: Where are the kids?
   B: I don't know. I've been calling them for ten minutes.
4. A: Who have you met tonight?
   B: Actually, I've met a few people from your office. How about you? Who have you met?
   A: I've met some interesting artists and musicians.

Exercise 37, p. 104.

A common illness

LARA: Hi, Mom. I was just calling to tell you that I can't come to your birthday party this weekend. I'm afraid I'm sick.

MOM: Oh, I'm sorry to hear that.

LARA: Yeah, I got sick Wednesday night, and it's just been getting worse.

MOM: Are you going to see a doctor?

LARA: I don't know. I don't want to go to a doctor if it's not serious.

MOM: Well, what symptoms have you been having?

LARA: I've had a cough, and now I have a fever.

MOM: Have you been taking any medicine?

LARA: Just over-the-counter stuff.

MOM: If your fever doesn't go away, I think you need to call a doctor.

LARA: Yeah, I probably will.
MOM: Well, call me tomorrow and let me know how you're doing.
LARA: Okay. I'll call you in the morning.

Exercise 43, p. 110.

1. A: Oh, no! We're too late. The train has already left.
   B: That's okay. We'll catch the next one.

2. A: Last Thursday we went to the station to catch the train, but we were too late.
   B: Yeah, the train had already left.

3. A: You sure woke up early this morning!
   B: Well, I wasn't sleepy. I had already slept for eight hours.

4. A: Go back to sleep. It's only six o'clock in the morning.
   B: I'm not sleepy. I'm going to get up. I have already slept for eight hours.

Chapter 5: Asking Questions

Exercise 4, p. 113.

Leaving for the airport

1. Do you have your passport?
2. Did you remember to pack a snack for the plane?
3. Will your carry-on bag fit under the seat?
4. Is your taxi coming soon?
5. Will you call me when you get there?

Exercise 6, p. 113.

Part I.

1. Is he absent?	becomes	*Ih-ze* absent? 或 *Ze* absent?
2. Is she absent?	becomes	*Ih-she* absent?
3. Does it work?	becomes	*Zit* work?
4. Did it break?	becomes	*Dih-dit* break? 或 *Dit* break?
5. Has he been sick?	becomes	*Ze* been sick? 或 *A-ze* been sick?
6. Is there enough?	becomes	*Zere* enough?
7. Is that okay?	becomes	*Zat* okay?

Part II.

At the grocery store

1. I need to see the manager. Is she available?
2. I need to see the manager. Is he in the store today?
3. Here is one bag of apples. Is that enough?
4. I need a drink of water. Is there a drinking fountain?
5. My credit card isn't working. Hmmm. Did it expire?
6. Where's Simon? Has he left?
7. The price seems high. Does it include the tax?

Exercise 9, p. 116.

Where are Roberto and Isabel?

A: Do you know Roberto and Isabel?
B: Yes, I do. They live around the corner from me.
A: Have you seen them lately?
B: No, I haven't. They're out of town.
A: Did they go to their parents? I heard Roberto's parents are ill.
B: Yes, they did. They went to help them.
A: Are you going to see them soon?
B: Yes, I am. In fact, I'm going to pick them up at the airport.
A: Will they be back this weekend? I'm having a party, and I'd like to invite them.
B: No, they won't. They won't be back until Monday.

Exercise 14, p. 118.

1. Do you want to go to the mall?
2. When are the Waltons coming?
3. Where will I meet you?
4. Why were you late?
5. What did you buy?

Exercise 19, p. 120.

A secret

A: John told me something.
B: What did he tell you?
A: It's confidential. I can't tell you.
B: Did he tell anyone else?
A: He told a few other people.
B: Who did he tell?
A: Some friends.
B: Then it's not a secret. What did he say?
A: I can't tell you.
B: Why can't you tell me?
A: Because it's about you. But don't worry. It's nothing bad.
B: Gee. Thanks a lot. That sure makes me feel better.

Exercise 29, p. 126.

1. Who's ringing the doorbell?
2. Whose coat is on the floor?
3. Whose glasses are those?
4. Who's sitting next to you?
5. Whose seat is next to yours?
6. Who's out in the hallway?

Exercise 30, p. 126.

An old vacation photo

1. Whose picture is this?
2. Who's in the picture?
3. Who's standing in back?
4. You don't wear glasses. Whose glasses are you wearing?
5. Who's the woman in the purple jacket?
6. Whose cabin are you at?

Exercise 34, p. 128.

1. A: How fresh are these eggs?
   B: I just bought them at the Farmers' Market, so they should be fine.

2. A: How cheap were the tickets?
   B: They were 50% off.

3. A: How hard was the driver's test?
   B: Well, I didn't pass, so that gives you an idea.

4. A: How clean is the car?
   B: There's dirt on the floor. We need to vacuum it inside.

5. A: How hot is the frying pan?
   B: Don't touch it! You'll burn yourself.

6. A: How noisy is the street you live on?
   B: There is a lot of traffic, so we keep the windows closed a lot.

7. A: How serious are you about interviewing for the job?
   B: Very. I already scheduled an interview with the company.

Exercise 37, p. 130.

Questions:

1. How old are you?
2. How tall are you?
3. How much do you weigh?
4. In general, how well do you sleep at night?
5. How quickly do you fall asleep?
6. How often do you wake up during the night?
7. How tired are you in the mornings?
8. How many times a week do you exercise?
9. How are you feeling right now?
10. How soon can you come in for an overnight appointment?

Exercise 44, p. 134.

A birthday

1. When's your birthday?
2. When'll your party be?
3. Where'd you decide to have it?
4. Who're you inviting?

Exercise 45, p. 135.

1. Where's my key?
2. Where're my keys?
3. Who're those people?
4. What's in that box?
5. What're you doing?
6. Where'd Bob go last night?
7. Who'll be at the party?
8. Why's the teacher absent?
9. Who's that?
10. Why'd you say that?
11. Who'd you talk to at the party?

12. How're we going to get to work?
13. What'd you say?
14. How'll you do that?

Exercise 46, p. 135.

On an airplane

1. Who're you going to sit with?
2. How're you going to get your suitcase under the seat?
3. What'd the flight attendant just say?
4. Why'd we need to put our seat belts back on?
5. Why's the plane descending?
6. Why're we going down?
7. When'll the pilot tell us what's going on?
8. Who'll meet you when you land?
9. When's our connecting flight?
10. How'll we get from the airport to our hotel?

Exercise 47, p. 135.

A mother talking to her teenage daughter

1. Where're you going?
2. Who're you going with?
3. Who's that?
4. How long've you known him?
5. Where'd you meet him?
6. Where's he go to school?
7. Is he a good student?
8. What time'll you be back?
9. Why're you wearing that outfit?
10. Why're you giving me that look?
11. Why am I asking so many questions? Because I love you!

Exercise 48, p. 136.

1. What do you want to do?
2. What are you doing?
3. What are you having for dinner?
4. What are you doing that for?
5. What do you think about that?
6. What are you laughing for?
7. What do you need?
8. What do you have in your pocket?

Exercise 53, p. 138.

1. A: Did you like the movie?
   B: It was okay, I guess. How about you?

2. A: Are you going to the company party?
   B: I haven't decided yet. What about you?

3. A: Do you like living in this city?
   B: Sort of. How about you?

4. A: What are you going to have?
   B: Well, I'm not really hungry. I think I might order just a salad. How about you?

Exercise 56, p. 140.

1. a. You're Mrs. Rose, aren't you?
   b. Are you Mrs. Rose?
2. a. Do you take cream with your coffee?
   b. You take cream with your coffee, don't you?
3. a. You don't want to leave, do you?
   b. Do you want to leave?

Exercise 57, p. 141.

1. Simple Present
   a. You like strong coffee, don't you?
   b. David goes to Ames High School, doesn't he?
   c. Leila and Sara live on Tree Road, don't they?
   d. Jane has the keys to the storeroom, doesn't she?
   e. Jane's in her office, isn't she?
   f. You're a member of this class, aren't you?
   g. Oleg doesn't have a car, does he?
   h. Lisa isn't from around here, is she?
   i. I'm in trouble, aren't I?

2. Simple Past
   a. Paul went to Indonesia, didn't he?
   b. You didn't talk to the boss, did you?
   c. Ted's parents weren't at home, were they?
   d. That was Pat's idea, wasn't it?

3. Present Progressive, *Be Going To,* and Past Progressive
   a. You're studying hard, aren't you?
   b. Greg isn't working at the bank, is he?
   c. It isn't going to rain today, is it?
   d. Michelle and Yoko were helping, weren't they?
   e. He wasn't listening, was he?

4. Present Perfect
   a. It has been warmer than usual, hasn't it?
   b. You've had a lot of homework, haven't you?
   c. We haven't spent much time together, have we?
   d. Fatima has started her new job, hasn't she?
   e. Bruno hasn't finished his sales report yet, has he?
   f. Steve's had to leave early, hasn't he?

Exercise 59, p. 142.

Checking in at a hotel

1. You have our reservation, don't you?
2. We have a non-smoking room, don't we?
3. There's a view of the city, isn't there?
4. I didn't give you my credit card yet, did I?
5. The room rate doesn't include tax, does it?
6. Breakfast is included in the price, right?
7. Check-out time's noon, isn't it?
8. You don't have a pool, do you?
9. There are hair dryers in the rooms, aren't there?
10. Kids aren't allowed in the hot tub, are they?

Exercise 61, p. 143.

Part I.

1. What kind of music do you enjoy listening to?
2. I just saw you for a few minutes last night. What did you leave so early for?

3. How are you feeling?
4. How long does the bus ride take?
5. Whose children are those?
6. When did the Browns move into their new apartment?

Part II.

7. A: We only have a few minutes before the movie starts.
   B: I'm hurrying.
   A: Do you have enough money for the tickets?

8. A: Is the mail here yet?
   B: No, I just checked.
   A: I'm expecting a package. How soon will it be here?

9. A: I start my new job next week.
   B: Wow, that's soon.
   A: Yeah, I wanted to start as soon as possible.
   B: Now, how come you're changing jobs?

10. A: Are you new to the area?
    B: Yes, I moved here last month. My company transferred me here.
    A: Oh, so what do you do?

Exercise 62, p. 143.

Ordering at a fast-food restaurant

Cashier: So, what'll it be?
Customer: I'll have a burger.
Cashier: Would you like fries or a salad with your burger?
Customer: I'll have fries.
Cashier: What size?
Customer: Medium.
Cashier: Anything to drink?
Customer: I'll have a vanilla shake.
Cashier: Size?
Customer: Medium.
Cashier: Okay. So that's a burger, fries, vanilla shake.
Customer: About how long'll it take?
Cashier: We're pretty crowded right now. Probably 10 minutes or so. That'll be $6.50. Your number's on the receipt. I'll call the number when your order's ready.
Customer: Thanks.

Chapter 6: Nouns and Pronouns

Exercise 6, p. 149.

1. hat	3. pages	5. keys
2. toys	4. bridge	6. dish

Exercise 7, p. 150.

1. pants	3. boxes	5. wishes
2. cars	4. pens	6. lakes

Exercise 8, p. 150.

1. prizes   ways
2. lips   pants
3. glasses   matches
4. taxes   shirts
5. plates   stars
6. toes   fingers
7. laws   maps
8. lights   places

Exercise 9, p. 150.

1. names
2. clocks
3. eyes
4. boats
5. eyelashes
6. ways
7. lips
8. bridges
9. cars

Exercise 10, p. 150.

1. This shirt comes in three sizes: small, medium, and large.
2. I found this fax on my desk. It's for you.
3. I found these faxes on my desk. They're for you.
4. I'm not going to buy this car. The price is too high.
5. I can't find my glasses anywhere. Have you seen them?
6. The prize for the contest is a new bike.

Exercise 28, p. 159.

How Some Animals Stay Cool

How do animals stay cool in hot weather? Many animals don't sweat like humans, so they have other ways to cool themselves.

Dogs, for example, have a lot of fur and can become very hot. They stay cool mainly by panting. By the way, if you don't know what panting means, this is the sound of panting.

Cats lick their paws and chests. When their fur is wet, they become cooler.

Elephants have very large ears. When they are hot, they can flap their huge ears. The flapping ear acts like a fan and it cools them. Elephants also like to roll in the mud to stay cool.

Exercise 36, p. 163.

A: I'm looking for a new place to live.
B: How come?
A: My two roommates are moving out. I can't afford my apartment. I need a one-bedroom.
B: I just helped a friend find one. I can help you. What else do you want?
A: I want to be near the subway . . . within walking distance. But I want a quiet location. I don't want to be on a busy street.
B: Anything else?
A: A small balcony would be nice.
B: That's expensive.
A: Yeah. I guess I'm dreaming.

Exercise 49, p. 170.

1. Be careful with that knife! It's very sharp. If you're not careful, you'll cut . . .
2. My wife and I have our own business. We don't have a boss. In other words, we work for . . .
3. Rebecca is home in bed because she has the flu. She's resting and drinking plenty of fluids. She's being careful about her health. In other words, she is taking care of . . .
4. In a cafeteria, people walk through a section of the restaurant and pick up their food. They are not served by waiters. In other words, in a cafeteria people serve . . .
5. When Joe walked into the room, he didn't know anyone. He smiled confidently and began introducing . . .
6. When I didn't get the new job, I felt sad and depressed. I sat in my apartment and felt sorry for . . .

Exercise 58, p. 176.

1. A: Did you buy the black jacket?
   B: No. I bought the other one.

2. A: One of my favorite colors is dark blue. Another one is red.
   B: Me too.

3. A: This looks like the wrong street. Let's go back and take the other road.
   B: Okay.

4. A: What's the best way to get downtown from here?
   B: It's pretty far to walk. Some people take the bus. Others prefer the subway.

5. A: When I was a kid, I had lots of pets. One was a black dog. Another was an orange cat. Some others were a goldfish and a turtle.
   B: Pets are great for kids.

Exercise 59, p. 177.

A: What do you do when you're feeling lonely?
B: I go someplace where I can be around other people. Even if they are strangers, I feel better when there are others around me. How about you?
A: That doesn't work for me. For example, if I'm feeling lonely and I go to a movie by myself, I look at all the other people who are there with their friends and family, and I start to feel even lonelier. So I try to find other things to do to keep myself busy. When I'm busy, I don't feel lonely.

Chapter 7: Modal Auxiliaries

Exercise 3, p. 179.

1. I have to go downtown tomorrow.
2. You must fasten your seat belt.
3. Could you please open the window?

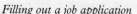

4. May I borrow your eraser?
5. I'm not able to sign the contract today.
6. Today is the deadline. You must sign it!
7. I have got to go to the post office this afternoon.
8. Shouldn't you save some of your money for emergencies?
9. I feel bad for Elena. She has to have more surgery.
10. Alexa! Stop! You must not run into the street!

Exercise 7, p. 181.

In the classroom

A: I can't understand this math assignment.
B: I can help you with that.
A: Really? Can you explain this problem to me?
B: Well, we can't figure out the answer unless we do this part first.
A: Okay! But it's so hard.
B: Yeah, but I know you can do it. Just go slowly.
A: Class is almost over. Can you meet me after school today to finish this?
B: Well, I can't meet you right after school, but how about at 5:00?
A: Great!

Exercise 13, p. 184.

1. A: Mom, are these oranges sweet?
   B: I don't know. I can't tell if an orange is sweet just by looking at it.

2. A: What are you going to order?
   B: I'm not sure. I might have pasta, or I might have pizza.

3. A: Mom, can I have some candy?
   B: No, but you can have an apple.

4. A: What are you doing this weekend?
   B: I don't know yet. I may go snowboarding with friends, or I may try to fix my motorcycle.

5. May I have everyone's attention? The test is about to begin. If you need to leave the room during the examination, please raise your hand. You may not leave the room without asking. Are there any questions? No? Then you may open your test booklets and begin.

Exercise 17, p. 186.

In a home office

A: Look at this cord. Do you know what it's for?
B: I don't know. We have so many cords around here with all our electronic equipment. It could be for the printer, I guess.
A: No, I checked. The printer isn't missing a cord.
B: It might be for one of the kid's toys.
A: Yeah, I could ask. But they don't have many electronic toys.
B: I have an idea. It may be for the cell phone. You know—the one I had before this one.
A: I bet that's it. We can probably throw this out.
B: Well, let's be sure before we do that.

Exercise 32, p. 194.

Filling out a job application

1. The application has to be complete. You shouldn't skip any parts. If a section doesn't fit your situation, you can write N/A (not applicable).
2. You don't have to type it, but your writing has to be easy to read.
3. You've got to use your full legal name, not your nickname.
4. You've got to list the names and places of your previous employers.
5. You have to list your education, beginning with either high school or college.
6. You don't always have to apply in person. Sometimes you can do it online.
7. You don't have to write some things, like the same telephone number, twice. You can write "same as above."
8. All spelling has to be correct.

Exercise 45, p. 201.

Puzzle steps

1. Write down the number of the month you were born. For example, write the number 2 if you were born in February. Write 3 if you were born in March, etc.
2. Double the number.
3. Add 5 to it.
4. Multiply it by 50.
5. Add your age.
6. Subtract 250.

Exercise 50, p. 204.

A: Why don't we go dancing tonight?
B: I don't know how to dance.
A: Oh. Then why don't we go to a movie?
B: I don't like movies.
A: You don't like movies?!
B: No.
A: Well then, let's go to a restaurant for dinner.
B: That's a waste of money.
A: Well, you do what you want tonight, but I'm going to go out and have a good time.

Chapter 8: Connecting Ideas

Exercise 11, p. 213.

Paying It Forward

A few days ago, a friend and I were driving from Benton Harbor to Chicago. We didn't have any delays for the first hour, but we ran into some highway construction near Chicago. The traffic wasn't moving. My friend and I sat and waited. We talked about our jobs, our families, and the terrible traffic. Slowly it started to move.

We noticed a black sports car on the shoulder. Its blinker was on. The driver obviously wanted to get back into traffic. Car after car passed without letting him in. I decided to do a good deed, so I motioned for him to get in line ahead of me. He waved thanks, and I waved back at him.

All the cars had to stop at a toll booth a short way down the road. I held out my money to pay my toll, but the toll-taker just smiled and waved me on. She told me that the man in the black sports car had already paid my toll. Wasn't that a nice way of saying thank you?

Exercise 15, p. 215.

A strong storm

1. The noise lasted only a short time, but the wind and rain . . .
2. Some roads were under water, but ours . . .
3. Our neighbors didn't lose any trees, but we . . .
4. My son got scared, but my daughter . . .
5. My son couldn't sleep, but my daughter . . .
6. My daughter can sleep through anything, but my son . . .
7. We still need help cleaning up from the storm, but our neighbors . . .
8. We will be okay, but some people . . .

Exercise 21, p. 219.

Part I.

To get more information:

1. A: I'm going to drop this class.
   B: You are? Why? What's the matter?

2. A: My laptop doesn't have enough memory for this application.
   B: Really? Are you sure?

3. A: I can read Braille.
   B: You can? How did you learn to do that?

Part II.

To disagree:

4. A: I love this weather.
   B: I don't.

5. A: I didn't like the movie.
   B: I did!

6. A: I'm excited about graduation.
   B: I'm not.

Exercise 28, p. 223.

Understanding the Scientific Term "Matter"

The word *matter* is a chemical term. Matter is anything that has weight. This book, your finger, water, a rock, air, and the moon are all examples of matter. Heat and radio waves are not matter because they do not have weight. Happiness, dreams, and fears have no weight and are not matter.

Exercise 33, p. 225.

1. Even though I looked all over the house for my keys, . . .
2. Although it was a hot summer night, we went inside and shut the windows because . . .
3. My brother came to my graduation ceremony although . . .
4. Because the package cost so much to send, . . .
5. Even though the soccer team won the game, . . .

Chapter 9: Comparisons

Exercise 4, p. 231.

1. Lara is as old as Tanya.
2. Sylvia isn't as old as Lara.
3. Sylvia and Brigita aren't as old as Tanya.
4. Brigita isn't quite as old as Sylvia.
5. Brigita is almost as old as Sylvia.

Exercise 8, p. 234.

1. Old shoes are more comfortable for me than new shoes.
2. I like food from other countries better than food from my country.
3. Winter is more enjoyable than summer for me.
4. I am the most talkative person in my family.
5. I am the friendliest person in my family.
6. Cooked vegetables are tastier than raw vegetables.
7. Taking a bath is more relaxing than taking a shower.
8. Speaking English is the easiest of all the English skills for me.

Exercise 12, p. 237.

My family

1. My father is younger than my mother.
2. My mother is the tallest person in our family.
3. My father is a fun person to be around. He seems happy all the time.
4. My mother was happier when she was younger.
5. I have twin sisters. They are older than me.
6. I have one brother. He is the funniest person in our family.
7. He is a doctor. He works hard every day.
8. My sisters just like to have fun. I don't think they work hard at all.

Exercise 15, p. 238.

1. Frank owns a coffee shop. Business is busier this year for him than last year.
2. I've known Steven for years. He's the friendliest person I know.
3. Sam expected a hard test, but it wasn't as hard as he expected.

4. The road ends here. This is as far as we can go.
5. Jon's decision to leave his job was the worst decision he has ever made.
6. I don't know if we'll get to the theater on time, but I'm driving as fast as I can.
7. When you do the next assignment, please be more careful.
8. The dessert looks delicious, but I've eaten as much as I can.
9. It takes about an hour to drive to the airport and my flight takes an hour. So the drive takes as long as my flight.

Exercise 23, p. 242.

1. a sidewalk, a road
   a. A sidewalk is as wide as a road.
   b. A road is wider than a sidewalk.
2. a hill, a mountain
   a. A hill isn't as high as a mountain.
   b. A hill is higher than a mountain.
3. a mountain path, a mountain peak
   a. In general, hiking along a mountain path is more dangerous than climbing a mountain peak.
   b. In general, hiking along a mountain path is less dangerous than climbing a mountain peak.
4. toes, fingers
   a. Toes are longer than fingers.
   b. Fingers aren't as long as toes.
   c. Toes are shorter than fingers.
5. basic math, algebra
   a. Basic math isn't as hard as algebra.
   b. Algebra is harder than basic math.
   c. Basic math is as confusing as algebra.
   d. Basic math is less confusing than algebra.

Exercise 36, p. 249.

5. Tom has never told a funny joke.
6. Food has never tasted better.
7. I've never slept on a hard mattress.
8. I've never seen a scarier movie.

Exercise 42, p. 253.

Gold vs. Silver

Gold is similar to silver. They are both valuable metals that people use for jewelry, but they aren't the same. Gold is not the same color as silver. Gold is also different from silver in cost: gold is more expensive than silver.

Two Zebras

Look at the two zebras in the picture. Their names are Zee and Bee. Zee looks like Bee. Is Zee exactly the same as Bee? The pattern of the stripes on each zebra in the world is unique. No two zebras are exactly alike. Even though Zee and Bee are similar to each other, they are different from each other in the exact pattern of their stripes.

Chapter 10: The Passive

Exercise 3, p. 260.

An office building at night

1. The janitors clean the building at night.
   The building is cleaned by the janitors at night.
2. Window washers wash the windows.
   The windows are washed by window washers.
3. A window washer is washing a window right now.
   A window is being washed by a window washer right now.
4. The security guard has checked the offices.
   The offices have been checked by the security guard.
5. The security guard discovered an open window.
   An open window was discovered by the security guard.
6. The security guard found an unlocked door.
   An unlocked door was found by the security guard.
7. The owner will visit the building tomorrow.
   The building will be visited by the owner tomorrow.
8. The owner is going to announce new parking fees.
   New parking fees are going to be announced by the owner.

Exercise 15, p. 267.

A bike accident

A: Did you hear about the accident outside the dorm entrance?
B: No. What happened?
A: A guy on a bike was hit by a taxi.
B: Was he injured?
A: Yeah. Someone called an ambulance. He was taken to City Hospital and treated in the emergency room for cuts and bruises.
B: What happened to the taxi driver?
A: He was arrested for reckless driving.
B: He's lucky that the bicyclist wasn't killed.

Exercise 17, p. 268.

Swimming Pools

Swimming pools are very popular nowadays, but can you guess when swimming pools were first built? Was it 100 years ago? Five hundred years ago? A thousand years ago? Actually, ancient Romans and Greeks built the first swimming pools. Male athletes and soldiers swam in them for training. Believe it or not, as early as 1 B.C., a heated swimming pool was designed for a wealthy Roman. But swimming pools did not become popular until the middle of the 1800s. The city of London built six indoor swimming pools. Soon after, the modern Olympic games began, and swimming races were included in the events. After this, swimming pools became even more popular, and now they are found all over the world.

Exercise 26, p. 274.

1. When will you be done with your work?
2. I hope it's sunny tomorrow. I'm tired of this rainy weather.
3. Jason is excited about going to Hollywood.
4. Are you prepared for the driver's license test?
5. The students are involved in many school activities.
6. The kids want some new toys. They're bored with their old ones.
7. Sam is engaged to his childhood sweetheart.
8. Some animals are terrified of thunderstorms.

Exercise 28, p. 275.

1. This fruit is spoiled. I think I'd better throw it out.
2. When we got to the post office, it was closed.
3. Oxford University is located in Oxford, England.
4. Haley doesn't like to ride in elevators. She's scared of small spaces.
5. What's the matter? Are you hurt?
6. Excuse me. Could you please tell me how to get to the bus station from here? I am lost.
7. Your name is Tom Hood? Are you related to Mary Hood?
8. Where's my wallet? It's gone! Did someone take it?
9. Oh, no! Look at my sunglasses. I sat on them and now they are broken.
10. It's starting to rain. Are all of the windows shut?

Exercise 31, p. 276.

1. Jane doesn't like school because of the boring classes and assignments.
2. The store manager stole money from the cash register. His shocked employees couldn't believe it.
3. I bought a new camera. I read the directions twice, but I didn't understand them. They were too confusing for me.
4. I was out to dinner with a friend and spilled a glass of water on his pants. I felt very embarrassed, but he was very nice about it.
5. Every year for their anniversary, I surprise my parents with dinner at a different restaurant.
6. We didn't enjoy the movie. It was too scary for the kids.

Exercise 33, p. 277.

Situation: Julie was walking along the edge of the fountain outside her office building. She was with her co-worker and friend Paul. Suddenly she lost her balance and accidentally fell into the water.

1. Julie was really embarrassed.
2. Falling into the fountain was really embarrassing.
3. Her friend Paul was shocked by the sight.
4. It was a shocking sight.
5. The people around the office building were very surprised when they saw Julie in the fountain.

6. And Julie had a surprised look on her face.
7. When she fell into the fountain, some people laughed at her. It was an upsetting experience.
8. The next day Julie was a little depressed because she thought she had made a fool of herself.
9. Her friend Paul told her not to lose her sense of humor. He told her it was just another interesting experience in life.
10. He said that people were probably interested in hearing about how she fell into the fountain.

Exercise 37, p. 280.

1. In winter, the weather gets . . .
2. In summer, the weather gets . . .
3. I think I'll stop working. I'm getting . . .
4. My brother is losing some of his hair. He's getting . . .
5. Could I have a glass of water? I'm getting really . . .
6. You don't look well. Are you getting . . .

Exercise 42, p. 282.

1. What are you accustomed to doing in the evenings?
2. What time are you used to going to bed?
3. What are you accustomed to having for breakfast?
4. Are you accustomed to living in this area?
5. Do you live with someone, or do you live alone? Are you used to that?
6. Are you used to speaking English every day?
7. What are you accustomed to doing on weekends?
8. What do you think about the weather here? Are you used to it?

Exercise 51, p. 286.

1. Doctors are supposed to take good care of their patients.
2. Passengers in a car are not supposed to buckle their seat belts.
3. Teachers are supposed to help their students.
4. Airline pilots are supposed to sleep during short flights.
5. People who live in apartments are supposed to pay the rent on time.
6. A dog is not supposed to obey its master.
7. People in a movie theater are supposed to turn off their cell phones.
8. People in libraries are supposed to speak quietly.

Exercise 52, p. 286.

Zoos

Zoos are common around the world. The first zoo was established around 3,500 years ago by an Egyptian queen for her enjoyment. Five hundred years later, a Chinese emperor established a huge zoo to show his power and wealth. Later, zoos were established for the purpose of studying animals.

Zoos were supposed to take good care of animals, but some of the early ones were dark holes or dirty cages. At that time, people became disgusted with the poor care the animals were given. Later, these early zoos were replaced by scientific institutions. Animals were studied and kept in better conditions there. These research centers became the first modern zoos.

Because zoos want to treat animals well and encourage breeding, animals today are put in large, natural settings instead of small cages. They are fed a healthy diet and are watched carefully for any signs of disease. Most zoos have specially trained veterinarians and a hospital for their animals. Today, animals in these zoos are treated well, and zoo breeding programs have saved many different types of animals.

Chapter 11: Count/Noncount Nouns and Articles

Exercise 3, p. 291.

1. We have a holiday next week.
2. What are you going to do?
3. Thomas told an unusual story.
4. Thomas often tells unusual stories.
5. I have an idea!
6. Let's go shopping.
7. There's a sale on shirts and jeans.
8. Let's leave in an hour.
9. Here's a message for you.
10. You need to call your boss.

Exercise 11, p. 296.

1. At our school, teachers don't use chalk anymore.
2. Where is the soap? Did you use all of it?
3. The manager's suggestions were very helpful.
4. Which suggestion sounded best to you?
5. Is this ring made of real gold?
6. We have a lot of storms with thunder and lightning.
7. During the last storm, I found my daughter under her bed.
8. Please put the cap back on the toothpaste.
9. What do you want to do with all this stuff in the hall closet?
10. We have too much soccer and hockey equipment.

Exercise 34, p. 313.

Ice-Cream Headaches

Have you ever eaten something really cold like ice cream and suddenly gotten a headache? This is known as an "ice-cream headache." About 30 percent of the population gets this type of headache. Here is one theory about why ice-cream headaches occur. The roof of your mouth has a lot of nerves. When something cold touches these nerves, they want to warm up your brain. They make your blood vessels swell up (get bigger), and this causes a lot of pain. Ice-cream headaches generally go away after about 30–60 seconds. The best way to avoid these headaches is to keep cold food off the roof of your mouth.

Chapter 12: Adjective Clauses

Exercise 20, p. 329.

My mother's hospital stay

1. The doctor who my mother saw first spent a lot of time with her.
2. The doctor I called for a second opinion was very patient and understanding.
3. The room that my mother had was private.
4. The medicine which she took worked better than she expected.
5. The hospital that my mom chose specializes in women's care.
6. The day my mom came home happened to be her birthday.
7. I thanked the people that helped my mom.
8. The staff whom I met were all excellent.

Exercise 28, p. 334.

1. The plane which I'm taking to Denver leaves at 7:00 A.M.
2. The store that has the best vegetables is also the most expensive.
3. The eggs which my husband made for our breakfast were cold.
4. The person who sent me an email was trying to get my bank account number.
5. The hotel clerk my wife spoke with on the phone is going to give us a room with a view.

Exercise 33, p. 337.

1. I like the people whose house we went to.
2. The man whose daughter is a doctor is very proud.
3. The man who's standing by the window has a daughter at Oxford University.
4. I know a girl whose parents are both airline pilots.
5. I know a girl who's lonely because her parents travel a lot.
6. I met a 70-year-old woman who's planning to go to college.

Exercise 36, p. 339.

Friendly advice

A: A magazine that I saw at the doctor's office had an article you ought to read. It's about the importance of exercise in dealing with stress.

B: Why do you think I should read an article which deals with exercise and stress?

A: If you stop and think for a minute, you can answer that question yourself. You're under a lot of stress, and you don't get any exercise.

B: The stress that I have at work doesn't bother me. It's just a normal part of my job. And I don't have time to exercise.

A: Well, you should make time. Anyone whose job is as stressful as yours should make physical exercise part of their daily routine.

Chapter 13: Gerunds and Infinitives

Exercise 4, p. 343.

1. A: When you finish doing your homework, could you help me in the kitchen?
   B: Sure.

2. A: Do you have any plans for this weekend?
   B: Henry and I talked about seeing the dinosaur exhibit at the museum.

3. A: I didn't understand the answer. Would you mind explaining it?
   B: I'd be happy to.

4. A: I'm thinking about not attending the meeting tomorrow.
   B: Really? Why? I hope you go. We need your input.

5. A: I've been working on this math problem for the last half hour, and I still don't understand it.
   B: Well, don't give up. Keep trying.

Exercise 22, p. 354.

A: Have you made any vacation plans?
B: Well, I wanted to stay home because I don't like traveling. I hate packing and unpacking suitcases. But my wife loves to travel and wanted to take a boat trip somewhere.
A: So, what are you going to do?
B: Well, we couldn't agree, so we decided to stay home and be tourists in our own town.
A: Interesting. What are you planning to do?
B: Well, we haven't seen the new Museum of Space yet. There's also a new art exhibit downtown. And my wife would like to take a boat trip in the harbor. Actually, when we began talking about it, we discovered there were lots of things to do.
A: Sounds like a great solution!
B: Yeah, we're both really excited about seeing more of our own town.

Exercise 44, p. 366.

1. My professor goes through the lecture material too quickly. It is difficult for us to follow him. He needs to slow down and give us time to understand the key points.

2. Asking others about themselves and their lives is one of the secrets of getting along with other people. If you want to make and keep friends, it is important to be sincerely interested in other people's lives.

3. Large bee colonies have 80,000 workers. These worker bees must visit 50 million flowers to make one kilogram, or 2.2 pounds, of honey. It's easy to see why "busy as a bee" is a common expression.

Chapter 14: Noun Clauses

Exercise 21, p. 381.

1. WOMAN: My English teacher is really good. I like her a lot.
   MAN: That's great! I'm glad you're enjoying your class.

2. MOM: How do you feel, honey? You might have the flu.
   SON: I'm okay, Mom. Honest. I don't have the flu.

3. MAN: Did you really fail your chemistry course? How is that possible?
   WOMAN: I didn't study hard enough. Now I won't be able to graduate on time.

4. MAN: Rachel! Hello! It's nice to see you.
   WOMAN: Hi, it's nice to be here. Thank you for inviting me.

5. WOMAN: Carol has left. Look. Her closet is empty. Her suitcases are gone. She won't be back. I just know it!
   MAN: She'll be back.

Exercise 39, p. 392.

Angela called and asked me where Bill was. I told her he was in the lunchroom. She asked when he would be back. I said he would be back around 2:00. I asked her if I could do something for her.

She said that Bill had the information she needed, and only he could help her. I told her that I would leave him a message. She thanked me and hung up.

關鍵字索引

專有名詞索引

6–10 畫

常見不規則動詞變化一覽表

原形	過去式	過去分詞	原形	過去式	過去分詞
awake	awoke	awoken	fall	fell	fallen
be	was, were	been	feed	fed	fed
beat	beat	beaten	feel	felt	felt
become	became	become	fight	fought	fought
begin	began	begun	find	found	found
bend	bent	bent	fit	fit	fit
bite	bit	bitten	fly	flew	flown
blow	blew	blown	forget	forgot	forgotten
break	broke	broken	forgive	forgave	forgiven
bring	brought	brought	freeze	froze	frozen
broadcast	broadcast	broadcast	get	got	got/gotten
build	built	built	give	gave	given
burn	burned/burnt	burned/burnt	go	went	gone
buy	bought	bought	grow	grew	grown
catch	caught	caught	hang	hung	hung
choose	chose	chosen	have	had	had
come	came	come	hear	heard	heard
cost	cost	cost	hide	hid	hidden
cut	cut	cut	hit	hit	hit
dig	dug	dug	hold	held	held
dive	dived/dove	dived	hurt	hurt	hurt
do	did	done	keep	kept	kept
draw	drew	drawn	know	knew	known
dream	dreamed/dreamt	dreamed/dreamt	lay	laid	laid
drink	drank	drunk	lead	led	led
drive	drove	driven	leave	left	left
eat	ate	eaten	lend	lent	lent

常見不規則動詞變化一覽表

原形	過去式	過去分詞	原形	過去式	過去分詞
let	let	let	sit	sat	sat
lie	lay	lain	sleep	slept	slept
light	lit/lighted	lit/lighted	slide	slid	slid
lose	lost	lost	speak	spoke	spoken
make	made	made	spend	spent	spent
mean	meant	meant	spread	spread	spread
meet	met	met	stand	stood	stood
pay	paid	paid	steal	stole	stolen
prove	proved	proved/proven	stick	stuck	stuck
put	put	put	strike	struck	struck
quit	quit	quit	swear	swore	sworn
read	read	read	sweep	swept	swept
ride	rode	ridden	swim	swam	swum
ring	rang	rung	take	took	taken
rise	rose	risen	teach	taught	taught
run	ran	run	tear	tore	torn
say	said	said	tell	told	told
see	saw	seen	think	thought	thought
seek	sought	sought	throw	threw	thrown
sell	sold	sold	understand	understood	understood
send	sent	sent	upset	upset	upset
set	set	set	wake	woke/waked	woken/waked
shake	shook	shaken	wear	wore	worn
shave	shaved	shaved/shaven	weave	wove	woven
shoot	shot	shot	weep	wept	wept
shut	shut	shut	win	won	won
sing	sang	sung	withdraw	withdrew	withdrawn
sink	sank	sunk	write	wrote	written

CD 分軌表

CD 1	軌數	練習	CD 2	軌數	練習
版權聲明	1		第六章	1	Exercise 6, p. 149
第一章	2	Exercise 1, p. 1		2	Exercise 7, p. 150
	3	Exercise 5, p. 4		3	Exercise 8, p. 150
	4	Exercise 6, p. 5		4	Exercise 9, p. 150
	5	Exercise 9, p. 6		5	Exercise 10, p. 150
	6	Exercise 21, p. 14		6	Exercise 28, p. 159
	7	Exercise 24, p. 15		7	Exercise 36, p. 163
	8	Exercise 33, p. 21		8	Exercise 49, p. 170
	9	Exercise 35, p. 22		9	Exercise 58, p. 176
	10	Exercise 37, p. 24		10	Exercise 59, p. 177
第二章	11	Exercise 4, p. 27	第七章	11	Exercise 3, p. 179
	12	Exercise 5, p. 28		12	Exercise 7, p. 181
	13	Exercise 8, p. 30		13	Exercise 13, p. 184
	14	Exercise 16, p. 37		14	Exercise 17, p. 186
	15	Exercise 17, p. 37		15	Exercise 32, p. 194
	16	Exercise 19, p. 38		16	Exercise 45, p. 201
	17	Exercise 20, p. 39		17	Exercise 50, p. 204
	18	Exercise 21, p. 39	第八章	18	Exercise 11, p. 213
	19	Exercise 22, p. 40		19	Exercise 15, p. 215
	20	Exercise 23, p. 40		20	Exercise 21, p. 219
	21	Exercise 24, p. 40		21	Exercise 28, p. 223
	22	Exercise 31, p. 46		22	Exercise 33, p. 225
	23	Exercise 39, p. 51	第九章	23	Exercise 4, p. 231
	24	Exercise 43, p. 53		24	Exercise 8, p. 234
第三章	25	Exercise 2, p. 56		25	Exercise 12, p. 237
	26	Exercise 6, p. 58		26	Exercise 15, p. 238
	27	Exercise 10, p. 60		27	Exercise 23, p. 242
	28	Exercise 11, p. 61		28	Exercise 36, p. 249
	29	Exercise 13, p. 62		29	Exercise 42, p. 253
	30	Exercise 17, p. 64	第十章	30	Exercise 3, p. 260
	31	Exercise 23, p. 67		31	Exercise 15, p. 267
	32	Exercise 33, p. 73		32	Exercise 17, p. 268
	33	Exercise 44, p. 79		33	Exercise 26, p. 274
第四章	34	Exercise 2, p. 82		34	Exercise 28, p. 275
	35	Exercise 12, p. 88		35	Exercise 31, p. 276
	36	Exercise 17, p. 91		36	Exercise 33, p. 277
	37	Exercise 19, p. 92		37	Exercise 37, p. 280
	38	Exercise 20, p. 93		38	Exercise 42, p. 282
	39	Exercise 26, p. 97		39	Exercise 51, p. 286
	40	Exercise 31, p. 100		40	Exercise 52, p. 286
	41	Exercise 34, p. 103	第十一章	41	Exercise 3, p. 291
	42	Exercise 36, p. 104		42	Exercise 11, p. 296
	43	Exercise 37, p. 104		43	Exercise 34, p. 313
	44	Exercise 43, p. 110	第十二章	44	Exercise 20, p. 329
第五章	45	Exercise 4, p. 113		45	Exercise 28, p. 334
	46	Exercise 6, p. 113		46	Exercise 33, p. 337
	47	Exercise 9, p. 116		47	Exercise 36, p. 339
	48	Exercise 14, p. 118	第十三章	48	Exercise 4, p. 343
	49	Exercise 19, p. 120		49	Exercise 22, p. 354
	50	Exercise 29, p. 126		50	Exercise 44, p. 366
	51	Exercise 30, p. 126	第十四章	51	Exercise 21, p. 381
	52	Exercise 34, p. 128		52	Exercise 39, p. 392
	53	Exercise 37, p. 130			
	54	Exercise 44, p. 134			
	55	Exercise 45, p. 135			
	56	Exercise 46, p. 135			
	57	Exercise 47, p. 135			
	58	Exercise 48, p. 136			
	59	Exercise 53, p. 138			
	60	Exercise 56, p. 140			
	61	Exercise 57, p. 141			
	62	Exercise 59, p. 142			
	63	Exercise 61, p. 143			
	64	Exercise 62, p. 143			

Fundamentals of English Grammar, Fourth Edition

Authorized Adaptation from the U.S. edition, entitled FUNDAMENTALS OF ENGLISH GRAMMAR (INTERNATIONAL) SB W/Audio CD; W/AK, 4th Edition, 0132315130 by Azar, Hagen, published by Pearson Education, Inc, publishing as Pearson Education ESL, Copyright © 2011 by Betty Schrampfer Azar

Chinese edition published by PEARSON EDUCATION TAIWAN and CAVES BOOKS, LTD., Copyright © 2012

Azar Associates: Shelley Hartle, Editor, and Sue Van Etten, Manager
Staff credits: The people who made up the *Fundamentals of English Grammar, Fourth Edition* team, representing editorial, production, design, and manufacturing, are, Dave Dickey, Christine Edmonds, Ann France, Amy McCormick, Robert Ruvo, and Ruth Voetmann.
Illustrations: Don Martinetti and Chris Pavely

中文版

著　作　人：Betty S. Azar, Stacy A. Hagen
發　行　人：陳文良
出版部經理：謝靜惠
翻　　　譯：吳姿璇
編　　　輯：蘇麗娟、吳姿璇、葛淑瑄
美術編輯：楊方瑋
電腦排版：辰皓國際出版製作有限公司
發　行　所：敦煌書局股份有限公司
地　　　址：台北市內湖區堤頂大道一段 207 號
電　　　話：(02) 8792-5001
版　　　次：2012 年 8 月第四版
　　　　　　2016 年 7 月第四版第七刷

ISBN 978-957-606-677-1
著作權所有・侵權必究
www.cavesbooks.com.tw